McCOOK
Learn

D1038259

DATE DUE

THE STONE OF KANNON

THE STONE
OF KANNON

O. A. Bushnell

PUBLISHED FOR THE FRIENDS
OF THE LIBRARY OF HAWAII
BY THE UNIVERSITY PRESS OF HAWAII
Honolulu

Library of Congress Cataloging in Publication Data

Bushnell, Oswald A
   The stone of Kannon.

   1. Hawaii—History—Fiction. 2. Japanese in
Hawaii—Fiction. I. Title.
PZ4.B979St [PS3552.U823]   813'.5'4   79-2563
ISBN 0-8248-0663-8

First printing 1979
Second printing 1980

CONTENTS

To the Gannen Mono, the First-year Men
who came to Hawaii, and to their
descendants who live here still

PREFACE

Most people who live in Hawaii today know nothing at all about the circumstances under which, in 1868, the first group of contract laborers from Japan was brought to these islands to work upon sugar plantations. And few people today are even vaguely aware of the trials that plantation laborers imported from any foreign country had to endure as they adjusted to the utterly alien environment they found in the Kingdom of Hawaii.

The Stone of Kannon attempts to tell in fictional form the story of the Gannen Mono, the First-year Men, as eventually those pioneer immigrants called themselves with great pride. (In true Japanese fashion, the name and the pride referred not to themselves but to the fact that they came to Hawaii during the first year of the Meiji emperor's reign.)

If you are wondering why a writer who cannot claim a Japanese ancestor is telling this story, the answer is both simple and saddening: no novelist of Japanese ancestry has yet done so. Accordingly, for lack of such a writer, I have decided to tell it myself. Not incidentally, I have written this story as much for nisei, sansei, yonsei, and gosei, as for all those other haoles of any ethnic group who don't know anything about either the Gannen Mono or Hawaii in 1868.

I have ventured to write this novel only after studying for many years the language and culture of Japan, and only after having lived in that country for seventeen instructive months. This preparation is supported by a lifetime's interest in things Japanese and by valued friendships with people of Japanese ancestry found among schoolmates, former students, and colleagues both in Hawaii and in Tokyo.

Because this is a novel I have imagined most of its characters as well as the little incidents, the thoughts, and the conversations by which their personalities are developed. But because this is also a historical novel I have tried most carefully to relate its heroes and its villains to important political events that actually did occur in both Japan and Hawaii. The places, circumstances, attitudes, beliefs, and customs described here were very real to Japanese, Hawaiians, and haoles in 1868. The sequence of events, from the time the First-year Men were recruited in Edo and Yokohama until they were dispersed among the sugarcane plantations of Hawaii, has not been invented. It follows accounts written by Hilary Conroy, Roy M. Shinsato, and Masaji Marumoto—whose works are available in our public libraries.

In order to represent the spirit of the time among Japan's commoners at the end of the Tokugawa Shogunate, I have written this account in a manner that suggests the style of popular novels and plays of that brilliant era. The most prominent of those, but by no means the only one, is Ikku Jippensha's picaresque novel, the vulgar, comical, and satirical *Hizakurige,* or *Shank's Mare.* Interestingly enough, several European novelists wrote about life among the commoners of their countries in much the same amused fashion as did their Japanese contemporaries. All those writers, whether from East or West, have influenced to a considerable degree the vocabulary, the shifting perspectives, the moments of unabashed sentimentality, the gossipy tone, the proverbs and the clichés, and especially the relieving irony with which I have chosen to tell the story of Ishi, my hero of many names, and his companions.

Borrowings from Japan's novels, plays, songs, poems, and especially from its abundance of "wise sayings" are scattered throughout the tale. So also are more dramatic techniques of acting employed in Kabuki (such as the mie, or dramatic posture, and passed-along dialogue), and numerous instances of the universal Japanese delight in quoting or composing or adapting a short poem suitable for an occasion. These touches are introduced in order to achieve verisimilitude—or, as a cynical Japanese playwright wrote long ago, "something with an air of truth to it." In short, this monogatari, or tale, has something for everybody—except for the purists who like to see diacritical marks in a serious scholarly work like this. Mercifully, for the sake of economy and readability those diacritical marks (and italics) have been omitted from Hawaiian and Japanese words.

If at times some of my characters act like theatrical hams, or speak with the wisdom of philosophers, or muse like sensitive poets they can do so quite naturally because, to me, they are creations of their admirably ingenious society. Although they were fleeing from its crueler constraints, they also carried with them most of its intangible gifts, the ones that sharpened the mind and strengthened the spirit and gave them the courage to escape from a homeland they could endure no longer. Even though few Gannen Mono could read or write, all had been taught the virtues that count in the shaping of a man. Those important virtues of *on, giri,* and *gimu*—in other words, the values of loyalty, gratitude, obligation, honor, courtesy, and industry—have enriched the lives of all of us who have grown up in the Hawaii the settlers from Japan and their descendants have helped to make.

The Stone of Kannon tells how 154 of those First-year Men came to Hawaii and what happened to eleven of the brave wanderers who were assigned to the plantation in "Wailuku of Maui" in 1868. It tells also how, in their turn, the people of Maui responded to the alien newcomers. A sequel, *The Water of Life,* takes up eight years later, when the Gannen Mono are no longer Japanese but are not yet Hawaiian. It describes the adventures of five survivors as they help to construct the spectacular Hamakua irrigation ditch along the northern flank of Maui's Mount Haleakala. Their bosses on that difficult job are a pair of struggling young sugarcane planters, just beginning upon a long partnership: Samuel T. Alexander and Henry Perrine Baldwin.

Honolulu, Hawaii
11 May 1978

CHAPTER 1
THE SHRINE OF KANNON

In her mercy Kannon answered Genzo's plea almost as soon as he uttered it. Standing among all the other petitioners for her help, amid the chatter of people entering into the space before her shrine, the clapping of many pairs of hands, and the rattling of coins against the sides of the offering chest, he too tossed a copper zeni into the box and clapped his hands to draw her attention to his need. With head raised, hands lifted palm to palm before his face, he who never asked for help from anyone on earth asked her for help from Heaven. Show me a way, he begged, wondering even then how she could hear his cry among all the others being sent up to her in that same instant.

His moment having ended, he bowed his thanks toward the high altar, decked with tall candles each ending in an unwavering flame, surrounded by great gleaming vessels wrought in gold or brass and by the holy images whose countenances are as inscrutable as is the will of Heaven. Pushing his way among the waiting pilgrims, he came down the long flight of stairs that brought him back to reality. Already the hope that had flickered briefly in him was waning, going back into the dark hole from which it rarely came forth. Fool!, he jeered, why should she care about you and your small worries? Why should she care whether you live or die? No one else does. Soothing himself with the thought that he had not asked her for much, compared with all those who besought the Goddess of Infinite Compassion for nothing less than miracles, he promised that never again would he do so foolish a thing.

Yet who can say that, in her great power, she did not hear him? When he touched again the trampled earth a way was opened up to him.

A two-sworded man stood before him, blocking his path. "You are Genzo of Shimoda in Izu?," the warrior asked. He put the question politely, he did not bark or snarl, as is the usual manner with samurai who deign to speak to creatures of Genzo's low position. He carried himself with the assurance of one who knows his worth and is certain of his facts, just as a policeman does, or an official of the Shogun's government. Feeling both frightened and betrayed, Genzo bent his knees, prepared to make the required obeisance, not seeing in this samurai the emissary of Kannon.

Genzo had gone to Kannon's great shrine at Sensoji in Asakusa of Edo with another of Lord Okubo's footmen. Early that morning ten retainers had been ordered to attend Lord Okubo's second son and two of his friends while they went from the daimyo's great mansion in Nagata-cho to visit in the Yoshiwara, and to bring the young gentlemen safely home again before the Shogun's police closed all the barriers at nightfall. Ordinarily, gentlemen in search of the assorted pleasures available in the flower pavilions of the Lucky Plain would spend the night there. But in these uncertain times the Bakufu, the Government of the Tent, as the people of Nippon called the Shogun's rule, allowed no one to escape its surveillance. Therefore, it decreed that every man, woman, and child of Edo must be present in his registered household during the hours of darkness.

Ordinarily, too, such ventures from Lord Okubo's mansion to the Gay Quarter would be made in riverboats, with oarsmen to take the painted vessels and their festive passengers through the streams and moats and canals of the city until they reached the Yoshiwara, waiting there, a garden of delights, beyond the Great Dike of Nippon, near the last bend of the Sumida River before it approaches the Bay of Edo. On this day, however, Lord Okubo's son wished to go first to Echigoya, the fashionable draper's shop in Suruga-cho, in order to buy some silks and brocades from the large stock the Mitsui had just received from Kyoto.

He was no languid, feckless spendthrift, this second son of Okubo Ichio, Lord of Odawara. Inasmuch as the chimbun, the pacification forces despatched by order of the young Meiji emperor, were marching eastward from Kyoto, intending to subdue once and for all the Shogun's rebellious warriors assembled in Edo, Lord Okubo's son foresaw some inconveniences in the days ahead. His father and elder brother being very much occupied as members of the Shogun's council, this second son had instructed the clan's chamberlain and his agents to buy up all the rice and pickled vegetables and salted fish they could put into the mansion's storehouses (a maneuver the chamberlain did not tell him he had completed several weeks before), while he himself would undertake the arduous task of acquiring stocks of precious brocades and more common silks.

Alas for foresight. Some men are endowed with a considerable measure of it, but others acquire more. The double-dealing Mitsui, having been in the business of outwitting everyone in Nippon for almost two hundred years, generously permitted Lord Okubo's son to buy a single bolt of silk and none of the brocade. To add to his vexation the head of their shop—a vulgar merchant named Minomura Rinzaemon, who laughed loudly and had very bad teeth—politely but firmly explained that all the rest of Echigoya's costly fabrics had been "committed."

All this sipping of tea and chaffering over unattainable bargains at Echigoya used up most of the morning and every bit of the young master's good temper. Storming out of that den of duplicity, he flung himself into his palanquin, snarling a command to hurry. Each distressed friend scrambled into his separate norimono. Jiro, the officious sergeant in charge of the group, bellowed his orders, and in fine array the procession set out at last for the Yoshiwara.

Trotting along beside the norimono of gentlefolk was no great hardship for Genzo and his fellows. "Flying feet," as footmen are called, soon become accustomed to the pace. Their chief duty in Edo was to provide care and honor for their august lord and the eminent members of his clan whenever they travelled along the huge city's busy streets. "Down! Down!," they would shout. "Off with your head gear! Get out of the way!," warning commoners and samurai who might not see them coming or notice the fluttering banners with the bold Okubo crests.

In Edo, full of policemen and warriors as it was, showing the crest of a daimyo was more important than offering a pretense of protection. Especially during these troubled times, when the country was divided among several factions, as the great lords vied for power among themselves and the manlier nobles in Kyoto plotted to restore the emperor to his rightful place as ruler, the daimyo still supporting the Shogun took every opportunity to display their crests in Edo. Among those the famed Aotari Fuji no Daimonji of the Okubo clan—the white circle enclosing a wreath of wistaria leaves surrounding the arrogant character for dai—commanded respect wherever it appeared. To even the most illiterate peasant that dai (which can also be read as o, as it is in Okubo) means "great." And every one who saw the Okubo mon —upon banners, kimono, liveries, palanquins—knew that, by his very presence, the powerful Okubo no Ichio, Odawara no Kami, helped to keep the peace in Edo.

On this day Genzo fretted at the thought of those hours of waiting about in the tiny tea shops or steamy bathhouses or cold alleys in Sanya or Imado, the wards just outside the Gay Quarter, while inside its walls the young gentlemen disported themselves with geisha, maiko, prostitutes, and dissolute Kabuki actors. Genzo's companions, however, did not mind the respite. They were delighted to be set free for several hours, to seek whatever pleasures their desires yearned for and their light money pouches allowed. In this fabled quarter of three thousand courtesans —where for every thousand registered whores there were two thousand willing servant girls and beguiling servant boys, not to mention uncounted numbers of places in which to lay them— most of Genzo's companions were too poor to go anywhere except to the public bath houses. There they could keep warm at least—and with luck they might find a woman, or a boy, who did not cost more than a zeni or two.

Genzo, somewhat older than his associates—and therefore less interested in hunting out a bed mate than he had been at their age—found himself becoming increasingly bored by these expeditions to the Flower Quarter. He had no right to complain, as he knew very well; but on this day especially he could admit to himself that no prospect pleased him. The very idea of steeping himself in a common bath while listening to his fellows' banter, unvarying and coarse and loud, depressed him. He did not have enough money to buy a good meal in a quiet restaurant. Going to one or the other of the theatres in the neighborhood, to see whatever plays or dances the actors and other river-bank folk happened to be presenting, held no attractions. Thinking only that he must get away from this noisy Okubo pack, he planned to escape at the earliest chance.

After leaving the Mitsui's shop, the party ran past the area of devastation in Nihonbashi, not yet entirely rebuilt since the great fire of the year before, dashed through the districts of Kanda, Ueno, and Asakusa. A long hour later the ten guardian footmen and the six grunting norimono bearers, all sweating and steaming like hard-run horses, arrived at the summit of the Great Dike. Below them lay the Yoshiwara, the "Nightless City" now denied its night.

A walled enclosure, more than a thousand feet long on two of its sides, more than seven hundred feet wide on the others, it covers with stones and houses and streets the place where once upon a time only swamp reeds and rushes grew. Through its middle, straight as a spear shaft, from the Great Gate in the eastern wall to the Water Works Gate in the western, runs the Naka-no-cho, the Yoshiwara's central thoroughfare. The most famous and the costliest brothels in Nippon line both sides of this wide avenue. From it, at right angles, open the three streets that divide the Pleasure Quarter into its tiny wards; and from these side-streets lanes and alleys branch off, like twigs in the crown of a pine tree. Along these side streets and byways stand the lesser brothels, houses of assignation, tea houses, bath houses, and dwelling places of the folk who serve the courtesans of the Yoshiwara.

Moving slowly, because of the scores of people going to the Flower Pavilions, Lord Okubo's norimono bearers carried their precious freight down the Emon-zaka, the sloping road connecting the Great Dike with Go-jikken-machi, the wide causeway that crosses the moat and leads to the Great Gate. Beyond that barrier no palanquins can go, no samurai can carry his swords, no man of any rank or name can take in any weapon save the one he is born with.

Lord Okubo's bearers moved carefully to the causeway's side, gently lowered the three norimono to the gravel in front of one of the fifty teahouses that give the causeway its name. The footmen ran forward to help their young gentlemen crawl out of those slings of torment. Daimyo and their sons would be more comfortable if they simply walked, or rode white horses, to the Yoshiwara, as was the custom in older times. But they can not depart from this newer style because pride will not permit them to travel on foot, as vulgar commoners do, and the Shogun's sumptuary laws proscribe the use of horses for such frivolous purposes.

The three young lords struggled forth from those boxes in which they'd been bounced about like dice in a gambler's cupped hands. Genzo felt a touch of pity for the young aristocrat to whom he offered knee and shoulder for support. Even if he was a daimyo's son the poor youth was as pale as the undergarment next to his delicate skin. While kneeling footmen helped to arrange the folds of their kimono the venturesome three managed to straighten backs and legs. They gave their pairs of swords to sergeant Jiro for safekeeping and tottered bravely toward the O-Mon. Policemen at the Great Gate bowed low as they entered the City of Joy. No one ordered them to register at the Police Box. The Okubo crest, borne in the five prescribed places upon the young lord's kimono, more than made up for the obscurity of those upon his friends'. As everyone knew, inside the gate or outside it, upon this day, as always, they were going to the Nishida-ya, the House of the Western Ricefield, in Edo-cho I-chome, the first street to the right, because for 246 years all the sons of all the successive daimyo of Odawara have frequented that palace of

pleasures, inasmuch as it was founded by Shoji Jinemon of Odawara. Not only loyalty to a clansman took them there. The wish to
honor a great thinker was even stronger. For, as everyone should
know, Shoji Jinemon (may his name be forever remembered!) was
the far-sighted man who, after sixteen years of striving, finally
persuaded the Bakufu to permit the building of this New Yoshiwara, after the old one had burned down.

When his three charges were safely delivered to higher authority, Jiro dismissed the footmen but not the norimono bearers.
"Everybody back by four o'clock!," he bawled, and Genzo fled.
"But not you!," he barked at the bearers, lower than flying feet
in the destined order among men. "You carry those rattling seed-
pods off to my teahouse in Imado. Then take a rest. There. But
bring 'em back here by four o'clock. You hear? If you don't come
back in time, I'll slice off your noses. Both of 'em!—Now go!"

Genzo was hurrying back toward the Dike when his hope of escape was shattered. "Genzo-san! Wait a moment, please . . ." He
knew without looking who called him. That ear-piercing cry could
come only out of Kosaburo, the youth from Ajiro in Izu, who last
week had been added to Lord Okubo's household in Edo. Like
Genzo himself, Kosaburo was one more of Izu's many payments
of taxes in living man flesh to its honorable lord.

Genzo waited for the boy, unable to ignore him. Shikata ga nai,
he shrugged, with the patient Nipponjin's admission that a thing
can't be helped. Shikata ga nai, he says when he can still laugh,
at least a little, is not yet needing to cry. Shikata ga nai, he
groans, because he has never learned to swear. At least Kosaburo
would be different, being new. His chatter had not yet staled;
and, as the older retainers discovered almost in the moment he
arrived, he seemed to be a good-hearted fellow who responded
well to teasing. Sometimes, to tell the truth, Genzo was not sure
who was teasing whom. The manner in which Kosaburo introduced himself should have warned everyone that he was no ordinary country lout. "Kosaburo of Ajiro in Izu am I," he declared,
bowing low in proper respect for the men in the barrack. "Kosaburo. Written with the character for BIG, not small." As he spoke

he arranged hands and body in such a way that no one could have the slightest doubt about his meaning. Everyone roared with laughter at such a cocky, comical fellow, and they had been enjoying his company ever since. He had a fisherman's strong body, this Kosaburo, and certainly a quicker mind than most provincial folk possessed. Genzo could not help smiling as he watched the lad running toward him, the bushy topknot bouncing above his shaven forehead, the wide smiling mouth showing so many big white teeth.

"So, then," he said as Kosaburo fell into step beside him. "This is your first visit to the Lucky Plain?"

"Yes. And to all this part of Edo as well."

"Don't you want to see the Gay Quarter? If so, you are going the wrong way."

"Yes, of course I want to see it. But first I thought I must say a prayer at the shrine, before I enter the O-Mon."

"Good idea. We can go together that far, before we part."

"Aren't you going inside?"

"No. I've been inside before. Too often."

"Oh?" The boy sounded disappointed. "Isn't it—well, worth looking at?"

"Oh, I guess so. Once or twice, perhaps. After that, it's always the same. Especially if you have no money to spend." He tried to think of the Pleasure Quarter as this seventeen year-old Kosaburo must be imagining it, as once, not so long ago, he himself had imagined it. Six winters ago that had been, when he was twenty-two years old. Saa, how quickly time passes. Even at that advanced age he, too, had been fascinated by these throngs of laughing men and women, clad in gorgeous kimono that boasted more than words ever could how little heed they gave to the Bakufu's edicts against the wearing of costly raiment. And almost all these people, walking in the Yoshiwara's avenues or frolicking in its houses, were searching for pleasures the Bakufu did not approve but understood only too well it could not forbid.

"Here's the shrine," he stopped before the red torii marking the entrance to Yoshiwara Jinja. Beyond the gray leafless trees the little shrine itself, painted in vermilion, furnished with vessels bought with harlots' gold, glowed like a single ember in the ashes of a poor man's brazier. Residents of the Houses of Happiness went there to pray for good fortune, if not for contentment, addressing their gifts and their hopes to the deity of the place, Akaishi Inari, the Bright Stone Inari. Black as the hair on a head, and just as shining, the stone had been found in this very Moor of Reeds more than nine hundred years ago, more than seven hundred years before this New Yoshiwara was built. Because the stone bore a rude resemblance to a fox, the sacred messenger of Inari, the God of Rice—and therefore of wealth—no sensible man or woman neglected to pray to Akaishi Inari for the riches that might ease the pangs of sorrow. Needless to say, among the whores of Yoshiwara, too many of whom had been sold into bondage in this "sea of trouble and bitterness," Akaishi Inari was a popular deity. Through the god's intercession many a beautiful courtesan had been set free by a wealthy lover. And sometimes a plainer girl, by diligence and thrift, had been able to save enough money to buy her own liberty, before she sank forever into that greedy sea.

"You are not coming in?," asked Kosaburo.

"No." Shrines and temples are for people who want something, and Genzo asked nothing from gods or men except to be alone for a while. He hoped the boy would say goodbye, that they could part company now before unfriendliness hurt him.

"Then please wait for me here. I'll be back in a few breaths." He raced off under the bare trees, his straw slippers making no sound upon the mossy path.

Genzo waited, like a patient ox tied to a post, chiding himself for being so soft-hearted.

Having nothing to fear, Genzo and Kosaburo registered their names with the policeman at the O-Mon and stood at last within the Yoshiwara. Most obviously having nothing to spend, they received some fatherly advice from the policeman: "Stay away from the cheap ones. They're just as likely to be diseased."

Before them stretched the wide Naka-no-cho. At either side of the avenue two-storied brothels painted green rose up, high above all heads. Wide galleries on the second stories extended over the street and the entrance ways and cages below, making an arcade that protected passersby from rain or snow or summer's sun. Upon these galleries sat many happy people, drinking tea or saké, talking, watching the crowds moving along the pavement below.

The cherry trees for which the Naka-no-cho is so famous had been brought in, but were not yet put in the ground. Already in full bud, they waited in wooden tubs or clay pots or, in the case of the biggest trees, with their roots bound up in matting made of rice straw. Laborers were digging the pits along the middle of the avenue in which those largest trees would be placed. In two or three weeks all those swelling buds would burst open, and from one end to the other the street would be filled with the soft white haze. And crowds of people, vying with the flowers in number, would come from all the wards of Edo, from all the sixty-six provinces of Nippon, to view these sakura blossoms, because here they would be enhanced by the beauty of the Yoshiwara's other flowers.

Genzo knew the song they would sing, but not he nor Kosaburo. Viewing cherry blossoms anywhere, except while they worked in the yard of their lord's mansion, was a pleasure that flying footmen could enjoy only in passing.

> Tilling spring fields—
> We leave that to others.
> And the whole long day
> We spend
> Among the cherry blossoms.

On this day Genzo and Kosaburo saw only the flowers that are always there, regardless of the season. Genzo guided his companion from the country. Stretching his neck like a heron, in order not to miss a single one of the Famous Sights of the Yoshiwara, Kosaburo did not know that his feet touched earth instead of the clouds in dreams. Men in a hurry to find a courtesan brushed past him, but he did not notice. Loafers lounging about studied him to see if he were worth the trouble of fleecing, but he did not see when they dismissed him with a sneer. Hawkers and peddlers tried to sell him things—rice and flour cracknels from Takemura, the bean curd of Sanya, the sushi of Aoyagi, rice balls and pickled greens, rice dumplings of Shinowara, the sweet cakes and candies of famed Futaba-ya, good luck charms, potions for love, colored prints of celebrated beauties past and present, prayers for potency, medicines for diseases, and lists of harlots, complete with addresses and prices—but he only smiled at them, as if he were deaf and could not hear a word they said.

Seeing Kosaburo so entranced, Genzo looked with a fresh eye upon the scene, and admitted that it had beauty and interest—if one did not examine too deep. Better to gaze at the paper lanterns swaying from the galleries overhead, the many colored banners fluttering in the wind, gaudy with advertisements presented as simple pictures or in the complex characters borrowed from China. The fact that he could not read most of those kanji did not disturb him. Few people could decipher them, other than scholars and officials—and sign makers. But they were beautiful in themselves, those kanji, like the patterns that weeping willow leaves make by chance when they fall upon wet earth.

He admired the handsome woods, new or weathered, of the house fronts, and the elegant bars to the cages in which the courtesans sat. He inhaled the scent of eel or fish or shrimp being broiled for hungry customers, the very aroma of the smoke itself, swirling up from scores of kitchens in this little city of so many people, hungry for so many things.—Ah, the pleasures of this floating world, fleeting as they must be, can hold a man captive for the whole of his life, if he is not stronger in will than are the brothel-keepers of the Yoshiwara.

—Or weaker in purse. In a whisper, because he feared to be heard by the harlots who awaited a man's choice beyond those bars, Kosaburo said, "This place scares me, to tell the truth. So many beautiful women smiling at us. So many expensive kimono.

And I," he sighed, "with no money to spend. Not a zeni. Only the hole in a zeni's middle do I carry in my sleeve." He mimed his plight so comically that younger whores beyond the bars tittered, hiding their laughter behind dainty hands or painted fans.

The youth's honesty pleased Genzo. "That is how most of us feel," he said. Our lords collect the taxes, and their sons spend the money, he thought. And, he was exceedingly careful not to say, most of our pleasures come from attending them at theirs. For expressing such an opinion Genzo would have been beaten with cudgels of split bamboo, until his flesh hung in shreds and his blood dyed the white sands of justice. Genzo, a man most wary, did not utter such opinions to any one because he did not want to be overheard by the Shogun's spies and informers. The Tokugawa shoguns, who had been ruling Nippon by the Will of Heaven for 268 years, did not like people to say or do anything that would disturb the harmony of their realm.

Most people in Nippon, whether they were great or small, thought nothing, said nothing, did nothing to upset the serenity of their august rulers. Nobles, samurai, and commoners alike had been taught to believe that their shoguns were providing them with the best of all possible governments. The shoguns, having borrowed from China the constraints of Confucianism but few of its liberations, used Kung Fu Tze's precepts to rule their state and all the people in it. "Live contentedly, and await Heaven's will," the people were reminded of the ancient sage's summary message, in almost every pronouncement of the Bakufu.

To this had been added the passiveness commended by Buddhism. Accordingly, the people of Nippon believed that nothing they might do in this life could change the flow of events ordained by Heaven, or could alter their relationships either with the lords who governed them while they lived or with the grasses that covered their bodies when they died. Change, if it came, could come only in the next life, with the next turning of the Great Wheel of Karma.

Thus, comfortingly, the precepts of Confucianism were conjoined with those of Buddhism, and—because death is the way out of it—no one in this world of sufferings was left without hope of improving his lot in the next.

Moreover, as all men of sense agreed, the course of events which affected them during this present life had been determined by their behavior in earlier incarnations. Genzo had been such a man of sense—until recently.

Strolling from one cage to the next, acting like wealthy merchants who lacked neither money nor time, Genzo and Kosaburo examined "the flowers of Yoshiwara budding and blossoming" for their enjoyment. Some of the older flowers, already withering and fading at the edges perhaps, and fearing to be without admirers for the day, smiled prettily at the two young men, showing their attractively blackened teeth. Some of the buds, knowing that they would not lack attention, pretended not to see them, or flirted coyly, with many an artful lifting of full sleeve or opened fan. Some affected to be reading long letters from absent lovers. The newest buds of all, not yet learned in the ways, fidgeted with playthings, made paper frogs, or chewed noisily upon the berries of the winter cherry. To Kosaburo, all were beautiful. To Genzo, all were saddening. For both, all were beyond attaining.

Thus they were walking along, engaged in a "spree without money" as annoyed whoremasters say, when suddenly Kosaburo stopped, his mouth opened like a fish's gaping in air. "Maa!," he pointed, unable to say more. Genzo saw the cause of his confusion and drew him back, joining other folk who gathered to watch the oiran pass.

Like a slow-moving pillar of fire she seemed, a blaze of red and orange and gold burning in the wide road, hedged in by serving men and women clad in drab kimono the color of wood, and attended by two little page girls resembling sparks from her flame. Before her walked a man holding a large paper lantern, lighted even at this midday. Characters brushed in red and black upon its surface told spectators the name of the brothel she served and where it could be found. To instruct people who could not read, the lantern bearer called out the information in a proud voice. Behind the oiran walked a younger man. Upon his right shoulder he bore the pole of a huge scarlet umbrella opened high above her head, to shield her from the cold gray sky. And behind him tripped a sharp-eyed woman, who watched over the oiran and all her company.

The courtesan moved past, stepping in the difficult and famous uchi hachimonji style, sliding her feet, with toes pointed inward, as if they inscribed upon the pavement the Chinese symbol for eight. The height of the lacquered geta supporting her small feet, the great weight of the many under-robes and the stiff crimson outer-robe covering the slender body, prevented her walking without assistance. At the left side a handsome young wakaimono kept her mincing pace, while she, with ineffable grace, supporting herself with a small white hand laid upon his shoulder, glided slowly forward, like a puppet responding to the touch of its master. Her right arm helped to ease the burden of the enormous bow of the obi: a confection of shining silks and ornate brocades, embroidered with threads of gold, silver, and new-leaf green, tied about with thick cords and freighted with tassels, it was half as big as herself. She wore it high upon her belly, in the oirans' outrageous celebration of their difference from women of virtue.

She moved past, as if dancing to the stately music of flutes and samisen being played in a distant shrine. Her gorgeous clothes; her head held high in pride, weighted though it was by the crown of black hair dressed in the Oshidori style, pierced with long pins fashioned of finest tortoise shell and luminous amber, which glowed like the nimbus upon the image of a bodhisattva; her face, a mask of white powder upon which two tiny lips were painted in brightest red; her eyes modestly lowered, that she might not look upon men in the street, proclaimed to everyone her profession and her use: she was a walking doll, a plaything for sale only to the wealthiest of buyers. Never had Kosaburo seen anything so beautiful!

Unable to contain themselves, lustful men called out their admiration for her loveliness, their approval of her profession. Wives and virtuous women forgot to sniff their disdain as they envied the splendor of her apparel. Kosaburo the Stunned sighed, because such loveliness lay beyond his grasp, forever. He might more easily build a bridge to the clouds than lie with a courtesan of her worth.

"Who is she?," he asked, before only the memory of her remained.

" 'A bride of one night,' " explained Genzo. "Tamakoto is her name. She is the ninth one to bear that famous title. A new yujo, soon to be one of the Celebrated Beauties of the Yoshiwara, I suspect. And very expensive. One hundred momme, for the night. Including the supper, of course. But not the rest of the fees. The bill for the man who marries her tonight will be six feet long, you can be sure."

"How do you know all this?"

Genzo laughed, looking down at the youth, so full of questions, so full of innocence. "Didn't you hear the man with the lantern, telling us all this? Didn't you read her name and house on the lantern he carried?"

"No. I heard nothing. I saw nothing else but her."

"Well! She stole your heart so soon? Shall we go after her?"

Shaking his head, waking from a dream, Kosaburo said, "In the next life, perhaps, I shall have that much money to spend upon a woman. But not in this. In this round I must be content with kitchen maids, until my father finds me a wife. Long ago I decided that all my lays must be free."

"A wise decision," said Genzo as they started walking again, edging their way through the crowds of men around the cages. "If you can keep to it. But in the Yoshiwara you will find nothing that is free. Not even a piece of ground to sit upon when you are tired." He wondered if he should offer to lend Kosaburo a few zeni from his own light pouch, then fell to worrying whether doing so would be a favor or a hurt for the youth. Starting him off with a debt, no matter how small, might be a bad beginning for his life in this big expensive city. Not to mention the burden of gratitude he would have to assume in accepting the loan. What, Genzo pondered, never knowing how to gain the answer, what is the Will of Heaven in these matters of insignificant cause and incalculable effect? One act, no matter how small, is linked to all other acts, past or future.

"To tell the truth," Kosaburo showed him how a man shapes his fate by his own deeds, "now that I've seen this much of the Yoshiwara—and in return have been shown how poor I am—I think I'd better go to Sensoji in Asakusa. It is quite close, is it not? Have you been there? Do you know the way? A brother of my father lives in Asakusa and owns a noodle shop in the temple yard. If we can find him, maybe he'll give us a bowl of soba. I could use a couple of them, right now."

"A pinch of dry salt, more likely—thrown at us when we come through the door. As if we were demons." Genzo put no faith in the charity of Edo's shopkeepers. And Kosaburo would learn soon enough that no merchant owned a shop of any kind, not even a peddler's tray, in Sensoji's extensive compound. The temple itself owned the land, the shops, and all the spaces around them. And it rented those at high fees to vendors of trinkets and comforts. They in turn, if they wanted to be successful, had to count every single small coin that came into their hands. Their stinginess was notorious, as the wealth of the temple was notable. Genzo did not care much for merchants, but he had even less liking for temples like Sensoji, ancient and grand and rich though it might be. And he had not the slightest regard for the sleek priests who profitted from them.

He did not especially want to go to Sensoji. Yet accompanying Kosaburo was better than wandering aimlessly and alone through the cold lanes of Sanyo and Imado, dodging gangs of kabuki-mono, those roistering young men who strutted about like noisy actors in search of a stage; or ducking the rival groups of hata-moto, who tried to maintain some degree of order in the Yoshi-wara; or fleeing from the soshi, those brutal bands recruited from the city's gamblers, confidence men, bribe-collectors, and heavy-handed bullies, whom the Bakufu hired to provoke "trouble" among people the Bakufu wanted to eliminate; or fighting off pimps trying to sell their women; or rejecting "foxes" of the lowest class, trying to sell themselves.

"Yes. I know the way." He yielded to the impulse, not knowing that his guardian deity was drawing him, too, toward his destined fate. "Let's go to Sensoji. In hope of a bowl of soba."

"Not only that. An uncle, too, don't forget. A family nearer to me than Ajiro. I have been in Edo for only a week, and already I am longing for home."

Fierce and swift the grief rose in Genzo. The ache of it made him want to howl. But, as always, the face revealed nothing, the body showed no sign of his struggle to force the demon of sorrow back into its abode. Why grieve?, he taunted himself, scorn being the only remedy he knew for quieting such pain. This is your karma, he reminded his rebelling self.

Kosaburo, following behind, knew nothing of the turmoil he had stirred up in Genzo. As is the way of the young, who suffer from lesser troubles, he had not yet learned the meanings of those sudden silences which sometimes gripped his elders, he had not yet studied the language of sorrow. In this, the springtime of his life, he was happy to be a part of the floating world, not yet realizing how treacherous are its lures, how transient its pleasures.

Some of his present happiness, he knew, came from walking with this serious mystifying man, whom all the lower people in Lord Okubo's household respected but few could like. Kosaburo, from the day he arrived at Lord Okubo's mansion in Edo, had cast many a quick glance at Genzo, not in longing but in fascination. He was so different from all other commoners who served in the yashiki. Although in the clan's office he was registered as nothing more than a peasant from Shimoda in Izu, he looked like a samurai—and, even more impressive, he bore himself like a two-sworded man. Indeed, as Kosaburo soon learned from the more romantical females in the household, to them Genzo looked like a nobleman, as much out of place among peasants as a crane among crows. They lusted for his body, tall and lean, wide at the shoulders, narrow at the hips. They admired the elegant curve of his nose, the high cheekbones, the sunken cheeks, the full lips and resolute chin. If he seemed to take notice of them, with his deep-set eyes, they fluttered about like hens being hunted by a cock. They fought among themselves to wash his clothes, to scrub his back in the barrack bath house, to lie with him in one of those little rooms set apart for that purpose by the kind providence of the clan's chamberlain. And when, as happened on occasion (for he was most definitely a man in this respect), he chose one of them to ease his need, she was the envy of her companions—until someone else replaced her on the next occasion. Never had the same wench been chosen twice. Why this should be so they did not know. More practical folk guessed that he was one of those men who did not want to be bothered with a wife and children. Others said that he was afraid to love, because he had been hurt by a faithless woman. And the younger maids, of course, quoted the ancient explanation for all such mysteries. "A man's heart and the autumn sky: both alike are fickle."

The older servants, no longer heated, filled only with the cold ashes of fires long since burned out, were the ones who whispered that, of course, Genzo must be the lost son of some young lord, pushed into a servant girl in Shimoda, and that he had been brought up in poverty because his father, having gone upon his merry way (as all young lords are wont to do), never knew that he existed. Such accidents of bedding happen often, as everyone can see all about her, every day in her life; and no one sneered either at Genzo or at his misfortuned mother because he lacked a father to claim him. No, the mystery that excited those happy gossips was the identity of his father. And the fuel that kept their kitchen fantasies alive was the expectation that someday, somehow, his true father's family would discover that he lived—the very son and heir they had been praying for and had been denied all these years by the justice of the Lord Buddha. Why, such things happen all the time, they assured each other, their eyes moistening at the thought of the great lineage and the immense fortune that Genzo would gain when his family found him. "Breeding, rather than birth," they said knowingly, nodding wisely over their cups of weak tea.

But no one among Lord Okubo's army of retainers ever saw a

man of any rank who looked like he might have fathered Genzo.
And if Lord Okubo and the officials of his clan knew who that
man might be, they did not tell him where he might find his mis-
laid son. They treated Genzo in exactly the same manner as they
treated all commoners—that is to say as something less than the
mud under their feet. Only the commoners among whom he lived
and served thought that Genzo was different.

Genzo could have ended their fancies about his father, but he
did not care to do so. Let them talk, let them guess, he thought.
The less they know about me, the better. He knew very well who
his father was. Neither could deny the other. The father and his
three sons were as alike as brothers born a generation apart. And,
indeed, Genzo's father was nothing more than a poor farmer
from Shimoda of Izu.

Genzo's grandfather was the one those foolish gossips in Edo
would have sold their last teeth to hear about. He was the one
who gave the men in Genzo's family their fine bodies, their in-
quiring minds, and their heavy burdens of sorrows. Although
when he was a youth he pretended to be only the spendthrift
younger son of a court official in Kyoto, in secret he read books
about the new learning from the West, about the new thoughts
stirring in Nippon. He would have been safe enough with his
reading if he had been as secret in his conversations. But, because he talked too openly about the teachings of men like
Motoori Norinaga, the master from Matsusaka near Ise, who ad-
vocated restoring the emperor to power, the Bakufu plucked this
young man out of Kyoto and dropped him down in Shimoda.

There, "eating cold rice" as the saying goes, at the end of the
world, without books, companions, money, or faith to sustain
him, the young exile lived long enough to father one son upon a
farmer's daughter before he went mad with despair and killed
himself. He was twenty-two years old when he cut the veins in
arms and legs with a grain sickle and watched his warm blood
flow out upon the mud of the fields he hated. The shame of his
banishment and destruction warped the life of his son, making

him a man cruel and bitter who hated learning of any kind. He never knew whether to love or to hate his own sons, born peasants, without even a memory of their ancestors' great name, but bearing still the stamp of their grandfather, a man so different from all the rest.

Different, a man apart, thought Genzo, striding toward Asakusa with Kosaburo at his heels. In its usual way Genzo's burst of grief had given way to questioning and despair. With them came thoughts that threatened to crack his strong will, to strip from him the mask of self control that he knew was as false as the smile upon a Yoshiwara harlot. And they were dangerous thoughts: if the Bakufu learned of them, policemen would come running in alarm, to cut him down where he stood.

Fortunately for harried men, few policemen can read their secret minds. Genzo and Kosaburo passed again without challenge through the O-Mon. The doshin, those constables of low rank who watch and listen for troublemakers in the wards of Edo, seemed not to notice them. Even so, Genzo knew, he and Kosaburo would be remembered in every detail, from the size of their topknots down to the pattern of mud spots on the gaiters that covered their legs.

Between the Yoshiwara and Asakusa lies one of Edo's poorer districts where artisans and workmen live and, in clusters of even meaner hovels, the eta, those outcasts who perform the most degrading of all services for the populace of the vast city. Yet, poor as these laborers might be in worldly goods, they own in plenty something that the Yoshiwara lacks entirely. Kosaburo, himself so recently a boy, did not see the children. But Genzo looked upon them with envy. To him, so recently robbed of his own, they were the greatest of riches.

The children, as is their habit, played in the streets, dodging among their elders, shouting, shrieking, intent only upon games, heedless of running noses, half-opened kimono, and the cold wind. Here and there an older girl carried a baby brother or sister strapped to her back. From the rooftops a number of boys tried to send kites aloft, only to have them beaten back by the strong winds blowing in from the east. The noise and commotion, the "gata-gata" of their wooden clogs clacking on the street, the happy faces, reminded Genzo that children can find fun anywhere, even in the midst of poverty. This is Nippon, he said to himself, sure that he came close to treason with the thought. The land of promise and of want. The land of rosy cheeks and blue feet.

As they crossed the bridge over the canal flowing between Sanya and Asakusa the icy winds attacked them, piercing their padded kimono and tightly-wrapped leggings, finding even their hands, drawn into the sleeves of their short happi coats. As they hurried to reach the shelter of houses on the farther shore Genzo pointed with his chin. "Sensoji," he called, more cheerfully than he felt.

Dark against the bleak sky to the east, the five-storied pagoda stood up, the tallest structure in all Edo. On most days sunlight touched its graceful spire, causing to shine the nine copper rings, representing the Spheres of Paradise, that support the brazen flames telling of a buddha's spirit mounting to Heaven. But on this day the spire was as black as the inside of a demon's heart. People in this world below who looked up to it for an omen would find no joy in it this day.

To the left of the pagoda the great gray curved roof of Sensoji's main hall loomed above the houses of Asakusa.

Not until they were caught up in the horde of pilgrims, coming from all parts of Nippon to worship at Kannon's shrine, did Genzo remember that this was the central day in the week-long festival of Higan. After this holy day, which marks the beginning of spring, the hours of sunlight will prevail over the hours of darkness. And on this very day the sun whirls round and round, in a dance of triumph, before it sinks to its rest beyond the western sea.

Pushed along by the tide of people, as driftwood is carried by a running sea, Genzo and Kosaburo entered the narrow gate that is the entrance to Sensoji. Just so, the gateway reminds those who wish to think that far ahead just so is the entrance to the next world: narrow is the gate, and numerous are the spirits of those who die. But, among the many that must pass through, who will achieve enlightenment and eternal peace? And who will be sent to the Netherworld for judgment by the tribunal of Emma-o, the King of the Dead?

Among the living, alas, especially on festival days at famous temples and shrines, not many people have time to think about dying and judgment. Once they've burst through a temple's narrow gate they rush about in search of their goals upon this earth as if they have just entered Mount Potalaka itself, the Lord Buddha's own Paradise. Fighting their way to the edge of the maddened horde, Genzo and Kosaburo finally reached the harbor of an unoccupied space beside a mountain of rubbish, the harvest and memorial of yesterday's visitors. "In the Name of the Thunder God!," cried Kosaburo, who had never even imagined so many people gathered in one place. Looking ahead, where the multitudes seemed to have increased tenfold, he moaned, "How shall we find my uncle in this Hell?"

Genzo, a man of unshakable calm, experienced in the ways of humankind, said, "Let us ask the priests. If they do not know, no one on this earth will."

At the counter of a nearby booth, served by two novices trying to keep their composure amid the wails of lost children, the importunities of old ladies in immediate need of a place of convenience, and insistent folk determined to leave messages for unfound friends, Kosaburo learned where, in the maze, his uncle's noodle shop might be. "But even they are not sure," he complained to Genzo. "Three different soba shops here are run by men named Mampei. They do not know which one might be Mampei of Ajiro in Izu. How can this be? When they are so learned?"

At last, after much asking about among wandering vendors of trinkets and people selling things from booths, and after much puzzling over conflicting instructions, all pointing in different directions, they happened by accident upon the soba shop managed by Mampei of Ajiro in Izu. Genzo refused to enter the place, so small as to be invisible, and already overfilled with customers. He very much doubted whether Kosaburo could thrust himself into the cell, more packed with bodies than is a holy painting showing the disciples of Buddha gathered beside his deathbed. And Genzo was willing to bet that Kosaburo's frantic uncle would spare him neither nod, noodles, nor dry salt on this busy day. Hastily agreeing to meet at the bridge to Sanya soon after the temple bell announced the third hour, they parted.

Hungry by then, irritated more by his stupidity in having come to this frenzied place than by the people themselves, Genzo wanted only to be alone. He plunged once more into the crowd on the Nakamise, shuffled along with it toward the Great Shrine, scarcely visible beyond the banners flapping on their bamboo poles and the smoke rising from hundreds of cooking-fires. At one of the stalls along the way he bought a broiled squid impaled upon a spit of bamboo. Then, eager to get away from the mob, from the Nakamise where—as Kichibei and Kisaburo did observe—"the smell of eels is changed into the sound of money," he set out in search of a quiet spot where he might decently eat the tough thing, without being seen at his chewing by a host of disapproving countrymen.

He turned into one of the narrow alleys that led to the far side of the temple yard. Unlike the main approach to the Grand Shrine, so holy, so crowded, and so dirty, the side street was almost deserted. It was clean as well, and the farther he went the quieter it became. Gnawing furtively at his lunch while he walked, he began to feel less annoyed. Now, if he could only find a place to sit, alone, in peace and quiet, while he waited for time to pass, he would consider that the day was not being misspent after all.

He passed through the gate that opened the way to the chapel of Kannon in her guise as Nyo-i-rin: Kannon the Precious Stone Able to Fulfill All the Desires of Those Who Possess It.

Peace awaited him there, and beauty. Long ago, in less populous times, a priest had made a small garden in the chapel's forecourt. Now, hundreds of years later, the rocks mottled with lichens, the clear water in the little pond, the carefully trimmed azalea and camellia bushes, growing exactly where he had planted their predecessors, showed that successive generations of priests had cherished this garden, caring for it as its maker must have hoped they would. A plum tree in full blossom leaned over the pond, like a drift of mist surprised before it could vanish.

Drawn by such loveliness, Genzo walked slowly toward the chapel. On this cold afternoon no one else had come to it. For once he was alone. The noises of the crowds streaming toward the main hall, the cries of the merchants who profitted from the needs of pilgrims and increased the wealth of priests, were so muted that he did not hear them. Anger and grief forgotten, misery put aside for the while, he did not ask why now he rejoiced.

He stood beside the pond, studying this garden, as he studied every such garden he was given the chance to see. He examined the sizes and shapes of the rocks, their colors, textures, planes, and furrowings, the positions in which they had been laid, the places in which the shrubs and grasses had been planted, the areas in which the mosses were allowed to grow, the art with which the stepping stones had been fitted each to the other as well as to the tread of pilgrims who approached. In the beautiful silence he heard, as one hears the sound of a koto from a neighbor's house, the chiming of wind bells in the eaves of the pagoda, the soft murmur of water flowing down the face of the rounded boulder serving as mountain to the lake of the pond. He looked up into the cloud of the plum tree, put there to flower in its brief season.

Genzo, who could never hope to own such a garden, did not covet it or envy the priests who shared it. The fact that such a refuge existed, to comfort him when most he needed help, was enough. In the midst of pain and grief a man can find solace in beauty, it said to him, as the priest who planned this garden knew that it would before ever he made it. In the contemplation of beauty the spirit understands that this world holds more than dirt and ugliness. And the man who understands this message is wise, for then he knows that, in the long span of eternity, struggle is useless and sorrow is meaningless.

He stood beneath the plum tree. Only a few of its blossoms had fallen. They lay like snowflakes upon the cold gray pebbles, like the first warriors slain upon a field of battle. Like sons lost too soon to death. This, too, was the garden's reason, and the message of the plum blossoms in their glory. Death will come in time, they warned, knowing their fate before they fell. This floating world: it is also a sad world. But just as after a blossom flowers it must also wither and die, so also out of death new life must grow. The unchanging rocks, the unfailing water, the nourishing earth: they give that new life a place to grow.

Looking down at the fallen blossoms, white upon the rounded pebbles fetched from some unknown river's bed, Genzo saw a stone that was different. It was black and hard and dense, shaped rather like a pillow block, resisting the forces that had rounded and polished the millions of gray pebbles among which it lay. Thinking that it might be a thing of value, he picked it up, that one among many. It was no jewel, no object fashioned by the hand of man. Nor was it as black as he had thought. Little flecks of green and yellow glowed in its surface, like lamps seen through mist on a dark night. It was a pebble like all the others, in one sense. Yet, in another sense, it was a pebble unlike all those others. But where did it come from? And how did it get there?

When he examined the curved bed with its countless little stones, seeming as alike as one grain of sand is to another, Genzo discovered a few other black pebbles similar to the one he held. Seeing them there filled him with relief. This stone lying in his hand was no miracle, no particular sign from Heaven given only to him. It was only a fragment from a far off mountain which had fallen into a stream, and then, in time, had been swept along by the waters of that stream until it rested among fragments of other mountains which were being gathered in the course of a mighty river. It was only a stone, then, like myriads of others. Yet it was different . . .

Warming it in his hand, Genzo knew that he must take this stone with him. It would be his one treasure, the one thing in his life that would be his own. No daimyo would deign to take it from him, and no thief would bother to steal it. This stone, he knew in his heart, was destined for him. Just as—the thought rose with a certainty that mounted almost to joy—this visit to Sensoji must have been destined.

But why had Kannon-sama directed him to this garden? And why had she led him to this stone?

To these questions he could think of many answers, as can any man who is presented with mysteries. The more he pondered, the more confused he became. Until, at last, he remembered where he was. In awe he stared at the precious stone he held in his hand. In terror he sank to his knees, feeling the presence of the One Who Is Able To Fulfill All the Desires of Those Who Possess It.

Thus did it happen that Genzo, the one who was different, the questioner who scorned priests and did not believe in miracles, the man who refused to ask favors either from men or from gods, pushed and squeezed and fought his way to the shrine of Kannon, more desperate to get there than all those other beggers for her mercy. Like all the others he, too, purified hands and mouth with clear cold water, bought sticks of incense from the wrinkled old woman with blackened teeth, clutched at the eddying smoke to gain its benefits. He, too, mounted the steep flight of stairs leading up to the shrine, threw his zeni toward the collection box, clapped hands, bowed his head, and, driven by need yet divided by doubt, implored her to help him find a way. "O All-wise and All-powerful Goddess of Mercy," he murmured the ancient formula, "cleanse my heart from sins and deliver me from worldly ills." He stopped, for the briefest of moments. "Help me . . ." he begged.

No thunder sounded from Heaven, no blaze of fire enveloped him or illumined the shrine. To him, the clinking of common coins, the clatter of hundreds of feet pounding upon the stairs, seemed to beat back his prayers as sleet beats back tender rice plants set out too soon in the spring.

Feeling somewhat saddened, and not a little foolish, Genzo came down from the temple.

Yet the purpose of the benevolence of Kannon is, above all, to save a man who asks her help. She gives him the wisdom to know what is the truth. As the sutra promises, "no sooner do men's moanings of agony reach her than she takes pity on them and saves them from the tortures of Hell. If they offer a sincere prayer to Kannon, even fire cannot burn them, and water cannot drown them."

When Genzo's feet touched again the enduring earth a man stood before him, blocking his way.

CHAPTER 2
THE MESSENGER OF KANNON

"**S**tand up, Genzo-san, stand up," said the samurai, embarrassed by such a show of respect. "How can you fear me? Or have you forgotten?"

Never in Genzo's long years of service had a samurai spoken so kindly to him. He stood straight again, wondering what this extraordinary condescension might mean. "Excuse me, master," he replied, "this stupid thing does not remember. . ." Then, slowly, in the rounded head, the squinting sailor's eyes, the wide determined mouth, he recognized the man who had saved his life twelve years before. "Nakamura-san?," he asked, beginning again to make the deep bows a commoner owes to his superiors, only to be bumped from the rear by an annoyed citizen of Edo. "Stupid!," growled the important fellow, until he saw the two-sworded personage who stood beyond Genzo. Ducking his head, mumbling a string of excuses, he scuttled off, like a crab running from a net.

Looking grim, Nakamura-san said, "Let us find a quieter place. Before we are flattened underfoot."

As Genzo followed, marveling at this encounter, he could not help but think back to the time when Nakamura-san rescued him from violent death. That had been the most terrible day in his whole life. And before it ended he knew that, from that day forth, he would be forever marked.

Inasmuch as, in those peaceful years of Genzo's boyhood, few samurai of any rank lived in Shimoda of Izu, that remotest of provincial seaports, the master of the town's one school of martial

arts petitioned the Bakufu for permission to accept as paying pupils the sons of certain worthy merchants. The ryu master was
emboldened to make this request because he knew that teachers
of the martial arts in great cities such as Edo, Nagoya, Osaka,
and Kyoto had long ago been granted the privilege he solicited.
After suitable delay of several years, and with seemly reluctance,
the Bakufu consented to a temporary suspension of the warriors'
code—not out of consideration for Shimoda's hungry ryu master
but out of concern to sustain the school his grandfather had established. For once in their careers of bafflement and confusion,
the officials of the Bakufu were anticipating changes that might
be forced upon them in the future, rather than thinking merely of
safeguarding the unchanging order of the past. They suspected
that they would need both the school and the samurai who would
be trained in it if ever those prowling red-haired, green-eyed barbarians from the West sailed their black ships once again into
Shimoda's little harbor—as, alas, they gave every sign of being
about to do.

Even so, in their forethoughtfulness, the Bafuku's officials did
not forget duty to class: they kept the vulgar in place by decree-
ing that ryu masters, wherever they might be, must not teach
commoners' sons the art of using genuine swords. A sword is a
warrior's "living soul," and no low commoner is permitted to
carry such a treasure. Instruction in the use of the fukuro shinai,
the mock sword made of wood or light bamboo sheathed in
leather, was deemed good enough for commoners.

When they received this edict of consent Shimoda's ryu master, its pushing merchants, and their bored sons were overwhelmed by the Bakufu's benevolent kindness. Happily, instruction could begin at once, because Shimoda's ryu master, like his
ancestors before him, taught heiho, the art of protection, according to the principles of the Itto School, and therefore had been
using the mock sword for his novice students drawn from the sons
of samurai.

Genzo, being a poor farmer's son, would never be considered
worthy of training in any kind of martial art. If ever Shimoda's

men should be called to war Genzo and his base sort could never fight in it. They might carry baggage chests, and provide food and shelter to sustain the samurai, but they would never lift a weapon in combat with warriors of that prideful class. Yet, by one of those contrivings of Heaven which must cause thoughtful men to wonder, an opportunity was given to Genzo to learn more about budo, the way of the warrior, than is accorded to most peasants' sons.

As his very name reveals, Genzo was the family's third son and unlikely to inherit its small holdings. Therefore, his father took him out of the nearby temple school when he was twelve years old, before he had received even two years of instruction, and put him to work at odd jobs in the town. In his thirteenth year, by great good fortune, the ryu master (who had a keen eye for stalwart lads) chose him to be one of the boys to live in the hall for martial arts. Four peasant boys served the master and his family, and helped to clean the budokan, the large hall in which the teacher and his disciples practised the arts of martial men.

In the beginning Genzo spent his time wiping floors, fetching water for drinking and washing, removing at dawn the sliding panels of wood that served as walls to the budokan, and replacing them at dusk or during heavy rainstorms. Because he was a cheerful worker and a pleasing youth, taller and stronger than the usual, the ryu master and some of his disciples began to favor Genzo, according him privileges that few farmers' sons ever achieved. He was allowed to massage the tired limbs of samurai, to wash and mend the clothing they wore while exercising in the budokan, and even, in time, to help them dress in the formal attire they must wear in public when they left the hall.

Before long, in that relaxed town where no great lord ever came, and prying officials from the Bakufu rarely entered, and even the o-metsuke, "the honorable eyes in attendance" who served the Bakufu as spies and censors, were friends and neighbors to everyone else, no one saw any reason for protest when Genzo, as well as others of his fellow drudges, were pressed into service as partners to the merchants' sons in their harmless dances of thrust and parry with the wooden lath in its leather sheath. And no one ever thought to send them away when, entranced, they watched true samurai armed with sharp swords engaging in the elegant duels of budo.

During those happy years of friendly acceptance in the budokan, rich in the smells of man sweat and even richer in the sounds of laughter and good fellowship that men arouse when they are at play, Genzo learned not only how to attack and how to defend, whether with staff or with sword. He learned something far more important, not from any instruction given him directly, but from listening to the ryu master while he taught his samurai disciples. "To know and to act are one and the same," the master would say, day after day, to his students who were learning to "grow from within," in their search for the true wisdom that comes when the "inner light" is attained.

Unknown to those samurai, almost without knowing it himself, Genzo learned—and he embraced, as a youth will who is reaching for the inner calm that is the mark of a virtuous man—the principles of self-discipline through which a student of budo attains control over his body and his emotions, and in consequence of which he becomes a man of peace, not a wager of war.

So Genzo lived in such harmony and true content, knowing little of life beyond the budokan's walls and nothing of sorrow or of death. He grew from a pleasing boy to a handsome youth, drawing more than a fair share of side-long glances from amorous maids and men alike. But of these, too, he knew nothing, in his devotion to the discipline of budo. Because of this "spiritual forging," and the example, the "wordless teaching," of the ryu master and certain of the older samurai, Genzo acquired other habits of which he remained unaware: he carried himself as they did, with shoulders braced and head erect, walked with their swaggering strut, as though he wore two swords at his side instead of none, moved with the confidence of a young noble instead of with the deference proper to a peasant's son. Perhaps this was his own idea, perhaps it was his grandfather's way of avenging himself upon the Bakufu which had destroyed him.

And, because Genzo prized most of all the inner calm of hara, the coolness of mind that comes with mastery over body and thought, he imposed a control upon his spirit that put a mask upon his face. Serene to the point where he seemed to have no passions at all, he looked like a bodhisattva who has attained release from this world of suffering men. Seeing him like this, amorous maids and men were driven to despair and commoners of any kind into bursts of anger. Seeing him like this too late, the ryu master rejoiced at such proof of the power of budo—and worried about the troubles that in this bitter world must surely come to a youth who has made himself so different from all others of his kind.

They began, those troubles, in a way far worse than anything the ryu master feared, one day in Genzo's sixteenth year.

They came in the Seventh Month of the Year of the Dragon (which, according to the Western calendar, would be the month of August in the year 1856), during the week before a black ship from America brought Consul-General Townsend Harris to Nippon. The Americans sent him to demand a place to live in Shimoda, an audience with a person he called "the Emperor of Japan," and the opening of the seaports and cities of Great Nippon to commerce with all the nations of the world.

Informed by spies in China that this unwanted barbarian was about to sail from Canton, the Bakufu appointed Okada Tadayoshi, Lord of Bingo, as special Governor for Shimoda, charging him to deny the foreigner any opportunity to stay in the Shogun's domain. Lord Okada, accompanied by a cohort of officials, warriors, clerks, censors, retainers, and servants, hastened down the coastal road from Edo to Shimoda, five hot days away.

In the time of waiting following their arrival in Shimoda some tempers were frayed, no doubt, both in the daimyo's official residence (hastily built for him amid rice fields to the west of the port) as well as in the overcrowded town itself. Most of Shimoda's people were delighted, however, by the presence of such distinguished guests, not to mention by the prospect of a visit from those fascinating foreigners. Inns and brothels were packed to the corridors; happy merchants sent for more supplies to the nearest villages and towns in Izu, Suruga, and Sagami; urchins and housewives rushed into the streets to admire the splendid retinue from Edo. And the budokan received more practitioners of the martial arts than it could easily hold.

During one of those hot summer afternoons a samurai of high rank, wearing the crest of his lord, the Daimyo of Bingo, strode into the budokan. Red-faced from having drunk too much saké, angered perhaps by some disappointment or slight, he glared about the dim hall. He should have been lying on a cool tatami at an inn, sleeping off his hurt; his retainers should have been attending him; his years of training in budo should have helped him to control his anger. But on this day his karma—and Ichiro's —ordained that he should enter the budokan of Shimoda with no friend to restrain him and no remembrance of the discipline of budo.

The ryu master did not observe his arrival, which omission increased his anger. The pairs of students, busy with their dueling, did not put down their weapons. And the spectators continued their cheerful shouts of praise or encouragement.

Only when the samurai from Bingo rushed out upon the smooth boards of the floor, snarling with rage, did all those men heed him.

"What is this?," he cried, pointing at Ichiro, son of the merchant Gozaemon, the youth who happened to be nearest to his accusing finger. Ichiro, taken by surprise, lowered the leather-bound staff with which he had been challenging his partner. "What is this?," the samurai cried again, his eyes narrowed to slits of evil. Now everything stopped in the great hall, every motion and sound and thought, as though frozen stiff by the most intense cold of winter. At the far end of the budokan, in the shadows near the wall where he was massaging a samurai who had just finished a session of exercise, Genzo's very blood turned to ice.

"Budo is for samurai," the warrior shouted. "Not for beasts! Not for dog shit like you!"

Desperate to appease him, the ryu master scurried forth on hands and knees, calling apologies to the great man.

The warrior did not hear him. With a strangled cry, he whipped his long sword from its sheath. The gleaming blade flashed, once, twice. Before Ichiro's left ear touched the floor, his right ear was falling to join it, his bright red blood was pouring forth upon them. Screaming, not in pain but with shame at being so abused, Ichiro forgot his training, and lifted his weak wooden staff to strike the enemy who had disgraced him. Grinning with malice, for this was exactly the response he expected, the samurai drove his sword through Ichiro's body. Remembering discipline too late, Ichiro did not cry out. Clutching his belly, he sank slowly to the floor, slipping from the sharp blade even as he died.

Of all the men in the budokan only Genzo made a move to avenge his friend. Still on his knees, forgetting all that he had ever learned about the gentleness of budo, he seized the long sword of the samurai lying before him. The harsh god rose up in him: with a hatred such as he had never known, he sprang to his feet, wanting only to kill the brutal butcher.

At this instant a man blocked his way. Saying not a word, looking into Genzo's blazing eyes with his commanding own, he forced down the boy's arms, pushed him back into the shadows, prevented him from throwing his life away after Ichiro's.

At the center of the exercise mats, standing amid all those silent men touching hands and heads to the floor in deference to his exalted rank, the violent warrior drew the packet of heavy white papers from its accustomed place next to his breast. He wiped the sword clean of Ichiro's cheap blood and, in the manner prescribed for expert swordsmen, slipped the sacred blade into its scabbard. He dropped the dirtied papers upon Ichiro's body.

"Encourage virtue and chasten vice," he said, as he strutted from the hall.

"Nakamura-san remembers me, after so many years?," Genzo asked, as they walked away from the Grand Shrine of Kannon. The warrior took one of the side paths that followed the outermost edge of Sensoji's yard.

"Of course I remember. A brave lad is not easily forgotten."

"Excuse me, sir. For not remembering you, at first. You have changed."

"Fatter and older, I know," Nakamura said, with a twinkle in his eyes and the faintest of smiles, "and wiser, I hope. And what of you? Older and —," he cocked his head, appraising Genzo while the smile broadened. "I have thought of you often, wondering what happened to you after I sailed away from Shimoda."

Genzo smiled sheepishly, uncomfortable in the company of so important a person, even if he was also a most friendly man. He could not believe that Nakamura-san really wanted to know about him so he did not reply, and lagged behind even farther than the two paces that custom imposed between samurai and servant.

"But I did not expect to find you here in Edo. By Kannon's Kindness! Come here, where I can see you. Otherwise I'll twist my head off, looking for you back there. That's better. Now stay there. And don't, in Kompira's name, be afraid of me. You look like you've seen a fox-spirit following you in the night. Well I'm not. Flesh and blood and bone am I. And a lot of sea salt sprinkled over the fat, perhaps. You are in Lord Okubo's service now, I see. For how long?"

"Almost six years, sir."

"Six years of running up and down the Tokaido with that Great One? What a waste of muscles. Growing leeks would put your time and strength to better use. No family?" Noticing Genzo's reluctance to speak, he insisted. "Well? Tell me."

"Once I had a family. A wife. Two sons. But they died, six years ago, in the great sickness that killed many people in Shimoda."

The sickness had come while Genzo and many other men of Izu were accompanying their lord as he inspected the province for the Shogun. Weeks later, when they returned to Shimoda, they learned that death had robbed half of them of children and a quarter of wives or parents. Jizo, the bodhisattva who takes care of children, had been powerless against Shinigami, the God of Death. The round straw lid from the rice bale that Genzo's wife had hung over the head of Dosojin, the village's protecting spirit, could not ward off the pestilence when it came down the road from Atami, touching one town in Izu's peninsula after the other, all the way to Shimoda at the end.

Genzo returned to an empty house, holding neither wife nor sons. "Perhaps it is best so," the old priest in the temple tried to comfort him when he went there to offer prayers for their spirits. And Genzo felt that he must agree with the old man. "I suppose that was their fate," he said meekly. Better, certainly, for a sickness to take them, swiftly, than to watch them die slowly, in time of famine. Or to have to stifle one of those babes, or to abandon it on a wintry hillside, because doing so would mean one less mouth to feed. Farmers call this "a thinning out," mabiki, but none of them does this as heartlessly with children as with seedlings in a garden. But, thereafter, for Genzo, whose family had vanished like dew under the morning's sun, awareness of the brutal indifference of Death was a burden he could not shed.

"And then?" Nakamura demanded.

Genzo was glad that he did not waste his breath upon empty expressions of sorrow. "After a while, because not much food was grown in Shimoda that year, I asked to be sent to Lord Okubo's service. Hambei—he was the headman of Shimoda then—was glad to arrange that for me. I did not want to stay there any longer. And younger men—those few who were left—did not wish to go away. But for me," he stopped, not sure whether to continue but encouraged to go on by Nakamura-san's expression, "running up and down the Tokaido, as you call it, and through the wards of Edo also, helps me to forget my troubles. At times."

"The calamities of the wicked are punishments," Nakamura said loudly, "those of the good are trials." Skillful navigator on many a sea, he was plotting this course better than he knew. "In here," he muttered, turning through an opening in the hedge of tall camellias. "I like to come to this place," he explained as they approached a weather-stained chapel, "when I need to escape from crowds." After skirting the little building they entered the same peaceful garden Genzo had left only a short while before. "And," Nakamura inspected the place carefully, not forgetting the chapel's porch, "from the many eyes and ears of the honorable Bakufu.—May they all go blind and deaf. Together."

Genzo scarcely heard him. His surprise at being brought back to this beautiful place gave way to the thought that this garden, his prayer to Kannon-sama, and the sudden appearance of Nakamura-san were bound together, like the strands in a rope. Like the links in the endless Chain of Cause and Effect.

At a spot in the middle of the garden, from which he could see every approach to the forecourt, Nakamura sank into a peasant's comfortable squat. "Come down, come down," he beckoned, the while he pulled the two swords from under his obi and laid them on the ground beside him. Thoroughly confused by this person of quality who had the manners of a fisherman, Genzo squatted opposite him.

"And what brings you to Sensoji, on this busiest of all days?," Nakamura asked. Had any one among his fellows in Lord Okubo's household asked him that question Genzo would have found a dozen replies, all chosen to hide the truth. Never tell them the truth about yourself, he'd decided when first he came to Edo. Always keep them guessing. This was the only way he knew for holding within himself the little portion of his thoughts and hopes that belonged to him alone. He did not tell lies, of course, because lying is forbidden—and besides a man can be caught in the lies he tells. But he never told the truth about himself, or at least the whole truth. He told bits and pieces of the truth, and these, along with his bright smiles and his fair looks, gave people the feeling that he was the most honest and honorable of men.

To his credit, Genzo did not use these partial truths in order to cheat his fellows. In his relationships with them, insofar as these touched upon their lives, he was scrupulously honest. And he was generous with help, as with patience. They knew they could trust him, in good times or bad. For this reason they respected him. But they could never like him because he would not allow them to do so. The moment some one offered him a kindness, or sent a friendly glance, he would tighten up, inside and out. The others could see it happening. "He is as prickly as a sea urchin," said the men. "He is not interested in love," sighed the women. In this way Genzo cheated only himself. For, as he well knew, and as they came close to guessing, he was afraid of love.

But to Nakamura-san, already a benefactor, he wanted to tell the truth. His respect for the sea-faring samurai, put away for so long because he had forgotten him, revived immediately. Instinct told him that he could trust the man who had saved his life. Yet experience warned him that he should not trust any man untested, especially in Edo of the Bakufu. For all he knew, Nakamura might be another spy checking the temper of Edo's commoners, another pair of those watching eyes and pricked up ears he pretended to despise.

"To offer a prayer," Genzo chose his words carefully. "To ask for help." This was truth, if not as much of it as he might have told.

"Is that so?," Nakamura exclaimed, raising eyebrows and voice as if astonished beyond measure. "And does this make you different from all those others? Isn't this exactly what everyone else is doing over there, in that rattling cash box? Throwing away good money. Whining for help. At such a rate that I doubt if all the bodhisattva in the Lord Buddha's heaven can hear them. Or find the time to answer them."

"Perhaps so," said Genzo, recognizing the contempt as being very much like his own had been—until today. Surprised by his stubbornness, he went on. "But if a man believes?" Belief, or trust, or faith, whatever you called it, whether between a man and his gods, or between one man and another, must be the foundation upon which that man's life is built. He had known such faith, once. But then it had been cut away, in one brutal bloody instant, in the budokan at Shimoda.

"Ah, faith is it?" Nakamura picked up one of the fallen plum blossoms. "You have faith in her? In this Goddess of Mercy, who has never been seen by any mortal? Whose tiny little image"— between thumb and forefinger he measured the length of a toothpick—"the priests of Sensoji do not show, even to the most faithful of her worshippers?" Imitating the voice and gestures of a Kabuki actor playing the part of a woman, he quoted the famous line from a ribald play: " 'The cha . . . rity of the God . . . dess of Mercy is a *mirac* . . .ulous thing!' Saa!," he slapped his knee, a samurai again. "I was hoping you'd be a man who thought for himself."

"How can I think for myself? I who am only one of the lower people?" He who thought for himself during every waking moment of every day, reaching conclusions and making judgments that would have led to his execution if they were known: he could barely suppress a smile at the ease with which he brought out this pious answer. That should please this policeman, if he is one, thought Genzo, watching for Nakamura's response. It came, a little smile of his own, as difficult to interpret as the curve of the lips on an image of Kannon herself.

"Even so," Genzo decided to push this conversation along, if ever it was going to lead anywhere, "I believe that she sent you to me, in answer to my prayer."

"What? You asked for me? Hah! I cannot take you seriously. Why should she send me to you?" The very idea of his being Heaven's pawn seemed to annoy him, until his quick mind found another possibility to play with. "Perhaps," he laughed, "she sent you to me, in answer to my prayer. Have you thought of that?"

Genzo burst out laughing, feeling freer and easier with Nakamura than with any man he'd ever known. "No, that thought had not come to me, I admit," he said, seeing again how each one of us considers himself to be the center of the world. "But if it is as you say, then please tell me what I can do for you, in answer to your prayer."

"In this best of all possible lands," Nakamura intoned, a priest before his people, "when the benevolent rule of the government of the Shogun has spread far into the nine countries of pagans and the eight countries of barbarians," he paused for breath, "how can I want for anything?" The words were as devout as any the Bakufu could want to overhear. But Nakamura's smooth face, in which only the bright eyes seemed to be alive, told Genzo that he, too, was being tested.

In the instant of recognition both men gave up further pretense. Genzo rejoiced. Once again this strange man who was his only friend had come to help him. Whether or not Kannon-sama had sent him, he was here. Sinking to his knees, placing both hands flat upon the cold earth, he bowed low before the man who, having saved him once, would save him again.

"I saw you, as you approached the shrine," said Nakamura gently. "You went up looking like a monk in a holy trance. You came down looking like a man abandoned. Ahh, I said to myself, my friend Genzo is in need of help. Therefore, I offer you my help, for what it is worth."

No longer afraid, Genzo said, "I asked her to show me a way. A way out from the misery in which I dwell. Can you help me to find that way?"

"Misery, my young friend, is the common lot of man, in this sad world where all flowers must fade. You sorrow for your wife and sons? I cannot help you there."

"No, I do not sorrow for them. Not any more. No, I sorrow for myself. And for so many who are like me. For us who are trapped at the bottom of this pit the samurai have dug and over which the Shogun sits. We who have thoughts: can we never speak them? We who have hopes: can we never reach them? We who have nothing: can we never gain anything that is ours alone?" Free to speak his thoughts now, for the first time in his life, Genzo almost choked on the words dammed up behind his tongue.

From its resting place in the folds of his obi he drew forth his talisman. "This little stone," he held it out for Nakamura-san to see, "I found it here this morning, and I took it with me. I stole it, the priests of Sensoji would say. It is my only possession. Why? Because, like me, it has no value for any one else. No one will steal it from me, not even a beggar. The Bakufu will not take it, or put a tax on it." Excited now, he stood up, tossing the stone from one hand to the other. "Why, in this land of many things, is this stone the only thing that I can call my own? Why, in this land, am I to be denied—Ahh, why do I go on? I speak foolishness. I might as well try to throw this stone at the sun. And, because I ask for more than can be given, I am a fool."

Nakamura looked up at him, a squinting Buddha. "Just as I suspected. You do think for yourself. That is good. But you think like a foreigner. Even worse: like a Christian. That is bad."

"I know nothing about such people," said Genzo quickly, disclaiming any connection with that forbidden faith, those dangerous intruders.

"You talk like one of those 'Men of Men,' those kyokaku. Are you one of them?"

"No. I know nothing of such men."

"You certainly show the spirit of one. Full of defiance and rebellion. Then who has taught you such dangerous thoughts?"

"No one has taught me. They have come to me out of my own mind. Out of my own need. First, and always, I remember that murdering samurai in Shimoda. Always I see what all samurai— and the Bakufu—are doing to us, all the time, all through Nippon. And I compare them with the Americans who came to Shimoda for a few days, soon after that time of trouble in the budokan."

"What did they do to you?"

"Nothing. I did not speak with them. How could I? When I did not know their language? When I was only a peasant, on the edge of the crowd, watching them wherever they went, whatever they did? But I watched them, as they worked and as they played. They showed me, by their own behavior among themselves and by the way they treated us of Nippon, that there is another way to live than our way. When their officers went among the lowly soldiers and sailors from the black ship, those common ones did not have to fall upon their faces in the mud. Far from that. Often enough they would talk, with smiles and laughter, common men to officers, as if they were equals. And often the officers would join the commoners in games and sports or in doing the work of the ship. I never saw one sailor beaten or one soldier kicked. And not once did an officer from that great ship take out his sword and hack down one of his lowly men. I saw then that they were not the cruel barbarians that the Bakufu had told us they would be."

"You are right. That is the way they are in America. In that country they have a saying: 'each man is the equal of any other.'"

"Yet here in our country they treated us the same way. With smiles and kindnesses. They were men with good hearts. And seeing them among us started me to thinking—"

"And that, you realize, is the great reason why the Bakufu wants to keep those dangerous barbarians out of Nippon. Think of what would happen in this country, if each one of Nippon's commoners thought he was the equal of any samurai!"

"Why should he not be?" Genzo did not want to tell Nakamura-san how, by their example, the Americans had saved him from killing himself in the days of brooding after Ichiro's murder. Shame for his own weakness during that dreadful moment, not grief for Ichiro, had driven him to the edge of madness. For, in an instant of discovery, he understood how, in grasping the sword of vengeance, he had betrayed himself, the budo, the man of discipline he yearned to be. He could not recover from that "backward turning." Without a word to anyone, not even to Nakamura-san who had saved his life, he walked out of the budokan, never to return. The wound in his spirit did not heal. Like his father, and his grandfather before him, Genzo recognized that he was a man born only to suffer. But the example of the Americans kept him alive, in the hope that someday, somewhere, he could find something better in this world than the sorrow and the shame his countrymen were heaping upon him at home.

"Ho!" Nakamura put up his hand. "With such thoughts running around in your mind you are a most dangerous man. Beware the Bakufu."

"All of us know that fear who live below, in the muck of those who live above. In everything we say or do we must guard ourselves. Not only against the Bakufu's spies. Against our own kind, too, who in envy or in greed may report upon us to those spies. But we learn, very early, to be wary. The unwary man does not live long. How many times have I seen such a one taken away. Never to be seen again. Please teach me: where do they go, those men? We are never told."

"To the stinking prisons, first. Then, if they survive those, to the gold mines of Sado Island, perhaps. Or to the copper mines at Ashio. Or to the coal pits at Miike, in Fukuoka, now that foreigners want so much coal for their fire-ships. Into holes in the ground, before they are dead, never to come up again, until they are dead. A terrible fate."

"And one that I do not wish for myself. To avoid it, I have taught myself to be stupid. I am deaf and blind and without a tongue. Fifty times a day I repeat to myself the most important lesson I learned in the temple school in Shimoda: 'The mouth is the gateway to misfortune, the tongue the cause of disaster.' But inside of me my mind is full of bitter thoughts. And I do not know how much longer I can hide those thoughts, without blowing up in rage—or going crazy with hopelessness. A man who spends most of his time running through the streets of Edo has lots of time to see much and to hear much. And to think much. But what can I do with these thoughts, and my hopes, and my fears? In all my life, you are the first man I have been able to talk with so freely. And I do not know when I shall meet another one like you."

Nakamura pushed himself up, holding his long sword like a staff. "Only use I ever found for the damned thing," he growled. "And of what use are your thoughts to you? What do they tell you?"

"That I must get away from Lord Okubo's service. I am weary of trotting forth and back, up and down, day after day, a flying foot to Lord Okubo's household. Weary in the head, not in the legs. I feel like a rat in a cage. I am sick of being nothing more than a slave of samurai. Have you ever really looked at us, you who are a samurai? Have you ever imagined what we must feel and think, when the lordly ones come swaggering past? And we must throw ourselves down before them, or run the risk of being cut down by their swords? With our hands, knees, and toes pressed into the mud; head bowed low, eyes seeing nothing; ass reared high, ready for kicking; and nose breathing deep the stink of samurai shit... Ahh!" Trembling with anger too long suppressed, Genzo kicked at the pebbles beneath his feet. Embedded among others like themselves, not one of them moved. Count each pebble as a man of Nippon, Genzo thought, seeing how in them Kannon-sama might be teaching him a lesson.

"I was not born a samurai, my friend," said Nakamura-san quietly. "And please remember: not all samurai are as arrogant as you think."

"You may be right. But except for you I have not seen any polite ones. Nor have they kept us from falling on our faces. They live as samurai want to live. We live as we must live, as we are forced to live. But we do not like it, this life in the stinking mud."

" 'The decrees of the shoguns are like their perspiration,' I've been told. 'Once released, they can never go back.' Nevertheless, I hope for a change to better ways, and I work for that, with others who feel as I do. But, to be honest, I can not see it coming soon. Some people are saying that the Meiji emperor will bring this change. But I cannot see how he can do so. He is only sixteen years old, not of an age to rule, even if the nobles and the daimyos who control him now would permit him to rule. Unless the Tokugawa collapse, and I do not expect that they will, we shall have a long civil war, as in the time before the first Tokugawa became the Shogun." He shook his head, worrying over bigger problems than Genzo could know about. "I fear for the future. This is another Degenerate Age, another Mappo. If we can live through the next ten thousand years . . . But in times of troubles, as the annals tell us, great changes can be made. Perhaps before long you will be a merchant, or a general. Or—have you thought of it?—a sailor like me. Where will you go, when you leave Lord Okubo's service?"

Like a kite robbed of its wind Genzo's fine thoughts fell back to the hard ground. "Where can I go? How can I go anywhere, when I am bound to his service for life? I have thought of running off to Yokohama, to steal away on one of those foreign ships. But I know nothing of the world beyond. How can I know which foreign ship will take me? I don't want to end up on Sado Island, or in a prison, like Yoshida Shoin, that time he tried to go with the Americans when their black ships lay in Shimoda bay. I was there when the Bakufu's officials took him away, chained in a cage, like a wild beast. For the crime of wanting to leave this fine country.''

''What? Do you mean to say that you want to leave Nippon?''

''Yes! That most of all! Have I not said so? I must leave Nippon soon. Or die.''

''Well! That's another matter entirely, from what I was thinking. What will you do to get out?''

''Anything!''

''Anything? That's a big word.''

''Anything that does not cost a life. I will not kill another man. I will not fight in the Shogun's army. Or in the young Emperor's. Even then, Lord Okubo may order me to fight, if the Emperor's army does come here. They are talking now of using even peasants like me in the defense of Edo. And I am not yet too old to be given a spear to throw.''

''A spear? Stupid things! They are 'idiot frogs fretting at the bottom of their well.' When the Emperor's soldiers are bringing rifles from England and cannon from France, these fools of Edo will arm their men with spears and swords. And what will you do if Lord Okubo gives you a spear?''

''I will not take up the spear.''

''That will mean your death.''

''I know. And a quicker end to this life, and earlier beginning upon the next round, when I can hope my karma will be better. Unless,'' like a boy with a ball he tossed the black stone in the air, caught it as it fell, ''Kannon-sama shows me another way. Soon.''

''There is another way,'' said Nakamura-san.

CHAPTER 3
THE PLOTTING

For a long moment Genzo looked down upon the stone in his hand. The prayer he had sent up to Kannon-sama was answered. The priests are right, he told himself, almost in awe: "Heaven has a voice which is heard upon the earth."

But now he did not know what to do. He felt like a man who had been clinging to a cliff for so long, afraid to move lest he fall into the abyss below, that he dares not reach out to grasp the rope of the rescuer. In the silence of the garden, as Heaven listened, Genzo knew how a plum blossom must feel the instant before it parts from the branch.

"How?," he asked, willing to be rescued—or fall.

"I do not know yet," honest Nakamura said. Genzo felt his stomach sink within him, just as a man does when he falls from a high place into the depths below. "This is a matter I must think more about," Nakamura continued. "But where does the way lead? This much I can tell you, for I have gone to that very place. And, as you see, I have come back from it."

"Where?," asked Genzo, beginning to breathe again.

"A place called Hawai. A group of islands, lying almost in the middle of the Great Peaceful Ocean, about thirty days' sailing to the south and east of Yokohama. Although they are not as big as the islands of Nippon they are large enough. And they rise high above the level of the sea. I am told, but I cannot say for I did not see them, that some of their mountains are even higher than is our Fujisan. Some parts of the islands that I did see are beautiful. Green and well watered. Comfortable to live upon. They look very much like your homeland of Izu. Other parts seemed to be nothing but bare dry rock. No water, I guess. But the green parts are better than Izu is, in many ways. The people in those islands know no winter. Neither do they have our hot and sticky summers. No typhoons, no earthquakes, no tsunami, no snakes afflict them. And—you will like this—no samurai. Although they do have a few Americans, and Englishmen, and foreigners of other kinds. Some white men, please remember, can be just as proud as samurai. And just as evil."

Genzo listened to all this with disbelief and a swelling uneasiness. Like everyone else in Nippon he knew that for more than two hundred years the Tokugawa shoguns had forbidden their subjects to visit foreign countries and had prevented their coming back again to Nippon if they were foolish enough to go away. Even if they were fishermen driven away by typhoons, or cast upon foreign coasts, they could not come back. The penalty for either crime, going or coming, was death, as notices posted in public places warned all Nipponjin throughout the nation. But here was Nakamura-san, the man to whom he had given his trust, blandly telling him things that could be nothing more than lies. How, then, could he trust such a false man? And, even more alarming, what was Nakamura-san's purpose in telling all these falsehoods?

Genzo, older and wiser than he had been when last he tried to challenge a samurai, hid mistrust behind politeness. "Excuse me, sir. How could you know all this? How could you go to this foreign land?"

Nakamura groaned, recognizing the suspicions that provoked Genzo's questions. Ignorance, alas, is the mother of suspicion. And fear is its father. In order to control the people of Nippon the Bakufu never told them about events happening in their country or beyond its borders. For the same reason it did not publish all the laws by which the lives of the people were regulated and their conduct was judged. Ignorance and fear, although they bred suspicion and poverty and hatred and many another ugly child, were the Bakufu's most powerful servants.

"Eight years ago," Nakamura began impatiently. "But wait.

I'm freezing my ears off, in this place. Let's go to an inn I know, where we can be warm while we talk. I still expect one of those o-metsuke to poke his head up from this pond. Or to drop out of that cloud of plum blossoms. In a land where walls have ears and stones tell tales we cannot be too careful. Let's go.''

A few minutes later they sat, warm and comfortable, in a sailors' inn, near the canal separating Asakusa from Imado. Nakamura ordered hot saké to take the chill off the liver and other parts of the body, to be followed as soon as possible by a hot meal for expelling the cold vapors from their bellies. ''This plump sailor was not always plump,'' he said, pouring saké into Genzo's cup. ''And this life, at best, is all too short. Drink it down, so we can have some more.''

Somehow or other he had assured himself that he could speak here without fear of being overheard by informers. Nevertheless, he kept his voice low; and even when, later, the saké and the good food made him merry, he did not relax his guard.

While those first sips of saké still slipped down their gullets he started upon his tale. ''Eight years ago I was chosen to be one of our countrymen who went to America on a mission for the Bakufu. That's when I got these grass-cutters,'' he tapped the swords lying on the mat beside him. ''The Bakufu was ashamed to send a mere commoner as an officer on its ship. But they could find no fancy samurai to do the job I had to do. So they solved the problem by making a samurai and a gentleman out of me, a fisherman's son from Tanabe of Kii. When needs mount, my friend, barriers go down. Happens all the time.'' Just to be sure Nakamura looked behind him as he talked, and to either side. But even nervous Genzo could not suspect the diners at other tables of trying to hear what Nakamura was saying. Chatting noisily, eating and drinking, they were all too busy with themselves to pay heed to anyone else.

The sailor-warrior drained another cup of saké. ''That's why I hope for change in this country of ours. The needs are mounting, faster than the Bakufu can meet them. Rough seas are ahead for

Nippon . . . " And Genzo wondered what more astonishing things he would hear from his friend before he learned how to reach the land called Hawai.

"Anyhow, as I was saying. The mission to America went to that far-off country aboard the *Kanrin Maru*, the Bakufu's first steamship-of-war. Ever hear of it? No? I thought as much. I went as assistant to Nakahama Manjiro, another fisherman's son they had to make a samurai because of his skills. Ever hear of him? No. Of course not. One of the finest minds in Nippon. *And* Nippon's best sailor. But no one's ever heard of him. He was the navigator of the ship. He told it where to go, I mean to say. And he told it to go to exactly the right place. Even though we sailed for thirty-seven days upon that heaving ocean, without seeing a speck of land upon the way. I was worried, I can tell you now, even though I had great respect for Nakahama-san. But I kept my worries to myself, like a good Nipponjin. And he got us there all right. He had to, because no one else aboard that pitching ship could do it. The captain—that same Katsu no Yoshikuni, Lord of Awa, who is so much talked about these days here in Edo—was sick in his bunk all the way. I hope he's a better diplomat than he was a sailor. Well, anyhow, on the thirty-sixth day, rising up out of the rolling waves, just as Nakahama-san said it would be, was the land called Kariforunia. And on the thirty-seventh day we sailed grandly into the harbor of San Furanshishiko, the very place to which we wanted to go. Nakahama-san, a remarkable man, learned that great skill from the Americans. And they taught it to him when he was only a boy. Ahh, but that is another story. You are wanting to hear about Hawai." He wet his throat with a sip of saké. "Only a tidbit to a ravenous gut," he laughed, tossing down the whole cupful.

"Well, then. On our way home again from Kariforunia to Nippon, we visited for a few days in Honoruru, the chief city of Hawai. It is there, I promise you. As you will see, when you go there."

"But how can I go there? Will the Bakufu send me, too, on that ship-of-war?"

"Be patient, my friend. I shall tell you, if only you will let me finish. Those islands of Hawai are almost empty of people. Too many of the Hawaijin who once lived there have died. Of sicknesses that have gone among them from foreign lands. A sad thing. And not enough new ones are being born. An even sadder thing. In whole valleys, on some islands, no one is living. And on others the plains and grasslands are deserted. To fill those empty valleys and silent plains the King of Hawai is asking people from other countries to go there to live and work."

"But will they not die, in that unhealthy place?"

"No. People from other countries do not seem to be affected. Only the Hawaijin are struck down. That is why their king is inviting foreigners to go there. At this very time, as I heard only yesterday when I brought my ship to Edo, some agents in Yokohama and Edo are looking for men of Nippon who will go to Hawai. Nipponjin are strong. And they are not afraid of hard work. Any man of Nippon who goes will receive free passage and a certain amount of money, just for going. And when he works in Hawai he will receive a certain amount of money for each day of labor. I am sorry that I do not remember all the details. I did not listen very carefully yesterday because I had no reason to be interested in that sailors' talk. But I can learn these matters easily enough, if you are interested."

"Yes! This sounds—"

"And how long has it been since you were home in Shizuoka?," asked Nakamura, in this way warning Genzo that the serving girl was bringing their food. For the few minutes she needed to put before them the fine dishes Nakamura had ordered they talked about matters in which the Bakufu could find no hint of danger.

But as soon as she had gone Genzo asked, "And can I go to this new land, if I wish? You mean the Bakufu will let me go, and all those other people who may want to leave Nippon?"

"I believe so. The Bakufu must have given its consent. These agents seem to be talking quite openly, without fear of the police."

"Such an astonishing thing! When most of us here in Edo cannot walk from Shimbashi to Shinjuku without obtaining written permission from some daimyo, or some magistrate, or some policeman, or some other official."

"In times like these," Nakamura put the fingers of one hand into the palm of the other, "all things are possible to those who spend honorable money. Obviously, those agents have lots of honorable money, which they are happy to share with certain officials. And, clearly, these officials in turn are happy to share with the King of Hawai any number of Nippon's people. 'We have too many of 'em anyhow,' seems to be their attitude. They're quite willing to ship out a few, I guess, in exchange for a bu or two a head. Nonetheless, something good will come of all this traffic. For the first time in the history of Nippon our people are being encouraged to leave it. To me this is a sign of progress. Once the door is opened wide—"

"I wish to go with them," said Genzo, putting a halt to Nakamura's vision of the future.

"Don't be too hasty. Should you not learn what kind of work you must do when you get there?"

"I don't care what it is. How can that matter? I will work at anything."

"Even laboring like a farmer in the fields' growing sugarcane?"

"What is that?"

"Eh?" Nakamura put a hand to his mouth. "Come to think of it, I don't know. Never saw one. Some kind of tree, I guess. Or maybe a vine. That makes sugar in its fruits. But growing it is hard work I've been told. Much harder, and less interesting, than trotting about with Lord Okubo."

Genzo realized that he was being tested still, although in another way. "Such work does not scare me. I am a farmer's son. And, for a while, when my family lived, I helped my father-in-law in his rice fields."

"Very well, then. As long as you know what to expect. I am glad that you want to go. From what you've told me about yourself you'd better go. From what I saw of Hawai, I believe that you will be safer there. Happiness I do not promise, for each man, I have learned, must find his own way to happiness. But the people there are kind, perhaps because they are so few. And you are still young. You could start another family."

"That is more than I ask for at this time—although perhaps it will come, as this feast has come after my hunger of this morning. For now all I want is to go away from this land of samurai. But teach me, please: how can I get away? Do I need papers? And how can I get them, if I have no honorable money for changing officials' frowns into smiles? And why should Lord Okubo's chamberlain release me from service to the clan? They have bound me. For life."

Nakamura-san nodded. "Those are difficulties that must be faced. Please give me a few days to think about them, and to get in touch with those agents in Yokohama. They must be having the same problems with other people wanting to go. We have plenty of time, I believe. As I recall, those agents have just begun their recruiting."

"Excuse me, please, Nakamura-san. I fear that we do not have much time. The Meiji emperor's army is coming."

"But it is still closer to Kyoto than to Edo. Staggering along in fits and starts, like a man taken with a loosening of the bowels. Although they haven't enough money to buy rice with, let alone enough food to make shit. At their rate of march, you will be working under the warm sun of Hawai before they see the smoke of Edo's kitchen fires. Don't worry." He lifted his cup of saké toward Genzo. "Just leave everything to me. How can I reach you, when I need to tell you what I've learned?"

Genzo shook his head, sucked air through his teeth.

"Saa!" Nakamura rubbed his nose. "I forgot. A running footman with a tether tied to his ankle . . . This will be a problem."

The more they thought about it the more nervous they became about finding a place in which a warrior could safely meet a lowly footman. In that vast city, filled with homes and inns and teahouses and theatres for almost a million people, they could not think of a single place where they might meet without arousing suspicion. Fixing upon a definite time for returning to Sensoji was impossible, because Genzo never knew from one day to the next where the clan office would send him. All other public places were too far away from Lord Okubo's mansion for Genzo to reach easily, or too closely watched by the police and their spies.

As they stared at each other over the empty dishes, the great bell of Sensoji boomed the third hour. "I must go," said Genzo, remembering Jiro's command, imagining his companions as they straggled back to duty.

"Ho!" He snapped his fingers. Those noisy fellows were of some use to him after all. "If Nakamura-san agrees, I can suggest a place for us to meet."

Sages have said, more in jest than in truthful attention to detail, that when they are naked all men are equal. However that may be, without his kimono and those two swords, wearing only his white breechcloth, Nakamura-san did not look like a samurai when he entered the washing room of the public bathhouse "Fuji" that Genzo had chosen for their meeting. It had been given the name Wistaria in honor of the Okubo clan's crest—and in anticipation of the Okubo retainers' patronage.

Genzo had chosen most sensibly. Even commoners are allowed to bathe. And he himself went to Furoya Fuji whenever he did not feel like bathing with his fellows in the barrack's busy o-furo. Furoya Fuji stood in the valley that winds between Lord Okubo's mansion in Nagata-cho on the east and the hill of Hie Shrine on the west. In order to reach this bathhouse Genzo had only to slip through the back gate in the high wall surrounding the Okubo yashiki. Inasmuch as all commoners who served in Lord Okubo's household passed through this gate as often as bees leave and return to the hive, the clansmen who guarded the approach would not question him. Whether or not they knew him at sight they would accept the livery he wore, marked with the Okubo crest, as surer proof of loyalty than his face.

For Nakamura-san, too, the bathhouse was convenient. He would walk to it from Shimbashi, where he was staying at an inn while his ship lay in port. He was an important man now, captain of a Kimizawa ship, one of the Bakufu's fast new two-masted sailing vessels built in the Western style.

Three days had passed since their encounter at the temple of Kannon. During those three days and two wakeful nights Genzo's hopes and fears rose and fell like ocean waves upon Cape Iro, the southernmost tip of Izu. Am I a fool for trusting a man I scarcely know? Genzo asked himself in the times when his courage ebbed. How soon can I sail for that land of promise? he wondered when his need mounted. And in all the moments between he questioned how he could endure to wait until, at last, he would be safe at sea, aboard that unknown ship taking him to that beckoning land.

Taro, the ancient bathhouse attendant, splashing about the wet floor in bare feet, was annoyed when Genzo arrived only a half hour before the curfew. "Nasakenai hito," he hissed, a serpent without fangs. "You're hopeless. Warm water will be your lot, for hot it will be not. I've already put out the fire." He'd also put out half of the eight rapeseed-oil lamps that the Bakufu prescribed for a bathhouse of this size. The clothes-changing room was so dark that Genzo could scarcely see where to walk. Taro beat his hardwood clappers loudly enough to make everyone wince. To the dark heads floating upon the surface of the water in the great wooden tub he begged to announce that the sorrowful hour of their honorable departure drew nigh. A chorus of grunts and shouts and squeals, as from frogs big and little, male and female, thanked him for his concern. Everyone who came to Furoya Fuji, Genzo not least of all, knew that old Taro would have perished from boredom if his clients gave him no cause for complaint or retort.

On this special evening Taro's delight in being grievously oppressed was increased twice more, in rapid succession. Genzo, crouched on the low bench that was one of Taro-san's few contributions to comfort, dipped hot water out of the trough, to use in washing his body from forehead to heel. He was rinsing himself off, with clean hot water, when Nakamura arrived, looking very much like a prosperous merchant. He nodded a greeting to Genzo over Taro's noise. Happy to see him there, Genzo responded with a quick smile. Thanks be to Kannon, he was thinking, as once more all his doubts and fears receded. Now he'll tell me what I must do.

But, as men of more experience might have told Genzo, what one deity can arrange another can undo. Kannon's power, perhaps, did not prevail in the neighborhood of Hie Shrine, where Sanno the jocose Monkey God presides. Just as Nakamura removed his loincloth and, bulging like a younger Hotei, sat down on a stool beside Genzo, Kosaburo came clattering in.

With the eyes of an owl Kosaburo found his friend, even in that murky gloom. With the voice of a crow he began to talk, as if he had been forced to keep silent for a week.

Fortunately for everyone in that echoing room Kosaburo was in a hurry. Genzo could thank Kannon for this intervention. The ardent youth informed Genzo, and therefore everyone else in the o-furo, that one of his free lays awaited him this very night. Shouts of encouragement from the men, and salacious observations about his endowments from the women, helped him to achieve one of the fastest washings in the history of Edokko, one of the briefest immersions ever noted for Taro's tub, and certainly the noisiest departure the neighborhood had ever enjoyed. Still wet, from top-knot to toes, still talking, yet managing to bow like an actor acknowledging applause—while Taro beat his wooden clappers as if he accompanied an actor at a kabukiza, and the bathers cheered him on, crying, "Brace up!," and "Keep a tight fundoshi!," and "What happens twice, must happen thrice!"— he wrapped his fundoshi, just in time, about that impetuous swelling at his loins, and rushed off into the night. Taro-san, cackling lasciviously, sped him on his way with a tremendous clatter from those hard blocks.

Nakamura, laughing with the others, turned to Genzo. "Deities, Buddha, love, heartlessness—all are visitors at the public bath," he quoted the famous novelist of Edo, Shikitei Samba, of whom Genzo had never heard. "Who is that small typhoon?"

Before Genzo could answer the other bathers left the tub,

yielding to Taro's renewed invitations to take their honorable carcasses where they belonged, and perhaps to stirrings in their own warmed flesh aroused by Kosaburo's excitement. Nakamura and Genzo exchanged places with them, settling into the water. Taro was right: it was no longer stinging hot. But it was still warm enough to be comfortable. And, mercifully, the tub was still new enough that it did not stink of rotting wood and moldy jointures.

Genzo related the short and uncomplicated history of Kosaburo, "written with the character for BIG."

Nakamura surprised him. "A good lad, that. Every ship needs such a fellow aboard, to make life easier for the rest. But is it possible for you Okubo men to stay out overnight?"

"We're not supposed to, without permission. But the guards are not strict, and usually we can manage to stay away, as long as we return to the yashiki by sunrise. And do not have to pass any ward gate or police barrier. The police make more trouble for us than do the guards at the yashiki."

"Very good. That will make matters easier for you, when the time comes." After that Nakamura would say no more, not wanting to be overheard by Taro, of necessity an informer, or by any of the others lingering in the dressing room.

Genzo and Nakamura left Taro's hospitality a few minutes later. The night, cold and misty, seemed all the darker when Taro shut the bathhouse door after them.

"I want you to meet the chief of those recruiting agents," said Nakamura after they had walked a few paces. "He waits for us not far from here, in one of the houses he keeps in Edo." Near the mouth of the valley, where it meets the Outer Moat, they came to a short lane. That passageway led them to a small house, distinguished from its neighbors only by the number tag and name plate on its gatepost. "In here," said Nakamura, a man not easily lost on land or sea.

An aged servant led them to an eight-mat room at the rear of the quiet house. A single rush lamp near the entrance gave enough light to see by.

A thin little man sat cross-legged upon a zabuton at one side of the room. Two swords were aligned upon the mat at his left. Seeing them, Genzo went down on his knees, preparing to touch his forehead to the floor. "Not necessary," the thin man said, pushing a zabuton forward for him to sit upon. Nakamura, he insisted, should take the place of honor, upon a flat cushion already waiting for him before the post of the tokonoma.

The concession to sit embarrassed Genzo. Never before had he been allowed to sit in the presence of samurai—except for Nakamura-san, of course, whom he did not think of anymore as a fearsome warrior.

With a slight bow to the stranger Nakamura introduced himself and Genzo. To Genzo he explained that the man they had come to see was Hamada Hikizo-san, also known as "Amerika" Hikizo, because he had lived for a while in that country and knew something of its speech.

Hamada acknowledged the introduction with a rapid blink of the eyes, a single brief nod. Every one of his motions, Genzo soon found, was quick, suddenly begun and suddenly ended. He moved like a lizard. He looked like a lizard. In the dim light the small head, the pouches beneath his narrow eyes, the sharp pointed nose, the wrinkled skin at his throat, the small teeth, even the long, narrow, curved finger nails, suggested a resemblance which Hamada-san himself always used to his advantage.

"Nakamura-san tells me you want to go to Hawai," he said. "Good. I am looking for men like you. Permit me to explain my position. I am the chief agent for Mr. Van Reed at Yokohama, who is Consul-General for the Kingdom of Hawai. He has instructed me to find three or four hundred men wanting to go there to work. So far, after only two weeks of talking about in Yokohama and Edo, more than a thousand people have told my assistants that they are interested. Not all will sign the papers, of course, for one reason or another. But I believe that we shall have no trouble in recruiting more than three hundred. If you are as eager to go as Nakamura-san says, I can put your name upon my list. His word, your appearance, are warrant enough for me."

Bewildered by Hamada-san's talk Genzo looked to Nakamura

for help. This lizard man used so many strange words, for one thing, that he could not be sure whether or not he understood them. And he was honestly shocked to learn that hundreds, if not thousands, of his countrymen wanted to leave Nippon just as much as he did.

"No question about his suitability, of course," Nakamura said in his grandest manner, "or about your accepting him. As I've told you, he's a farmer first, a footman only under orders from his village headman. I think you'll agree that he's a man of better quality than those wharf-rats from Yokohama and those gambling bums and gangsters from Edo who are trying to get on your list. For that very reason, however, he'll have more trouble receiving permission to go. The Bakufu will be glad to get rid of them. But Genzo's clan will not want to lose him. Please instruct us. What are your thoughts about obtaining his release from service to Lord Okubo?"

Hamada flicked his tongue over those pale lips. "Depends ... We have a choice of a number of ways here. Who is Lord Okubo's chamberlain?" Genzo named that powerful person, in truth the man who governed the clan and Lord Okubo as well. Hamada smiled wryly. "I've not heard of him. He must be an honest man."

"As are the assistant chamberlains," Genzo said. Down at the bottom of the heap of officials, however, honesty got lost among papers and ledgers and whispered conversations from men who always need money.

"Then we cannot buy your release, as we could if they were more—well, approachable," said Hamada. "No matter. Other ways can be found." He ticked them off on his long fingers. "You could die. Or disappear. Or suffer an accident. Or fall sick with a loathsome disease. Or be adopted by a rich man, who wants you for his son. Or—and this is very popular right now—run away to join the new emperor's 'stability and comfort' forces." He flicked all those fingers at Genzo. "Many ways. But most of them are too slow, or too expensive. We need 'something with an air of truth about it,' as that rascal priest says in the play.

In your case, I believe, everything would be much simpler if you just disappear."

"Disappear?" Genzo could not imagine how he could accomplish such a feat in Nippon.

"Like night mist in the morning's sun on yonder plain of Musashi. One evening you will be present, along with your fellow footmen, in Lord Okubo's yashiki. The next morning you will not be present. By the time they realize that they are missing you, then check in all directions to make sure that indeed you are not present, and then report your absence, first to the assistant chamberlains, then to the chamberlain himself, then to the Bakufu —saa, a whole week will have passed. But on the very first day we shall take you to Yokohama, and put you aboard the ship that will carry you to Hawai. No one will think to look for you there. And when, on a certain day after that ship has sailed, the police find your bloodied clothes under some tree near a ditch in Aoyama, or out beyond Shinjuku—" his face wrinkled up in a cheerful grin, "what else can they do but conclude, with happiness and relief, that you have been murdered? They will so report to Lord Okubo's chamberlain, and that will be the end of the matter— and of Genzo. Believe me, in this big city, and in this land of identification papers, officials, spies, and police, a man can easily disappear forever—and still go right on living in it."

"But," said Genzo, unable to shed his respect for officials, in or out of the clan, "are the police so stupid?"

"Not stupid. Just—let us say, just trusting. And, perhaps, weary. Also one more thing, which none of us likes to think about, but which is the greatest truth of all: in this land of many people, who cares about the life of a mere commoner? Who would be disturbed if a hundred Genzos, a thousand Genzos, were to disappear? No one. They would not be missed. That is why the Bakufu is not preventing my efforts to recruit these workers for the sugar planters of Hawai. 'Let them go,' an official has told me, 'take them off our hands.' As Nakamura-san has said, many of them are bums and wharf-rats now, in Edo and Yokohama. But they were not always so. Before that they were farmers, or brewers of saké or of shoyu, or fishermen, carpenters, potters, stone masons, and so on and so on. Something has happened here to make failures of them in their own land. But I like to think that, if they have a chance to start over again, in a new land, they will not fail a second time. For this reason I am trying to pick the best men I can find, among the many who are asking to go."

"You think, then, that the Bakufu will not let Genzo go openly?," Nakamura asked.

"The Bakufu would not care a hempen thread about him. Especially now, when it is falling apart, at all its joints and seams. No. The man to be feared here is Lord Okubo's chamberlain. He will look upon Genzo as an animal too valuable to lose. My advice is not to ask for something you are not sure to receive. The plan I suggest, in which he simply drops from sight, is the best. Believe me. I have been managing such disappearances for years. And—I must be honest with you—I have very few failures to my discredit."

"That's why I picked you, the best man in Edo for the job," said Nakamura.

"Then we agree?," Hamada asked Genzo. More than ever he looked like a lizard watching his prey, waiting for the instant when he would flick that long tongue and catch his helpless victim. Feeling lost in this meeting of men who knew how to manage the affairs of this world with a power that he thought only gods and daimyo possessed, Genzo nodded his acceptance of the plan.

"Good. When you leave Edo you'll be given a new set of papers, complete with official seals and signatures, telling anyone who asks that you are whatever you want to be, known by whatever new name you choose. By what name shall we call you from that day forth?"

"Why must I have a new name?"

"Because when I submit to the government officials at Kanagawa the list of people who are going away on that ship, I do not want them to read your true name on it, and connect it with you, the missing footman of Lord Okubo. The whole purpose of giving you a new name is to prevent any possibility that they will drag you off the ship before it sails. I do not expect that they will know about your—ahh, disappearance before then," he flicked his tongue, "but just in case they do, I want to make their search as difficult as possible."

"Ah, ah, now I understand. Forgive me for being so stupid. Then, for my new name—" He reached into his obi, brought out the stone of Kannon. It lay in the palm of his hand, for the others to see. "Ishi shall be my name, for this stone which has brought to me this second chance. And I wish to be put down for a—a stone mason." He who had been a farmer, who had intended to be nothing more than a farmer in the sugarcane fields of Hawai, found himself saying "stone mason" without knowing how the word had come to his tongue.

"So shall I write it. And the place of your birth? Most necessary. I suspect that we shall have a few other stone masons aboard our ship."

Nakamura slapped his knee, laughing heartily. "Use 'em for ballast."

Genzo, the man who was not so different after all, thought for a moment, seeking a birthplace. "Put me down as a man from Asakusa," he said, thinking that, in a way, this was true, for at Sensoji in Asakusa he had been reborn.

"Ishi of Asakusa, stone mason," said Hamada. "It has a good sound. After tonight, say it to yourself, now and then, so that you will get used to it before you go aboard the ship. Now let us talk about how you will know when to be ready. To be honest, I do not know when that ship will sail. Mr. Van Reed has not yet hired one. I expect that we will have enough people on our list by the middle of the Fifth Month. Perhaps sooner, perhaps later. Therefore, on the first night of the Fifth Month you must come here, to this house, for a message from me. In that message I shall tell you when you are to disappear from Edo."

"How will that be done?," Nakamura asked, more for Genzo's sake than his own. "I am curious about the details."

"Easily and quietly. One of my men will meet him here on the appointed night. He will enter this house as Genzo, a footman for Lord Okubo. He will leave it as Ishi of Asakusa, stone mason. If the police are still closing the barriers early, my man and he must spend the night here. Then, the next morning, after the gates are opened, they will go to a fish market at Furukawa. From there one of my fishing boats will take him to Yokohama. A very simple plan, really. Nothing to worry about. Not even the harbor police. For one reason or another they never stop my boats." He grimaced comfortingly at Genzo. "We help people to disappear quite often, for—let us say, for one reason or another." The lizard's grin turned on, then off. "And sometimes, when the need has ended, we help them to reappear. As good as new. Any questions?"

"None. I understand. And I thank you for your help."

"Not necessary. My business. Thank him." Hamada waved a talon at Nakamura. He was picking up his swords, preparing to leave.

Cloaked by darkness and mist the two walked up the gentle slope to Lord Okubo's yashiki. Genzo spoke from a full heart, readily accepting the burden of a lifetime of gratitude. "Once again you have saved me. This time from a useless life. How can I ever thank you?" Knowing very well that Hamada Hikizo was not helping him just out of good will, he faltered. "I—I am ashamed ... I cannot return to you the money you must be paying him."

Nakamura clapped a hand on his shoulder. "Say no more about money. What else is money for, but to spend?—If one has it to spend, I mean.—This little arrangement with Hamada is costing only a few bu. But I think that it is silver well spent. On him, because he's the most powerful of the waterfront bosses, and therefore a man to be trusted. On you, because—well, because you're a good man. And you, in your turn, when you are a rich farmer or prosperous stone mason in Hawai: well, then you can help someone who is in need. Who knows? Perhaps I may be the one to knock at your gate, asking for help. Such things have been known to happen. And Kannon-sama—as we have reason to know—is even more wonderful in the arrangements she makes than is this clever Amerika Hikizo."

"Why do you not come too? Are you not unhappy here?"

"I have thought of doing so, believe me. But for me, you see, my unhappiness does not have the same causes as yours. Nor is it as heavy as yours. This land, the Bakufu, even those samurai you do not like, they have been good to me, although I was born a commoner. Karma perhaps? Chance perhaps? Ability to do certain things with ships probably. Who knows? Who can say, until a man's life is ended, whether something happens to him for good or for bad? Only the Great Goddess of Fortune can say, and she never speaks. But for you, this land has not been good. You are trapped at the bottom of the pit, as you say. For you to go to a new place, to make a new life, is only right. But I," he concluded firmly, "I cannot go. I shall stay here. I am thinking that, in this time of Mappo, I can be of some use to my country. You see? I do not believe in karma. I believe that a man can shape his own course as he sails into the future."

With this long answer, which he did not fully understand, Genzo knew he must be content. He realized that Nakamura-san had reasons of his own for staying, hidden behind words referring to sentiments that no one had ever defined for him. In all the great land of Nippon no one save Nakamura had ever given him any reason to love the nation or its people.

They parted at the edge of the great sphere of luminous mist, set aglow by pine roots burning in cressets before the gate of Lord Okubo's yashiki.

"Thank you," said Genzo, bowing to his friend. "Until we meet again."

"See you in Yokohama," said Nakamura quietly, before he turned back into the dark.

CHAPTER 4
A MATTER OF LOYALTY

Hamada Hikizo's confidence and Genzo's hopes were swept aside by the perils that threatened Edo. Sooner than anyone expected the Meiji emperor's pacification forces came down from the mountain pass at Hakone and advanced upon Edo across the wide greening plains of Musashi. In the heart of Edo, within his vast castle ringed about by three broad moats and many high ramparts of great stones, the last of the shoguns, Tokugawa Keiki, Lord of Hitotsubashi, resigned once again from the position he had given up five months before. The ministers who advised him to take this peaceful course were Katsu Yoshikuni, Lord of Awa, and Okubo Ichio, hereditary Lord of Odawara as well as titular Governor of Izu.

Once again, as before, many others of the Inside Lords, whose families for so many generations had been helping the Tokugawa to rule Nippon to their profit, urged the young Shogun not to yield, for the sake of his glory and their privileges. To their dismay the Shogun resisted only their persuasions, and declared once more his submission to the Meiji emperor. Whereupon some of the more determined daimyo resolved to wage a decisive battle at Edo, with all Nippon for the prize.

Never before touched by war, the common people of Edo rushed about the city in great excitement, like ants disturbed at their labors. Rumors spread among them faster than the flames which so often consume their shops and homes. Many Edokko talked about fleeing to the northern provinces, or to mountain retreats in the west. A very few faint-hearted ones actually did run away, but most of Edo's citizens could not bear to leave the city at this most exciting of all times. They chose to stay behind, not to fight—for they were as sensible as the Shogun in this respect—but to cheer on those heroic samurai as they marched off to fight the daimyos' war, and to squeeze from them, going and coming, as much money as the warriors could shed. No matter which set of glaring overlords lost the battle on Musashino, the businessmen of Edo knew who would win the war.

Always, of course, with the qualification that in the confusion the city did not burn down around their heads. To forfend such a catastrophe those provident businessmen sent their women and children to invoke the protection of all the gods and deified heroes who are worshipped at every temple and shrine within the city's limits, and for a few ri beyond.

In the midst of all this excitement Genzo found himself holding a spear. Lord Okubo, even though he had counselled the Shogun to choose the way of peace, could not very well sit idly by while so many other Inside Lords prepared to fight to keep their power. Not yet sure which side would win, he bargained with the one and armed with the other. He instructed his chamberlain to give weapons to all the clan's retainers in Edo, even the commoners. This appalling lowering of military standards he justified with an argument no modern samurai could condemn, much as he might regret it: "The Outside Lords have trained their farmers' sons and merchants' clerks to be soldiers. Unnatural and ignoble as that may be, we must do the same."

As he leaned on his spear, while waiting to be trained in the wielding of it, Genzo was disheartened by the turn of events. If Nakamura-san is not a reliable prophet in this business of war, he pondered, how trustworthy then is the Lizard in his business of smuggling me out of Edo? Illusions, dreams, hopes, all fell to pieces, while new worries took their places. Things move too fast these days, he complained. Among them bullets, one of which he feared was destined to find its way into him. Despite the confused and contradictory accounts that trickled down to retainers at his low level, Genzo and his fellow spearmen were impressed with the size of the emperor's army and most especially with the valor of the warriors those Outside Lords had brought from Satsuma, Choshu, Tosa, and other such country provinces in the south. And every one of those enemy warriors, according to rumor, carried at least one bullet-spitting weapon.

Genzo was even more impressed with his cowardice. He, the man with the brave mouth, the one who had declared that he would rather die than carry a spear for his daimyo, meekly caught that ancient weapon when sergeant Jiro tossed it at him. Not once did he even think of letting it fall to the armory floor. Nor did he give a second thought to the idea of refusing to learn how to use it. Along with the other footmen, gardeners, cooks, scribes, and carpenters who were well enough to stand up, he dutifully practised how to use the awkward thing against an enemy he did not hate and certainly did not want to meet.

But what else can I do? he argued with himself as with an accuser. Why choose to die now, when escape is so close at hand? Foolishly, he had not thought to arrange a plan by which he might meet either Nakamura-san or Hamada-san in the event of an emergency. Therefore, he must wait until the first night of the Fifth Month. Try as he might, he could think of no way by which he could reach Hamada-san. Nor could he think of an alternative to holding the spear—except for that decisive one which he did not want to think about.

Trapped in the rush of forces let loose by stronger men, he could do only what every person in Nippon learns early in life to do: bend in the wind, like the supple bamboo, and hope that, when the storm was ended, he would be neither beheaded nor uprooted, but upright again, and whole. Am I any the worse for this? he asked the accuser in himself, annoyed to have to admit that in this, as in so many other matters, he was no different from most other men.

Besides, something about this crisis—no doubt the very lightheartedness with which all Edokko greeted it—warned him that this was not the time to lose his head for the sake of an opinion few others of his countrymen would share. There will be time enough for dying later, he convinced himself, if he could not manage to escape from Edo before the battle of Musashi Plain began. In short, like a true Edokko, Genzo valued his life. Instead of considering death in battle as the most glorious of destinies, he thought that samurai who chose to die in that way must be somewhat worse than fools.

During those days of uncertainty and futility, Genzo enjoyed few comforts of the body. But, in common with many another soldier, he found many comforts for the spirit. The beauties of the unfolding spring; the sight of the perfect peak of snow-capped Fuji, lifted high above the haze of Edo's cherry blossoms; the jests and ribald talk of his comrades at their drill; the aroma of steaming rice; the hot bath at the end of a long day: these and all the other good things in life reminded him, as they were supposed to do, that death comes too soon when it takes a man in the spring of his life. No, not yet, said Genzo to death's offer to come for him at once, if he but put down Lord Okubo's useless spear. This world, 'tis true, is but a temporary abode, he thought, but, somewhat to my surprise, it is not so full of sorrows that I want to leave it quite yet.

Among his greatest comforts, he realized one day, was the pleasure he gained from Kosaburo's company. In this he was not alone. The youth's quickness of wit, his accomplishments as a mimic, brought the help of humor to most of their companions, including the samurai of low rank who taught them the rudiments of spearmanship. The sour-faced ones who would not laugh, whether samurai or commoner, did not matter. Watching Kosaburo, and the ease with which he moved among his comrades, Genzo understood what Nakamura-san meant with his praise for that "small typhoon."

Fortunately for Genzo, his self-esteem was given another source of comfort during this time of preparation for strife. The clan chamberlain ordered Lord Okubo's footmen to learn judo, the "empty hands" form of the martial art, in which no weapons at all are used. Although Genzo had not entered a budokan since the day he left the school in Shimoda, he had never forgotten the instruction he received there. In Edo, he felt, his training took up again where it had stopped, twelve years before, in Shimoda. This time, possibly because he was older, undoubtedly because the instructors put no restraints upon his learning the art, he made good progress toward attaining that inner calm of the spirit through the disciplining of the body.

In truth, Genzo liked judo, the "pliant way," because he recognized that it was an art more helpful to commoners than any others they were permitted to study. A samurai could always count upon his swords to help him. But a commoner could count upon nothing but his body and his spirit. Yet, relying only upon his empty hands (with assistance, if need be, from fists, elbows, legs, and feet), he could defend himself against even a strong foe—provided that he possessed also the tranquil mind and the good heart that judo could give him. For Genzo, after twelve years of deprivation, judo was like a salve laid upon a wound that would not heal. With this new teaching his wounded spirit began to grow strong again.

Their trust in the gods served the Edokko well. They were spared the horrors of war without being denied a single one of its numerous pleasures. At the height of the suspense the Shogun's chief ministers, Katsu Yoshikuni, Lord of Awa, and Okubo Ichio, Lord of Odawara, met with Saigo Takamori of Satsuma, a general from the emperor's army. The entreaties of the ministers confirmed the humaneness of the general: as old friends who were becoming statesmen of the new Nippon, they agreed that a battle fought for Edo was neither necessary nor desirable. The city was saved, with all its treasures and all its joyful people. Only the Bakufu perished, and in the celebrations over the coming of peace only a few officials could have mourned the Shogunate's passing. Edokko welcomed the victorious pacification forces, who had conquered the nation's largest city without firing a pistol or dodging a spear. To help everyone enjoy those festive days and nights, merchants opened their warehouses, policemen the barriers, shopkeepers their doors, the Yoshiwara its Great Gate. And the Mitsui, in their famous store at Suruga-cho, held a big sale—"fine quality goods, at fixed prices"—of silks and brocades "recently imported from the Imperial City."

Lord Okubo's footmen heard little about his part in the negotiations over Edo. They lived at the lantern's base, so to speak, where everything is in darkness. But the lantern's light streamed far abroad, and in time some of it was reflected upon the folk below. After a while the clan officials told them to put back their weapons in the armory and to resume their usual duties. For Genzo, Kosaburo, and the other footmen these consisted in cleaning the yashiki's courtyards, refurbishing the barracks, mending horses' accouterment or burnishing samurai armor, sadly tarnished during the last few weeks' neglect. Some men, like Genzo and Kosaburo, continued to practise judo, even though this was no longer required of them. Runners and footmen were seldom called, inasmuch as Lord Okubo and his clansmen did not go out much during those days of change, when the Outside Lords (now suddenly become the Topmost Lords) and their bragging troops moved back into the city they had won in the emperor's name. Of those returning daimyo and their men, the ones most dreaded were the warriors from Satsuma. As everyone in Edo knew, the Satsuma vassals were determined to avenge the burning of their several yashiki in Edo, set afire by cowardly—but unidentified—enemies only four months ago.

During those quiet weeks of the Fourth Month, while the beauties of spring unfolded, one after the ordered other, Genzo could not forget that he was seeing them for the last time. The certainty that soon he would be leaving all this beauty forever often moved him to tears. And now that he was about to leave it Nippon had never looked so fair. The bright green hues in the new leaves unfolding upon the rounded cherry trees and the towering gingkoes; the coppery flush in the new shoots rising up in the bamboo groves; the heavy-scented flowers of sweet daphne; the masses of azaleas, white and pink and purple; and, startling amid all the expanses of grasses and shrubs, the splashes of scarlet, like drops of blood, which are the flowers of the boke, the lowly quince, his favorite among all the gifts of spring: he must look his fill upon these now, storing them in his memory, to think about during the years when he could not see them ever again. And oftentimes he would wonder what he would find to take their place, in a land that knew no winter, and therefore could enjoy no spring.

Flowers, plants, trees, rocks, gardens, birds, clouds, Fujisan rising white against the clear blue sky: none of these did he own, but all of them he loved, with the passion of a pauper who can have no other loves. For him these were not proofs that this is a floating world, a place of things which live briefly, only to fade and to die. To him they were promises that this world is a place bursting with life and with hope, and that out of life comes change, and that out of death new life will come.

At times like these Genzo would ask himself if he had not been too hasty in his decision to leave Nippon, would wonder if he should not stay in his homeland, in a place where he belonged. But when, on the few occasions he was sent from the yashiki upon an errand and, while running through the streets of Edo, saw the mud beneath his feet instead of tree tops and clouds above, he knew that he would not stay here at home. Beyond the jostling cheerful throngs of Edokko he saw the sick, the dying, the dead, abandoned by the wayside. He smelled the stink of too many living people, the stench of too many dead, thrown into canals and rivers and open fields to rot. And the pleas of shivering beggars, clustered at temple gates or huddled beneath Edo's many bridges, spurred him faster upon his way. He could almost feel the crawling of their lice and the itching of their sores.

And always, wherever he went, he saw the two-sworded men. Every one of them, lean or fat, tall or short, bathed or dirty, high or low, reminded him of the one who murdered Ichiro. "Everything will change in Nippon now," its people were being told, since the ministers of the Meiji emperor had taken over the rule of the land. But when Genzo looked close he saw that nothing had changed, that nothing would ever change in this country ruled by samurai. In a land where might takes charge, as the people whispered among themselves, justice cannot be found. "Tsuyoi mono

gachi," they muttered among themselves, and Genzo agreed with
them. "The powerful will prevail."

Strengthened in his resolve to leave, Genzo practised listening
to the sound of his new name whenever he could be alone. "I-
shi" gave a good rhythm for his feet to follow as he ran. "Ishi of
Asakusa" fitted better the scratching of the bamboo rake when,
early each morning, he helped to clean the courtyards. Before
long he became so accustomed to the new name that he was in
danger of failing to hear the old when someone called to him.

At long last the first day of the Fifth Month arrived. After dark
that evening Genzo went to the house near the Outer Moat, half
expecting to be disappointed. But Hamada Hikizo's message
awaited him, exactly as promised: "Hamada-san says, 'Come
here on the seventh night,' " the old servant said, happy with the
good news he delivered. " 'The ship will sail at dawn on the tenth
day.' You understand?" Genzo thanked him profusely, with
many bows and polite expressions, for he was a kind old man who
could be finding little joy in his caretaker's lonely life.

When, all but bursting with relief, Genzo returned to the footmen's barrack, he found the place in a state far worse than any
the threat of war had caused. Kosaburo, they shouted, had just
been taken to the yashiki's house for the sick. Some men said that
he was dead, some that he was dying, while still others insisted
that he was only slightly hurt. Although no two could agree upon
the extent of his injuries, everyone declared that yes, indeed, the
wounded man was Kosaburo.

"But why Kosaburo?," asked Genzo. "And who did this to
him?"

"Why?," answered Jiro. "Karma, that's why."

"You know how he is," said another, coming closer to a more
immediate cause. "He was rushing off, to meet one of his light-
assed women, when it happened."

"The people who brought him to the gate saw the whole thing.
Satsuma men did it. Three of them. Looking for a fight. And
ready to jump on any one who wears the crest of an Inside Lord."

Genzo hurried to the sick-house, the only one of his barrack mates willing to be Kosaburo's nurse, if he lived, or the washer of his body, if he died. The hospital was a small house, little more than a single room, set apart from all other parts of the yashiki because of the defilement that accompanies illnesses and the pollutions that issue from the bodies of sick or wounded people. Satsuma men! he raged. Chikusho! Beasts! How like them to pick upon a defenseless boy. And an innocent one, too, who was not even living in Edo at the time of the raids upon those mansions of the several Satsuma lords. And, furthermore, one who belonged to a clan that had taken no part in the cowardly attack upon the empty Satsuma yashiki.

In the sick room, lighted by one of those new rock-oil lamps the Western barbarians have invented, Kosaburo lay upon a pallet. Naked and bloody, he looked small, and lifeless. The clan physician, with kimono sleeves tied back, knelt beside the boy, touching limbs and bruises, lifting his eyelids. In a corner sat an old man, carefully folding the bloodied kimono and the damp loincloth Kosaburo had been wearing.

Genzo sank to his knees, bowing low to the doctor. He was only a one-sworded man, a commoner. But he bore two names, the mark of a favored commoner. And in his mind he carried much learning, in his fingers much skill. Where samurai hacked and slaughtered, he tried to mend and save. Genzo and ignorant folk like him respected physicians above all other men in Nippon. "Please tell me, sir: how is he?"

The doctor, a good-hearted man, did not ignore Genzo. "Oh, he'll live all right. He's a tough fellow. Unconscious now because he's been hit on the head. But he'll wake up, after a while. A good thing they did not think him worthy of their swords. However," he shook his head, disapproving all men of violence, "he will not be as good to look upon as before. With a smashed nose—split lips—a few teeth knocked out—a cut on the cheek that will leave an ugly scar. But no broken bones, as far as I can tell. They seem to have taken a great dislike to his face, those Satsuma men."

His accounting completed, the doctor turned away from Kosaburo. "He will know the meaning of pain, during the next few days. But," he could not keep from smiling, "fortunately they did not damage the part of him that he cherishes the most. That's as good as new. A tight fundoshi, especially if it is wet, can be like a coat of armor for a man beset." He comforted Genzo, this physician: in the midst of trouble, he was a man who gave help. In the face of death, he would smile and recommend a tight fundoshi. Kosaburo, when he awakened, would like this doctor.

Two kitchen maids came to the door, carrying wooden pails filled with hot water, baskets full of clean rags. "Maa, the poor boy," said the elder, seeing the blood and the bruises. "Ahh, the poor man!," exclaimed the younger, her glance lingering over the parts of Kosaburo he revealed only on special occasions.

"Put those things down. And go!," the physician waved them off like gnats. To the old man and Genzo he said, "Wash him. I'll come back when you're done."

Blood and wounds, battered bodies and broken bones are nothing new to retainers of daimyo. The old man and Genzo did their work swiftly, the old man impersonally, as one who has spent his lifetime in such employment, Genzo with a tenderness such as he had not felt for anyone since he had put his sweet-smelling sons into their beds. Am I falling in love with this boy? he wondered, knowing about the kind of love that is so widespread and so honored among samurai, and mariners, and among retainers of daimyo who are denied the chance to have families. But no, he soon concluded, his was not that kind of love: his was made of tenderness and pity, and of concern and enjoyment, too, but not of lust for this smooth firm flesh, or of yearning and jealous ownership. With a shock that quickly gave way to contentment, he recognized that what he felt for Kosaburo was something like a father's love for a favored son. And why should this not be so, he asked, when I am almost old enough to be his father? And lonely enough to need a son?

The doctor returned, followed by a serious young man carrying a small medicine chest. At the physician's direction the apprentice put a certain kind of poultice upon the cut in Kosaburo's cheek, applied a greasy ointment to the swollen nose and puffed lips, the bruises on neck and shoulders. With the doctor's help he tied bandages of white cotton cloth around Kosaburo's head, to hold the poultice against the wounded cheek. The other places, impossible to bandage, they left uncovered. When they were finished, the doctor gave to Genzo a glass vial holding a dark brown fluid. "You will stay with him for the next few days.—I shall arrange with the office for you to be here.—When he awakens, and begins to complain of great pain, give him this medicine to drink. All of it. This is opium, from China. A most kind thing, at first. Later, worse than a thousand devils. It will ease his pain, and put him to sleep again. Tomorrow I shall give him one more drink of this medicine. After that he must suffer the pain as best he can."

While the apprentice closed up the lacquered medicine chest the doctor lifted Kosaburo's eyelids, peered again at those bloodshot eyes. "In the morning they will look like the purple irises of summer, in full bloom," he told Genzo. "But, like irises, they too will fade in time." Then he and his sober assistant went away.

The quiet old man covered Kosaburo with a clean sheet, over which he drew a padded futon to keep the boy warm during the night. After putting the room in order he brought in a pallet and a futon for Genzo to use, and a small brazier holding three glowing coals. Just before he put out the lamp he said softly, "The boy will be all right. Do not worry." In the darkness, made all the more pressing by the three fiery eyes in the hibachi, Genzo thought those were the kindest words he had ever heard.

Two nights and a day went by before Kosaburo awakened from the combined effects of the blow to his head and the Chinese medicine. By then the aches and pains were easier for him to bear. Except for the times when he forgot them, and tried to raise his head or to laugh at one of Genzo's remarks, he did not suffer overmuch. He was a good patient, uncomplaining and grateful. Genzo fed the boy, washed him, massaged his arms and legs and back, talked when he felt like speaking, kept silent when he wanted to sleep. But, unknown to Genzo, Kosaburo slept less than he pretended. When, at length, on the fourth day, he had thought a great deal and was ready to speak, he startled Genzo almost out of his skin.

"Beasts!," he exploded. "Fools! All of them! Small-minded,

greedy, cringing, bowing, stupid, damned offspring of slaves!''
The number of curse words and insulting epithets available to the
polite people of Nippon is exceedingly limited, but Kosaburo
used as many of them as his bruised head could recall. ''Dung!
Sons of shit!'' He ran out of words long before his breath could
fail him.

Genzo sat up in alarm, fearing that his patient was having a fit
caused by the blow to his skull. With those inflamed eyes ringed
in black and blue he resembed an angry badger routed from his
lair. Angry he was, that much Genzo could see. But certainly he
was not crazed. ''Who?,'' he asked quietly. ''The men of Satsuma?''

''What do you mean, the men of Satsuma?'' Kosaburo lisped,
his tongue sticking in those places once filled with white teeth.
''The whole damned lot of them, I mean. Every man, woman, and
child in the country, I mean. Including you and me. Everyone
who sits here on his heels, licking the ass of the policeman above
him—''

''Stop! Remember where you are!''

''How can I forget where I am? That's exactly what I'm talking
about.'' Even so, checked by Genzo's fears, he lowered his voice.
''Let me tell you something. The men who beat me up the other
night: they were not Satsuma men. I am not as stupid as I let people think. I could have run away from the Satsuma men—or from
any other bunch I didn't know. But the gang who jumped on me
were men I knew and trusted. Why should I run from them,
standing there in the street? They were men I knew.'' His voice
rose in a fury of protest. ''From this very yashiki. They were men
of Izu!''

''What?'' Genzo did not want to hear that such treachery was
possible. And yet, in his heart, he knew that it could happen.
Since the beginning, the history of Nippon, of its people both
high and low, is filled with accounts of deceit and violent be-
trayal.

''I'm telling you the truth. The men of Satsuma were the ones
who came to help me, when those mad dogs of Okubo—Ahh, who
can I trust, after that?''

"A terrible thing!" Genzo did not have to ask the reason for their turning upon Kosaburo. A tongue six inches long can kill a man six feet high. And a faithful woman, as country folk say, is as hard to find as an honest whore or a square egg.

"And must I go on living with them? Why? Why? How can I get away from them, from this place, without being caught when I run? Where can I go? I who wanted so much to come to this fine place: now I hate it. 'Hearing is paradise. Seeing is hell.' "

The cry was Genzo's own. He recognized it at once, and the desperate need that made Kosaburo so furious and so helpless. But how could he tell the boy of his own hopes and plans, of the way Kannon-sama had given him to escape from oppression? This was his secret, and he dared not tell it to anyone else, for fear that when he did it would be a secret no longer.

"They remind me of cormorants," said Kosaburo, in disgust.

"Who?," asked Genzo, lost now among the profusion of Kosaburo's targets.

"Who else but the people of Nippon? I wonder if people in other lands are as stupid?"

Inasmuch as neither of them had any knowledge about other lands or other people, they realized at once that this was an unprofitable line of inquiry. "The frog in the well knows not the great ocean," croaked Genzo, and Kosaburo had to laugh with him. "Why cormorants?," asked Genzo. Not being a fisherman, he knew very little about those peculiar birds.

"Well, to begin with, they're trained to obey their master's commands. They work long hours, without complaint, in all kinds of weather, for very little reward. Because of that ring around the neck, they can swallow only the smallest fry. The bigger fish, of course, they will cough up for the master."

"But, in return, doesn't the master take good care of his flock?," Genzo asked most virtuously, signaling with eyes and hands to put an end to this dangerous conversation. Ko's tongue, clacking away, would soon kill them both.

"Oh, to be sure," Ko's scorn was so obvious that a spy as dull as a daimyo could have understood it. "He gives 'em fine homes made of reeds and rotting straw to live in. Beds of deep mud and manure to raise their young in. And just enough food to keep them alive—but always eager to work for more.''

Delighted by the fable he was imagining, Kosaburo forgot to be angry. Raising himself up, to rest his weight upon an elbow, he rushed on. ''And, oh my! How we—I mean they—how they love being so well treated by their master. How loyal they are! And how jealously they guard their rightful places in the flock, in the pen, in the fishing boat. Old Ichi is the Boss, he is Number One. Number Two knows it. Just as he keeps Number Three in his place. And so we go, down the line.'' With his wonderful ability, he imitated, with hands, neck, head, eyes, lips, suckings, snufflings, gurglings, and squealings, a giddy cormorant in the very bliss of happiness with his position in the obedient flock. ''We have the Inside Cormorants, the Outside Cormorants, and, at the very front, the Shogun Cormorant.'' Laughing, the tears trickling down from those black and blue sockets, he could hardly finish. ''Reminds me of—a daimyo's procession ... Reminds me of— us ... ''

Although he, too, was laughing at Kosaburo's show, Genzo could no longer overcome his fear that an ear in attendance might be listening to them playing this hazardous game. Folly, passing by, must not be allowed to chase reason away. He sped to the door, dashed to the nearest place of convenience. While engaged in that permissible errand he could see into the space beneath the hospital house as well as the area around it.

''Nobody's there,'' Kosaburo sneered when Genzo came back. ''Nobody ever is. But they've got us trained to *think* that someone is there. And so we're afraid to talk, almost afraid to think. Why should they listen to what we say? Why should they be afraid of us? We who are Numbers 501 and 509 in Lord Okubo's cormorants' procession? They've got us trained to obey. And they've got those rings clamped so tight around our necks ... '' He groaned in rage. ''A grasshopper trying to climb a mountain,'' he sobbed. ''That's me.''

''Be glad that no one was listening, friend. Otherwise tomorrow's sun would find two birds less in this fouled nest. And not because they've flown away."

"Flown away?" Ko sank back upon his pallet. "You have failed to realize the most important fact about cormorants. They have been taught the Five Cardinal Virtues of Confucius: benevolence, justice, courtesy, wisdom, and loyalty. Oh, especially that last. Above all, they are *loyal.* They *never* run away." After a long pause, he sighed, all laughter spent. "Because they can't. Where would they go, in this big pen?"

During this spinning of Kosaburo's parable Genzo was doubly uneasy: he feared not only the ears outside but also the eyes within that single room. He could not be sure that the boy might not be testing him in this devious way. He did not want to believe that Ko had been ordered to spy upon Lord Okubo's retainers. But such spies had been found before, in other yashiki, and perhaps now was the turn of Lord Okubo's men to be observed. He had to consider the possibility that Ko had been beaten by Okubo men because they suspected him of being an informer. Genzo was caught between his affection for Kosaburo, so recently acknowledged, and this sudden suspicion of the boy, so recently introduced into the yashiki.

Very carefully, for this was the pivot about which their whole world revolved, past, present, and future, Genzo said, not for the listening spy but for the two of them who were alone in this room: "And is loyalty not a good thing?"

"Yes," said Kosaburo, quietly now. "Without it, I suppose, the world would fall apart. But in my opinion, loyalty should go both ways: up to the lord, and down from the lord. Up to you from me, and down to me from you. You and I: we are loyal, each to the other. I know this. I feel this in my belly. But I do not see Lord Okubo being loyal to me or to you. Or any of his officials being loyal to us. Or any of his two-sworded men. They could slice us up as a tunafish is sliced into sashimi, if they felt like doing so, and no one would tell them that they shouldn't do that to us. And while we're on this subject, what loyalty did certain men of Izu show to me the other night?" This time the tears creeping out from those bruised eyes did not come from laughter. "Loyalty is a good thing. But I find no loyalty among the cormorants of this pen. For such as them, there is no place in Heaven or on Earth. As for me, 'Nothing but pain and shame do I feel in this world of men,' " he muttered. " 'But I can not fly away, lacking the wings of a bird.' "

Genzo laid his hand upon the boy's arm. "You are right, my friend. Loyalty is a good thing. And you will find it, even here, among certain Okubo men. 'Right's sure to win, even if it cannot speak.' "

"I wonder," said Ko, settling back into his gloom.

Once again Genzo went out into the courtyard, walked around the little house, stretching arms and legs, scanning the heavens for signs about the weather, checking the yard for evidence of spies. After five minutes of caution and deepest thought, he returned to Ko's bedside. "Please listen. Listen carefully," he began to whisper. Kosaburo lifted one sleepy eyelid, opened his scabbed lips. Go on, they said, without making a sound, I am listening.

"Here is one cormorant who is running away."

Ko's eyes opened wide. He sat up. The battered face expressed surprise, belief, and then joy. "Where?," he whispered. "When?"

Genzo told him as much as he needed to know: about the islands of Hawai and their need for men from Nippon, about Hamada Hikizo, who was looking for people who wanted to work in that far-off land. Kosaburo understood at once, faster than Genzo had, everything that the land of promise offered. "A country almost empty of people ... Then there is room in it for me. Please take me with you."

"You're sure you want to go? To leave your family in Ajiro? Your uncle in Asakusa?"

"They are nothing, compared with my wish to live without this ring around my neck. And how often shall I see them, my mother in Ajiro, my kind uncle in Asakusa, tied as I am to this—to this stinking boat?"

"Then I shall ask if you can go with me. 'The best thing in traveling is a companion.' I cannot promise, you understand. But I shall try to get you a place on the next ship, if this one is already filled."

"That is all I ask," Ko said, lying back in his bed. " 'The best thing in the world is kindness,' " he completed the proverb Genzo had begun, but his thoughts were already far away.

Even though he was still defiled, because of his association with the impurities issuing from Kosaburo, Genzo went that same evening to the house near the Outer Moat, hoping to find Hamada-san. But the man servant said that his master was not at home, and that he never knew where to find him. Genzo returned to the yashiki. Unable to tell Ko the truth, he put on a cheerful face, saying that he had started a message on its way to Hamada-san. With all his power, Genzo told himself, surely Hamada-san can help both of us to disappear.

In the morning of the seventh day of the Fifth Month the doctor released Ko from the hospital. "Go out," he ordered. "Sit in the sun. Get your strength back. But don't start a fight with any warriors yet," he wagged a finger at the boy of many colors. "Wait a week or so, until that cut is healed."

They could not return to the barrack until they had been cleansed of their defilement. By the time the priest came half the morning was gone. He himself took only a few minutes to sprinkle them with salt water, wave over their heads a branch of the sacred sasaki tree decked with pendant paper gohei and chant a ritual prayer in an archaic language, no word of which they understood.

When Genzo reported for duty to the clan office the minor clerk who assigned jobs to footmen scowled like the God of Thunder in a rage. Fumbling through his papers, clearing his throat, he looked everywhere but at Genzo. "Too late for man's work today. Come back tomorrow. About eight o'clock. You get to be first messenger." Thanking the honorable official for his kind notice of this lowly person, Genzo bowed, was turning away, when the clerk said, without looking up, "Today you watch the hinin."

For the rest of the day Genzo watched over the hinin, the not-people, as the eta were called, the wretched and untouchable folk who did the scavenging work for lordly samurai and their retainers. He guarded the yashiki's treasures—its people, buildings, and very stones—from their polluting touch. He allowed them to remove manure from the stables, excrement from the places of convenience, refuse from the several kitchen middens. But he could not permit them to wash their filthy hands at one of the mansion's lavatories or to drink the cold water that flowed from one of its springs. Although Genzo had been assigned this duty before, he had never thought much about hinin, or about their place among the other people of Nippon. He had accepted them unquestioningly, as everyone else did. And, like everyone else, he had trained himself never to see the not-people. Their lot was ordained: the revolting labors they performed were only one of the consequences of their karma. The disgust and fear they aroused in true people, the separation and the shunning, were even worse consequences. And nothing in this life could change either their position or the revulsion with which clean people regarded them.

But on this special day, after so much had happened that promised to change the lot which was supposed to have been ordained for him, Genzo saw those eta in a new light. They are no different from true people, he understood at last. Even though they wear little more than rags, even though they stink because of this filthy kind of work, they laugh and talk and look like all other men and women I have ever seen. That girl, there, who is washing out the refuse buckets: if she were cleaned, and dressed in a pretty kimono, and he saw her on one of Edo's streets, he would think that she was a merchant's daughter, or even a rich man's concubine. That fatherly old fellow, with the white hair and the cheerful talk, who was their headman: in some other place, and in proper clothing, he could be taken for a good-natured priest or some clever artisan.

Genzo, seeing at last with opened eyes, knew how these eta must feel and think and suffer as do all other people. And, he asked, why, then, are they set apart?

His spirit shuddered. Ko and I, he thought: we are not the last in this cage of cormorants. We do not live at the bottom of the pit.

When he found compassion for the hinin in his belly he discovered also a new depth of rebellion against the priests, the samurai, the shoguns who, with this evil doctrine of karma, kept not only the eta in bondage but all the people of Nippon. More than once he was tempted to whisper to the leader of these eta a word of encouragement, a hint about Hamada Hikizo's search for men to go to Hawai. But always his fears overcame his pity. He said nothing. Not even seven words of friendliness could he find to speak.

In discovering the not-people Genzo found a new way to look upon himself. Ishi of Asakusa, he told himself more than once during that last day of his service in Lord Okubo's yashiki, you are a most fortunate man. And always, as he touched the smooth black stone in his obi, he murmured his thanks to Kannon for being so kind to him.

That evening, after supper, Genzo went over to Kosaburo, sitting cross-legged in the space which was his home and bed. "Let's go down to the bath house," he said. This was the signal they had agreed upon before leaving the hospital.

"You think I can go?" In this fateful moment Ko looked more stricken than ever he had seemed in the sick room. The black and blue marks around his eyes were fading, the jagged cut in his cheek was healing nicely, the nose and lips were no longer swollen and sore. But worry drained the blood from his face and, as he stared up at Genzo, he resembled a small boy about to be whipped by his angry father.

"I am sure you can," Genzo said quietly. "It's not very far." Around them their barrack mates, sprawled upon mats or sitting at low tables playing cards or Go, paid them not the slightest attention.

"Then I am ready," said Ko, rising from his mat.

Genzo owned a stone, given to him by Kannon, and a few copper coins, saved from six years of service given to Lord Okubo. But Ko had nothing of his own to take away except the fundoshi he wore. Not even the crested kimono that covered his body belonged to him.

Dressed in the livery of Lord Okubo's footmen, they walked through the servants' gate into the street, warm and mellow in the last light of day. Neither the guards nor the household folk gossiping there, with Okubo men or with servants from neighboring yashiki, noticed them. When they had gone off a safe distance Ko began to giggle. "Two cormorants," he said, "slipping out of the flock. And no one sees them going."

After a few more steps he started to sing. A geisha's love song it had been, but he changed the words to please his humor:

> He rises and goes.
> There are some dark clouds.
> Shall I be a singing nightingale,
> Or a firefly burning in silence?
> But dumb grief, a tearful parting, are not for me . . .

Fluttering his eyelids, making his head wobble like a geisha setting all her hairpins aquiver, he warbled, as he looked up at Genzo:

> And when I think we might never have met,
> Been utter strangers. . . .

Laughter. This is the best farewell, thought Genzo. And the best beginning to a new life.

At the bathhouse Taro-san welcomed them with extraordinary friendliness. "I've heard of your troubles, Honorable Stud," he leered. "For you," he touched Ko's breastbone, "but not for you," he pushed Genzo away, "a free bath tonight. Courtesy of the management."

After a leisurely soak, during which no one teased the battered lover, they walked down the valley road to the Outer Moat, reaching the house of mystery at the appointed time. Hamada's messenger waited for Genzo in the eight-mat room. If the old servant attached to the house had not presented him Genzo would never have believed in him as a man to be trusted. He was a huge fellow gone to fat, with the belly of a failed sumo wrestler and the shifty eyes of a gambler who has been caught too often at cheating.

"Hah! What's this?," he complained the instant they came in. "I am told about one passenger, not two."

"Can't you take two as well as one?," Genzo began hopefully.

"Yes, indeed," the fellow wheezed, in that high hoarse voice that so many fat men have. "A dozen. Fifty. Any number at all. I don't mind. But if I bring him more than one tomorrow, my boss will slit my throat. With his own dagger. And use my eyes for fishbait. Therefore, I believe in doing what I am told." He held up one fat finger. "Only one. Which one, then," he looked down at a document lying on the mat beside him, "is—What? How is it read, this kanji? Seki of Asakusa? Ishi of Asakusa? Koku? Shaku? What?"

"Ishi," said Genzo. "Here he is," and he pushed Kosaburo forward.

"What do you mean?," cried Ko. "Ishi is not my name!"

"Listen to me," said Genzo, holding him by the arms, "and be sensible. Ishi is my new name, for now, so that the police will not find me under my old name. You take it, and use it, in place of me." As Ko started to object Genzo tightened his hold, began to shake him as he might a rebellious son. "Be sensible! I know the way to Yokohama. You do not. I can walk to Yokohama. You cannot. So go with him on that fisherman's boat. I shall meet you there tomorrow evening." He turned to the fat man. "You can tell me, at least, where I can find Hamada-san?"

"To be sure. He'll not be hard to find." Like most bullies, this one could be pleasant enough when not crossed. "Just look for the milling mob of idiots, all wanting to sail off to Tenjiku. They'll be pushing their way into Fujimi Inn. What a name! No one can ever see Fujisan from there, even on a clear day, but that's what they call it. Yet it's close to the harbor. You'll have no trouble finding it. If you ever get there."

"Thanks. That's all I need to know." Releasing Kosaburo, he said, "You're on your way now, Ko. See you tomorrow night, at Fujimi Inn. Wait for me there. I'll do my best to join you, there. If I don't—go without me, on that ship. You hear me?"

Ko nodded unhappily. "But how are you—" he began, as Genzo turned and hurried from the room.

"What's happened to your face?," the fat man was asking Ko, as the old servant led Genzo to the front of the house.

Early the next morning, lighted by the rays of the rising sun slanting through the pine trees, Genzo departed from Lord Okubo's yashiki and service in the most conspicuous manner he could contrive. Wearing the livery that distinguishes the runners who carry the clan's messages, from the conical hat woven of sedge to the gaiters tied about his shins; flaunting his daimyo's crest in the five prescribed places; and carrying the long staff to which is lashed the lacquered case that holds the august messages, Genzo trotted forth for the last time from the yashiki's gate.

The sleepy guards saw only another runner, starting upon another round, carrying one more message in exactly the same manner that all messages have been carried, since the beginning of time. "Genzo of Shimoda in Izu," he mumbled, even then not wanting to tell an outright lie, letting them think that he was going to Shimoda, five days away. "Something with an air of truth about it," as Hamada-san had said. So they heard him, and so they repeated to their superior sitting in his warm cubicle in the gate house, and so he wrote it down in the logbook his superiors required him to keep.

Turning for the last time toward the Outer Moat and, beyond that, the road that leads to the Tokaido, Genzo smiled at the ease with which he had started on his way to freedom. Hamada-san is right about officials, he grinned. They'll not miss me for two weeks, or more. " 'While the hunter looks afar after birds,' " he sang, " 'they fly up and escape at his feet.' "

CHAPTER 5
THE BARRIERS

Genzo's great worry was not Lord Okubo's guards at the yashiki's gates but the Bakufu's policemen at the two stations on the Tokaido through which he must pass before he reached Yokohama. Although the Bakufu ceased to exist with the entry of the emperor's ministers into Edo, its system for controlling the people did not come to an end. In the hope of keeping their jobs under the new rulers the Bakufu's officials still performed their duties in all departments of government. In the hope of keeping order throughout the country the imperial ministers accepted, for the time being, the services of those officials who once had served the shoguns. The Bakufu's policemen still managed the barriers across the country's highways, its spies still watched for troublemakers in cities, towns, and villages. And, out of habit as well as in ignorance, the docile people of Nippon went on living as before. For them only the masters, not the rules, had changed. "Nagai mono ni wa makeru yo," the people said behind their hands, "yield to the men of power."

Genzo never questioned the fact that policemen would be watching the barriers on the Tokaido. Those checking points were as much a part of Nippon as were daimyo castles, Buddhist temples, Shinto shrines, farmers' hovels, and pine trees shaped by the winds. He could not conceive of a country without barriers across its roads or police to watch them. The problem was to get past those strong gates without being caught as a man running away from fealty to his lord. The penalty for that crime, as no one in Nippon could ever forget, was crucifixion—the most agonizing of all deaths. And his name would be reviled through all the nine generations of men.

During the sleepless night after he left Kosaburo in the care of Hamada-san's fat minion Genzo thought long about his predicament. The usual method of presenting a document issued by the clan office, bearing the seals of the clan chamberlain and of some minor functionary in the Bakufu, he dismissed at once as being beyond his reach. How could he ask for papers sending him on a mission to which he was not assigned? Remembering Hamada's precept—"Do not ask for something you are not sure you will receive"—he concluded that he must go without a passport, trusting to the laziness of constables at the barriers and to his own wits in the event of an emergency. And, above all, to the devisings of Kannon-sama, who makes all things possible to men who call upon her in true faith.

Kannon helped him, more than he dared to hope.

She put into his mind the thought of leaving the yashiki in full sight of anyone who happened to see him. She put the slowness of sleep into the minds of the yashiki's guards, and bright morning sunlight into their eyes, so that his departure from Lord Okubo's household was made easy. She harried the constables at the barrier of Shinagawa. Squeezed as it is between mudflats and swamps on the one hand, and the slow Shina River on the other, it is the busiest checking point in all Nippon, the sole mouth through which all traffic to and from southeastern Edo must flow.

The great gate stood wide open. On either side, merchants with carts and pack trains, fishermen and farmers with shoulder-poles and swaying baskets, pilgrims on journeys to holy shrines and famous places, even great lords and retainers in their caravans, must wait for inspection. For every one of them the police must make certain that they presented the necessary permits for going or coming, and that they smuggled no contraband goods or weapons into Edo, no treasures or women out of it. In such a confusion no busy policemen could find the time or the strength to suspect a lone messenger, clearly unarmed and as obviously serving a powerful lord. And so they waved Genzo through the gate, happy to be rid of the one man who was no problem at all. He had counted upon this very probability (which in truth he'd experienced often enough before), and he was neither much surprised by it nor unduly grateful to Kannon-sama for this rather ordinary intervention. But the next barrier, he foresaw, would put her to the test—and himself as well.

Once safely through the drab town of Shinagawa he slowed his pace to the usual trot of the long-distance runner. He felt no need to hurry, with only five ri to travel before nightfall. And he did not want to reach the next barrier before its guards had any business to employ them. Therefore, he decided to enjoy while he could the pleasures of the road.

"The water is deep and the river wide," sing the people of Edo, "you can rave all you like on the other side." The weather was perfect, clear and cool, with the brightest of blue skies overhead, coloring the ruffled waters of Edo's wide bay to his left and the smooth surfaces in swamps and unplanted rice fields to his right. The blue of the sky, the green of pine trees and other fresh growing things: these are the colors of spring, these are the promises of good fortune. And the breeze singing in the pines marking the course of the Tokaido reminded him of the famous storyteller's poem, comparing that murmuring with "the sounds of someone singing to the koto, of how the pine trees at the gate bring wealth, freedom, and happiness." The day, the poem, the promise: these were the best of omens. And the poem led him, quite naturally to think of himself as a joyful Hachirobei, going to meet his comrade, a friend even better than Kitahachi because he was neither as stupid nor as gross. Who could say what strange adventures Kosaburo and Genzo might not experience, as they sailed across the sea to a foreign land, as they lived and worked in that rich earth? Wealth and freedom would be theirs, assuredly, as Hamada-san and Nakamura-san had said. And perhaps even happiness would be granted to him, who had known so little of it in this land of his birth.

But this was not a day for looking back, for grieving. Already he was thinking of himself as being free—a little too soon, he warned himself, although not very successfully. But how could he be sad and dispirited on such an exciting day? For him, too, as for Hachirobei, the horses on the road where whinnying "hin-hin-hin," their bells were ringing "shan-shan-shan." As always, postboys argued and teased among themselves, or offered to rent their drooping nags, at remarkably variable rates, to travelers tired of walking.

In Omori, where the people plait straw into so many useful things, their children cried out to passing folk, "To give us food, please buy our wares." Before every inn and eating-place, servant girls plucked at the sleeves of wayfarers, inviting them to "Stop here," or to "Walk in, walk in, and try our special kind of soup." Many a wench, with brazen stares or provocative gestures, tried to lure Genzo in for something more than a cup of tea, but he managed to dodge around her, always with the laughing promise that he'd have more time to stop on the way back.

Beyond Omori, however, he was almost alone, having overtaken the travelers who had started early from Edo and not yet having met those who approached from Kanagawa or Odagaya. Now, with little to distract him, his anxiety about the rest of this day pushed more pleasant thoughts from his mind, and soon he was using those flying feet as if all the constables in Edo pursued him.

"It is not far between the barriers," as Sankoku has written about the fifty-three stages of the Tokaido. Even so, Genzo amazed himself at the speed with which he raced from Shinagawa to the edge of Kawasaki village. He went almost as fast as Idaten, the Buddhist god famed for his swiftness: in little more than two hours he had run half the distance to Yokohama.

Kannon-sama! Hail, Goddess of Great Mercy and Great Compassion! Help me now, he begged, as he drew near Kawasaki and the last police barrier in his way. He had chosen to come by this new road, rather than by the old one farther inland, where travelers cross the southernmost branch of Rokugo River in a flat-bottomed ferry boat. Without a passport to show the constables, and without money for bribing the ferryman, the ticket seller, and the guards, he could not possibly try the older route. The new road, using the high bridge across the Rokugo that had been built recently in order to accommodate the increased traffic between Edo and Yokohama caused by the presence of foreigners at the new port, would be dangerous, because both police and spies gather there in great numbers. But it also offered him more opportunities to slip past the guards upon some pretext or another.

When he came to the wide road leading to the bridge, his belly sank. The barrier was closed tighter than an abbot's fist, impounding crowds of travelers on either side. Kannon-sama, he prayed, what shall I do? As he drew near Genzo saw all the signs and trappings of a daimyo's procession: the long lances, their blades sheathed in coverings of fur to show that the great name traveled on a peaceful mission; the escort of many samurai, clad in armor and mounted upon horses; and, closest to him, at the rear of the long parade, bearers of his own low station, supporting heavy boxes hung upon their shoulders or great wooden chests slung from carrying-poles. The crest of their livery—a bold circle enclosing two thick bars crossed at right angles—told him that these were the men of Lord Shimazu Hisamitsu, the redoubtable Daimyo of Satsuma. Ahh, Kannon-sama, I thank you, Genzo rejoiced, seeing how easily she had arranged this meeting for him.

Inasmuch as Lord Shimazu was one of the new rulers of Nippon, the keepers of the barrier found themselves in a most delicate position. If they allowed his procession to pass without checking its papers, they could be charged with failing to perform their duty. If they delayed the procession merely to check a sheaf of unnecessary documents, they could be accused of showing an insulting lack of respect for the august dignity of Lord Shimazu and his paramount clan. Even more agonizing was the fear that some of these Satsuma hotheads might cut down the guards where they stood, accusing them of being loyal to the Bakufu instead of to the young emperor.

Following a set of instincts that needed no instructions from Edo, the head constable succeeded in avoiding all perils. With much bowing and scraping and drawing of air through teeth, he begged to be allowed to explain that, of course, the stupidly closed gate, the presumptuous request to be favored with a view of the honorable official passports, were only concessions to established form, required by the exalted government of all esteemed and august daimyo only because these humble servants, the guardians of the gates, must set a good example for vulgar commoners, who so often, as everyone knew, tried to escape the just rule of the honorable law. The clan officer who led the procession—fortunately for everyone the hot-tempered if exalted daimyo himself was dozing in his palanquin—smiled grimly, bracing himself to hear this identical apology at all the other fifty-one stages along the road, and gave the documents to the terrified constable. He received them in trembling hands, bowed to them as if they were sacred relics and, without pretending to examine anything in it, returned the packet to the officer, who graciously accepted it. The forms having been observed, both commanders started bellowing at the same instant, the one to open the gate, the other to start the procession moving.

While this ritual of protocol was occupying the personages at the head of the procession, Genzo attached himself to the worthless ones at its tail. Just as daimyo assist each other in times of need, so do footmen, bearers, and other lowly folk.

"Morning," said Yukio, one of his old friends among the Satsuma footmen, as Genzo approached. Like patient oxen the bearers stood there, resting their burdens against the walls of houses or upon staves thrust into the road. "Where you bound for? Odawara?"

"No," said Genzo, relieved at finding an ally so soon. "Only to Kamakura." This would be a fair compromise, he thought, between his actual destination and the pretended one. "And you? Home to Kagoshima?"

"Nah, nah. To Kyoto again. Reporting to the new master. The one they call Meiji Tenno, whatever that means. Our lord spends more time traveling along this stinking road than he does in any of his many mansions." Lifting one plump shoulder, then the other, wincing dramatically, he delivered the necessary complaint: "This bloody box is heavy. When my back learns it has to carry this stupid thing all the way to Kyoto, my legs will want to stay behind. Kamakura, eh? That bloody hole. Stinks of priests and seaweeds."

And, alas, just as daimyo gossip so do common footmen. "About a pilgrimage Lady Okubo wishes to make, to the temple of the Great Buddha," Genzo said, enlarging upon a rumor he'd heard in the servants' quarters. "But," he leaned toward Yukio-san, "on the way I want to stop in at Yokohama. To visit a woman I know." He winked, Yukio leered, the command to prepare to march came from the head of the column, and the barrier swung open, all in the same moment.

Bending low, in deference to the Lord of Satsuma and his noble escort, the head constable hissed to his minions. Prostrating themselves at the side of the road, they smelled for a while the Tokaido's dirt.

Trudging among his providential friends, rump thrust high, head bent low in proper humility, Genzo passed, uncounted and unremarked, through the gate at Kawasaki. And the footmen, glad to be on their way again, sang out:

> Fluttering our papers,
> The spring winds blow,
> When through the open barriers,
> How gratefully we go . . .

After Kawasaki he should be safe, at least from all predictable traps. Yet Genzo did not become overconfident. He stayed with the Lord of Satsuma's slow procession for another hour or so, listening to their chatter, no different from that of Lord Okubo's men, until they reached a crossroads near the northern slope of the hill known as Takashimadai. There he dropped out of line, leaving them to continue along the broad Tokaido, toward the next barrier at Kanagawa. "So long," he called to the men nearest him, "keep trying."

"Keep it UP!," Yukio shouted him on, lifting his staff in tribute to Genzo's profane mission in Yokohama, rather than to his spiritual one in Kamakura.

Genzo turned into the side road leading toward the hills west of the Tokaido. Although the sun was nearing its peak the air was still cool, the wayside grasses and weeds were still fresh. Soon a curve and a hill shut him off from the Eastern Coast Road. A few minutes later he found the place where he would be transformed: a dell too small for a farmer's use, yet large enough to have grown a thicket of trees. No one saw him when he left the road, waded through the fast-flowing stream, and entered the silent grove.

In the soft light, beneath the angular nurude trees and the bending young maples, their leaves not yet fully green, he shed the livery of Lord Okubo, without hate, with few regrets, and feeling not the slightest qualm of guilt. At the foot of a wild azalea bush, its scarlet blossoms seeming to burn like little flames, he dug a hole in the earth, using his staff for a spade. Keeping only the plaited sandals as a remembrance of Lord Okubo's care, he laid in the pit the kimono, gaiters, sedge hat, and the pieces of the broken staff, covered them with dirt and leaves, until no trace of them could be found, even by the cleverest policeman.

Like a yamabushi, a recluse who draws power from the spirits dwelling upon a mountain and from the austerities he practises, Genzo purified his body and possessions in the cold waters of the stream. He washed himself from shaven pate to muddied feet, his loincloth, the stone of Kannon, the coin pouch with its eleven zeni, even the straw sandals. Then, a cleansed man, he went out, a new man. He bound the wet fundoshi tight about his loins, placed the purse, holding the dark stone and the bright coins, under the folds of cloth next to his navel. He slipped his feet into those soggy sandals, and set forth upon the last stage of his journey to Yokohama.

In a nameless village, sheltered in a fold of hills near the great Soto temple of Hongaku, he went to the pawnbroker's shop. She was a bent and toothless old woman, sitting forlornly in a sagging house, among musty articles held too long in forfeit. Perhaps Kannon persuaded her to be generous, perhaps she was kind by nature, who rarely sold anything in that hamlet of poor folk. In exchange for his eleven zeni she sold Genzo a used kimono of outmoded style, made of dark brown hempen cloth rusty with age, but suitable for a peasant to wear on festival days. It was too small for him, and rather frayed at the edges, but he took it anyway because he liked its sober color and its lack of any pattern or ornament that suggested a daimyo's crest.

He put on the kimono at once, while the old woman exclaimed and admired. She was so taken with this handsome stranger that she insisted upon giving him an obi of dark green brocade that cost ten times the price of the kimono when it was new. "My late husband's, this was," she said, as she brought it out from a storing place in her room at the rear of the house. "He came from Edo," she added proudly, as if that fact alone had made him a most distinguished man. Genzo declined the gift, not so much out of politeness as from a notion that he should start his new life only with things that he himself would earn.

"Please take it," she insisted, brushing wisps of white hair from her cheeks. "What shall I do with it, who have no husband and no sons? Please wear it, and allow it to fulfill its destiny. It will bring you good luck. See," she made him feel the several places in the narrow band, "images of the Lord Buddha, of Kannon-sama, and of Saint Jizo are sewn into it. And they have great power to help the traveler on his way."

Genzo looked sharply at this old woman, trying to tell if she were a seeress, or perhaps a fox-spirit in human guise, who knew his secrets and sought now to hold him with her magical spells. But her eyes did not shine with that mad glitter by which a fox-spirit is detected. Nor did they show the vague and clouded gaze of the seeress. She was just a lonely old woman, full of memories and unspent love, who was preparing to be a traveler soon upon another road than the one he was taking.

"Thank you, honorable mother," he said gently, who could not remember his own mother being so kind to him. "I shall think of you each day I wear this gift. And please do you pray for me, that good luck will be mine, as I wander far away."

"How can it fail you, a man so good?," she bowed low before him, convinced that he must be some god come to earth for reasons she might never know.

He tied the obi about his hips. Against the kimono the green silk looked like the leaves of spring appearing upon the brown hills of Kanagawa. "Farewell," he said, bowing three times, not knowing how else to thank her.

"Farewell," she called after him, her eyes dimmed with tears.

When he took off his livery in that little valley Genzo became a new man inwardly as well as outwardly. No longer did he think like a servile footman or act like the frightened fugitive. He became a free man, who owed allegiance to no daimyo, who took orders from no clansman. The weight of twelve years of fear and servitude was lifted from him that day, and both his spirit and his body recognized this release.

Although in his thoughts he was conscious of this change, he did not realize how his body was responding to it. He did not see how, once again, he held his head high or how, clad in his own brown kimono and beautiful green obi, he fell into the swaggering strut of his unthinking youth, when he imitated the ryu master and his disciples in Shimoda. He did not realize that the quick glances he cast about, searching for policemen who might be hunting for him, looked exactly like the haughty stares he so hated in samurai.

He came down from the hills and entered the Kangai section of Yokohama by one of the lanes connecting the town with farms and villages south of Noge bluff. In this way he avoided the barrier at Kanagawa.

When they saw him the people in Kangai did not doubt that he was a ronin, a masterless samurai, who had put aside his swords when he left the service of his lord. They looked for a moment at that lean body and those piercing eyes, then they drew back, opening a path for him, as they did for all ronin. Samurai are dangerous enough, but ronin are terrors to be fled. Without any restraints placed upon them either by clansmen or by law, they can be as treacherous as earthquakes, as mean as a mother-in-law to a young and ugly bride.

For Genzo, however, this busy seaport town, which had not existed ten years before, was full of fascinations. His eagerness to see all of them made him as harmless as the country farmers who entered the town every day. He would have been astonished had he been told that the people of Kangai feared him.

Meat-eating barbarians of all sizes and colors and ranks thronged the streets of Yokohama: huge black men from Africa; blonde blue-eyed giants from Europe and America; slim Lascars with rings in their ears; bearded Sikhs with twisted turbans; laughing brown men from Polynesia's scattered islands; and Chinese compradors, wearing black gowns, black skullcaps, and queues of braided black hair hanging down their backs. Genzo had seen a few foreigners in Edo: Europe's proud ambassadors being drawn through the streets in splendid carriages, escorted by mounted soldiers in gorgeous uniforms and plumed helmets; or, rarely, an anxious Christian preacher or a furtive schoolteacher, scuttling through alleys, in terror of being cut down by samurai who still resented the presence of aliens in Nippon, the Land of the Gods. But never had he seen so many gaijin at one time, or such a variety of clothing.

And never before had he seen a foreign woman. The first one he encountered caused him to stop and stare, just as Kosaburo had gaped at the oiran in the Yoshiwara. But this woman, he could tell, was no harlot: clinging to a merchant's arm, her head and pale face all but hidden by a covering that looked like a bucket stuffed with yellow hair and blue silk, her waist pinched in like a bee's, she seemed to be floating upon an enormous bell-shaped skirt of black silk that covered half the width of the street. Poor woman, he thought, if she needs to wear such a huge kimono she must have a bottom as big and rounded as that of a daruma doll. Small wonder her husband must pull her along. How strange the world is, he mused, that gives our women such pleasing shapes, and makes the women of gaijin so deformed. Not until later, when he saw a foreign woman of another sort, painted and bold, lifting her full skirts to enter a carriage, did he understand that, at bottom, beneath all those layers of clothes, foreign women are very much the same as are the women of Nippon.

Bakamono! he scolded himself. You should have known. He was so stupid! In his youth, he hated to remember, he'd actually believed—along with most Nipponjin—that foreigners were "one-toed folk." Not until he saw the American sailors at Shimoda take off their shoes did he realize that they, too, have five toes on each foot, just as did the men of Nippon. And yet people who had never seen foreigners still believed all those lies about the visitors that the Bakufu had invented . . .

By the time he reached the inner section of the city—called Kannai, or Inside the Barrier, because of the gate that in earlier days cut off the foreign settlement from the rest of the Shogun's forbidden land—no one could have mistaken Genzo for a ronin. Gone were the suspicious stare and the martial step. Now he looked like every other Nipponjin coming for the first time into this mad amazing city. He wandered along, seeing the shops full of strange new things from the West, the splendid carriages with their prancing horses and extravagant passengers, the long drays laden with crates and barrels sent from half the world away, the solid massive buildings in the Western style, made of stone rather than of wood, with broad verandahs both upstairs and down, and tall windows covered with sheets of clear glass. Genzo could scarcely believe the things he saw, the sounds he heard. Unlike those fanatical samurai whose war-cry is "Sonno Joi," because they want only to revere the emperor and expel the barbarians, he admired everything the foreigners had done. Compared with Edo, staid and grim and bound, Yokohama was exciting, gaudy, turbulent. It was alive with busy people, full of wonders, bursting with wealth. The foreign people impressed him most of all: they seemed to be happy, and free of fear. They reminded him of those Americans he had watched so long ago, for so short

a time, in Shimoda. Even the people of Nippon who lived in Yokohama behaved more like foreigners than Nipponjin: they were
friendlier and kinder and ruder to each other, much less bothered
with bowings and the formulas of meaningless politeness, than
ever the people of Edo had learned to be.

Well! said delighted Genzo to himself, if this is what the great
world is like into which I am going, then indeed am I the most
fortunate of men. Kannon-sama: I thank you for taking such good
care of me.

But where, in all this frenzy, was Fujimi Inn? The few people
he asked had never heard of it, being strangers here too, they
confessed. And, as usual, in trying to be helpful they succeeded
only in contradicting each other with their instructions. Sensibly
disregarding them he pushed on, keeping close to the water's
edge, hoping the while that Hamada's fat henchman had not lied
in his throat.

The harbor was larger than he expected, much broader than
Shimoda's little pocket, and busier by far than that place could
ever be. A dozen great ships lay moored in the bay; and, near the
southern shore, several others were warped in along both sides of
a long stone quay. Their bowsprits extended over the jetty like
stiff branches growing out from the forest of masts. An offshore
breeze brought the familiar scent of seaweed and brine, mixed
with smells that clean Shimoda never knew: the reek of rotting
garbage and excrement, thrown into the water from those many
ships, joining the stench of rubbish and excrement and mud
washed in from the town.

At long last, tired, hungry, and worried, Genzo found Fujimi
Inn, at the far end of the harbor, near where the bay curves back
toward the sea, bent to it by the bluff of Yamate. Just as the fat
man promised, the inn squatted near the water's edge, like an old
woman resting on her haunches. And, as he had jeered, even if a
man stood on its roof on the clearest of days, it could not possibly
have presented him with a view of Fuji. A narrow weatherbeaten
structure, hemmed in by grog shops and stores full of cheap trin-

kets, it announced its identity in two syllabaries. Flowing Chinese characters, carved in a large slab of wood, the grooves brightened with vermilion, told Genzo that this was Fujimi Ryokan. Roman letters that Genzo could not read, painted upon the building's face, informed Westerners that this was Veiw of Foogee Hotel. Much relieved by this proof that even cheats can be honest when they have nothing to gain, Genzo approached Hamada's haven.

But where was the milling mob the fat man promised? No crowds of eager applicants stood in the street. When he entered the tawdry inn Genzo found a dozen or so men sitting on the tatami, looking bored and unhappy, as if they had been waiting there for many weeks. A scrawnier, shabbier lot of city bums he had never seen. Most of them were unshaven, a few even looked unbathed. But the bleary eyes with which all peered at him for a dispirited moment told him that they were not so poor that they couldn't afford to drink too much saké the night before.

Drunkards and bums he did not mind, having seen many in his life. But the thing that made him shudder was the livery they wore: each one was wrapped, more or less, in a happi coat made of cheap cotton cloth, dark blue in color, except for an enormous crest on the back—a white circle enclosing the character ki, printed in black. And whose mon is this? What does this ki mean? Genzo asked himself, unhappy at the very sight of it.

The innkeeper, guessing what he wanted, waved Genzo toward a large room at the rear. There he found Hamada-san, sitting cross-legged upon the tatami, explaining something to a group of men sitting or squatting before him. Slowly and patiently, using simple words of the sort that one directs toward children and peasants, avoiding the honorifics and the phrases of politeness and indirection that superior people must employ, he told them about the kind of work they were supposed to do in Hawai as well as the wages they would receive for this labor. The whole idea of a detailed and written contract between an employer and a worker was so new to Nipponjin that some could not accept it as an arrangement to be trusted. Hamada-san, by this time an experienced recruiting agent, offered to explain the contract system more fully, but later, to those suspicious folk. Meanwhile, he said smoothly, he wanted to sum up the entire proposal, for the sake of those who, having understood, wished to sign the contract immediately.

"First," he started, holding up a finger for each point as he made it, "you will work on a sugar plantation for three years. Second, for each month you work you will receive four American dollars—that's twelve bu in Nippon—as well as a free house to live in, free food to eat, free medicine if you get sick, and one set of free clothes, when you arrive in Hawai, to start you off when you begin to work in the fields. But," he held up both hands, "remember this third point: this is very important: to help you save some of that money for the time when you come back to Nippon, the sugar plantation company will give you only half of your wages each month. The other half, as writing on a piece of paper, will be put in a strong-box for you, until you come home. Then you will bring those papers here with you, to the Consul-General for Hawai in Yokohama. He will give you your money in bu. You understood this important point?"

"Yes. Yes, it is a good thing," some replied. Others nodded, coughed, grunted their acceptance of the plan. No one objected to it.

"Fourth," Hamada continued, "when you sign the contract here, today, you will receive, here, today, ten American dollars—that's thirty bu—as an advance payment on your wages. With this money you should buy the things you will want for the trip on the boat, or for starting your new life in Hawai. Do not buy food for the journey. The ship will feed you, free. Three times each day. But if you want to take saké, or tobacco, or cakes and candies, or pickled vegetables and other such delicacies, then you must buy them before the ship sails.

"Fifth: the passage on the boat, both ways, is free. You do not pay for that. And, finally, sixth: if you are married and wish to take your wife with you, she can go. But she too must work when she gets there, although perhaps not in the fields. She will receive two American dollars each month. That is good pay, you will agree, for a mere woman."

The listeners rumbled their agreement. To them, accustomed to receiving no money at all for labor, only payment in kind, those sums in dollars and bu sounded like great fortunes. And for all of them the thought of receiving thirty bu right now, to spend upon themselves, was beyond resisting. If they worked for a hundred years in Nippon few of them could ever amass thirty bu to spend upon themselves at one time. This lure, more than anything else, brought them in from Yokohama's streets to listen to Hamada's proposition. And this immediate gain, more than any sums they might earn later in Hawai, was the inducement that made most men sign the paper that put them under contract for three years. In the confusions of new thoughts and sounds, however, no one, not even Genzo, caught a detail that Hamada-san carefully neglected to explain: this was the fact that those ten American dollars were offered not as a gift but as an advance payment against their wages. According to the contract, which no one was given a chance to read—if indeed he could read—the amount of this loan would be deducted from the wages they earned on the plantations, at the rate of fifty cents a month.

"One more thing," Hamada drew them past that sticky point, "because only healthy men are wanted, men who are free from sickness or deformities, applicants for these fine jobs must pass a medical inspection. My personal physician awaits you beyond that screen over there. He will give you this examination right here, without any further trouble for you. It's quick, but thorough. You must be inspected, I repeat, before you sign the contract, not after. Now, do you have any questions to ask of me?"

"Yes. Teach me, please," said a thin little man, in a deep voice, surprisingly resonant for so small a body. "If I do not like that strange land, or the work I must do there: I mean, if I do not wish to stay there for three years—"

Hamada interrupted him, having heard the question before. "The contract is for three years. When you sign it, you belong first to me, then to the captain of the ship, then to the sugar planters of Hawai. For three years. Make no mistake about this. Just as a farmer in Nippon very often belongs to his lord, or an apprentice to his master, so do you belong to the holder of the contract. You cannot come home until you have served out your term. But," he held their attention by drawing out the word, "remember this: you are bound for only three years, not for life. Those three years will pass quickly. And when you come home, with all those American dollars, you will be a very rich man. That's one of the reasons, I might add, why the Bakufu—the emperor's government, I should say—has agreed to let you go. The need for foreign money increases each year . . . " Somehow, with a meaningful glance, a stiffening of the neck, a slight gesture with the lizard's paw, he managed to convey to his listeners the idea that when they returned with the enormous fortunes they had acquired they would be received with expressions of gratitude and honor by the government of Nippon itself.

Once again the men nodded soberly. Hamada-san, this generous go-between, was speaking only the obvious truth. What are three years of hard work in a man's life, if at their end he can pass the rest of his years rich, honored, respected—and envied? Three years are as nothing in the long string of them that is life. Why, even a hard working wife does not grow wrinkled and gray in so short a span.

Like a schoolboy, a pale nervous fellow raised his hand for permission to speak. Having received it, he cleared his throat several times before he could begin. "If a man should die, in that faraway place, what will happen to his spirit? Will it wander alone, in darkness? Or will it come home, across the sea, to the shrine of his ancestors?"

Now and then, since he'd crept into the room to listen to Hamada's discourse, Genzo would look about for some sign of Kosaburo. He found the youth at this juncture, leaning against a post at the far end of the hall, talking very happily with someone hidden by a partition. Judging by the boy's rapid chatter, excited hands, and frequent laughter, Genzo suspected that he was working up to some kind of contractual relationship of his own with one of the housemaids. And only yesterday, Genzo shook his head in wonder, he was in the hospital . . .

Ko had acquired a new kimono for his flight from Edo. And

Genzo did not have to think twice about who had chosen it. Made of pale green cloth, the color of stagnant pond water in the heat of summer, it was plentifully adorned with colored koi. When, in the pleasures of conversation, Ko waved his arms or wriggled his rump, the carps seemed to come alive, leaping and thrashing about as if determined to swim their way up a watercourse as tall as Kosaburo and as wide. Even at rest, on a clothes rack, that kimono was enough to make most people dizzy. But on jumping Kosaburo it threatened to make them sick.

Shaking his head to ease his eyes, Genzo found relief in the sober grays and browns and blues worn by the men closer to him. Hamada was answering the nervous man's question. "On this, too, you need not go in doubt. We have asked the learned Reverend Abbot of Hongakuji for his opinion on this most serious matter. And he has declared that, of course, it is the duty of the guardian god of a man's family shrine to watch over him at all times, wherever he may go in this world, and to escort his spirit back to that shrine if, by some unlikely misfortune, spirit and body should be parted in a foreign land. So, you see, the gods, too, give their blessings to this auspicious enterprise."

Kosaburo, naturally, found time to send no more than an occasional glance into the room in search of Genzo. Not until Hamada was soothing the nervous man's disquieted spirit did Ko discover his friend. Clapping a hand to his mouth, rolling his eyes at the girl he'd been entertaining with an Edokko's urbanities, he excused himself with a dozen quick bows, and hurried over to Genzo's side. Fortunately Genzo did not see him coming, a veritable pondful of writhing goldfish, all rushing toward him as if lifted up in a whirlwind.

As Ko squatted beside Genzo, greeting him with bobbing head, smiles, and bright eyes, Hamada said, "If you have no further questions, I'll turn you over to—Ah. Yes? You have a question?," he pointed to a bored and pockmarked youth, sprawled at the far side of the group.

"Yes. It is this: what if a man should sign your contract, take your money, and then—well, disappear?"

"Ah, yes. A matter of honesty, isn't it?," Hamada replied

suavely. "The answer is easy. We don't have that problem, any-more. We had it only once—only once—at the beginning. But not anymore. Most of our people in Nippon are honest, of course, as we all know. But once in a while, unfortunately, we meet with a fellow who is not. He thinks he's smarter than we are. But soon he learns, to his regret, that he is not. For one thing, I too have my honorable eyes in attendance. They watch every one of you who signs the contract. For another thing, whenever you leave this inn, you are required to wear the happi coat we give you. That is the uniform of our band of honest men." Never had he looked more like a lizard, never had his grin revealed more sharp little teeth.

"Let me show you what happened to the one man who took our money and then tried to run away." He snapped his fingers. An assistant snatched away the cloth that covered something every-one had assumed was a doll in a case, or a valued bowl, belonging to the inn. It was nothing so ordinary. It was a sealed glass jar filled with some kind of clear fluid. Steeped in that fluid was the head of a young man, his eyes raised in agony, his mouth opened in mid-scream.

In absolute silence they stared at that ghastly thing.

"Oh, by the way," said Hamada-san, "in case some of you have wondered what the 'ki' on our crest means, now is the time for me to explain it to you. It does not stand for Kimura Hambei, as some people have thought. It stands for kiru, which means to cut.—A little something to remember us by." He snapped his fingers again, the assistant covered the gruesome persuader.

"In the absence of further questions," Hamada said pleasant-ly, "I'll turn you over to my assistants. If you wish to join this group going off to make a fortune—and *if* you pass the physical examination—these two honest men will help you sign the con-tracts. And they will give you the money, the uniform, and such other prizes as you will receive when you become a member of our band. If you do not wish to join, you are free to leave at once. I certainly do not want you to feel in any way that you are being forced to join. We want only people who want to go. We have lots of interest in our proposal, I might add, from people in Edo and Yokohama. But the ship leaves day after tomorrow, let me remind you. You have little time to waste."

Of the twenty-eight men sitting before him, nine hurried away. Among them were the man who worried about his spirit, and the sullen youth, strangely green under his pockmarks.

As the nineteen who remained waited in line for the physician's attention, Hamada-san came up to Genzo. "Ah, the stone mason from Asakusa," he said affably. "You got here, I see. I've been wondering about you. And you sent another recruit in your place, I hear. Very brave. Is this the one?"

"Yes, sir. Do you have space for him?"

"Sure. Still plenty of room. Glad to have him join us. A lad who likes fish, I believe?"

Kosaburo, still awed by the great man, and even more so by the pickled head, made not a sound. Neither fin nor tail moved on his fish.

"But tell me," Hamada turned to Genzo. "How did you get here, without my help?"

"With Kannon-sama's help, and your advice. I remembered your opinion of officials, and proved it to myself. You were right." He gave Hamada-san a brief account of his escape from Edo.

Hamada grinned wickedly. "A good pupil. Too bad you're going away. I could use you here, in my organization. Perhaps when you come back, in three years or so, Ishi-san."

Genzo chose to overlook the invitation. "Is Ishi still my name? Does it not belong to Kosaburo?"

"No need to change. Ishi was your choice. It fits you, I think. Certainly more than it does this—this creature from another element. We'll give him a passport of his own, with a name of his choice. What'll it be, young fellow?"

"Koi," said Kosaburo promptly. "Koi of Yokohama."

"That, too, is a good choice, I must say. We'll get the papers right away. Come with me."

They followed him to the older of his assistants. Kimura Hambei, plump yet hard, had the moon face of a man who eats too much and drinks too much, even as he works all day and all night for his boss. He sat at a low table, piled deep with writing brushes, papers, documents. In unpainted wooden boxes beside and behind him lay mounds of strings of cash.

"Kimura-san: take care of these two very special men, will you? New identification for one. Remember that one for Ishi-san has already been made. Passports. Contracts. Accommodations at the inn. All the rest. They won't need a medical inspection. I vouch for them. But make sure they know what to do. And when."

Kimura Hambei accepted the assignment with a series of nods and grunts, all signifying that he knew exactly what to do and say. Hamada-san, blinking sleepily, said to the two valorous recruits, "Sit down, while he takes care of you. Relax. You're safe now. And this evening, enjoy your last night ashore. Tomorrow everybody goes aboard. Early next morning, at ebbtide, your ship sails. On schedule."

Bowing repeatedly, they thanked him for his great help and personal concern. If Kannon-sama can choose him for an instrument of her designs, Genzo had concluded long before, he cannot be entirely an evil man.

"Not necessary. My business." Hamada-san seemed to be pleased by their gratitude, yet unwilling to accept it. He turned to leave. Then, remembering something else, he looked up at Genzo. "Ah, yes. Too bad about Nakamura-san."

"Ho! And what has happened to him?" Genzo feared that Heaven was exacting from Nakamura-san the payment for his own release.

"He cannot be here, although he told me that he planned to come to say goodbye to you. He's been ordered to chase after Admiral Enomoto and whatever's left of the Bakufu's navy. Those die-hards have retreated to Yezo. Nakamura-san, my men tell me, sailed yesterday from Edo. For Hakodate."

Kimura Hambei was efficient, impersonal, and scrupulously honest. "Here's the contract," he said, thrusting across the table a piece of paper covered with very small print, giving them no time to read it even if they could have deciphered all those difficult characters. "You've heard the terms. Sign here. If you can't write, I'll do it for you."

Genzo's new name was easy enough for him to write. Taking the brush, he put that strong new character in its proper place at the top of the paper, feeling a great pride as he did so. First the horizontal stroke, representing the surface of the earth. Then, descending from it, at the left, the oblique stroke representing the side of a hill, or the slope of a quarry. And finally, close beside this slanted line, the little square denoting a stone resting at the foot of the hill. Five strokes in all, a good solid angular character, with nothing soft or curving about it: this is me, the *new* me, thought Ishi, congratulating himself on his choice of a name. "From now on," he said, to himself as much as to Kosaburo, "we must call me Ishi."

Kosaburo had no idea how to put together the eighteen interconnected strokes in the two complex characters he wanted for his new name, so Hambei wrote them for him. Possibly because he was tired at that late hour, perhaps because he did not see all those cavorting fish on Koi's kimono, probably because he chose to play a joke upon the illiterate boy, he did not write down the character for carp. He brushed instead the intricate and complex character identifying another meaning for the sound "koi," thereby making the fisherman something quite different from the intent of his chosen name.

"Here are your passports," Hambei said. Ishi's, having been prepared earlier in Edo, he slid across the table. Koi's took him a few seconds, while he wrote the new name for the second time in a minute, stamped the paper in black ink, using a seal carved in ivory for the purpose. "Here. Signed. Sealed. And delivered," he rumbled, without the faintest trace of good will. "Fast service, courtesy of the Kimura Hambei branch of the new Ministry of Foreign Affairs. Tell your friends about our efficient agency." Ishi and Koi, never having seen a passport, and unable to read the ancient and elaborate characters printed upon any of those papers, had to accept them on faith.

"Here's your money," Hambei heaved a small mountain of strung zeni toward each convert. "Less deductions."

"Deductions?," asked alert Ishi. "For what?"

"Minus three bu for your happi coats—which you will receive as you go out that passage over there. Less three bu for food and bed in this fine inn."

"Three bu, for one night's lodging?—That's money enough to keep both of us for a month!"

"Things are expensive here in Yokohama, friend," said Hambei the imperturbable, pulling a jug of saké from under the table. "Because of all these foreigners, crowding around. Less five bu for passports and other official documents."

"But—," Ishi began, thinking of Nakamura-san's good money, already spent for him. Or worse: pocketed by these pombiki, these confidence men.

In the face of such impertinence, Hambei sustained himself with a long pull at the saké jug. As he put it back upon the floor he resumed his instruction. "Less three bu for personal services from Hamada-san and his able staff."

Ishi and Koi knew when to admit defeat. Without wasting another word each one scooped up the strings of cash lying before him and rose to go. Ishi stormed out like a raging samurai. His fury was diminished not a whit when, passing the screen behind which the medical examinations were being conducted, he saw Hamada's fat henchman playing the part of doctor.

Koi, taking a bit more time, gave a fine imitation of a cormorant spewing fish, trying to dodge the excrement of the bird above him, uttering frantic cries of distress, the while he hopped across the hall to the door.

"Trouble makers," scowled Hambei, settling back, waiting for the rest of those innocents to come his way.

CHAPTER 6
OF MISERS
AND SPENDTHRIFTS

Even after Hambei's raid they still had so much money that they didn't know what to do with it. They sat down to count it all, in a corner of the inn. Each carried forty strings of cash. They could count that high. But when they tried to calculate the total number of zeni each possessed (at the prevailing rate of 960 zeni to a single string) they became thoroughly confused. After much writing of imagined figures with index fingers upon palms of hands, much scratching of heads, they decided they couldn't do a thing without an abacus. "These numbers are too big," complained Koi. "Why do we waste our time on such foolishness?"

"You're right," agreed Ishi, as inept as a nobleman from Kyoto in matters in finance. "A man needs a chamberlain to do this sort of work."

"Money is made to be spent, not counted," declared Koi, the born spendthrift, fondly picking up his half of the treasure. "I never did like misers."

This, too, was a consequence of Hamada Hikizo's planning: the men who signed his contract received no encouragement to be thrifty. They were given no coin worth more than a single zeni. A forethoughtful man, as Hamada knew very well, might yield to the temptation to hide in his breechcloth a thin gold koban, worth four bu. And such a miser-in-the-making would think long and hard about spending a silver momme, valued at sixty-four zeni. But what man in his right mind would want to save a heavy string of these cheap common copper coins, let alone a single zeni, which in these days buys little more than a cup of tea and two small sugared wafers? Hamada-san, a man of the world, understood the science of keeping money in circulation. For this wisdom compounded with generosity his clients in stores, inns, restaurants, and brothels near Fujimi Ryokan called down blessings upon his name, thinking it only fair that they should return to him (through the hands of his amiable agents who visited them each morning) ten zeni for every hundred taken in during business hours of the preceding day.

Unlike Hamada-san, however, Ishi and Koi, beginners in avarice as in almost anything else, could trust no one with their wealth, even for only a short time. Therefore, they dragged those 76,800 heavy zeni around with them, wherever they went. No one in the inn laughed at them for this, because every other guest at the moment was having the same trying experience. As they rattled through the corridors, going to and from the baths, latrines, dining rooms, they sounded like whole temples-full of praying monks fingering rosaries made of metal tags. But they looked, every one of them, like Ministers of Finance brooding over the country's needs for more guns, more ships, more money to keep out the barbarians. After that harrowing day many a man resolved never again to allow himself to be freighted with such cares. And, indeed, so attentive is Heaven to a man's wishes, events in his life were so arranged that never again did he have to take up such worrisome burdens.

Nevertheless, by sitting on their money, like quails trying to nest upon swans' eggs, Ishi and Koi contrived to eat a good dinner. In spite of the shabby appearance of the inn its cooks took pride in their art. Urged on by Ohta-san, the proprietor, because he was overjoyed at receiving a whole bu in payment for each guest's sojourn, the cooks prepared the best meal served anywhere in Yokohama that evening. Although the laborers bound for Hawai did not realize this, it would be the most tasty, the most satisfying, the most beautiful meal they would ever eat, during all their days in this floating world.

It began with fresh slices of red sashimi resting upon mounds of finely shredded snow-white daikon, served with a sauce composed of shoyu, a pinch of horseradish, and a dash of vinegar. It proceeded to fillets of young eel broiled over charcoals, then to a delectable hot custard in which morsels of tender chicken, slivers of water chestnuts, and slices of young green leeks were embedded. (Although in this land of many Buddhists, well-intentioned people are not supposed to eat the flesh of animals the cooks were well aware that the Law wisely allows occasional dispensations, especially in behalf of people who are about to depart upon extended and hazardous journeys. "Besides," as one of those hard-working artists said, quoting some earlier master of irony, "a good Buddhist is as rare as a tiger in a market place.") Next, they sent on the sea bream, a white fish of incomparable texture and taste, cooked in the Suruga style, that is, encrusted in rock salt then baked in embers covered with moist seaweed. While the guests ate, flicking their chopsticks faster than tongues can shape words, waitresses brought them side-dishes of pickled vegetables, crisp, salty, and cool, with others of hot soybean curd smothered in sweet-sour sauce. Serving maids poured all the hot saké or new spring tea they cared to drink. The feast concluded with bowls of steaming white rice, to fill in the empty spaces left in their bellies; and, an elegant touch rather wasted upon most of those gluttons, a clear broth graced with tiny shrimps, delicate white mushrooms, and a single green sprig of wild cress.

Belching frequently to show their great appreciation, greeting each new dish with exclamations of wonder (for in truth never had these peasants from Kanagawa's fields, these failures from the wards of Edo and Yokohama, or these footmen from Izu, ever eaten so much or so splendidly), the guests devoured everything placed before them, including the finely shredded white radish under the sashimi and the aojiso leaves laid as garnishes upon the plates.

Belching now in distress, reeling under a triple load, yet not so drunk that they forgot to don their happi coats, the fifty men who signed Hamada's contract during that busy day fared forth to lose their fortunes. Clattering about in geta borrowed from the inn, and arrayed in those distinguishing coats bearing Hamada's warning written large on every back, they resembled guests at a hot springs resort as they wander about in search of gifts to take with them to friends when they must go home again.

The last trace of day, still streaking the heavens high in the west, went unnoticed in the brilliance that had sprung up on earth. The brightness of whale-oil lamps or paraffin-oil lanterns streamed out from doors and windows of stores, restaurants, and grog shops. Paper lanterns, lighted by flickering candles, hung like necklaces of luminous pearls above the streets. At this magical hour more people promenaded through those narrow streets than ever walked in them by day.

"Ishi-san," said Koi, rather tipsy, unnaturally serious, "what are we going to do? How can we possibly spend all this honorable money?"

Ishi, equally concerned, but ready heroically to make the attempt, gazed at all those dancing lights. "Brace up," he said, gripping his friend's shoulder with his free hand. "Ducks can swim on a daimyo's moat, just as well as swans."

The friendly merchants of Yokohama hurried to their aid. Before they were sober again Koi had parted company with his entire fortune, and Ishi had spent all but one string of cash. But they thought their money was well spent, and therefore were perfectly happy: at long last, each had been able to buy all the things he'd ever yearned for, whether or not they would be useful. Is this not one of the greatest satisfactions a man can experience? Pity the rich merchant, or the bored daimyo, who has bought everything already, at least once, and does not know what to spend his money upon tomorrow.

Ishi, thinking ahead, recommended at the start that each should equip himself with articles absolutely essential to surviving in that empty foreign land, where no neighbors would be at hand to help them and they would have to shift for themselves. "Good idea," said Koi. Whereupon each bought a pair of scissors and a pocket knife with three blades, made by ingenious artisans in Sheffield of England, and a woodsman's ax, fashioned—

according to the shopkeeper's explanation of the vivid picture painted on its haft—by an Indian chief in America who dwelled upon a great grassy plain called Shi-ka-go, which is all but covered with fierce shaggy beasts called ba-fa-ro. Ishi, vain about his appearance at all times and most careful about his grooming, felt that he must buy an English razor, a cake of soap, a shaving brush, and a small mirror, now that he could no longer receive the attention of the Okubo footmen's barbers. Koi, who at his age did not care how he looked, contributed to the extent of buying a native whetstone with which to sharpen all those assorted blades, knowing that he could borrow Ishi's razor whenever he needed it.

By this time Ishi was beginning to respond again to all those fish frolicking along with Koi, amid splashes of shoyu, sashimi sauce, and tea. Looking down at his own ill-fitting kimono, he decreed, "We must be properly dressed. From now on we cannot bring shame upon ourselves, or upon our families."

"Agreed," said Koi, somewhat missing Ishi's point. "I suppose we ought to have a change of clothing. At least for festival days."

Inasmuch as the hot season had almost arrived in Nippon, and winter never arrived in Hawai, they bought kimono made of summer cottons. Ishi chose a staid pattern of small dark blue squares laid upon a light blue ground, Koi an exuberant thing bedecked with enormous blue-black dice falling singly and in pairs upon a blue and white ground, showing all the conceivable faces a gambler can throw. Restraining himself still in his role as elder brother and substitute father, not to mention as traveling companion foredoomed to see those monstrous eyes for the rest of their days, Ishi thought to impart some message to Koi by buying for him, as a gift, a quieter pattern showing fine bamboo leaves, done in light green, disposed upon a faintly golden background. Whereupon, in gratitude and obligation, Koi bought one of identical style as his gift for Ishi.

So they went, scattering strings and half-strings of cash in store after store, rejoicing everyone, not least themselves. They bought several new fundoshi apiece, this being the fundamental

garment of the well dressed male; they discussed the need to buy
haramaki, or belly bands, and decided that they really didn't
need those, inasmuch as neither was ever sick and never gave a
thought to keeping his liver warm. They bought splendid geta,
fashioned of beautifully grained persimmon wood, with thongs
woven of cords dyed black, and manly black tabi to cover their
feet on festival days.

When the pile of purchases grew unwieldy each bought a canvas bag of the kind they'd seen foreign sailors carrying as they
swarmed ashore on leave, and stuffed their prizes into those.
Then, because the bags were only half full, they went in quest of
luxuries.

Koi led the way in this hunt. He bought something his fingers
had always coveted: an inro, one of those elegant sets of small
nesting boxes a city gentleman wears at his waist, wherein he car-
ries medicine, or his favorite tea, or powders to enhance his virility, if perchance he stands in such need. And, of course, it had to
be provided with a netsuke, the carved little figure on a cord, by
which the inro is fastened to its owner's obi. Inevitably, for his
netsuke Koi selected a lively carp with a curved tail. Fins, scales,
gills, eyes, and all, this koi was carved from a whale's tooth. Mercifully, the artist had disdained to tint his handiwork.

Ishi did not approve of such extravagances. They reminded
him of greedy, paunchy merchants, as well as of strutting samurai. He almost yielded to the impulse to buy a tiny and intricate
image in ivory of Kannon trampling upon the demon of evil. But
then he remembered that he already possessed a symbol of her in
another guise, and put aside the costly carving. Instead, thinking
ahead to the time of need, he bought an implement that had fascinated him since he'd seen the American sailors using one at Shimoda: a small burning-glass, and a brass tripod upon which to
rest it.

Because Ishi bought so many expensive things imported from
foreign countries, and therefore had to pay high taxes upon
them, he was running out of money before Koi did. "Let me give
you some, then," said gallant Koi, holding out his remaining

strings of cash. But Ishi sternly refused, preferring to show now the frowning face of Emma-o rather than the smiling one of a borrowing Jizo. That was the moment when he resolved to save his last string of cash, until he was sure that he had not forgotten to buy something important. Thereafter, the suggestions of shop girls, the appalling example of his wastrel companion, could not weaken him. "Cheap things bought," he replied to one and all, "mean money lost." And he would stalk away, as if he were indeed the richest miser in Nippon, sneering at all those trinkets set out before weaker men.

Koi tossed his zeni about with the speed of a typhoon devastating a seaside village. Although he did not smoke, he bought a brass-and-bamboo pipe, with a tiny bowl the size of a shallow thimble, and tobacco enough to keep it filled for half a year. Although he could not play a single musical instrument, he bought three different kinds: a samisen, with its three silken strings and its sound box of catskin edged with snakeskin from Okinawa; a fue, the small horizontal flute of shrill tone; and a shakuhachi, the vertical flute made of bamboo which sings of loneliness and melancholy. In the future, with so much time on his hands, said Koi, he was going to learn how to draw music from all these instruments. Ishi, forced to concede that the boy must know how to fish, did not protest overmuch when he acquired a metal box filled with shining steel fish hooks of assorted sizes, ranging from some to catch minnows with up to a fearsome barb big enough to snare a shark.

In a final burst of pleasure Koi spent the last of his zeni upon a pack of hanafuda, those little playing cards with pictures of Nippon's most famous flowers printed upon them; two pairs of gamblers' dice; packages of sour pickles, sweet cookies, rock sugar candy; and—being suddenly reminded of the awful fate in store for him—a tiny and ugly image cast in brass of Benten, the Goddess of Love.

By the time they were drained of money they were almost sober. Feeling somewhat like spirits who, having known the bliss of dwelling for a while in the Pure Land, must be reborn again in the world of sentient creatures, they walked back to Fujimi Ryo-kan, back into the world of troubled men. In this fleeting world, alas, the most fleeting of its things are its pleasures, the most en-during are its sorrows.

The streets were less crowded with people, no longer brilliant with lights. Joy was gone from their world, not so much because their money was spent but because they were tired, after a day full of worries, and most especially because now, on this last night they would spend in the homeland, they had time to look about and to realize what they were leaving behind. Joy was gone from them, perhaps, but beauty was still there, in the loveliness of the spring night, in the peace which lay over the houses in the ci-ty, over the ships in harbor, almost as visible as the haze com-pounded of mist and smoke that hung like incense upon Yokoha-ma. Above the height of Yamate, lifted from beyond the sea, floated a swelling moon, clear and cold and pure. Upon the smooth waters of the bay she laid a path of silver, pointing to the southeast, toward the land across the sea. A good omen, thought Ishi, not wanting to break the spell by speaking. Good weather to-morrow, thought Koi, in the fisherman's way of arriving at the same consolation.

Afraid to speak of the future, unwilling to speak of Izu, they hurried back to the inn.

At the foot of the stairs leading up to the second floor where, amid a maze of corridors and sliding partitions, the guests of Fujimi-ya slept, Koi handed his sailor's bag to Ishi. "Please take this up for me," he whispered. "I must go now. To—ahh—to meet a girl . . . "

"You certainly didn't lose much time over this one," ex-claimed Ishi, shaking his head, yet laughing. "Are you sure she's safe to be with? Or, rather, that you're going to be safe?" Only a week had passed since Koi's beating and already he'd forgotten the lesson.

"But this is my last chance! What am I going to do on that ship, without a woman? Thirty days. Thirty nights! I shall swell up, and burst." Winking with both eyes, first one, then the other, he said, "See you later," and pattered off, trailing the school of fish after him as he loosened his obi.

Young men for women head, old men for the benjo and bed, thought Ishi, not much helped by his crabbed wisdom. Thus does one hole take the place of another, until at last the last hole of all does swallow us all . . .

Later, when, relieved in bladder and bowels, cleansed once more in the ryokan's bath house, he slipped between the cool sheets, he fell at once, as story tellers say, into a deep and untroubled sleep.

In the morning, following the habit of a daimyo's retainers, they awoke at dawn. From beyond the paper partitions the sounds of coughing and muttered conversations, the scent of morning pipes, told them that they were not the only ones to be awake. For once they lay abed, enjoying the pleasures of not having to get up, until long after the sun had risen above flat Kazusa to pour its warmth upon Edo Bay and Yokohama.

Koi lay with hands behind his head, staring at the ceiling. The strong body, uncovered by futon or sheet, was that of a man, but the face was that of a puzzled boy. The unnatural silence disturbed Ishi. "What's the matter? You sick?"

"No."

After another long silence Ishi tried again. "Wasn't it good, last night? Or wasn't she there?"

"Nothing like that. It's me. I—I'm ashamed of myself." To his further shame, and Ishi's surprise, tears gathered in his eyes.

"Why should you be ashamed? She was willing, was she not?"

"Yes. But for her it was the first time. I didn't know that until too late."

"Saa. That can't be helped. You make too much of this. There's a first time for everybody. If it wasn't you, it would have been another." For his friend's sake he did not tell him what no sinner ever heeds at the time of sinning: 'Repentance comes too late.'

"I know, I know. But why her? And why me?"

"As people say, 'It's her karma.' If not yours also."

"She did it for me, she says. All that blood, all that pain, for me. Because I wanted her. And because she liked me." He touched his cheek. "Even with this." He touched the spoiled mouth. "Even without teeth. She liked me."

"You liked her?"

"Sure. But I like 'em all. You know how I am. To me they are just things to be screwed. I didn't think about anything else. To me, yesterday, she was just another legspreader. But now, since last night, she is something different. I can not forget her."

"You will," said Ishi, with much assurance. "When the next one comes along. That is the pleasure of being a man."

CHAPTER 7
THE TRAP

At eight o'clock in the morning of the ninth day of the Fifth Month in the first year of the Meiji emperor's reign, the people who had signed Hamada Hikizo's contract began to gather in the street outside Fujimi Ryokan. They were both excited and afraid, welcoming the day because it brought an end to waiting, yet regretting it because with it would disappear all the certainties around which they had fixed their lives. It was like the hour before dying, when a man does not know whether his spirit is going to Paradise or is to be caught up in another life, in one of the Six Realms of Rebirth. In that hour of mystery, from his knowledge of himself, he must expect the worst while hoping for the best.

How can we be sure that we have chosen well? these people wondered. How can we know that we go to a land of wealth and comforts, such as is offered, or to a land of toil and hardships, no better than the one we are leaving? So must the spirit of a dying man question what is to be its fate. If it must be reborn, will it be rewarded for the merit it has earned in this life by being graced with the body and mind of a man? Or will it be punished for its sins by being forced to spend some time in the body of a lower creature, such as a woman or a cockroach, a hungry ghost or a foul demon?

Worries of this profound nature might have added an undercurrent of doubting to the thoughts of 174 of the folk who accepted Hamada's passport to Hawai. The other six passengers could not possibly have entertained such deep thoughts, because four of them were women, two were boys not yet men. As everyone knows, women can not think, and boys of that age do not take the time to think.

Freshly shaven on skull and face with Ishi's new English razor, the two runaway footmen came out of the inn. They found hundreds of people milling about in the street, just as Hamada's fat messenger had said. "Saa!," exclaimed Koi, "is the boat made, which can carry so many passengers at the same time?" "Maa!," said Ishi, "will it have space in its bowels for the two of us?" Poised on the stairs, they tried to find some beginning or end to this flood of shimmering kimono and bobbing black heads to which they might attach themselves. After a moment they realized that no one in that crowd was wearing Hamada's uniform. "They've just come to say goodbye," said Ishi. "Kimura! Over there!," shouted Koi, pointing to the left, at the far edge of the mob. There, with waving arms and repeated roarings, Hambei and his assistants were pushing their charges into a double file, practically awash by the sea. "Let's go," cried Ishi, plunging into the horde, like a swimmer venturing into the swirling waters between Awaji Island and Honshu.

Eventually the current carried them to its farther edge, to the double row of emigrants. Koi and Ishi took their places at the end of the group. Soon other folk emerged from the crush of bystanders, to extend the double line. "How many of us are going?," Ishi asked his neighbors. "Don't know," one replied, "too many, looks like." "Three hundred, I heard," said another. "Nah, nah, five hundred," said a third. "Can't you see?"

Everyone, whether going or staying, was talking as loudly as possible. Everything was going along cheerfully, with only the normal amount of confusion, or slowness to comply with Hambei's instructions, or sudden decision to change a place in the line for another position three persons away. Not too many recruits forgot to stay in line when they saw friends bearing small farewell gifts come to wish them good fortune. Hambei, most of all, seemed to be enjoying himself, judging by the ribald jokes and heavy-handed pats he distributed indiscriminately among the women in the crowd and the men in his lines. Shrieks of laughter from the delighted women, snickers from the lewd men, accompanied his progress. He, more than anyone else, had reason to be happy. Now at last the weeks of hard work and planning which Hamada-san had delegated to him were coming to their end. All in all, he was thinking, he'd done a good job for the boss—and for himself.

Ahh, but this was an event worthy of celebration in the young city of Yokohama, which has almost no history to recall. No more than a score or two of its oldest residents could remember the occasion, almost eight years before, when the last group of Nipponjin to sail away to a foreign land left from this very beach. That was the time when the Shogun Tokugawa Iemochi sent abroad a Grand Embassy, the first to depart from Japan for more than 200 years. The Grand Embassy to the United States of America was made up of nobles and daimyo, with their retinues of samurai and servants, sailing aboard a powerful American warship named *Powhatan* and the Bakufu's pride, its first steamship, *Kanrin Maru*. Yet those ambassadors had gone away for only half a year, because every one was eager to return to his duty in Nippon. But the people going today were different, in every respect: they were commoners, nothing more than third and fourth sons of poor farmers and humble merchants, the first such low persons to be permitted to leave the homeland since the time of Iemitsu, the third Tokugawa shogun. And these today were going as laborers, not as diplomats. And they would be gone for at least three years before they would come home again to Nippon—always provided the Lord Buddha was willing that they should return to where they belonged, bringing their wealth and their tales with them. All in all, the few elders agreed, this is indeed a memorable day for Yokohama.

The cheerful throng, the warm morning's sun, full bellies under their obi made Ishi and Koi very happy members of Hambei's disordered troop. They were among the few recruits who looked upon this day as a time of release, as an occasion of escape in every sense of the word. For they, among all those chattering others, had broken more than one rule in order to stand here on this fateful morning. And, happy though they were, they could not dismiss the fear that they would not be safe from punishment until the ship carried them beyond the grasp of Lord Okubo's officials, beyond the sound of their families' cries of shame at the way these two sons had betrayed their mighty lord and master.

Ishi looked out upon the festive crowd, fixing the picture forever in his memory because he knew that never would he see its like again. He felt no great tugging at the heart because he was leaving his own people. Is it wrong, he asked, for a man to take a chance to make a better life? I cannot think so, he decided, therewith burying doubts if not the small remnants of guilt. The sound of the new name he had chosen, he remembered, can also mean "will." And how can a man endure, if he lacks will?

Idly, listening to the friendly conversations, the raucous cries of vendors and children, the whole joyful babble, noisier than a dozen temple schools and O-Bon festivals all at once, he allowed his eye to roam across the bright scene. He was thoroughly content—until he saw the samurai. He stiffened, gasped almost in pain. Koi looked up in alarm.

"What are they doing here?," Ishi growled, indicating the four samurai standing in the entrance to Fujimi-ya. Two swords in their belts, crests on their kimonos, white tabi on their feet, the haughtiest of postures: beyond any doubt they were samurai. And Kimura Hambei cringing before them, with a sweep of his arm inviting them to join his happy troop. As Ishi watched, the four accepted Hambei's welcoming. Swaggering down the stairs, without pretending to accompany him, they strutted over to the head of his grubby line. Behind them four hired bearers carried fine woven baskets and lacquered chests of the kind in which samurais' possessions are packed when they travel far from home.

"Dame desu!," Ishi snarled. "Not good!"

"What are you so mad about?," demanded Koi, too short to see anything beyond the giggling girls he had been teasing ever since they'd found him.

When Ishi told him he shrugged, not at all disturbed. "Maybe they're going with us?" He did not share his friend's hatred of warriors. Like most commoners, he endured his betters by avoiding them as much as possible while fearing them at all times.

"Leave the powerful alone, and they will not harm you," said most of the people of Nippon, despite the evidence presented to their eyes and ears. And to this advice Koi added his variation upon the Law of the Fishes: "The big ones eat the little ones, and little ones have to be smart. I shall be smarter than they, all the time."

"To work in sugarcane fields?," Ishi cried. "To be farmers scratching about in mud? I cannot believe it."

"Cows herd with cows," said a plump farmer, whose big eyes looked off in different directions. "And horses with horses."

The man next to Ishi spat toward the shore. "Or to spy on us, when we are there."

A neighbor lifted his hands to stop them. Don't let those lordly ones hear you, those tongueless hands warned. Just in case ears in attendance happened to be close by, he said, "I am sure they go to protect us."

"Or to kick us down," said Ishi, refusing the warning. "There, as they do here."

"I knew it, I knew it," whined another fellow, already limp with fright. "They've come to arrest us. For wanting to leave Nippon. We should never have put our names on those pieces of paper."

"Yosh! That's enough!," cried another man. "Fools!" He stepped out of line, waving hands, rattling his long tongue. "What are you afraid of? Those samurai stayed in the same part of the inn as we did. All four of them. They're quite decent. The big one especially. And they signed the contracts, like all the rest of us."

"I don't believe that," said Ishi. "Why should they go with rubbish like us, when they have everything they want here, in this fine land made for samurai?"

"Oi! Where have you been lately?," cried the defender of warriors. "Times have changed. Some samurai are as poor as we are."

"Nasakenai," whined the frightened man. "How terrible. We've been trapped. What jail will they take us to, I wonder? Where do you suppose they'll send us to die?"

"Ah, shut up, you wind-passing ass hole!," shouted the defender, drawing back the sleeves of his kimono, revealing two muscular arms ready to hammer sense into unbelievers. "Give 'em a chance."

"Make a lid for that fool," said another. "Cover him up."

"Ten men, ten minds," giggled the wall-eyed farmer, backing away.

Seeing that a splendid brawl was about to start, Koi dodged about among the arguers, waving his hands, playing the peacemaker, looking like a wall of fighting carps. "Easy now, easy now . . . Let's wait and see. Maybe they're only going to take us to the boat. Maybe the Bakufu sent 'em—"

"Bakufu!," a dozen fellows bawled, rounding upon Koi, subjecting him to the usual fate of peacemakers. "Where have you been?"

Ready for sport, bystanders and recruits alike urged them on, laying bets. "I'll take the handsome young fisherman!," cried a retired prostitute with freshly-blackened teeth, wrinkles no amount of rice powder could hide from the morning's light, and a very good eye for man-flesh.

"Saa koi," growled the man with drawn-back sleeves. "All right! Come on. You're asking for it."

But events occurring on a larger stage disappointed all humbler folk in their expectations. A foreign carriage drew near, coming from the heart of Yokohama. Interest shifted to its two occupants: on the instant everyone was transformed into a rokurokubi, one of those long-necked creatures who never misses a thing that is happening. The ones with the longest necks and sharpest eyes informed the rest that Hamada Hikizo-san was the important rider in the Western-style norimono. Sitting beside him, they said, was a thin little gaijin, who might have been Hamada's brother except for the curling yellow locks springing out on either side from a part at the very middle of his head. "Maa! Look at all that beautiful hair!," exclaimed the retired prostitute, not loosing her hold on the sleeve of Koi's kimono.

The carriage drew up beside Hambei. Grim as one of Emmao's demons, his face as mottled as the back of a frog, Hamada-san summoned Hambei less with sound than with furious handwavings. The gaijin, no longer having to worry about the speed of his carriage, put a tall stove-pipe hat upon the crest of that shining halo. "Ahh, too bad," sighed the retired prostitute, as Koi moved her hand away from a place much lower than his kimono sleeve.

"Hurry!," Hamada order his lieutenant. "Take them aboard as fast as you can!"

"Why?," asked the quick-thinking Hambei. "We've got all day ..."

"Hurry, I say!" Hamada opened the door of the phaeton and leaped to the ground. "Show them the way! We have no time to waste!"

"Just what I was about to do," said amiable Hambei, backing away from his boss, a snake with teeth, about to bite. Trudging over to the head of his column of converts, he yelled, "Let's go," and without another word or look started on his way. Joking among themselves at this martial command, the four samurai followed him immediately.

But their porters and all the emigrants after them, scrambling to pick up their bundles and baskets, shouting farewells at their friends, were too slow for Hamada Hikizo. "Hurry!," he screamed. "Run!"

In running to catch up with the samurai, some commoners transformed their fear of Hamada's rage into a general suspicion that something had gone terribly wrong with his plans. Not knowing what had gone wrong, they could only guess—and the more they guessed the more frightened they became. Wondering why they ran, not even knowing where they were supposed to go, they ran. Treading upon the heels of the samurai, they forced the warriors too to run, and Hambei ahead of them. In a few minutes every recruit in the whole long line—less one worried man and one stolid woman—was running. Not as gracefully or as fast as a herd of Nara's deer did they go, but just as determined to follow their wise leader. And much more noisily. For, as they fled from the unnameable terror loosed among them by Hamada's anger, they began, as nervous people will, to laugh and to whoop. The women, and the more womanly men, even screeched. "Komatta naa!," they bawled, and "Shimatta!," they screamed, holding up kimono skirts in one hand, bouncing bundles in the other.

The one most worried man, however, certain that they were running straight for the gold mines on Sado Island, without even the briefest of stops at the prison in Edo, raced away in the opposite direction, peeling off that happi coat as he ran. He vanished among the narrow alleys beyond Fujimi Inn. The stolid woman would not have run from an incoming tidal wave as high as a house. Following the pulse of her own sluggish blood, she walked at her invariable pace, not bothering to step from the path of people rushing past her.

Hambei, puffing along at the head of this rout, led them along the waterfront road until he came to the stone jetty. There he turned right, drawing the whole train after him. Like a swarm of buzzing bees following their scout to a new hive they followed him. At the fourth berth he stopped, panting for breath, holding out his arms in such a manner that the left pointed to the ship, the right instructed the runners to turn at that spot. Without missing a step the samurai raced up the long gangway slanting from the jetty to the ship's main deck. Up they went and over the rail, and the whooping mob went up after them. Alerted by their noise some of the ship's officers reached the deck in time to wave their passengers along, pointing to companionways and ladders that would take them down into the holds below.

Of all the Nipponjin who hurried aboard, not one had the chance to see the vessel's figurehead, the carven bust of an Indian warrior, with eagle's feathers tied in his braided hair. Nor did anyone notice the yellow letters, painted on the curve of her bow, that spelled her alien name: *Scioto* they said, in symbols that only one of her passengers could read and no Nipponjin could pronounce. And only Hamada Hikizo and Eugene Van Reed, the man with the yellow hair, knew that this low, black, three-masted schooner flew the ensign of Great Britain, not that of the Republic of the United States of America nor that of the Kingdom of Hawaii.

Assuming that the four samurai had gone below at the bow,

Ishi dashed for the stern, as far away from them as he could go. He and Koi stumbled down the steep ladder into the afterhold, almost falling into what seemed to be a huge cavern, gloomy and cold. As their vision adjusted to the dim light, they made out the bare planks of the deck beneath their feet, the pale round eyes of portholes in the ship's sides. Swept along by passengers already in the hold, each gripped the other's obi to keep from being separated. "To the back," shouted Koi, finally remembering that he knew something about the insides of ships.

Almost in the same moment Koi realized that tiers of bunks lined the sides of the hold. "In here," he yelled, scrambling into the topmost bunk, pulling Ishi up after him. The space could scarcely accommodate the two of them. "Not good," said Koi, "I'm going below," as he slipped into the bunk beneath.

Safely installed, each in his own cell in this buzzing hive, Koi and Ishi pushed away latecomers who tried to climb in with them. The hold was full of shouting, laughing, cackling, swearing people, behaving like mad folk in prisons, like tormented souls in one of Emma-o's many hells. Some squatted on the floor, not knowing what else to do. Others climbed up and down the scaffolding of bunks, much as Kyoto's monkeys do when they raid the forest temples of Ranzan for food-offerings laid upon the altars. Friend called to friend, changing places, entreating strangers to exchange spaces with them. New-found enemies fought with tongues and talons. Koi looked down upon all that commotion with disgust: "Look at them!," he called up to Ishi. "A bunch of cormorants. A bunch of stupid cormorants . . . "

Into this madhouse, bold as Izanagi the Father God going into the Land of Yomi, the World of the Nether Plain, that time he went in search of his beloved wife Izanami, descended a samurai. At the foot of the ladder he stopped. In a voice that sounded like thunder cracking over Edo on a hot summer day, he cried: "Quiet! Quiet!" At the first roar they looked to see who commanded them so powerfully. With the second they obeyed. No third roar was needed from this fighting man.

When the last scuttling fellow had settled into place, and the hold was so still that the waves of the sea could be heard lapping against the hull, the samurai spoke. "Hamada-san sends me here. He asks me to say, 'Do not worry. Here on this ship you have no need to fear.' " He had a big voice, in talk as in command. He was a big man, perhaps the tallest Nipponjin the people in that cavern had ever seen. "Somehow or other," he continued, laughing deep in his throat, as does a kabuki actor giving a performance in the theatre, "outside there we became too excited. Now we need be excited no longer. Therefore, let us be easy again. And let me tell you what we must do to make ourselves comfortable in this ship."

He went to the nearest bunk, laid one of his huge hands upon its side. "This, in the foreigners' tongue, is called a bunk. In our country we have nothing like it. This is a place for you to sleep in, or to sit in, if you wish. Each of you should claim one such bunk. It is to be your home for as long as we must live in this ship. Each bunk in this ship is made to hold two people. If all were filled, then four hundred passengers would go with us. We number only 180. So, therefore, we have plenty of space for all. At this time take up your belongings and go into your bunk. Sit there for now, to keep out of the way. Later, when the ship is at sea, we can find space on the floor for sitting and we can ask about bringing more light and air into this dark hole."

Within one minute he restored calm and order among the emigrants. Within three minutes he became their master. Against his will, Ishi was impressed by this tall samurai who knew so well how to command. So must Oda Nobunaga have led his warriors, once upon a time, when he ended the Age of Warring States. And Ieyasu, also, the first of the Tokugawa, who mastered all of Nippon.

"Who is this lord?," the people whispered. No one could say, because no one knew his name or the crest he wore. Ishi wondered about him, along with the rest. He seemed to be a good man as well as a fine samurai. But that was exactly the trouble: he was too good to be trusted. Ishi was willing to concede that he might be a kind and generous man, like Nakamura-san. But until he proved himself, beyond any doubt, Ishi would suspect him of being as proud and arrogant a warrior as were all other samurai he had ever known.

Someone asked a question, in a polite voice few could hear. The samurai repeated it for all to understand. "Why did Hamada-san tell us to hurry? A good question." He returned to the foot of the ladder. Light streaming through the hatch fell upon his back and the wide pointed shoulders of his kataginu, the prescribed surcoat for samurai. But his face was hidden in shadow. "E ... to ... ," he dragged out the word by which a man signals to his listeners that he is weighing his thoughts even as he speaks. "I do not know the answer in full. Only in part. The rest I must guess. But, I confess, I ran, too. Yet why I ran I cannot say. A foolishness seized us all, I think. Nevertheless, I have learned not to talk about guesses. Too often they are wrong, and being wrong they can cause troubles. When I am sure that I have the right information, I shall tell you what I learn. Do you agree?"

Ishi heard this explanation in utmost amazement. Here was a samurai who as much as admitted that he did not know everything under the arch of heaven! Who acknowledged that he could make mistakes! And who, in his manner of speaking, did not set himself so far above mere low commoners that all they might ever see of him were the toes of his feet!

He spoke to them in just the same language as they used among themselves, in the common words of common men, without calling upon those roundabout expressions, those haughty verbs, with which an exalted warrior, merely with his speech, imposes authority upon inferiors. When such a man talks, commoners are reminded constantly, almost with every word he utters, that they are far beneath him in everything, even in the words they are allowed to use when they presume to address him.

"Yes!," the men cried out, some bowing where they sat, others kneeling to touch foreheads to the deck. "Thank you, honorable master," they said, over and over again. They were so delighted with this new kind of lord who had come among them so providentially, who would be here in the future to tell them what to do, what to think, what to believe.

Of them all only Ishi saw how the old patterns of submission,

the heavy yoke of dependence, were being laid upon them still.
And only Ishi protested. Groaning aloud, he beat his fist against
the side of the bunk. For the second time in his life he felt the
harsh god raging within him. For the first time in his life he committed an open act of rebellion.

"What's the matter?," Koi whispered. "You sick?"

"Yes, in my spirit," said Ishi loudly, wanting to be heard by
everyone in that dark pit. "I do not like what is happening here. I
feel betrayed."

The samurai heard him. Resting his hands upon the hilts of
those two sharp swords, he looked toward the bunk from which
that challenge issued, he remarked the face of the challenger.
Then, turning soundlessly on his stockinged feet, he strutted off
to the far end of the hold. Seeing the arrogant back, the very
swirling of the hakama about those warrior's legs, reminded Ishi
of Ichiro's murderer. The harsh god breathed hard within him,
struggling to break out.

Suddenly, before Ishi could groan again, in rage at what he
was thinking, in fright at what he had done, the light at the head
of the companionway was shut off. Everyone in the hold looked
up, some in curiosity, most in alarm, fearing the closing of a trap.
But this was no trap for them. Nor was it a jailer. This was a prisoner, carrying her prison within.

Slowly, as though aching with great pain at every step, a
woman came down the staircase, moving only by the power of her
will. The companionway shuddered under that tread, as if her
spirit as well as her flesh and bones were made of heaviest iron.
Down she came, the light flowing after to fill the space she had
emptied, but seeming to be unwilling to pass around her to shine
upon the deck below. The people in the hold, who only moments
before had feared her shadow, now shrank before that weighted
body. Everyone looked at her, seeing the staring bulging eyes,
the puffed face, the body filling its kimono as a caterpillar fills its
skin.

A man called gently to her. "Over here," he said. Unable to
see, she followed the sound of his voice, plodding toward him

with unconquerable determination, utterly indifferent to the people she must pass. When she came close, he stood up and drew her to the lowest bunk. "Here is where you will live, as our leader has said," he explained lightly. "And I shall live in the space just above."

At either side neighbors listened for her reply, their ears stretched out and quivering, like the noses of mice in quest of grain. By her response they would know if she were mad, or blind, or only simple-minded. But she did not speak. Nor did she smile, or gesture in dumb show, or snarl at him crazily. She just sat down on the edge of the bunk, folded her hands in her lap, and waited. Smiling to himself—the devil!—the man sat down beside her.

Gradually the passengers settled in, the excitement of their arrival aboard this strange ship subsided. With nothing to do, and —as they interpreted the samurai's advice—strict instructions not to move from their bunks, they made the best of the situation, as all Nipponjin learn to do early in life. With the ease of long practice, most went promptly to sleep. Some did not even lie down in order to sleep. A few, who had caught up with their need for rest during the nights before, talked quietly from neighboring bunks. A rare scholar crouched next to a porthole, reading a book by the greenish light coming through the thick glass. And in one bunk, huddled against the porthole, looking like a humpbacked fish hiding in a grotto, Yonekichi of Imado in Edo wrote rapidly in his journal, relating the events of the morning, anticipating with an excellent sense of budding scandal the events that would enliven the voyage. "If only it would begin today," he wrote. "I am tired of waiting for so long." Yonekichi, a scrivener, and one of the first of Hamada's converts, had been waiting for a month. With thirty or so others, mostly potters from Imado, he had been living aboard the *Scioto* for four days and nights.

In their bunks Koi and Ishi tried to think, the one about last night and the experience which had robbed him as well as a maid of innocence, the other about a future most clouded. But the gentle rocking of the ship, the murmurous darkness in the hold, soon put them to sleep, chasing away guilt as easily as they banished care.

A door in the forward bulkhead crashed open. "Everybody up! Everybody up!," cried a militant voice. Startled out of wits and sleep, passengers sat up in a hurry, hearts pounding, hands clutching at empty air. "Cursed samurai!," said Ishi, knowing exactly who this must be, beginning too soon to speak his secret thoughts.

Through the doorway filed a peculiar procession: a short bony Nipponjin carrying a lighted paraffin-oil lantern, followed by three red-haired barbarians from the West. Two of these were ship's officers, wearing the navy blue tunics and high-peaked caps identifying Great Britain's lords of the sea. The third seemed more like a prosperous foreign merchant, dressed in the height of fashion of ten years before.

"I am Sato Ryonosuke," announced the no-sworded man in a ringing voice worthy of a shogun's grand chamberlain, shining the lantern's light upon his scrawny self, "Yokohama representative of the esteemed company that owns this honorable ship, and official translator for same. These," he swept the light briefly across the row of foreigners before returning it to his imposing person, "these are your honorable masters aboard this ship. Obey them, in all things, and nothing will go wrong. Disobey, and troubles will befall you and this worthy ship. Understand?" His speech, brusque and commanding, loaded with demeaning imperatives and calculated rudenesses, informed his listeners that a most superior personage condescended to address creatures in their most inferior station. Easy-going Koi, who could scarcely understand the language of this martinet, curled his lips in hatred at the mere sound of that voice. Ishi, who had encountered a few men of this self-satisfied breed—they congregate in clan offices and in the lower levels of the Bakufu—simply yawned at the fool, wishing he would go away. "Ei kuso," said someone out of the twilight, "oh shit."

"Kapitanu Ri-gan," Sato allowed his lantern's light to fall upon a short, thick, red-faced Irishman, gone all to belly, his face furbished with huge Burnsides that swirled inward to meet an enormous flowing mustache, a petulant moist little mouth, and a rounded beardless chin. Captain Reagan glared out upon his invisible charges, hating this exhibition of his busy self, not understanding a single syllable of the long-winded speech this bloody little Nip had already delivered in the two forward holds to all them other ruttin' Nips squattin' there in the stinkin' dark. Spoilin' for a fight, thirstin' for a sip of the brew (Jesus, Mary, and Joseph, a whole hour had passed since last he'd quaffed a bit of the stuff!), he rose up and down on the toes of his heavy boots, thinking of directing one of 'em at the bleedin' arse of this blinkin' sod with his blindin' goddam lantern.

"Mistah Jaakusonu, Fahsto Metto of this ship," intoned Sato, shifting the light to the tall willowy Englishman standing loyally beside his captain. Mister Jackson, under his peaked cap and high-collared tunic, was not the whole man he appeared to be. Because he entertained strange ideas about many things, including God's purpose in putting hair upon the human body, Jackson simply could not abide the presence of it above his waist, and spent much of his free time directing a Chinese servant-boy in shaving off every trace of hair that could be found on his person, from crown to midriff. Naturally, he hated his hairy captain, and simply adored the boys of Asia, "so slim, so smooth-skinned, so hairless—except on their dark heads, of course . . . "

"He is the honorable hands and honorable feet of Kapitanu Rigan," explained Sato to his audience, all enchanted by the strange and difficult names these funny-looking gaijin bore. "He will inspect his esteemed ship in all its honorable parts, from front to back, and bottom to top, once during each day. You will not disappoint him in his high expectations of a clean ship." Mr. Jackson, lost in reveries about expectations of other sorts, did not notice when the light descended upon him, or when it was whisked away.

It turned next on Doctor Lee, a cheerful graying man, with a trim gray mustache and beard, and a body which, for lack of exercise, was beginning to assume the feel of fat and the luster of wax. "Dokutah Ri, of Amerika," Sato announced, "will keep you in good health, if you obey his instructions each day. He cannot promise to make you well if you neglect them." Doctor Lee would have been much surprised had he understood what his interpreter was saying. But at least he seemed to care about his charges: when the light came to him, fleeting as Heaven's grace upon an Irish sinner, he smiled brightly and waved a genial hand.

Out of the darkness came a single word from Captain Reagan. "Ah, yes. The new master," Sato translated smoothly, "not of the ship, but of you." Now the light played lovingly upon the tall samurai who had quieted the emigrants in Hold 3. Ishi, Koi, all the others, except the Slow Woman, leaned forward, the better to hear the name of this splendid leader. "Makino Tomosaburo-san of Sendai. Hamada Hikizo-san has appointed him to be in charge of all passengers during the time of this voyage." Makino Tomosaburo made a stiff bow, an inclination of the head and shoulders, not so deep as to be fawning, yet something more than the disdainful neglect with which samurai usually regard peasants.

"And that's enough," growled Captain Reagan in good plain English. "Let's shove off." Without waiting for his assistants, he marched toward the companionway, they treading close upon his heels.

Left in command, Sato seemed to swell like the king of frogs. "Here are the orders of the captain," he said, no longer hiding his dislike for these traitors who, by leaving it, betrayed their country and presumed to think that they could find a better one anywhere else in the realms under Heaven. While in his secret thoughts he hoped they would drown in the depths of Edo Bay, within sight of the very fatherland they were deserting, yet far enough out to be beyond rescue by any soft-hearted countrymen, he shouted at them the commandments that were intended to keep them alive during the weeks of their voyaging upon the Great Peaceful Ocean.

"First: passengers will keep walkways and stairways clear at all times.

"Second: No open fires, of any kind, at any time, will be allowed below decks. Lanterns may be lighted only during evenings, between the time of darkness and 9 o'clock. Remember: fire is the enemy, fire is the greatest danger.

"Third: Smoking of tobacco is forbidden from now until you leave the ship. Smoking is not permitted at any time, in any place. If you wish to smoke, you must not. Fire is the greatest danger.

"Fourth: Serious sickness, not merely that caused by the motion of the ship at sea, must be reported to Doctor Ri or to Makino Tomosaburo-san.

"Fifth: No fighting, no drunkenness, no gambling is allowed, at any time.

"Sixth: If storms happen, passengers must stay in their bunks. Do not go above. That place is for the sailors.

"Seventh: Food will be prepared by Chinese cooks in kitchens above, and will be carried to holds for serving at six o'clock in the morning, at mid-day, and at six o'clock in the night. Meals will be eaten in the holds. Passengers will take turns in serving food and washing dishes. Everyone will help. No one will neglect his duty.

"Eighth: Save water! Washing of bodies and of loincloths is permitted. But do not wash large articles, such as kimono or blankets. Do not waste water! Washrooms and places of convenience are located behind walls at the rear of the ship, in the middle, and at the front. Wait in line for your turn to enter. Do not push past people waiting before you. These places of convenience are made in the foreign style, much different from the Nippon style. Signs and drawings in the rooms will show you how to use them. Passengers will be responsible for keeping these little rooms clean.

"Ninth: Men who break these laws will be punished."

He stopped for a moment, searching among the four corners of his small mind for a last warning, a missing command. Makino whispered a suggestion. "Ah, yes. The cooks will fix no mid-day meal today, because they are still ashore buying vegetables. However, box lunches will be brought aboard at twelve o'clock. Courtesy of Hamada Hikizo-san." Annoyed at such consideration being shown to traitors, he blew out the light in his lantern and raced for the untainted air above.

"After taking all that crap," announced Koi, leaping from his bunk, "my bung wishes to relieve my belly. Where's that benjo?"

Relief at Sato's departure, the general good fellowship that swelled up among the inmates of Hold 3, were sorely strained by courteous Hamada's box lunch. The fine dinner they'd eaten the night before could not be repeated, they knew; but after such a treat they were not expecting the two-day-old rice balls and twigs of dried fish that Hamada's minions sent aboard.

"Of course! What do you suppose?," a neighbor said in answer to Koi's loud complaint. "Hamada must pay for this prison food out of his own money bag, not out of our little pouches."

Nevertheless, being a long-suffering folk, they greeted Hamada-san politely when he arrived, in a rustle of silken robes, soon after 2 o'clock. Kimura Hambei, the voice as well as the hands and feet of his master, blew in like the God of Wind in league with the God of Thunder, banging open the door, bellowing like both raging deities, shouting, "Everybody kindly shut up!" Makino quietly closed the door after them.

"You may have been wondering," Hamada began, but could not find the will to finish the sentence. "Here is the reason. Early this morning new officials of the Meiji emperor's government took over the former Bakufu's duties at Kanagawa and Yokohama. Our friends of the Bakufu are no longer in control. No longer in power ... " Regret for all those misspent golden kobans and obans, all those wasted hours of patient persuasion, flowed out of him like smoke from a fire smothering under wet grass.

When troubles begin, for honest men as for scoundrels, they come, as everyone knows, not singly, not in pairs, but in swarms.

Scarcely breathing, almost enjoying his anguish, the passengers waited for Hamada to tell them the rest of his afflictions. "From Edo orders have come to stop this ship from sailing tomorrow."

"Hah!," gasped scores of trusting men, made too suddenly aware that Hamada-san's troubles were also their own. "Why?," some men cried, seeing the frail vessel of their hopes being wrecked upon the coasts of officialdom. "What's going to happen to us, then?," demanded others, looking far enough ahead to see that from this shipwreck no survivors would reach the hostile shore and live.

"Why?," said Hamada, sneering his disgust with unreasonable officials. "Who can say what those honorable daimyo in Edo are thinking, from one day to the next? But I can tell you that Mr. Van Reed and I are quite sure that this ship will sail tomorrow, as planned. Mr. Van Reed is conferring now with those new officials, up there in Kanagawa. I believe that he has justice on his side. After all, the Hawaiian government has spent too much money on you already, to give you up now without a protest. The Meiji government, we are sure, will see the justice of our claim."

Justice being a new word to Nipponjin and foreigners alike, it being still the catchword of certain high-minded diplomats and many a conniving businessman, few of Hamada's converts knew what he meant at this point. But they heard very clearly the message behind his next words.

"Please be patient. And please be careful. Stay right here, on this ship, in this hold. Whatever you may think or want, *do not go ashore!* The new government's police are outside now, on the jetty, on the road beyond. And I do not need to tell you what will happen if you leave this ship and fall into their hands."

A woman wailed, forgetting good manners in her fear.

"Don't worry. They cannot arrest you while you are here. This is a British ship. It is the same as land in the country of Great Britain. The Meiji police cannot come aboard. This is what the captain and Mr. Van Reed tell me."

Ishi sprang up, his heart in his mouth, from fear of the police, from shame at attracting attention. "If this is a British ship, why doesn't the captain sail away? Why doesn't he save us from those policemen by taking us away from them?"

Hamada recognized him, even in that gloom. "My friend," he replied, "foreign ships cannot come and go as easily as you think. Just as there are barriers on the roads for ordinary people like us," he purred, without a suspicion of guile, "so are there barriers of a sort for ships upon the sea. Especially for foreign ships. They must receive permission from the government of a country to enter a port, and to sail out of it again. The officials at Kanagawa have not yet given Captain Reagan that permission. As I have said, Mr. Van Reed is with them now, trying to get that piece of paper. One way or another. I believe that he will succeed. He has much, ahh—ahh, power."

Once more the door in the wall opened, once more the dark belly of the ship swallowed up the messengers of good and evil who came and went so frequently. In their gloomy cave, a refuge from nothing but the sunlight, Ishi and Koi and all those other people, once so full of hope, lay silent in their bunks. Like men laid out in coffins. Like men put into holes in the ground before they are dead.

CHAPTER 8
THE ANCHORED WANDERERS

S even days later the *Scioto* still lay in Yokohama's port, still tied to the stone jetty. The Meiji government's officials still declined to grant Captain Reagan his clearance papers. Each day the Consul-General for Hawaii made ritual calls upon the officials, although on both sides the proferring of smiles, compliments, tea, and other pleasantries became increasingly strained. Between courting bureaucrats and placating Captain Reagan, Van Reed was much tried and nearly exhausted. As he knew all too well, he had little money and no power with which to influence the new officials. And they, in the manner of zealots, could not be persuaded by any means known to Western diplomats. Neither outright pleas nor veiled threats, hints of bribes nor sumptuous entertainments—such as dinner parties attended by seductive geisha—had any perceptible effect upon their stubbornness.

"How?," they asked, always deeply pained with the need to be discourteous, "how can we permit 180 of His Imperial Majesty's subjects to live in a foreign land with which His Imperial Majesty has not arranged a treaty? How can his Imperial Majesty's Government release so many of his valued subjects to the rule of a foreign sovereign, when—because of the lack of a treaty—they will receive no protection either from Nippon or from the foreign nation? Who can promise that, under these most regrettable circumstances, they will not be seized and sold as slaves? Or, if not enslaved, abused as aliens in a foreign land? Or denied the right to return to Nippon when their contracts have terminated?"

All these instances, Mr. Van Reed professed himself most hap-

py to concede, were the proper concern of an established government for its citizens, and the regard His Imperial Majesty's Government showed for the well-being of its citizens abroad accorded
it great honor. But, Mr. Van Reed felt constrained to point out,
his negotiations had been conducted with officials of the previous
legitimate government of Nippon, who had placed no bar or hin-
drance upon his recruiting as many residents of the country as he
cared to take.

"Ah, yes, Mr. Van Reed," His Imperial Majesty's highest representative at Kanagawa replied, "you may have done so a month
or two ago. But since that time the government of our country
has changed. Without a treaty between our new government and
the one you represent, you have recruited our people illegally, I
am distressed to say. And by means most improper . . . "

To this allegation Mr. Van Reed begged to answer that, until a
treaty between the two countries could be prepared and ratified
he requested the honorable officers of His Imperial Majesty's
Government to remember that the Kingdom of Hawaii, too, was
an enlightened nation, blessed with a government as concerned
for the welfare of its people as is that of His Imperial Majesty in
Nippon. "The Hawaiian government," he explained, "eighteen
years ago established a law, 'A Masters and Servants Act,' in
order to protect the rights of both employers and workers. Laborers from China have gone to Hawaii for more than fifteen years,
without suffering harm to themselves or arousing complaint from
their home government. Moreover," he played his trump card in
this gamblers' game, "the people of Hawaii are famed throughout the world for their hospitality to foreigners. Most especially
have they been kind to castaways from Nippon, whose broken
ships have drifted across the Great Peaceful Ocean to the shores
of Hawaii's islands. Please to remember the happy experiences of
Jirokichi of Oshu and his shipmates in 1839, and of Nakahama
Manjiro and his shipmates in 1843—"

"Excuse us, please. Who are these men?," asked the officials,
sincerely puzzled. "We have never heard of them."

Aboard the *Scioto* the passengers who were going nowhere in body went in spirit from worry through terror to despair. For a time, at the beginning of that first week of waiting, when the Meiji officials did not seem to be especially fearsome after all, the passengers found a kind of grim humor in their condition. They spoke of themselves as "anchored wanderers," or "waveless things," or "barnacles of Yokohama," as "children in the Nether World waiting to be reborn." But, as the dreary days and dull nights followed, one after the other, the emigrants' fear of the policemen on the shore was compounded with irritations caused by the gloomy ship, the irascible Chinese cooks, and most especially by themselves. Humor and hope gave way to frustration and complaint and, as the week wore on, to apathy and despondency. By the sixteenth day of the Fifth Month most of the *Scioto*'s passengers would gladly have gone back to their homes on land. Only fear of Hamada's quick revenge and wariness for the government's slower punishment kept them from abandoning the ship, along with all their hopes for favor and fortune in the other country.

Yet even that double-jawed trap did not keep all of those restless children within the ship's protecting womb. By the end of the week twenty-seven men had slipped away, one by one, no longer able to endure uncertainty. Some went over the side of the ship, in the dark of night, and swam for shore. Others, not caring any longer what the government would do, simply walked down the gangway and surrendered to the police, waiting there like hungry crows at an execution ground. People who remained aboard ship saw how the constables escorted such a man to the shore, as if taking him to the execution place at Omori. After that no one could say what happened to him.

Not all passengers submitted to despair. Yonekichi the scrivener found much to keep both mind and brush very busy. He was the one who learned the story of the Slow Woman. Encouraged to do so by the man who was with her, Yonekichi spread it about so successfully that thereafter she was known as the Sad Woman, a cause for pity rather than an object to be feared. She and the man who accompanied her did not yield to despair: they knew that better times would come, because their god had promised this fate for them before they died.

This is their story, as Yonekichi of Imado wrote it down in his journal:

Katsuro, the only son of a prospering merchant in Nikko, took for his wife O-Yuki, the third daughter of a farmer's family in the countryside in nearby Imaichi. Theirs was a happy marriage because the young couple grew fond of each other, and because O-Yuki's mother-in-law was kind to her. The gods seemed to have blessed them, and they looked forward to a long and contented life in the busy shrine town of Nikko.

But what hopeful man expects is not always what the gods grant. Each year, for four years in succession, Yuki lost a child. The first one died soon after it was born, of a weakness that denied it strength to breathe. The three who followed did not stay long enough in their mother's belly to be born alive. They came into this world too soon, by three or four months. Katsuro and Yuki never saw the ill-formed bodies, hurried away from the birth-room by the saddened midwife.

As each calamity fell upon her, Yuki became more despondent, heavier in body as well as in spirit. Her flesh swelled up, as if with the water of tears she could not shed for her misfortunes. Her eyes started from their sockets, as if searching endlessly for the children she and Katsuro so yearned to have. Grieving, she found no joy anymore in life. Like one drugged by the day lily, she sat in her darkened room, moving only when she must, speaking only the most necessary of words. Katsuro, at first attentive to her in their sorrow, began to shun her, spending his time with prostitutes and loose women. She did not object, knowing that he could get neither pleasure nor children from her. Feeling herself accursed, for some reason she could not determine, she begged him to divorce her. "Some offense I committed in a previous life must be the cause of our sorrow in this," she said, as she urged him to free himself from this curse. But he would not put her aside, feeling some respect for her still, and in truth not needing the solace of a wife as long as he could employ servants to keep his household and could use harlots to ease his desire.

Then Yuki resolved to kill herself, in order to release him from all obligation to her, and to free herself from the bonds of this present stage in the cycle of her karma. But before committing the irrevocable deed, she went first to the great temple of Rinno in Nikko, there to apologize to the gods and to her husband's ancestors for failing to give him sons. So heavy were her limbs, so slowly did she move, that she needed a whole morning to walk up the long hill from her home to Rinnoji. Caught there by a heavy snowfall, she could not return home. The monks put her into the inn for pilgrims that they maintain outside the temple gate. There Katsuro found her the next day, having learned from his servants where she had gone.

When he met her she no longer thought of dying. During the night a vision had come to her: the Lord Buddha himself appeared, holding a beautiful child in his arms. He spoke to her, while the smiling child reached out his arms to her, the hopeful one. Yuki could not understand the words the Lord Buddha uttered. They seemed to be in a foreign tongue, as he seemed to be in a foreign land, full of strange trees and unusual birds, upon which a warm unclouded sun cast its shining light. Feeling certain that the vision was a promise from the Lord Buddha, she was much comforted in her heart when she awoke.

With Katsuro she went to consult Kitashirakawa-no-kami, the Imperial Prince-Abbot of Rinnoji. After hearing her story he agreed that, indeed, the vision must be a message from the Realm Beyond. Then, they asked, what did it mean for them, who still dwelled upon this earth? He told them to seek counsel from the oracle-priest of the temple.

They sought out the priest. Sitting in the immense Hall of the Three Buddhas, at the feet of the three great gilded images—of Thousand-handed Kannon to the right, Amida-Nyorai in the center, and Bato Kannon to the left—he bade them pray for help to the deities, while he cast the forty-nine yarrow sticks that might tell the meaning of O-Yuki's vision.

As the priest shook the bamboo container holding the yarrow sticks, tossed them upon the mat, flicked aside the ones that fell aright, added up the numbers written on their sides, Katsuro gazed up at the face of Bato Kannon, the god of animal spirits, who bears the figure of a horse's head upon his brow. Six times the priest threw down the oracle sticks, in order to learn the six signs that would tell him how to interpret O-Yuki's dream. On the sixth throw Katsuro slumped to the floor. When the priest and Yuki turned him on his back he groaned once and died.

During the forty-nine days of mourning for her husband, Yuki decided that she must leave that stricken household, that baleful town of Nikko. Katsuro's parents still lived, might yet adopt a son to carry on the family's name and business. But she, a misfortuned widow, unmarriageable and resented, would be in everyone's way. She could not go home to her parents in Imaichi for the same reasons. She would be better dead, but the vision of the Lord Buddha holding the child in his arms kept her alive with its temptation of hope. At length she resolved to take one of the few courses possible for an unwanted widow: she would make a pilgrimage. She decided to go to the famous temple of Shinso in Narita of Shimosa. She chose Shinsoji because the image of the god Fudo Myo-o which is venerated there is so heavy that it cannot be moved, and in this heaviness she saw some resemblance to her own. Moreover, because the sword presented to Fudo by the Emperor Shujaku is said to cure insanity and drive out fox-spirits, she thought that touching the sacred weapon might cure her if she were indeed possessed. If, at the end of the pilgrimage, no other answer was given her by gods or priests, she would shave off her hair and become a nun in another of Narita's many temples.

Yuki asked a younger brother to accompany her to Shinsoji. Being a fourth son having little else to do, Nagayuki was willing to accept the duty of protecting her while he saw a bit of the country beyond the limits of Imaichi. Moreover, for himself he would gain benefits from this pilgrimage to the Shrine of Fudo, who fights against the Three Poisons of Avarice, Anger, and Folly. Because he had nothing in this world Nagayuki feared that, in time, he would be attacked by these three evils, as well as by all the others that come in their wake, unless he took some action to forfend them.

They started upon their journey on the feast of Higan, the first day of spring. Horses shod with boots of plaited straw carried them through the deep mountain snows until they reached warmer Kanuma. From there they walked along country roads and main highways to Narita. Fortunately, Nagayuki, a plump and amiable young man who looked much like his sister, did not mind either her silence or her slowness.

At Shinsoji she prayed to O-Fudo and touched the healing sword. Neither Fudo-sama's furious expression and fiery halo nor the power in Shujaku Tenno's sword made her feel better immediately. But an incident happened there, in the forecourt of the temple, that did affect her profoundly.

While she prayed before the altar, Nagayuki bought for her one of those fortune papers which are sold for a zeni apiece at temples and shrines. Written by priests, who inscribe upon them thoughts prompted by the gods, all are different, no two are the same on any one day. She opened the folded paper and read:

> Happiness?
> Seek in far places.
> Water divides, water provides.
> And the sun above all shines.

Smiling wanly at this foolishness—for what right did she have, at any time, to seek happiness?—she was about to throw the paper down into the dust, when Nagayuki showed her his prophecy, written in a different hand:

> Fulfillment?
> Seek it not at home.
> From mountain cliffs it springs,
> Where water greets the sun.

How could they doubt such a pairing of oracles? This was more than the working of mere chance. But what did they mean, these riddles?

They asked a young priest what they meant. He, being young and imaginative, and not yet humble enough to have faith in the power of the gods, laughed as he said, "That sounds like Tenjiku."

"And where is that?," they asked, somewhat disappointed, knowing only that Tenjiku is another name for Paradise, the resting place of the Buddha.

"India," the young priest explained, proud of his learning.

"And where is that?," they asked, never having heard of the place.

"A land far away to the south," replied the priest, "across the dividing water. Beyond Kyushu. A place warm and bright, where the sun is always shining. That is the Lord Buddha's land."

Now everything was clear, to Yuki if not to the priest or her brother. "That is where I shall go," she said, doubting no more, yet not knowing that the shogun's laws allowed no one to journey to any foreign land.

They were in Yokohama, resting after the day's slow walk from Kawasaki, when they heard about Hamada-san's search for people to work in Hawai. "This Hawai must be a fine place," said people who had listened to Kimura Hambei's descriptions of the empty islands. "Another name for Tenjiku. A veritable Paradise. Warm and bright. Not like Nippon. A land of plenty . . . "

Many a city man scoffed at such talk, knowing that Edokko such as Kimura Hambei and his gang could think of new lies to tell faster than a female frog can spawn eggs. But Yuki, hearing only the enchanting words, knew that this was the goal to which the Lord Buddha sent her. When Kimura Hambei himself, at Fujimi-ya, confirmed as proven truth all the things she had heard as fables from others, she reached for his contract and signed it, saying, "That is where I must go."

"You may go home to Imaichi now," she told her brother. Unbothered Nagayuki, having nothing to go home for, signed a contract of his own. He was never a man to question the workings of karma. Through them, as through so many other devices they can arrange, do the gods direct the lives of mortal men.

With this pious utterance Nagayuki concluded, for the while, the story of his sad sister and of his unperturbed self. But Yonekichi of Imado, pondering over this tale as he wrote it all down in his diary, could not let it end there. Always seeking for a reason, for a moral, he found one ready-made in the verse of a priest much wiser than was the young one at the Temple of Fudo Myo-o who started O-Yuki upon her search for Tenjiku:

> Not knowing how near the Truth is,
> People seek it far away.—How strange!

In so borrowing the wisdom of Hakuin, Yonekichi showed how perceptive he could be when judging the lives of people around him. But nowhere, in his short journal, did he give any indication that he applied the meaning of this verse to his wandering self. Was he already so wise that he had accepted without question the haplessness of the wave-tossed wanderer? Or was he so worldly that he did not seek the Truth?

No matter. Whatever he may have thought, as he wrote so busily in the hold of the *Scioto,* clinging still to the shore of Nippon, the gods would reveal to him in time, as he labored in the mud of the sugarcane fields of Hawai, what they held in store for him.

Ishi, too, did not lose hope, although for a while he was both afraid and annoyed. He kept his faith in Kannon of Infinite Compassion and in himself, knowing by now that a man who seeks the way to freedom must pass first through the trials of adversity. He who had been tried so often had to admit, however, that this period of waiting aboard a big comfortable ship was more like the time of rest for a farmer during a bout of bad weather than an ordeal to be endured without hope of rescue.

Yet, when he least expected it, he was tried in a manner most exasperating. And in this trying the resented Makino Tomosaburo served as both judge and humbler.

On the day the recruits went aboard the *Scioto*, Hamada Hikizo and his assistants departed for Edo, their duties being ended. Before he left Yokohama, however, Hamada told Mr. Van Reed that, in his opinion, all those bewildered passengers needed some one in authority to tell them what to do each day, until they arrived at their destination. He suggested that Makino Tomosaburo be appointed to the position of headman. In support of this recómmendation he mentioned Makino's fine presence, his quieting of the nervous passengers soon after their entry into the ship, and the fact that, somehow, the samurai from Sendai had learned enough of the difficult English language to be useful as an interpreter during the voyage. Mr. Van Reed, favorably disposed by those qualifications, was even more impressed by Makino in person. He was the very model of a samurai as imagined by an American: tall, sound of limb, authoritative, responsible, and, withal, perhaps because of the big nose and the shaven forehead, looking very much like a balding Yankee in the days when Americans, too, wore queues. Van Reed offered the appointment to Makino, who accepted it with a dignity becoming to his rank and the occasion.

Before the day ended word of Makino's promotion to be their leader passed among the recruits. To call him a headman was unthinkable, that being a term applied only to commoners, so they referred to him as their daimyo. Everyone approved the choice of Makino, most with enthusiasm, some with reservations they would not express because they could not allow themselves to object to decisions made by superior persons. Ishi, too, conceded that he knew of no one aboard ship better qualified for the office. Yet in his thoughts he vowed to stay as far as possible from this new daimyo. He might be a good leader. He might be able to speak that strange foreign tongue with the glibness of a merchant and the persuasiveness of a priest. But first, last, and always he was a samurai. And Ishi had made up his mind about samurai.

As the promised day of departure wore on, and more and more signs told the passengers that they were not going to sail according to schedule, aggravations began to mount. They were too hot, the people said, buried in those stifling holds. Why couldn't they have some fresh air to breathe, seeing that air was free? And when could they go on deck, to walk about, seeing that the crew was not going to need that space for sailing this mud-stuck hulk. The latrines were beginning to stink, because no one cleaned them. And, as usual, only a dutiful few helped to serve the morning meal, while all those lazy others simply lay in their bunks until the food was ready for them to eat. Rubbish was strewn about. Some men talked loudly, with the foulest of mouths, when others wanted to sleep. Gambling and drunkenness led to many fights and not a few knife wounds and blackened eyes. In half a day the emigrants were making new enemies and losing old friends faster than fleas can leave a dying rat. Naturally everyone complained to his friends, no one did anything to correct the inconsiderate folk, and, of course, no one presumed to tell the honorable new daimyo how his little clan was falling apart before ever it had a chance to be united.

Makino, a wise observer of his fellow men, was better aware of these dangers than were any of the people under his command. Yet he also knew that discipline and order are best established when they come from within a group. They do not last if they are imposed from above. He could have installed a samurai as lieutenant in each hold, and thereby made a prison ship of the *Scioto* before she sailed. But he rejected this easy way because he wanted to try another plan.

During that first full day aboard ship Makino worked alone, without lieutenants and without his two swords. He wrapped those in their silken covers, laid them at the far side of his bunk, and never wore them again. Armed with nothing more than a philosopher's hopes and a bodhisattva's patience, he went forth to calm the rebellious and teach the ignorant.

Drunken or sober, Captain Reagan was not the brute he wished he might be. He readily agreed to Makino's request that more light and air be admitted to the holds. At his orders sailors removed the hatch covers, slung canvas awnings over the openings, strung ropes around them to prevent passengers from fall-

ing into those pits. The recruits came upon deck for their first
touch of the sun in more than twenty-four hours. In the beginning
they took care to cover their faces with fans or kimono sleeves, to
hide from the policemen on the jetty; but when they saw that the
lone constable on duty paid them not the slightest attention they
were almost angry at being thought so unimportant.

Makino's success with the captain increased their esteem for
this new lord. Because he happened to be standing by when the
midday meal was brought in, dozens of men got in each other's
way, striving to serve it. When he was seen coming out of a benjo
holding his breath for the stench within, people suddenly remembered Sato Ryonosuke's commandments of the day before. The
Sad Woman, prompted by no one, took it upon herself to trudge
about Hold 3, using a cast-off pair of chopsticks to pick up pieces
of paper, fragments of toothpicks, the souring remnants of earlier
meals spilled upon the deck.

Ishi himself led the way in cleaning the benjo at his end of
Hold 3. But he waited until Makino was out of sight before he
made a move. "Come on, Koi," he tugged at his friend's foot,
"yatchao. Let's get it over with." Yawning, complaining that he
was no filthy hinin, Koi did as he was bid. "Where hinin are not,
we are hinin," said Ishi, offering him a sodden brush and an
empty bucket. "It won't be the first time," he continued, pump-
ing water into another bucket.

"True, all too true," said his eager partner. "Which makes me
fear that it will not be the last."

Makino allowed his charges to do whatever they wished, that
first day. He said not a word in command, made few remarks of
any kind. And he did not make the mistake of being pleasant. He
watched everything and everyone, with the eyes of a falcon
searching for prey. In each of the three holds the people knew
what he wanted of them. And, so powerful is their habit of obedience, by mid-afternoon the holds were so clean and orderly that
First Mate Jackson could find no fault with them when he made
his inspection.

Makino disliked this shogun's way of using fear and guilt as means to achieve worthy ends. Nevertheless, by using it once he learned very quickly about the people who had been put under his care. He wanted lieutenants, chosen from among the commoners, to make sure that each day's work was done promptly and shared fairly. During that day of observing he concluded that the plan he had in mind might work.

The next morning, while making his rounds, Makino informed his lieutenants that they had been selected for the honor and the duty. In Hold 1 he chose Tetsuo of Edo, in Hold 2 Daigoro of Kamakura. When he came to Hold 3 he could not find the man he sought. Attending to another errand, Makino stepped into the benjo. Ishi, Koi, and Dembei of Meguro, barefoot, stripped to the skin, were scrubbing down the narrow room. They were singing a Shimoda song, while Ishi and Koi threw bucketsful of seawater upon the wooden walls, the high wooden seats raised in the Western style, the long slanting trough of discolored zinc. Dembei manned the pump, and at the same time beat out the rhythm of their song by striking a geta against the wooden privy, making it boom like a great drum:

> In Shimoda of Izu
> You need no anchor:
> The strings of geishas' samisens
> Will tie up your ship . . .

Makino stood in the doorway, enjoying their good humor, their willingness to work. Koi, seeing only his legs and feet, shouted "Not yet, not yet. Come back later." Then, recognizing those big feet and sturdy legs, the pattern of that kimono, he yelled, "Heads down!" Ishi and Dembei swung about. "Hah!," they said in unison, ducking low. "Please excuse us."

"Well done," Makino replied, with a laugh that he hoped would put them at ease. "I don't blame you. I would do the same." He looked squarely at Ishi. "When you are finished here I must talk with you. On the top deck. I'll wait for you up there."

Ishi was so surprised that, after Makino left, he stood as mo-

tionless and silent as the pump. Why me? What for? he asked
himself. A moment later, with a second thought, his stomach
sank. The clan has discovered where I am. The chamberlain has
sent men to get me. Koi had the same fear. "Not good," he
whispered. "Do you suppose . . . ?"

Ten minutes later, glistening with droplets from the half-
bucket of fresh water Koi had poured over him, dressed in his
blue summer kimono, Ishi appeared before Makino. Tall and
straight, refusing to bow even though this might be the last act of
rebellion he'd ever have the chance to make, he looked at Makino
through eyes cold and hostile.

Makino sighed to himself. Ah, these young men, so full of re-
sentment, so proud yet so unable to put off the yoke. And I, so
weary of contending with them, as I try to show them how the
yoke can be lifted, even in Nippon . . . Assuming what he called
his fatherly expression, he said, "You do not like me, I see."

This was not the sort of talk for which Ishi was prepared. But
his new resolve made him say what he thought. "I do not dislike
you, sir. I do not know you." He stopped for the moment, wondering if he had said too much. But Makino's expression invited
him to finish. "I do not like samurai."

"Ah, so. I should have been less concerned about me. All this
time I've been thinking that you had turned against my important self." He wrinkled his nose, in reference to the larger subject. "I don't like them much either. A useless lot, by and large.
But I hope you will agree that some exceptions are possible?"

Ishi scowled. This samurai was playing with him, like a boy
with a ball, before he threw him away. The samurai who killed
Ichiro had committed his murder swiftly. This one was slower
with his torture, but just as deadly: under his laugh he hid a
sword. Wanting to put an end to this torment, Ishi said nothing
to continue it.

"You are a hard man. Hard as rock." Seeing those lips, sticking out like the parapets around a daimyo's castle, Makino shook
his head, expressing admiration and exasperation, both at once.
"I need your help. And yet I find it difficult to ask for help from a

man who will not talk. And from a man whose name I do not know."

"You do not know my name?—Then—?"

"Yes? Then?"

By this time Ishi managed to pull his wits together. If Makino did not know his name, he could hardly be preparing to hand over a runaway footman to his vengeful clan. That being the case, perhaps he'd better listen to what this new daimyo wanted to say before he made any more foolish guesses that might be equally wrong. The sullen mouth relaxed a bit. "I am called Ishi. Ishi of Asakusa. A stone mason." He was almost polite.

"Ah, so? A stone mason?" Makino knew better than to smile at the rightness of the name, and the falseness of the profession. He looked down at those beautiful hands, the tapering fingers, the long clean nails. Those hands, he was willing to bet, had not touched anything rougher than a pair of chopsticks for at least a year. "How long has it been since you worked at your craft, Ishi-san?" He mixed apparent concern for an unemployed mason with just the right amount of suggestion that he knew when a man was not telling him the truth. Ishi heard the accusation, resumed his pouting.

"But no matter," Makino said with his most paternal smile. He wasn't much more than seven or eight years older than Ishi, but before him Ishi felt as young and inexperienced as the boy he'd been in Shimoda. "On this ship we have many stone masons. Times are bad, I know. Fortunately, the sugar plantations in Hawai seem to be in need of them. So Hamada-san told me, at least, when we read over the passenger list. But that's not what I wanted to talk with you about. On this ship we must work with people, with people made of flesh and blood, not with unfeeling stones. That is why I ask for your help."

Ishi the Suspicious turned a look upon him that would have made a lesser man throw up his hands in anger and rush away. Ishi, this imaginative fellow, believed that Makino wanted to put him to work as a body servant to his lordly self. Or—may the great gods help us all!—as his running footman, carrying messages to and fro in this floating village. This, he thought bitterly, is exactly the sort of revenge a samurai would exact for being insulted by a lowly commoner. Ishi the Rebel, alas, was so new to this game of rebelling that he believed the whole world took notice of his heroic deeds.

"As you know, I'm sure, I have been made responsible for the welfare of all our countrymen while we're aboard this ship. This duty means telling them what to do, when to do it, and how to do it, if necessary. Keeping them from fighting, from stealing, even from killing each other, for many of our group are vicious hoodlums. Also, if possible, preparing them for living in that foreign land, when we get there. Most certainly I can not do all this by myself. I need help from everyone. But most of all I need help from men I can trust, who will be my assistants. One assistant for each hold. I have chosen Tetsuo of Edo for Hold 1, Daigoro of Kamakura for Hold 2. I would like you to be my lieutenant for Hold 3."

Ishi fell back a step, as if Makino had threatened him. The sullen mouth opened in astonishment. Never in his whole life had he expected to hear such a request from any man. But to hear it from a samurai! "Why me, sir?," he managed to say. "Why not those—those other samurai?"

Patiently, realizing that he must lead this rebel carefully now, else he would lose him, Makino gave his reasons. "Because this is not a ship full of samurai. Nor is it a ship full of commoners. To me, this is a ship full of people who have chosen to go to a new land, to begin a new life in a place where they will have no samurai, no daimyo, no shogun to hold them down. Whether or not these people know this fact, it is the most important fact in their lives from this time forward. Think of it, Ishi-san, think of it!"

Ishi had thought of it, but only with respect to himself and to Koi. He was ashamed to realize how selfish he had been, compared with this man, who saw how the hopes and needs of all men were the same.

"I know very little about life in foreign lands," Makino continued, wondering if he had misjudged this silent hard man. This stone so well named. Was he all good looks, without any brains behind those eyes? Or did he have a mind, hidden behind those scowls? "What I do know I've learned only from reading a few books. I never saw a foreigner until last week, in Edo. I never talked with one until the day we came aboard this ship, when Mr. Van Reed chose me for this job. But I like what I've learned about some of those foreign countries. Especially about America and England. And about Hawai, too, which seems to be something like both, but yet is different.—Do you understand what I am saying, Ishi-san?"

"I do," Ishi replied, not trusting himself to say more. "But why me?," he asked again, not sure that he was good enough a man to be this good man's helper.

"Because you, like me, have begun to think. I heard you, the other day, when you groaned in your bunk. And I thought I understood at once why you cried out that you were being betrayed. Like me, but unlike most of our companions, you seem to be wanting a new and better way to live. In a land without samurai and without daimyo. These others aboard ship: some may take that new way to live, if it is offered. Most will not, because they will not care how they live. But you and I: we will not let it slip through our fingers, when it is offered to us." He saw now, in Ishi's bright eyes, in his eager attention, that he had not misjudged this man.

"Ishi-san: let me tell you how I obtained permission from the Bakufu to leave Nippon. My daimyo, Lord Date Muneki, said to the Shogun, 'Let him go. Rid me of this gadfly.' Why did he say that? Because I pestered him, stung him at times, almost to the point of anger, with my questions about this cause of unrest among our clansmen, my suggestions for removing that reason for trouble. Before long he saw that I was a danger to the harmony of the realm—and to his peace of mind as well. I saw it too. And when I could get nowhere with him, and with my clansmen, I began to punish myself. With drink, with women and wasteful debauchery. I brought so much disgrace upon myself that I was banished from Sendai. And only when, in the remoteness of the countryside, I lived alone and had time to think, did I see how foolish were those ways of protest and how useless were my attempts at making my clansmen change. I came to Edo, to ask my lord's forgiveness. And while I was there I heard about Hamada-san's search for laborers for Hawai. I went to my lord, asked him for forgiveness—and for something else, too: permission to go to Hawai. He freed me from my oath of loyalty, despite my skills as an armorer. 'Go,' he said, laughing in his friendly way, even while he scolded me, 'go and sting those foreign daimyo for a change. But come home again, when you are tired of living in those barbarian lands.' But I do not think that I shall go home again. I told him as much, when I said farewell to him."

This is how an honorable man behaves with his lord, thought Ishi. He walks out, in honor, in the sight of all, with his head held high. But I, the man without honor: I must run away in secret, to be forever in disgrace. Gazing deep within, I am humbled by shame . . .

"So must you have done with your lord," said Makino. "But I do not ask about your past. Now, for us, only the future is impor-tant. For me, you declared yourself with that cry of protest. I marked you then as a man I respect. For you, I declare myself to-day. And now I bring this long talk to its end. I ask you for your help."

Doubting only himself now, Ishi asked one more question. "How shall I know what to do?"

"How can any man know what to do at all times? We shall learn together. No doubt we shall make some mistakes. But I be-lieve that, we being men of good sense and good intention, the four of us will take care of our people without behaving like a gang of samurai. Or, even worse, like a band of crooks in Edo's darkest alleys. That's the most important thing for us to re-member."

"Then I wish to be your helper," said Ishi, in the happiest mo-ment he had ever known.

Koi, the jolly fisherman, least inclined to despair, proved to be one of the most desperate among the *Scioto*'s passengers.

On the fourth evening aboard ship he said to Ishi, "I can stand no more of this cocks' roost. Two nights without a woman I can survive. Three nights have driven me crazy. Four nights—I cannot imagine what will happen to me if I stay here tonight."

They were sitting on the top deck, along with many others, seeking a respite from worry and boredom in the cool evening, in the beauty of Yokohama's lights, and, above all, in viewing the moon, now nearing its full. From the shore the gentle breeze brought the sounds of merrymakers singing in geisha houses and brothels, the crack of a firewarden's heavy wooden clappers as he warned, "Hi no yojin, Beware of fire," the melancholy cry of a sweet-potato vendor, calling "O-imo . . . Ishiyaki imo . . . " And, most unnerving of all, that cruel breeze brought the scent of horse chestnut blossoms, which is the essence of sperm, which at this time of year is strong enough to drive every potent male in Nippon to thoughts of venery if not to wildest deeds. The night was charged with lust, and Koi was not its only victim.

Ishi, also feeling the call in his blood, did not wonder why Koi had been nervous and irritable the whole day long. He bristled when Ishi asked him, as his newly-appointed lieutenant, to oversee some minor detail in the housekeeping of Hold 3. Playing hanafuda bored him. Practising the samisen or the fue or the shakuhachi bored him. During the morning's barbering session when, this being the fourth day since the last scraping, each had shaved the other's head in order to give it that smoothness so important to the proper man, Koi had been as fidgety as a small boy. All the signs told Ishi the nature of Koi's affliction, but even so he was not prepared when, that evening, the youth muttered, "I'm going ashore. Right now."

"Just for a woman?" Ishi chose his argument carefully. "You'd lose your chances for freedom just for a mere woman?"

"Yes! What freedom do I have here, sitting around on this unmoving barge? What good is freedom without a woman?"

"What good is laboring in the gold mines, without freedom or woman?"

"I'll take my chances on prison. I think I can go ashore and come back, without being caught, if you'll help me climb aboard in the morning."

"You know I will."

"And please lend me some money. A hundred zeni. I may have to buy a lay tonight. For lack of time to make other arrangements ... "

While Ishi cut a hundred warm zeni from the string he wore around his waist, Koi took off his kimono, folded it into a small packet which he tied atop his head with the obi. The clean white fundoshi, wrapped tight about his flat belly, made him look like a prisoner about to be executed. Disturbed by this ill-omened thought, Ishi hurried to chase it away with good deeds. "Here's the money," he said. "Spend it for your pleasure, without thought of returning it. I have no use for it. All I ask is for you to return safely."

Koi slipped the pieces of cash into his loincloth. "I'll come back. And I'll pay you back tenfold, in that land of wealth to which we are going. But you may have to wait a month or two before you get it."

Their neighbors, noticing Koi's preparations, called out warnings or advice, according to their degree of envy. "Thaw it out with hot saké," cried one. "Nah, nah," said others, offering assorted ribald remedies, none of which Koi would need. "To go is easier than to return," said a worrier. "How do you expect to come back?"

"I'll be here at sunrise, down there in the water, by the rudder. If I can get here. Please help to pull me up."

"I'll be here," said Ishi. Several other men, early risers still, promised to help him at the appointed time.

To his friend Koi said in a low voice. "Tonight I must go ashore. But I'll come back, I promise you. I do not want to stay in Nippon."

"A man must follow his heart," said Ishi.

Two neighbors uncoiled a hawser, lowered it over the side. Koi slid down the rope, slipped into the cold water as smoothly as a fish. The last Ishi saw of him, moving without a splash toward the shore near Fujimi-ya, was that gaudy kimono tied to the top of his head. A carp is he, Ishi agreed, swimming bravely, against all obstacles ...

True to his word, Koi returned at sunrise. Ishi and their friends hauled him aboard, cold and tired from his swim, but happy and ready for sleep.

Koi's departure, that night, started other men to thinking. Not about swimming ashore—but rather about having certain of the comforts of the shore brought to them aboard ship. They talked with Ishi, who spoke with Makino, who conferred with a policeman on the jetty, who consulted his superior on the Bund. He, being a man first and an official only incidentally, said he would make the necessary arrangements. In consequence of this short Chain of Causes and Effects, each evening at dusk twenty-five of Yokohama's less expensive prostitutes tripped merrily aboard the *Scioto,* to please the men among passengers and crew who could afford to buy their favors. The ship's officers took no part in these connexions, they being ashore consorting with more costly whores. Everyone was delighted with this most sensible accommodation. Especially the cordial police official, who each evening received from the brothel mistress his percentage of the receipts, chastely wrapped in heavy white paper. Most especially the retired prostitute, called back to duty during this urgency. When some of the younger girls declared that they felt embarrassed at being associated with a colleague of such unseemly age, their mistress reproved them gently, exhibiting a charity that exceeded by far the courtesy of the police official. "In the dark," she said, "all bodies are equally beautiful."

Naturally, having done it once, Koi must try it again—and again. Each night he swam ashore, each morning he came back.

Until the sunrise of the eighth day. That morning he did not return.

CHAPTER 9
THE FLIGHT

After seven days of fruitless conversations with the bland officials of His Imperial Majesty's Government, Mr. Van Reed was convinced that they were playing with him a game much more deceitful than anything he had ever attempted to try with them. And, he realized, the recruits imprisoned aboard the *Scioto* served as nothing more than pawns in this ruthless maneuvering of forces by some very clever players in Edo. The officials of His Imperial Majesty's Government, in Kanagawa as in Edo, cared not a penny about the fate of Nipponjin in Hawaii, as they cared not a zeni about them in Nippon. The issue here, Van Reed perceived at last—as it is in so many other problems being thrust upon this tender young bureaucracy—was prestige, the saving of face. Because the Meiji emperor's government had not been involved in Van Reed's negotiations for sending laborers to Hawaii, its officials felt obliged to disown everything the Bakufu's officials had agreed to approve. Moreover, in dealing so stubbornly with a small and powerless country like the Kingdom of Hawaii, Japan's new rulers were beginning to assert their independence—in clear warning about things to come in their relationships with the powerful nations that had so often affronted the Bakufu.

While Eugene Van Reed could understand this attitude in principle, and, indeed, as a striving young diplomat of very low stature, felt a considerable sympathy for it, he also allowed, in private, that he'd be damned if he'd put up with another year of negotiating—and paying—just to please these newcomers to power.

By the evening of the seventh day, feeling himself something like a pawn at this point—and yet fired with true American impatience with "this typical Oriental duplicity"—Van Reed was reduced to using the worst and weakest of all a duplicitous diplomat's weapons. He demanded that His Imperial Majesty's concerned and benevolent Government reimburse him and the Government of His Majesty the King of Hawaii, to the amount of $10,000 American, "in compensation for all sums expended to date . . . upon the recruiting of laborers to work in the sugar plantations of Hawaii."

Not at all to Van Reed's surprise, but much sooner than he'd hoped, the presiding official called an abrupt end to their meeting.

Captain Reagan, fighting drunk most of the time, was furious over this idiots' delay. By Saturday morning he was wonderfully choleric when, for the eighth day, the troubled Consul-General called upon him with yet one more request for still another postponement of the *Scioto*'s departure.

"I know nothing of treaties or of diplomats, Mr. Van Reed," he growled, staring at those goddam golden locks, the smooth cheeks of this master nitwit of them all. "I know only that I am hired to sail this ship, with its cargo, wherever Jardine, Matheson tells me to take 'em. Get me them bleedin' clearance papers, so I can sail out of this stinkin' port. That's all I ask. Customs has given me clearance. But not the government. They're still as unwillin' to part with 'em, up there, as a hungry dog with a bone. Why? Get me them bleedin' bloody papers. So's I can be on my way. Or," he slapped the arm of his chair, sending his voice into a scream, "get them bloody Nips off me ship. They've eaten me out of a week's stores. And I'm not shippin' aboard any more to replace the vittles they've stowed away. Pay me for the damages they've inflicted upon me fine ship, what with their spillin' of food on the decks, their spittin' in the corners, and their stringin' of ropes about to hang their bloody underdrawers from. Me prideful ship looks like a blinkin' Chinee laundry, it does. And pay me and me crew for all the time you've cost us, makin' us sit here in this stinkin' pigstye, like old maids in a county workhouse, waitin' upon your lordship's pleasure." He couldn't have chosen a less appropriate figure of speech, or a more vulnerable set of lies, but both of them knew very well what he intended.

Van Reed winced with each new demand. Captain Reagan, this piggish son of a sea sow, was treating him to exactly the same strategy he had just used upon those blank-eyed sons of crows up in Kanagawa. And he was no more able to pay Reagan than, as he well knew, His Imperial Majesty's Government was able to pay him. The Hawaiian government had sent him a paltry $1925 American, to spend upon the recruiting of three or four hundred laborers, promising to pay the expenses of transporting those recruits to the captain of the ship that delivered them in Honolulu. Already, by his rough calculation, the costs of chartering the *Scioto* and of furbishing it to transport people rather than merchandise exceeded $4400. He couldn't pay Captain Reagan, or Jardine, Matheson either, even if he wanted to call off the whole botheration. And, to put the matter mildly, until this moment he hadn't wanted to call it off. He'd be damned to hell and back first, before he gave in to those imperial buzzards up there in Kanagawa. Stringing him along, with all that pious talk about protecting their people when, up there in Kanagawa, right here in Yokohama, they couldn't raise a jot's worth of concern for all the peasants in the country . . .

Suddenly he was sick of the whole baffling game. Sick of officials of any rank or color, sick as much of American and British ministers and minions, who gave him no support at all, as of their Japanese counterparts. The emperor's minions, to do them justice, were only beginning to learn the tricks of dealing with Westerners. And he was sick, most heartily sick, of this singular sea captain, reeking of whiskey and rancid sweat, bellowing and ranting as if consuls lived to serve only him. And he was sick—no, not sick, but weary—of those quiet, shrinking, fearful little Japanese hiding in the *Scioto*'s holds, with their pleading lustrous eyes and muted terror of whatever punishment those samurai devils in Kanagawa might have in store for them.

But most of all he was sadly sick of himself, of his ineptitude and failure, of his inability to rid himself of this shipful of lost souls with whom, despite his good sense, he had got so damnably entangled. This is what comes of allowing sentiment to take the place of reason, he saw all too clearly, now that the mistake was beyond correcting. This is what comes of trying to help a country almost empty of people gain a few from a country which has too many. His troubles began, he realized now, on the day when he decided that he liked the people of Japan. The common people, that is to say, not those haughty samurai, not those supercilious obstaculating bureaucrats . . .

"Why don't you just sail away?," he said wearily, scarcely thinking beyond his own need for relief. "And thumb your nose at the whole lot of us."

"Eh?" Captain Reagan sat up, all attention, putting his heavy boots back on the floor.

"Why not? What can they do to stop you?"

"Holy Mary, Mother of God." The captain's smile broadened as his brogue thickened. He saved that for moments when he was touched by reverence. "Sure, and it's the loveliest thought. 'Tis the best it's been me pleasure to hear from the lips of a buddin' diplomat." Rolling his eyes heavenward, as if conferring with the Virgin Mother Herself, he took stock of the hazards to such a leave taking. Satisfied with the reckoning, he slapped the desk this time, making a noise that gratified himself, as though he were laying a cannon shot across the bow of Japan's bureaucracy. "You've said it, me lad. What can they do to stop me? Nothin', nothin' at all. Not a single gun, not a single frigate, lies between me and freedom. Only a broken word. And who will blame me for that, when I have been held a veritable prisoner, much against me will?" The rogue's eyes began to twinkle, as he thought of the tales he would tell, in other ports, about the time he upped a fast sail on them saucy Nips, up there in Yokka-hamm-a. "By the Nails of the True Cross. I'll do it. But what of you, lad, what of you, left here in their heathen hands?"

This was a schemer's mind at work, Van Reed understood, not a friend's. "How can they blame me for something you do?," he said airily. "No, I'm in the clear. But are you sure you're safe? Any repercussions from the home office in Hong Kong? Or from your government in London?"

"On the contrary. The company'll keel-haul me and cut me loose if I waste much more of their precious time just gatherin' barnacles here. From London-town? Faith, now, would I be committin' an unfriendly deed? Or an act of war? No. Not a bit of it. The idea never crosses me mind. Me soul quivers at the very thought. And ye'll vouch for that, will ye not? 'Tis just that I, a helpless foreigner in this strange land, not knowin' the nytive tongue, did misconstrue those Customs House papers for the Government's. And in Hong Kong I can say that I, not being able to see an end to these diplomatic conversations, so to speak, in an access of true Christian compassion for me heathen charges quartered in the holds below, did put out to sea in order to ease their misery. 'Tis an act of Heaven's own mercy, I'd be showin'. I'll even swear to that on a heap of Bibles, I will, damme, because the more I think about this bloody business, damme, the more do I think 'tis God's own truth I am utterin'."

"Good. We see eye-to-eye in this matter of compassion. When do you begin your act of mercy?"

"Soon's wind and tide are runnin' right. My guess, from what I've seen of this mucky cove, is 'long about dawn. On the morrow. No sooner. No later."

"An excellent time, I'd say. All diplomats and officials of government, including this weary one, will be abed at that hour. And no policeman will be nigh. Your departure should be unobserved—at least until you're out yonder in the bigger bay—the more so because these clever people have noticed that most foreigners do no work on the seventh day of the week. By the time they discover that you are an exception to the holy rule," he stood up, restraining himself from flicking specks of captain's dirt from his frock coat, "and given the winds of the morning, you should be beyond their reach. I'll take my belated leave, then, Captain, wishing you a most pleasant voyage."

"Pleasant it may be not, but the goin' will be most pleasin'.

Meantime, say not a word of this to anyone. We'll go in a rush, when we go. I'll not even tell me crew, until the watch changes at midnight."

Knowing nothing of Van Reed's conspiring with Captain Reagan, the *Scioto*'s passengers and crew considered the day to be just one more in a series that threatened to go on forever. By then almost everyone aboard was reconciled to a long waiting, and no one tried any more to guess when their captivity would end. Each morning they awoke to the loss of a few more men, each night they wondered who would be gone when the next dawn came. Familiarity bred more quarrels among the people aboard the ship, while diminishing the number of enemies they imagined on shore. Yet without their fear of Hamada's knife-men to intimidate them even more of his converts would have fled. Remembrance of that preserved head, more than the presence of a bored constable or two on the quay, kept all but twenty-seven recruits honest if not patient. The fact that those who stayed never learned what happened to any of the men who ran away or who gave themselves up to the police merely added the terror of mystery to the grimness of certainty.

Ishi was not much surprised, therefore, when Koi did not return to the *Scioto* at dawn that Saturday morning. But he worried, nonetheless, about the reason for his friend's absence. He could not really believe that Koi had deserted. Necessarily, then, the boy was being kept ashore either by force or by accident. If by force, nothing could be done to rescue him. If by accident, then certainly he would be back by dawn the next morning. In the event that he did not return at that time, Ishi resolved to swim ashore during the next night, with the hope of learning what had happened to him. The one contingency that Ishi did not consider was the possibility that Koi might be tied to the shore by bonds of his own fashioning.

But precisely that had happened to Koi—although perhaps it would be more correct to say that he was entangled in a whole net of love, not in just a few trifling bonds. That maid in Fujimi

Ryokan, the virgin who had given herself to him, the girl whom he could not forget: she was the one who drew him back to shore, night after dangerous night, and who kept him in her toils on that important morning.

Yet she was no witch, this maid, no fox-spirit hiding in the body of a girl. In the eyes of most men she was not even beautiful, although they might have conceded that she was far from being ugly. But to Koi she was beautiful beyond all others he had ever seen. He loved her slender body, not yet a woman's, her thin and comely face, the way her eyes lighted up when she saw him, the softness of her touch and the gentleness in her voice. He loved the sweetness of her breath, the warmth of her body when he lay with her, and now, since he had taught her, the passion with which she responded to his own. He loved her more than just because she loved him. She gave him thoughts and hopes and yearnings, for the two of them together, such as he knew only a long lifetime spent with her would grant him.

And she loved him because he brought her fulfillment, with his laughter and his wit, his promises and great dreams, the strong hard body and its need of her, with the prospect of the handsome sons and beautiful daughters she would bear for him and for his family in Ajiro of Izu.

Their first night together left them both miserable. Their third convinced them that they were the most blissful pair of lovers in all Nippon. The fourth made them unhappy again, aching with the knowledge that soon they must part forever, weeping with the certainty that they would never survive such a separation. The fifth night—after they'd eased their bodies for the while—they spent in thinking about how they could arrange to go together to the land across the sea. Koi did not doubt that there was space for her beside him in his bunk. And surely provisions enough to feed her during the voyage could be found. But, try as he might, he could not think of a safe way by which he could take Aiko aboard that guarded ship.

Although she was not yet sixteen years old, Aiko could not have worked for three of those years in her uncle's inn without learning much about the world of men. Even so, she was slow to apply her learning to solving Koi's great problem. By the time she and Koi could arrange the details of her plan he had missed his chance to swim back to the *Scioto.*

In the quiet of the evening passengers who did not wish to lie with prostitutes gathered on the top deck, while their lustier associates rattled the bunks below. Lanterns hung in the rigging gave the loungers on deck enough light for playing Go or cards. But nothing could help to keep mosquitoes and midges at bay, or to subdue the scent of those libidinous chestnut blossoms, wafted out from the land.

Ishi, following his habit, sat on the deck near the wheelhouse, half listening to the chatter of the men around him the while he thought of many things. Underlying all of them was his concern for Koi. During the long warm day, while performing his duties as Makino's assistant, he almost managed to forget the boy. But now, with nothing to do, the absent Koi was more in his thoughts than he would have been if he were present in person. Foolish kid! Ishi clucked for at least the hundredth time. I'll bet the police caught him when he tried to swim back this morning. But how can I find out what's happened to him? Where shall I start to look, when I swim ashore tomorrow night?

"Ha! Just look at this!," he heard Dembei growl. Others exclaimed, "Maa!" and "Nanda?" and "Dame da!" and "Saa!" The expressions of surprise and disgust sputtered around him. He looked up to see what caused them, and promptly added his "Dame!" to the rest. Conversations stopped, games of chance waited, a woman tittered with embarrassment. All eyes turned upon that object of curiosity.

Mincing toward them on a harlot's high geta, lissome as the tendril of a wistaria vine swaying in a soft spring breeze, came a painted youth. Powdered and tinted like your cheapest of pluckable blossoms, his mouth puckered as though to give a filthy kiss, eyes modestly cast down, he brought shame upon all honest pleasure-boys and genuine whores. His shaven head and tight topknot showed that he was born a male. Most certainly he had not grown up to be a man.

The creature swayed toward them, leading by the hand a small and timid person, holding a kimono sleeve before its face. It appeared to be a girl, or possibly a woman, but, in the company of that bedizened male, who could be sure? "Nanda?," asked puzzled Dembei. "What is it?"

The dansho stopped near the wheelhouse. Without sense enough to be ashamed, it wagged its giddy head, stuck up on that long powdered neck, fluttered its eyelids, simpered in the direction of the fascinated men. "Excuse me," it said, in the high affected tones of one of the Yoshiwara's most expensive blossoms. "Forgive me for interrupting, but . . . is Ishi-san here? The handsome Ishi-san of Asakusa? He has sent for me. For tonight . . . "

Ishi could not believe his ears. "Yossh!," he snarled. "I did not!" He waved the creature off, while all true men hid smiles behind their hands or fans.

Recoiling as if he'd been struck, dangling that limp hand before his flat bosom, the dansho shrieked, "O, Ishi-san! There you are!—But you are so cruel! Don't you love me anymore? Have you forgotten me so soon?" Touched by this tender scene, some of the men looked away, pretending they had other claims upon their interest, while their ears stood up like sails on a ship, to catch every word of this lovers' reunion.

"Kono yaro," muttered Dembei, not pretending to be disinterested. "This varlet."

As Ishi flinched in horror from this brazen creature, wondering how to rid himself of it, wishing he could throw it overboard, the thing itself began to change before their very eyes. The tight painted lips stretched into a wide grin, opening a big mouth lacking a few teeth. A man's hearty laugh issued from that powdered throat. The hand, no longer limp, pulled down the shoulder of his yukata, revealing the carps on the kimono beneath.

"Koi!," everybody yelled at once, bursting into shouts of laughter that must have startled half the people in Yokohama. Ishi jumped up and hugged him, knowing no shame in embracing a real man. "You're back! You're here!," he cried, feeling his worries dropping away.

"Of course. I told you I'd come back. But this time I did not come alone." He drew to his side the one whose hand he had been holding. "Here is Aiko. My wife."

Ishi looked for the first time upon the wife of his friend. "Aiko-san," he said, bowing formally, "I am happy to meet you." She is so young, he marveled, and so small. In that light, with the flush of excitement still in her cheeks, he thought that she was beautiful. A fit mate for Koi.

"Now I won't have to swim ashore every night. She is going with us, when we sail. If we ever do sail."

"Welcome, welcome to our company," said Ishi, beckoning to the others to gather around, to greet Koi's chosen wife.

Before dawn the next morning, while the passengers slept, the *Scioto*'s full crew freed the ship for her run to the sea. Quietly they slipped the bowlines from the jetty's bollards, hauled up the gangway, and stood by the shrouds, awaiting orders. Slowly the dead weight of the *Scioto* yielded to the pull of the ebbing tide, the push of the offshore breeze. Silently, like a ghostly barque made of cobwebs and graveclothes, she drifted backwards, away from the jetty and neighboring ships, into the clear.

Because this first stage had progressed without accident or alarm, Mr. Jackson, with a wave of his lantern, sent the sailors aloft, to man the yards. When the helmsman swung the ship around, to face the bay of Edo beyond the point of Yokohama's Bluff, Mr. Jackson waved the lantern again. Far above, the sailors, clinging with their toes to foot ropes, unloosed the ties, pushed down the furled topgallants and tops'ls, and the great sheets fell free. Within the instant they took the wind. The drifting ship seemed to hesitate, as though deciding upon a course, and then she leaped toward the bay. With a joyful shout, for nothing could stop her now, the sailors began to unfurl all others of her wings, from skys'ls to mains'ls, hoisted the jibs and spanker, putting her under full canvas for the flight. Within two minutes they transformed her from a helpless drifting hulk to a sleek ship racing on her way.

The shouts of the crew awoke the passengers. The creak of timbers as the ship sprang into motion, the hiss of water against her hull, told them what was happening. "We're moving!," they cried. "We're going at last!," they shouted into the darkness, finding in such unnecessary noises, as well as in laughter and sobs and tears and other expressions of joy, relief from the strain of their long waiting. Hurriedly putting on their kimono, they waited patiently in the dark holds, until they might be allowed to go on deck. While crewmen aloft finished setting the sails, others on deck closed the hatches, coiled up the rope guards, preparing the *Scioto* for her dash down the Bay of Edo.

Captain Reagan, standing beside the wheelhouse, looked and listened for alarms from the shore. Not a voice cried out, not a light flared up. The fair-haired lad's right, the captain acknowledged, flicking a salute in the direction of the Bluff, where Consul-General Van Reed, beside his Japanese wife, enjoyed the sleep of the merciful, if not of the just. Sober as an Irish priest before his first mass of the morning—for Captain Reagan followed the rule of never sipping from the comforting cup while his vessel was under sail, never dashing away the cup from his lips while his craft lay in port—he studied the sky for signs of the weather, the stars for the course he wanted to set. Save for a few dim lights along the sweep of Yokohama's waterfront, he could see little of the land behind. Only the cold light of the dying moon showed him where the ruffled water lay. But Stella Polaris glittered on high, and all the constellations in the northern heavens; and by taking them for guides he could lay a track without need for compass or sextant or Admiralty charts.

"The next half hour will tell us whether or not we've done it," he confided to Mr. Jackson, standing near his captain. The adventure in this leave-taking, the ease with which it seemed to be going, made the two almost companionable.

"All hands are keeping their eyes peeled, sir," replied the First Mate respectfully. And what, in Heaven's Holy Name, he wondered, would a Japanese interpreter make of that remark? No longer nervous, relieved at the speed with which his crew had got the ship under way, Mr. Jackson had time now for philosophical thoughts.

Keeping their eyes peeled, they saw no dangers in the sea— and only glories in the firmament made by Captain Reagan's omnipotent Jehovah. No police boats fretted about, marking their unlawful departure. No warships of His Imperial Majesty's new navy rushed up, foaming at the bow, to intercept them. But while the *Scioto* raced out into Edo's bay, going far enough from its western coast to be safe from promontories, shoals, islets, shore batteries, and from most of those all but invisible fishermen's sampans, the eastern sky, above the long peninsula of Boso, began to glow. The hills of Kazusa, the higher ridges of remote Awa, stood up dark against the lightening blue of dawn.

Captain Reagan called an order to the helmsman. Gradually, grandly, the *Scioto* responded to the wheel, marking a curving wake in the black water. Aloft, yards shifted upon the masts, as sailors paid out lines, trimming the sheets to the freshening wind. Now she was ready for the most dangerous time in her flight, the long run down the narrow gullet of Uraga Channel. Beyond its mouth, near Miura, lay the open sea.

On the rim of the world, far beyond Kazusa, clouds scattered the blaze cast by the rising sun. Like the spokes of a mighty wheel the rays of light lay across the sky, changing their colors from blue to green to yellow as their source neared the moment of its revealing.

Sailors, their duties put off for the while, turned to watch. "A fine morning, Mr. Jackson," said Captain Reagan, offering silent thanks to the Jehovah who created such grandeur for the eye of mortal man to behold. "Tell our passengers they may come on deck, if they wish. They might be wantin' to bid a proper farewell to the auld country."

"A fine thought, sir," said Mr. Jackson, approving for once his captain's whim. Already a mass of black-topped heads and pale upturned faces waited on the companionway to Hold 3. With a

gesture worthy of the Bishop of Rome himself Jackson invited
them to come up. They rushed forth, bowing their thanks to him
and the captain before hurrying to the port rail. From the forward holds came similar eruptions of passengers. Without making a sound they gazed in awe at the beauty of this most special
dawn.

The hues of light, bringing Amaterasu-Omikami's gifts to a
grateful land, changed to richest copper, to flaming orange, at
the last to fiery red. The voyagers aboard the *Scioto* could not see
the horizon, hidden beyond the mountains of Awa, but they could
tell the moment when the sun burst forth, triumphant, above the
curve of the earth, for in that instant the floor of heaven turned
into a canopy of gold. There are the Five-colored Clouds of Paradise, thought some, certain now that they were sailing for Tenjiku. There is Nippon, the Source of Day, the Begetter of Light,
thought others, saddened at what they were leaving behind.

"Fuji-san!," a man cried out. Turning their backs upon the
east, they found Fuji in the west. In far-off Suruga, beyond the
low green hills of Kamakura, beyond the humped greening ridges
of Hakone, above the purple haze compounded of morning mist
and sea spray and wood smoke, rose the sacred mountain, clad in
snow.

"Ahh! Utsukushii," they murmured, "beautiful, so beautiful . . . " Except for Koi, the fisherman from Izu, never before
had any of the wanderers seen their beloved mountain from the
vantage of the sea. And now, as never before, they realized how
much they were leaving behind.

"Sayonara!," a man called, his voice breaking at the need to
say farewell to that beautiful land, to the familiar places of home.

As grief took hold of them, and fear and vain regret, each of
the emigrants bade farewell to the homeland in his own way.
Many wept, without shame for their tears. Others gazed out, dry-
eyed, yet weeping in their hearts. Some knelt upon the deck, or
upon the hatch covers, bowing low, doing ogamu, folding hands
in prayer, to Fujisan, to Dai Nippon. Others stood at the rail,
looking out over the dark blue waters tipped with crests of white,

toward the land they would not see again until three years and more had passed. A few, wiser than the rest, were saddened by the thought that they might never see this land again. For who can tell, in this world of troubles and perils, what travelers will return again to the home from which they depart?

Ishi would not permit himself to weep. But he was softened by the grief he felt, and the love for this vanishing land that lay in his heart, threatening to choke him with tears. Why do I grieve, he asked himself, for a land which has not treated me well? Why am I not dancing with joy, because I am leaving it behind? He saved himself from tears by offering thanks to Kannon Nyo-i-rin, for her compassion and intercession. As he touched her precious stone, safe in its carrying place in his fundoshi, he thought that perhaps he should return it to her, by dropping it overboard, into the deep water. But no, he remembered the words of the Lord Abbot of Hongakuji, assuring the emigrants that the powers of their guardian gods would accompany them wherever they might go. Not until my life is ended shall I cease to need the help of Kannon. I shall keep this stone with me, through all the days of my life.

Beside him stood Koi and Aiko, she drawn close to his body, he with his arms around her. In the general swell of emotion no one minded this unseemly display of tenderness between a man and his wife. Koi, as he felt his heart melt with love for Aiko, as he breathed the fragrance of her hair, gave thanks to Benten, the Goddess of Love, for bringing them together, for putting them aboard this wonderful ship just in time.

Makino Tomosaburo, standing near the stern, looked back toward the land he would not see again. It is so beautiful a land, he thought. So full of promise—and so crowded with disappointments. It is indeed a land of illusions and vanities. Why do I go? he asked himself, why do I abandon this beautiful country I have loved so much? Because I cannot bear to stay in it and see it despoiled, he answered himself. Because I cannot hope that it will be saved from the despoilers. But am I foolish to strive for anything else?

As tears of sorrow brimmed in his eyes, he murmured the lines of a poem, written more than 1100 years before by Priest Mansei:

> To what shall I compare this world?
> To the white wake behind
> A ship that has rowed away
> At dawn.

Of all the voyagers the only one who would not say farewell to Nippon was the Sad Woman. Standing beside the mizzenmast, she looked ahead, seeing nothing but the dazzling sail, swelling in the wind.

Each alone with his thoughts, the voyagers stood upon the deck of that black ship, like prisoners being taken into exile, like spirits of people already dead being ferried across the waters of the River Sai, to the Nether World.

Leaning with the wind, beyond stopping now, the *Scioto* bore them away, speeding across the waters of Uraga, toward the waves of the ocean sea.

CHAPTER 10
PERILS OF THE DEEP

Makino's lieutenants reported the presence of not one but two extra passengers.

Ishi took Koi and Aiko to Makino's office, his bunk in the forward hold. Makino could be calm about Aiko's addition, because he had not yet learned about the other one. Ishi told him the lovers' story, very briefly, mentioning not a word about the manner in which they had arrived. Seeing the two of them, so young and so pleasing (an effect that Ishi had counted upon), Makino did not have the heart to scold them for taking advantage of Captain Reagan's generosity. Besides, as everyone knew, he couldn't do anything anyway about putting Aiko back in Yokohama. Accepting the fact like a forgiving father, he said, "I must tell the captain about Aiko-san. He will put her name upon the passenger list."

Koi had never heard of a passenger list but he knew about passports. He pulled his own from a kimono sleeve and asked, very politely, "Will you give her a paper like this? Or can you write her name on this one, together with mine?"

Makino snorted at the sight of the flimsy document. "Not worth the trouble. Those are useless pieces of paper, I've been told. The government of our country has not yet begun to issue passports. And the government of Hawai does not require passports for hired laborers like us."

"What?," cried Ishi. "You mean—?" He tried to remember how much honorable money this piece of paper had cost him.

"I do. The list of names being taken by the captain from Mr. Van Reed is the only passport we'll need. That's why I must tell the captain to put Aiko-san's name on the list."

"And Hamada's papers?," Ishi persisted, hating to hear again that they'd been duped, yet needing to hear it too, just as a drunkard needs his saké.

"They're just another of Hamada-san's schemes for squeezing our money out of us. Someday I hope he has to work for his living. Under the hot sun. In the mud of a ricefield."

"Better the prison mines of Sado," said uncharitable Ishi, "for a man who loves gold so much."

" 'Whether in this life or the next we cheat,' " said a disgusted bystander, " 'in either case our punishment we'll meet.' "

"But what does it say, then, this writing?," asked Koi, more confused than ever.

Makino unfolded the paper and read:

THIS UNOFFICIAL DOCUMENT TELLS THE HONORABLE READER

of this writing that

KOI OF YOKOHAMA IN THE COUNTRY OF NIPPON

is allowed to enter the foreign ship that is named

SHIOTO

SEAL

Meiji 1 year, 5 month, 8 day   Signature

"As you might expect," Makino said, giving the folded paper to Koi, "the seal and signature are so made that they mean nothing."

"Screwed again!," cried Koi. "Those crooks! Makes me wonder why I try to be an honest man." The more he complained, the more he remembered. The more eloquent he became, the more people gathered around to hear him. "And all those stories they told us, about the policemen watching us from the jetty.—You know what happened to the passengers who gave themselves up to the police?"

"No, what?," several men asked. All waited, breathless, to learn their dreadful fate.

"Nothing! The policemen took them to the office on the shore, wrote down their names in a book, gave them a cup of tea, and sent them home, since that's where they wanted to go."

"That's all? You're sure?"

"Yes! One of them told me so himself. A Yokohama man. Free. And happy to be home again."

But suspicion dies hard. "Poor fellows," said a doubting man, his voice as lugubrious as his face. "They'll never sleep easy again."

"How do you know all this?," another directed his suspicion upon Koi.

"I was there." Not thinking to explain, he hurried on to the really delectable scandal. "And that pickled head. You remember it? It was the head of a man, all right. But he was not one of us, a recruit who tried to run away, as Hamada said. He was a prisoner of the Bakufu, executed in Osaka fifty or sixty years ago, after Oshio Heihachiro's rebellion."

"Ha! Wait a minute," Makino interrupted this bloodcooling tale. "Oshio's Rebellion? Not that long ago. I can remember hearing about it when I was a lad of six or seven. Let's settle for thirty years ago."

"Well, anyway, a very long time ago," Koi rushed on. "Hambei borrowed that terrible thing from a side-show manager in Yokohama. He's been letting people look at it for many years. Aiko told me so. She's seen it many times. So many times that now she and her friends are not afraid of it anymore. They just laugh. That's what she did, when she saw it sitting around in Fujimi-ya." Beside him, Aiko nodded repeatedly, proud to support her news-bringing husband.

Makino put an end to the mounting anger. "Perhaps we should thank them for scaring us with their lies," he said quietly, shocking them with his mildness. "Else how many of us would have stayed aboard ship during that week of waiting? Who can say that Hamada's schemes were not wise, and that his duplicity was not kindness in disguise?"

This was too heavy a dose of philosophy for his charges to take. The Great Chain of Cause and Effect was fashioned for priests and professors to ponder, not for honest working men to waste time upon. Muttering at Hamada the Cheat, puzzling over Makino the Meek, they backed away. Ishi and his friends were glad of the excuse to take leave of their daimyo.

But Makino tugged at Koi's sleeve, pulling the carps to a sudden halt. "One more thing. Your name, you say, is Koi?"

"Yes." His hands, waving over the bodyguard of fish, suggested that here was, indeed, a most foolish question. "Does not my paper say so?"

"It does. In a way. But with another character than the one you—and I—expected. The one written on your paper is not the kanji for carp." He waited for the effect of this revelation, as artful an actor as Koi could be.

"What! Don't tell me that dumpy Hambei screwed me there, too!"

"That will depend upon how you feel about it. The one he gave you is the kanji for 'love.' "

"You mean—you mean my name is 'Love'?"

Makino chuckled. "And most appropriately, I think."

"Old Hambei must have looked into your heart," said Ishi. "For this I can forgive him all his cheatings. But this name, I think, is not a cheat."

"Well," Koi scratched his head, "I think I like this meaning better. Once I thought only of being a fish-man. But this name: it shows that Aiko and I were fated to meet."

"So it seems," Ishi agreed. "You must have been a good man in your previous existence, to win such a name and so fine a wife in this."

"Which reminds me," said Makino. "Aiko-san *is* your wife? You've been formally married? Not that I care, one way or the other. But the captain will want to know. Foreign officials, I have heard, are a very strange lot. Especially where matters of sex are concerned."

"Of course we're married. Twice. We've drunk the San-San-Kudo two times. Yesterday afternoon, at Fujimi-ya, when Aiko's uncle and aunt gave us a marriage feast. Before we went to the brothel," he explained to Ishi.

Makino looked puzzled, not having heard about the style of their arrival aboard ship. "Later, I'll tell you later," Ishi whispered, hoping that the busy daimyo would forget to ask about that prank of Koi's.

"And again last night, when our friends in Hold 3 gave us another feast."

"Then the gods will bless you twice," said Makino. "Double fortune will be yours. And twice as much happiness as we bachelors will have."

"And only half as many troubles?," asked shy Aiko, worrying that the gods might be angered by such jesting about so serious a matter.

The second unexpected passenger had no friend to present her and no husband to stand beside—although more than a dozen men had served her in the part of husband since they'd boarded the *Scioto*. But she did not mind the absence of a registered mate: she herself stood up when Makino's lieutenant, Daigoro of Kamakura, passed her bunk in Hold 2.

"Excuse me, sir," she said. Already she knew who were the important men aboard this ship.

He stopped in some surprise. To save his life, he couldn't remember having seen her before. Small and neat, dressed in a summer kimono of plainest blue and white, she reminded him of someone's sister. "You're new," he finally guessed. "Where did you come from?"

"I came aboard last evening, sir. With the girls from Mother Hayashi's honorable House of Good Report."

He could not believe her. She did not look the part. She did not act it. But, taking her at her word (for, as everyone knows, many a whore is someone's sister, sold by her father into the profession), he cried, "Then why didn't you go back with them when they left?"

"Because I didn't want to go back. I preferred to stay." This was not the time, she decided, to tell him that she had got the idea for hiding aboard when Aiko and Koi came to her for help in smuggling them past the guards on the jetty. Nor did she want to say, quite yet, that if this ship had room enough to add one extra wife, then most certainly no one could honestly object to the presence of a second.

"And work your way across?," he leered, before he thought.

"No, dearie," she tapped his hand with her little fan, not in the least hurt by such coarseness. A girl in her calling has to put up with crudities of this nature, especially from men of his kind. Besides, he was attractive, with his warm brown flesh, full of a young man's juices, those teasing black eyes, and those strong arms and legs, made to clasp about a woman's yielding body. Not to mention other endowments she could guess at. Nonetheless, she could tell, being a woman of considerable experience, that he was a man not to be trusted with a woman's heart: vain and shallow, too conscious of his good looks, he was the sort of man who kept whores in business, to the sorrow of a wife and the neglect of parents and children.

"No, my dear," she smiled up at him, showing her blackened teeth, "I'm a retired prostitute now. Twice over. I've had enough of that frivolous life, and I've bought my freedom, fair and proper. Please remember: 'a woman's chastity is not of the body.' Now I'm looking for peace and quiet. And a husband. A good husband." She poked him gently in the ribs with the folded fan. "And I thought that on this ship, with all these lonely men, I'd have a wider selection of merchandise to choose from. Like going shopping at one of the big Mitsukoshi stores. And," she pressed ever so slightly upon his strong brown arm, not yet having given up that harlot's habit, "plenty of time for choosing."

"You're a smart businesswoman," he said, changing from leer to laugh, out of respect for such frankness. "But they may want to test your honorable wares, before they buy."

"Many have done so already. But I don't know them, not one from the other, even in the light of day. Just as, I'm sure, they won't know me—even after we're introduced. My! These holds are dark enough by day, but at night! May Benten have mercy on us . . . In any event, all that doesn't matter anymore. After last night, this shop is closed. Not permanently, you understand. But from now on the door opens only to a husband. And, you may be sure, I shall be a good wife to the man I choose."

"I believe you," he bowed, half in jest, half in honor. Despite her past (which he could not help thinking must also be her present and future), the little tell-tale signs of ageing, and the directness of her speech he could not help liking this forthright woman. And really, now that he'd had time to study her, she wasn't bad looking at all. In fact, he felt that most magical urge, he wouldn't mind flinging her into a bunk right now . . . "Please keep me in your favor," he said, intending to make his interest known, before all those other hard-up men got after her.

"As a brother, perhaps, but not as a husband. You're the sort of man a girl must never trust, either with her girdle or her heart. When I marry, dear, I want a husband who will want only me."

Daigoro shook his head, in respect for such determination, in tribute to such wisdom. "May the gods help the men on this ship!"

"Spread the news, like a good brother," she prodded him with the fan. "Tell the men that Miya is here, in search of a husband. But tell the gods that they need help only me."

As the *Scioto* sailed past Cape Nojima, far to larboard, and entered the western reaches of the Great Peaceful Ocean, many passengers began to feel sick. Paling at the thought of eating, they fled into their bunks. Makino's lieutenants and their assistants hurried about, distributing wooden pails for the sick to use, reminding the well to help the ailing. Aiko, trembling and faint, crept into her bunk, whereupon Koi became almost as green as she was, not with seasickness but with worry. The Sad Woman came to help them. Without a word she pushed Koi aside, placed a cold wet towel upon Aiko's forehead, gave her a dried mushroom to put into her navel, tucked two blankets about her, and trudged away. Soon Aiko slept, and Koi slipped in beside her, unable to leave his beloved.

Miya, in the way of women, knew how to help the ailing men in Hold 2. Moving from one to another, with wet towels, little cups of saké, cheerful talk, and cool hands, she soothed their thoughts if not their uneasy bellies.

Fortunately, toward evening the winds fell and the sea became smoother. Most of the sick passengers felt better. And, so great is the healing power in Inari-sama's rice, almost all pronounced themselves completely recovered after they had eaten the evening meal.

With stomachs quieted, the excitement of the long day waning, above all with the knowledge that they had begun the journey at last, their spirits quickened. They sat on the floor of the hold, beneath the unlighted lanterns, talking about what they expected to find in the new land, not about what they left behind in the old. They made bets about the length of the voyage. When some said thirty, or thirty-one, or thirty-two days (having heard these estimations from the Chinese cooks), others refused to believe such lies. They thought that Tenjiku lay only a few hours' sail east of Edo, not much farther away than Hachijoshima, the island south of Izu to which the Bakufu had exiled so many of its enemies. And those ignorant travelers were ready to weep when they learned that they could not easily sail home again, to celebrate O-Shogatsu, the Festival of the New Year, or the ceremonies of O-Bon, the Festival for the Dead, during the last weeks of summer. This is how ill-informed about the world the people of Nippon were in those days, and how cleverly Hamada Hikizo and his men invented lies to please the ears of their questioners.

Many voyagers went up to the maindeck at sunset, for a last glimpse of the homeland. It could not be seen, not even the high white head of Fujisan. As if she wished to forget them for deserting her, Nippon had withdrawn behind a screen of clouds and rain. Only the wide gray sea lay around them. And upon its surface only the waves moved, and the little vessel carrying them into the night.

Just before the lanterns were doused a strange thing happened. Dembei of Meguro near Edo, a bowlegged little man from Hold 3, having drunk too much saké since the evening meal, decided to go for a stroll. He walked from Hold 3 to Hold 1 and back again. With much dignity, not staggering, not bumping into things along the way, he made his round. But something raging within him caused him to lift his head every now and then, to shout in a voice hoarse with fury, "Bakayaro!"

The holds echoed with that cry. Astonished people looked up, wondering what he meant. Some laughed, thinking that he proved himself a fool. Some thought he loathed himself for being such a fool as to set out upon this journey. Others suspected that he accused them of being fools. A few disillusioned ones maintained that only now, when he was safe at sea, did he rail at the wife he dared not beat while he lived at home. "The drunkard belies not his true character," they whispered among themselves when Dembei had gone past.

They never did learn what he meant. In the morning, when they asked him, quite sober by then and friendly, he answered them with a shrug, a little laugh, and an infuriating retreat into private thoughts. "Oh, I don't know," he drawled, grinning like the mask for a demon in a Noh play. "Sometimes I get like that . . . "

At dawn the whole sky, filled with a light haze from east to west, seemed to take fire from the sun.

"Red sky in the morning, sailors take warning," Captain Reagan sighed, along with every other seaman on watch. Feeling his burdens, surer now than ever that he should not have offered his ship for this insane expedition across almost four thousand miles of the mightiest monster on this earth, he called for help upon Saint Christopher, who protects travelers where'er they may be, and upon the Christ who calms troubled waters.

"Sir, the glass is falling," reported the man at the wheel.

"Looks like we may be in for a bit of weather, Mr. Jackson," said Captain Reagan, glaring at the burning sky, the treacherous blood red sea. "Prepare for the worst."

"Aye, sir," replied Mr. Jackson, feeling some of Christ's compassion for all those heathen below, soon to be assailed by the perils of the sea.

The typhoon caught up with them during the night, announcing its coming with heavy rains and quickening seas, driven by gusts of wind hurrying up from the south, beyond the Loo Choo Islands. Then, blacker than the night, came the wall of violent wind and savage rain, rolling across the oppressed ocean, blotting out the stars in the heavens. Screaming with triumph, like a tiger leaping upon a babe, it threw itself upon the little ship. Faced head-on to the fury, she was as ready as the hands of frightened men could make her. Many hours earlier they had furled every inch of canvas, battened down the hatches, sealed the companionways, chained the wheelhouse to the deck and the rudder to its stanchions, tied ropes to themselves which they could fasten to hawsers strung the length of the deck.

She shuddered as the full force of the storm hit her, trying to push her down into the depths. She fought back, reeling and pitching, while the people in the holds cried out in terror and two sailors in the wheelhouse struggled to keep the helm from spinning. Refusing to submit, the *Scioto* recovered her balance in time to rise upon the following wave. In the wheelhouse Captain Reagan and his men shouted their praise for her, and gave thanks to all their guardian saints.

By morning—according to the *Scioto*'s chronometer, for the storm had ripped away the sky and put out the light of the sun—the wind was unrelenting. It howled through the rigging, screaming like the spirits of vengeful dead desperate to get at the flesh of the living.

For three more days and nights those unappeased ghosts fought to increase their number. The waves swelled to become rolling mountains, up which the *Scioto* must toil, down which she must plunge and rise again if she wanted to live. The summits of those foaming mountains were whipped away, but their sides would crash down upon the *Scioto*'s bow, jarring her to the keel. Icy green water would sweep the length of her deck and rush back to its home from the sides and stern, hissing with annoyance at its defeat. But always the carven figurehead of the Indian chief would rise again, pulling the ship after him.

In the three holds the emigrants knew the meaning of dread. They lay in their bunks, praying to Broken-nosed Jizo, the god of travelers; to Kompira of Kotohira, the protector of sailors and prostitutes; to the Kannon of Infinite Might and Mercy; to the Lord Buddha; and to all other gods, bodhisattvas, and spirit guardians they had any right to call upon. Some cried out, "The gods are angry with us, because we leave Nippon. Now they are sending to overtake us, before we can go beyond their reach." No one who disagreed with them ventured to say they were wrong, if only because in times like these even disbelievers must suspend their disbelief.

They tied themselves to their bunks, with obi and fundoshi and other rope-like things. They tried to sleep, hoping to ease hunger as well as fear. During such wild weather no fires could be lighted in the galleys and no food could be cooked. Once a day two cooks crept down from the galleys, bearing a cauldron half-filled with raw rice and cold water. With this hard gruel passengers and crew must satisfy both thirst and hunger. In the beginning they ate this tasteless mess, supplementing it with whatever remained of the pickled vegetables and dried fruits they had brought aboard. But by the third day of the typhoon they no longer cared to eat. They were so worn by the trial that many were ready to die. Death itself, they thought, would be more easeful than continuing to live in this storm-tossed grave. Gaman, the ability to endure, to persevere, ran out of many, as strength failed.

Water dripping into the holds from above, driven through the very cracks in the hull, made everything damp and cold. Reeking with the stink of vomit and excrement, lighted with only a single dim lantern lashed to a beam, each hold was like the tomb of an emperor in ancient times, before all the retainers who chose to follow him into the Realm of the Dead had perished in the great hole wherein they were buried with their lord.

"Why live?," the voyagers moaned, "if this is to be our life?" "Why clean the benjo, if we must drown?" They were wanting to die, in order to end their misery and fear.

Of them all only Makino Tomosaburo, the three other samurai, and Makino's lieutenants encouraged them. "Shikkari shiro," they said, over and over again, "take courage." "Gambare ne," they cried, "keep trying, don't give up." The samurai did not lose courage because they had been schooled against despair. Ishi, Daigoro, and Tetsuo did not despair because they could not let down their leader.

Makino Tomosaburo was everywhere, going from one hold to the next, like Broken-nosed Jizo himself descended into that tossing Hell to remind them of the hope of salvation. "We are all at sea," he told them in the words used by the priests of Buddha, "in every day of our lives. So, then, we must not fear overmuch now. The surface and the waves out there are very rough, indeed. But underneath is the boundless stillness that gives life to all the moving waves. And soon the moving waves will sink back into that great peace."

The screams of the wind haunted them in their sleep, maddened them when they were awake. This noise was the worst torment of all. But the sea, they knew, was the greatest danger. Often, at the portholes, they stared in awe at the water driven mad by the wind, until they could bear to look no longer. Then they would fall back, into the cold dark hold, certain that they would never survive.

Yet they did survive. On the fourth night the typhoon cast the *Scioto* out from its eastern edge. The scream of the wind sank to a whine, then to an occasional plaintive cry, then to whispers that their deafened ears could not hear. This quietness: this boundless stillness: it was the most welcome gift. For many hours they wanted to hear nothing else.

The tremendous waves did not diminish for still another day. Through the fourth day and the fifth night the people hungered, because the captain sternly refused permission to light fires in the galleys.

On the fifth day, as the crew hoisted again the *Scioto*'s sails, and she rode at last upon a subsiding sea, the galley fires were lighted. The meals were not much improved, the people noticed, but at least the rice was cooked and the bitter tea was hot.

Sailors unsealed the companionways, opened the hatches somewhat, releasing the foul air from the holds, permitting fresh air and cleansing sun to enter in. The passengers cheered at their first view of the sun. The teams appointed by Makino's men went gladly to their tasks of cleaning the holds. The people who had been sick came out of their bunks. Others hung up wet blankets and clothing to dry, waited in lines to wash their itching bodies and dirty fundoshi, first in cold harsh seawater, then in cold soft rainwater. Of this, they were assured, the storm had brought them plenty, and for once they did not have to measure it out with ladles.

On the pacified sea, in the light of the sun, the voyagers who had been spared found that life was good, after all.

The opinion spread among certain men in Hold 1 that they should give thanks to the gods for preserving them from the storm and the sea.

"And who are we to thank?," demanded Kuranosuke of Edo, once a maker of pickled vegetables. As befits a good city man, Kuranosuke had addressed his prayers to Kannon the Kind and to Daikoku, God of Wealth. But during the storm he could not fail to hear his neighbors calling for help to many a lesser kami, such as Never-slumbering Jizo, or Kompira, or even—may the great deities save us from such dark ignorance!—to that loutish pair of country clods, the coupling couple Dosojin. Kuranosuke of Edo asked his question before others could speak only because he wanted to propose that Kannon-sama be the one to receive the thanks of all.

"The gods have punished us for leaving Nippon," stated Seiichi of Kanagawa, foiling Kuranosuke's plan. "Why, then, should they even listen to our thanks?"

"Because they have stopped punishing us," broke in another contentious fellow. "Should we not thank them for that?"

"Yes, but which one should we thank?," began Kuranosuke, failing to foresee what troubles he invited with such an approach. Kuranosuke was a man accustomed to managing his former pickle factory by decree, not by this modern fashion of collecting opinions from everyone in order to arrange compromises that satisfied no one.

Sure enough, the responses poured forth, each one naming his private hope, no one paying any heed to the greater power of the superior divinities. One of the younger men, not much more than a boy, shouted "Tenno-sama!" But the elders stared him down, first for speaking out of turn in the presence of wiser men, as well as for other reasons, not the least of which was the self-evident fact that this new emperor had not yet been given enough time to demonstrate his power as a protector of his subjects.

Being very practical people—no doubt because they are born wise, to begin with, but also because each one is blessed with so many relatives, friends, and neighbors to counsel him—Nipponjin have a way of finding very sensible solutions to the most complicated problems. At length, after each man (except for the Meiji emperor's youthful admirer) had presented his opinion, and after much discussion, they agreed (with only Kuranosuke abstaining) that, in this most delicate situation, the sensible solution was to thank all the gods, separately and together, but all at the same time, for their aid.

"And how are you going to do this?," asked that argumentative Kuranosuke. He was thinking, of course, that while all gods, high and low, delight in being worshipped, no two of them like to receive exactly the same offerings, or to hear the same prayers. Such an affront! As Oda Nobunaga said of himself, in his lifetime, each likes to be first.

"E . . . to . . . ," Seiichi of Kanagawa conceded, "you have a point there . . . " After a moment of deep thought, he realized that this problem must be resolved by higher authority. "Let us go to Makino Tomosaburo-san for advice. He will tell us what to do."

They went in a body to the far end of Hold 1, to see Makino-sama. He was touched by their earnestness, and by their faith—of which he, alas, kept so little. He believed that the gods, and especially the Lord Buddha, lie within one's heart, not in temples and shrines. Gravely he listened to the delegation, solemnly he pondered the question they put to him.

"You are right," he replied. "Thanks should be given, by all of us, at once, to all the gods. And each of us will thank his personal god in the same way in which he besought help: with a personal prayer. I think that, our circumstances being such as they are, the gods will understand why we cannot present them with special offerings and sacrifices. And yet, of course," he placated those scowling men who would not presume to address a deity without first making a proper sacrifice, "we must, all of us at once, make an offering that will inform them of our gratitude. The one thing I know that is pleasing to all gods is incense. Therefore, we shall burn some sticks of incense, and in their fragrance we shall send our prayers heavenward. Do you approve of this?"

"Yes," they agreed, "it is good."

"Then I shall arrange a ceremony for us. Toward sunset, on deck. Tell everyone to be there."

"We shall tell them."

"But," Makino said, "should we not also express our thanks to the captain and the crew of this fine ship? They are the ones of this earth who, by their skill and unceasing work, kept this vessel afloat during those terrible days and nights."

"You are right. We did not think of them, in our respect for the gods. Please, do you tell the men of this ship of our gratitude."

"I shall, and willingly."

"And do you tell them, please, that if we were on land we would express our thanks with gifts of fish and rice, of saké and fruits and other good things. But that here, so far from land, we have no gifts to send up to them."

"They will be so informed. They will understand."

Captain Reagan, the pain of intense concentration written upon his face, upon his whole body, tried his damnedest to understand the tall samurai standing before him.

"Kapitanu, sah," Makino said slowly and carefully. "To you pahssangyas of you much sank you ahru prayingu, I sink."

What in God's Holy Name is this fella sayin'? Captain Reagan implored his attending angels. He could rarely catch a word of this man's lingo, even though that golden-haired whatshisname back there said that he spoke the King's English "like a native." Judging by the man's formal bows, the punctuating smiles, this speech was intended to be complimentary. He supposed.

As usual, he turned to the Chinese cabin-boy for interpretation and elucidation. A lift of the bushy eyebrows set off the heathen Chinee. "Him talkee, alla Japanee fella godown belowside likee sayee sankyou sankyou to Kapitansah, foa no godown below inside watah taifun time."

"Ah, ah," said Captain Reagan, immediately enlightened by this perfectly clear presentation in a perfectly recognizable variation upon the universal English tongue. Now why, in the Name of the Holy Pentecost, couldn't these blinkin' Nips learn to speak it as well? A simple language, really, a boon to commerce and industry ... Not like your Frog's Gabble, or the Spanish Flux, so damnably—Bowing in his turn to the samurai, beaming with happiness at being so kindly remembered, he said, remembering to shout, so that both infidels would be sure to hear, "Shure, and 'tis a foine kindness in them to be a-sayin' so. And yet, in truth, I must say, 'twas the Mercy of God and of His Blessed Mother—" Seeing the strained expressions on those two pagan countenances, he broke off. "Oh, Lord! God help us!"

Makino needed no translation for that. "Yesss," he said. "To orru godsu foru heruppu orru pahsangyas to givingu sanksu ah wanting, I sink. Kapitansu-sah say pahmission?"

"Permission granted," Captain Reagan cried, with enthusiasm, relieved that the man wished to withdraw so soon from his august presence. "Goodbye, goodbye," he crooned, as Makino bowed himself out of the cabin. The captain collapsed in his chair. Makino, proud of his success in negotiating an understanding in this berry difficurut Engrish ranguage, went below to call his countrymen.

Behold, now, Captain Reagan, clinging to the mainmast, scandalized beyond the verge of sanity, at sight of this heathen mummery taking place on the quarterdeck of his christened Christian ship. A veritable host of infidel Japanese, arrayed in rows upon that consecrated deck. Facing west, by God, toward darkest Japan, not east, toward the Holy Land of Our Holy Savior's birth. And, he fumed, while the tightening collar of his tunic damned near choked him, tossing stinkin' saké about his craft, sending clouds of heathenish smoke into the vault of spacious heaven! Pollution, he thought. "Abomination," he groaned, "Anathema!," he swore, too distraught to remember how, when he served as an altar boy, he loved most of all to swing the polished censer, sending puffs of Catholic incense into the cramped vault of his village church.

Knowing only one way to combat the forces of evil, he rushed to the foredeck, shouting for Mr. Jackson to come a-runnin'. Poor Mr. Jackson, interrupted in the midst of a most heavenly session of depilation—the first in six whole days!—came a-running, half dressed, half covered with unwanted hair, half wet with collapsing lather, half mad. "Mr. Jackson!," bellowed the maddened captain, "pipe all hands for'ard! For a *Christian* service of thanksgiving!"

While Mr. Jackson yelled for the bos'n, the captain dashed to his cabin. As the bos'n piped the dishevelled crew to his side, the captain joined them. Facing the hallowed east, turning his back upon the infidels who had taken possession of his own territory, by God, upon his own ship, by God, he glared at his wondering crew. With an exorcising flourish, he lifted the sacred book for all to see, rested it upon the bulge of his belly. It was a Church of England book, of course, this being a Jardine, Matheson vessel. But it was a Christian book, and that was the talisman he needed now.

It opened to a certain page. "Dearly Beloved," he began. "Oh, hell! Wrong place!," he grunted, flipping the pages violently until he found the right one. "Ah. Here 'tis. 'Oh, Thou Who hast delivered us from the perils of the deep . . . ' "

On the quarterdeck the Nipponjin, relieved by the ceremony from their double burden of guilt and gratitude, heard the sounds of strange and eery music. At first they thought it came from on high, the singing of apsara despatched from the Lord Buddha's Paradise. But keen ears soon traced it to the foredeck. Sharp eyes found the Fahsto Metto, half naked, waving his arms in a martial manner. Apparently he was exhorting the honorable sailors to emit a set of restrained battle cries, or possibly of ancient sacred chants. At that distance the respectful Nipponjin could not be quite sure.

The sailors sang a hymn of thanksgiving:

> From every stormy wind that blows,
> From every swelling tide of woes,
> There is a calm, a sure retreat,
> 'Tis found beneath the mercy seat.

"That's enough!," barked the captain, cutting short the upwelling of voices ruggedly bass and more or less tenor, all raised in praise of the Lord Jehovah. "Now," he looked uneasily over his shoulder, "sing 'My Soul, Be on Thy Guard.'"

Dutifully, with scarcely a pause for breath or pitch, they followed Captain's Orders and Mr. Jackson's lead:

> My soul, be on thy guard;
> Ten thousand foes arise;
> A host of sins are pressing hard,
> To draw thee from the skies.
>
> O watch and fight and pray!
> The battle ne'er give o'er;
> Renew it boldly ev'ry day,
> And help divine implore ...

"Ahh," the Nipponjin said, one to another, understanding not the words but sensing the anguish in this chanting. "The gaijin, too, are offering their thanks to the gods of Heaven and Earth.

But, certainly, theirs is a very strange way. Surely, the customs and ceremonies and thoughts of foreigners are most incomprehensible to us. Yet, equally surely, the goodness in their hearts is plain to see.''

Unknown to the voyagers, their rite too was about to end in a manner quite strange to most of them, if not actually incomprehensible. While the smoke of their incense swirled up, toward the approving gods, while Makino-sama led the people in the clapping of hands, the bowing, the saying of prayers, Koi was thinking that such gestures, while good in themselves, were not good enough in sum. In his opinion, a greater tribute was needed in thanks for rescue from such great dangers. He had lived in abject fear during the typhoon, not for himself but for Aiko, lying weak and helpless by his side. If they died together, he would not mind death's early claiming. But if she died and he did not, he knew that he would be crazed with grief during the few minutes that would pass between her death and his.

But she had not died. Pale and wan, she stood beside him now, while he thought of the greater gift he wanted to offer to the gods who had spared them. During the height of the storm, he remembered the votive offerings that fishermen and sailors make when they have been saved from death in the sea. While lying there in the narrow bunk, in the black box that might be their grave, he vowed that if Aiko and he were spared he, too, would make this sacrifice of the most apparent evidence of his manhood when the proper time came.

Now the time had come. Taking Aiko by the hand, he moved to the rail, above the greedy sea. While she watched, with more than her usual docility, he drew Ishi's sharp razor from his obi. Its bright glitter as he opened the blade attracted the attention of several men standing near, Ishi among them. While they stared at him and at that blade, he took hold of his topknot with his left hand. With the right hand he lifted the razor. In a few seconds the sharp steel cut through the rope of black hair. As the wind ruffled the strands still attached to his head, Koi held the severed topknot high, for the moment of his prayer, then let it fall into the water.

Nothing teaches better than good example, as priests and parents will say. The men who saw Koi offering his sacrifice recognized it at once as an example they wished to follow. Ishi took the razor from Koi's hand, saying, "Now it's my turn." Within a few seconds his topknot, too, fell into the sea, floated for a minute in the white wake, then sank to the realm of the gods who dwell at the bottom of the ocean. He stepped back from the rail, passing the razor to the next man. Some men, too eager to wait, ran down into the holds to fetch their razors or sharp knives, rushed back to the deck to make their offerings. Of the 147 male passengers aboard that lucky ship, 126 cut off "the hair of regret" that day.

The twenty-one others either scorned such a primitive practice ("only ignorant provincials would do a thing like that," sniffed Kuranosuke the pickler), or refused to part with their chommage because they believed that if they did so they would be parted, in time, from their manhood. "Saa," wondered Koi when he heard about this worrying man's excuse, "Do men exist who are not wholly men?" Koi was very young, not yet acquainted with the full list of tragedies that afflict all men in this world of evanescent things.

Of the trusting males who cut off their chommage only a few realized that, in doing so, they could also cut themselves free from some of the constraints that had kept them in subjection at home. Makino and Ishi, of course, recognized this at once, even before lifting the razor to do the deed. Gladly they threw away the hair of regret, asking only why they had not thought of doing so sooner. Those shaven foreheads: those cocks' combs of oiled and bound-up hair: those signs of rank, and therefore of servitude, so minutely prescribed by Tokugawa regulations with respect to size, shape, placement on the scalp, even to the quality of the oil a man might use in grooming it: they were thrown away without regret.

In the days following the cutting of his topknot Ishi enjoyed a new experience: shaking his head just to feel the soft caress of the loose unoiled hair still attached to the back of his scalp. Ahh, this is the very feel of freedom, he thought, vowing never again to shave the forepart of his head or to wear anything like the Toku-gawa topknot. Then, running a hand over his bristling pate, he would think of the future: with not a little vanity, he would won-der what style of foreigners' hairdress would be most becom-ing . . .

"You watch," said Makino one day, as they talked about the new freedoms the people were showing, along with the fuzz of new hair sprouting upon their heads. They were a funny-looking lot, to be sure, what with the long black hair waving around in the back, like tail feathers on a cock, while the front looked like garden patches in which seedlings were just beginning to poke up their heads. "They'll not grow those topknots again. They may not know this yet, but in time they will look upon the shaven pate as a badge of shame."

He was right. Many of the freed ones, after studying the heads of sailors and officers, started to cultivate heroic mustaches, bushy Burnsides, chin whiskers, and other hairy adornments, such as would have shocked everyone they'd left at home in Nippon.

Only a very few passengers could not grow a full head of hair. To his sorrow, if not his shame, Makino was one of these. "A cause of grief," he sighed, caressing the bald dome he'd never realized he owned. "It is ever the way of the gods, to deny a man the thing he most wants to have."

Yet to Ishi this hairless head of Makino-sama seemed to be on-ly the outward sign of his many great virtues. For, as is well known, do not the gods have their seat upon the brow of the just man?

Of the many males aboard the *Scioto,* only Mr. Jackson mourned the efflorescence of all that hair. He who loved those smooth-shaven faces, those gleaming skulls, especially those mar-velously suggestive topknots, cried in anguish to himself: Now they're going to be as hairy, and as *messy,* as everyone else . . .

CHAPTER 11

A FLOATING CLOUD,
A SAILING SHIP

For more than two weeks after the day of thanksgiving the voyagers prospered. Fair weather, good winds from the west, brisk sailing, and a general recovery of health made them think that even the most lingering curse had been lifted from them. As proof of recovering spirits, gamblers fell to fighting again, the chase after O-Miya resumed, and the four married women had to slap away the reaching hands of men hoping to enjoy privileges that are reserved for husbands. Even the Sad Woman was not safe from those men who agreed with Mother Hayashi's comment about lust being blind, whether by day or by night.

Yet, in general, this was a happy time. The players of samisen, shakuhachi, and fue, helped by thumpers of empty shoyu tubs, made music for many good-natured dances, especially of the kind from the villages around Yokohama and the districts of Edo. And Nagayuki did not hesitate to show the lusty Edokko that the people of Nikko, too, know how to dance and sing.

In Hold 2 thirteen-year old Ichigoro, dubbed the Viper for his viciousness, was cuffed into submission by some shipmates, coddled into good behavior by others. But when he was caught sneaking too many drinks from the private jug of saké belonging to Ozaemon, the Tattooed Juggler from Nipponbashi of Edo, the juggler's outraged friends threw the Viper headfirst into the privy and held him there for half a day. That treatment gained him both a bath and a long period of reform. But, alas, as the effects of the one wore off so did the controls of the other. Within the week he was just as nasty as ever, a far greater trial to Daigoro of Kamakura than any others of his charges.

The best of all possible omens was delivered to the wanderers in the fine son born to O-Tomi, the nineteen-year-old wife of Kintaro-san of Roppongi. Although this was her first child Tomi had an easy birthing, no doubt because of the placated gods. Daigoro was supposed to report the beginning of her labor pains, but at her entreaty he held back until the child was already born. She did not want that foreigner to help her bear a child of Nippon, she declared. When Daigoro said that no midwife was aboard to assist, she said that O-Yuki from Hold 3 knew enough about the bearing of children to be of great service to her. So Daigoro called the Sad Woman to Hold 2, and because of her skill all went well with O-Tomi. O-Yuki bathed the child, and swaddled it, before the doctor came.

Kintaro-san and his neighbors stood by to see that the foreign doctor did not exert any baleful influence upon either the child or the mother. Doctor Lee, seeing that he was not needed at all in this case, did not stay long. Kintaro politely thanked the doctor and, with a delegation of neighbors, accompanied him to the companionway. When the physician was safely gone the weary father and his friends hastened to salute the first-born son with gratulatory cups of saké. As a sign of forgiveness Ichigoro the Viper was allowed to pour the first cup of saké, offered to the gods who escorted this new spirit to its birthplace, so far from the land. But everyone carefully counted the cups that Ichigoro was permitted to drink for himself. At the seventh, when he showed signs of his usual contrariness, Ozaemon and Kintaro banished him to his bunk.

Makino-san, serving as priest, purified with sprinklings of salt water the infant, Tomi, the Sad Woman, the birthing place, and everything in reach of his aspersions.

"What will you name your son, Kintaro-san?," asked Makino as he joined the drinkers, now recovering from their ordeal.

"Ahh," Kintaro winked as a man will when he does not boast of his virility yet wants everyone to be thoroughly aware of it. "His name was chosen long ago. The day he was made."

"And?," said everyone.

"The male principle," said Kintaro, drawing from his fundoshi a small bronze amulet cast in the shape of that primal force, "is my first god. And," he winked again, "my great comforter. The boy's name, therefore, is decreed. 'Yotaro' it will be: Male Great Son."

"May he be a son worthy of his male great father," Makino lifted his cup in salute to the eternal verity.

"Ahh," intoned Ozaemon, rippling the muscles of his arms and chest in such a way that the tattooed dragons danced and the red, green, blue, and black flowers swayed, "the blessing of being a man."

"Almost everything goes well," wrote Yonekichi the diarist, "except for the food. It is bad. Very bad."

When the *Scioto* escaped from Yokohama she carried as provisions for her 155 passengers twenty sacks of white rice, five hundred sacks of unhulled rice, fifty tubs of miso paste, five tubs of shoyu, and one large chest of Chinese tea. That was all. No fish, no fowl, no seaweed wet or dried, no vegetables fresh or pickled were brought aboard because the quartermaster, a thrifty man, intended to buy all such stores the day before the ship sailed. Captain Reagan's sudden decision to hoist sail caught him unprepared.

"Not even the smallest of pickled plums," complained Yonekichi, "not even a moldy cabbage, or limp daikon." During the days of the typhoon they would have sold their sisters into whoredom for a bowl of cooked rice. But after a few days of eating nothing but a bowl of miso soup and a couple of bowls of rice—with shoyu or without shoyu—three times a day, their stomachs and mouths protested. Their memories played tricks on them, telling of all the good things they'd had to eat at home, saying nothing about the times of hunger and want. The men who, each day, were assigned to take the husks off the brown rice threatened to polish no more.

In that crowd of hungry tailors, cabinet makers, printers, potters, blacksmiths, cooks, barbers, stone masons, saké brewers, picklers of vegetables, candy makers, dyers of cloth, gamblers, drunkards, and city bums—all of whom had solemnly assured Hamada-san that they were expert farmers yearning to work as farmers in Hawai—only one happened to be a fisherman. And he was the last to remember his profession, possibly because so many months had passed since last he'd cast a hook into a fish's mouth.

They were sitting around on deck one afternoon, just after the midday meal. The belly is full, they mourned, but the mouth is empty. Only the taste of thin miso to linger on the tongue. Nothing pleasurable to recall in a good belch. Not a shred of fish between two teeth in shrinking gums, to be dug out with tooth-pick or long fingernail. Such suffering. Such privation!

"Miso that tastes of miso only," said Dembei, sounding worse than a nagging wife, "is not good miso."

"Ahh, what I wouldn't give for the taste of sashimi," said Eizo of Edo, the printer.

"Oh, for squid broiled over hot coals," sighed Ishi.

"I'd be happy with just a hand-long piece of takuan fresh from the pickle-crock," moaned Koi. "Good, cool, crisp, chewy takuan . . . *Fragrant* takuan . . . "

Watering mouths, tearful eyes forced them to stop such tortur-ing. It was like inviting a bee to sting a face already swollen with weeping.

"With a whole oceanful of fish out there, you'd think that we'd be able to sink our teeth into at least one," said the printer, gaz-ingly sadly at Koi's kimono, wishing that, by some god's timely intervention, all those painted fish could be made to come alive.

Only then did Koi wake up from his mixed-up fantasies of pickled daikon and passionate Aiko. Pressing his left forefinger to the left side of his mouth, he announced, "You are looking at the biggest fool afloat on this biggest of all fishponds." Saying no more, he rushed away, leaving them to think that, as usual, he went to throw himself atop Aiko. How he does it, with only miso and rice to eat, I can't imagine, the delicate printer was thinking, when Koi came rushing back.

By the providence of the gods who take care of fisherman

ashore and asea, the fish hooks he'd bought for use in Hawai proved to be much more valuable in the middle of the Great Peaceful Ocean. While Ishi went to gain Makino's help in winning the captain's permission, Koi rigged a trolling line, using several of his larger hooks and a long rope borrowed from that very friendly First Mate, who smiled upon Koi as fondly as does a shark about to devour a young tuna. Because tuna fish are so stupid that they will snap at naked hooks Koi needed no bait. But because fishermen must attract the attention of those stupid tunas to the hooks Koi cut small strips from a clean fundoshi and, near each hook, tied a piece of the cloth in a tight knot with long dangling ends. Having gained the captain's approval, he cast the line over the side, into the *Scioto*'s wake. Within a few minutes the prowling fish discovered this new kind of prey, and the fisherman enjoyed the applause of his shipmates while they hauled in two katsuo of moderate size. "Sometimes," he explained to his friends, "big fish are smarter than small ones."

Thereafter they never lacked at least a small piece of fish each day for everyone aboard, or men to haul in the line, or bait with which to catch other kinds of fish than tunas. Mindless tunas, hungry mackerel, and curious dolphins made up the usual catch, but on many occasions they pulled in strange creatures they'd never seen before yet ate just as readily.

One day they snagged a ragged lump of waxy, sweet-smelling golden stuff. They took turns at feeling it, sniffing at it. Then, deciding that it must be "sea rubbish," not fit to eat, not worth keeping, they threw the perfumed thing back into the water.

"Everything goes better now," wrote Yonekichi. "More than half our journey is done. The people are in high spirits."

The spirits of some were too high, too bothersome, decided Makino and his lieutenants one afternoon. They sentenced Takesuke and Torakichi, two young bullies from Edo, to twenty-four hours in the ship's brig, in irons, as punishment for a prank they played upon a "Nanking," as the Nipponjin called the five Chinese cooks. When his back was turned those two varlets dumped ashes from the galley stove into a pot of boiling water. This so angered the Nanking that he threw some of the hot water at them, but fortunately it did not scald them. Makino and his tribunal decided that Takesuke and Torakichi must be punished for the harm they caused. "The prank itself is a minor trouble," said Makino to the abashed pair, "the lack of respect shown to officials of this ship and to your shipmates is a serious one. And so is wasting precious water. Freedom does not mean that a man can do what he likes without regard for the welfare of other men around him." Unmentioned, but pressing upon the minds of all, was the delay of a whole hour in serving the evening meal, because the water in that dirtied pot had to be replaced.

Fist fights and stabbings happened so often among the city bums that the brig could not have held all the law-breakers. Makino punished them in other ways: they husked rice, washed dishes, cleaned benjos, swept decks. The ones who stabbed were made to take care of the ones they'd injured. Soon the rasher men learned to keep their fists in kimono sleeves, daggers in sheaths, and to fight only with their tongues. Lest tongues urge them into worser troubles, Makino ordered them to give all knives, daggers, scissors, and other sharp things, including razors, into the keeping of the women in each hold. They released those articles only when the owners actually needed to use them.

Makino did not attempt to stop drinking or gambling. "A foolish rule," he snorted, "made by fools who've never looked at life. Or spent long days and nights with nothing to do. How else can these men pass the time?"

"Especially," said Daigoro, speaking for many unmarried men aboard, "without women to help them while away those long hours."

O-Miya's search for a husband worthy of her helped somewhat to lighten those long hours—and gave gamblers endless reasons for laying bets, if not herself. Although a few men fled from her in terror, and others hid in the shadows—Yonekichi confessed to being one of these because, as he wrote, "I do not like a woman with her forward disposition"—she did not lack suitors. They surrounded her day and night, paying court. They played Go with her, at which she was very proficient, and hanafuda, at which she excelled, and guessing games of many kinds, at which she was very clever, having a mind that noticed everything and forgot nothing.

"I could let you win these games, you realize," she said, "and flatter you for now. But that would be most dishonest of me. And very disappointing for you, later," she looked around at all those men, panting like hounds on a hunt, "if you should be the one to marry me." She was a very intelligent woman.

She would not play for money. "I do not wish to win, and thereby become richer than my future husband. I wish to be as poor as he, sharing his poverty as well as his bed." She was a very generous woman.

On the first evening of the voyage she made known the kind of man she sought for a husband. "I don't care if he is not handsome. The beauty of his heart I seek, not of his body. And he need not be young—although, of course, he must not be too old to enjoy the excitements of bed. After all, I still do. But he must be a man who is in good health, who does not mind working hard for a living. I have seen too many women who are starving because their husbands are lazy, or sickly, or spendthrift. 'Extravagance can eat you up,' " she repeated the proverb that parents have mouthed ever since children learned to ask for money. "If he has a weak mind, I shall not care, as long as he has a good heart. And," she brought to an end her description of this paragon among husbands, a creature of her imagination who could not possibly exist in real life, the while she, a paragon of wifely virtue, turned only the most modest of glances upon those eager men, hoping to bed her before the night was ended, "he must not be the kind who spends his time and money on prostitutes. Why should he be searching for such diversion away from home, when he'll have me, in his home?"

"Saa," the men said, and "Dame da," and other less polite expressions of disgust and dismay, as they fell away in droves, dis-

couraged by so many obstacles to achievement, and much per-
plexed by this woman who behaved like a cloistered nun and
talked like a grand oiran. Nevertheless, after the storm many men
continued to be attentive to her, admiring her wit if not her
wisdom, enjoying her company if not her body. And certain of
them—but who knows who they are?—crept to her bunk during
the hours of darkness, thinking that what was denied by day
would be permitted by night. Foreseeing this, she put up a
"screen of state" across the opening to her bunk, which, in
prudence, she had chosen at the topmost level. To each whispered entreaty she replied, very distinctly, for everyone to hear,
"No. Only my husband can enter here. And I have not yet chosen
him."

But, as the sage has said, lust has no bottom. And hope has no
bounds. One night a man not easily rebuffed—and beyond any
doubt most desperate—tried to push beyond that screen of state.
A whole wind-chime of empty saké bottles, hung by samisen
strings, jangled and clanked long after he fell back and fled.

She was a very remarkable woman, that O-Miya. Nonetheless,
Yonekichi still could not like her, impressed though he was by
her good qualities. "I pity the man she chooses to be her mate,"
he wrote. "He will have no peace, from either end of her."

As they counted the days, felt the warming breezes blowing up
from the tropics, they were almost happy. Then, on the twentieth
day of the voyage, neighbors reported that Wakichi-san, a man in
Hold 3, was unable to rise from his bunk. Ishi went to ask what
might be wrong. He found the man beyond the reach of questions, sunk in his last sleep.

A neighbor whispered, "It is the kakke, I think."

"How can you tell?," asked Ishi, drawing back. The dreaded
kakke, a wasting disease that sometimes kills its victims, which
never fails to make them suffer most miserably: he did not want
this affliction to fall upon him, or upon any man.

"By the swollen legs. The flesh sinks in, when it is pressed, and
does not come out again until after a long time. By the sore

muscles, the trouble in walking. And, lately, Wakichi-san has had trouble just to breathe."

Other neighbors gathered around. Some confirmed the signs of Wakichi's sickness, but could not say what they meant. All expressed worry that now they would be possessed by this same evil.

"Why do you worry only now?," Nagayuki asked Ishi. "He's been sick since we came aboard. But only lately has he been too weak to eat with the rest of us."

"Did he not eat?," asked Ishi sharply. That gaunt body, not much more than skin and bones above, swollen in the legs below, made him suspect that Wakichi was starving to death. "And why did you not tell me before this that he was sick?"

"Oh, yes. We fed him," Nagayuki replied. "We brought him rice. Because he would eat nothing else, we brought him only white rice. The best. Three times a day. And we took turns carrying him to the benjo. We did not tell you because we felt you were busy enough with other duties."

Relieved to hear that Wakichi's friends had not neglected him, Ishi went off to call the doctor. He shook his head when he saw the unconscious man, he lifted up the eyelids, peered into those unseeing eyes, listened to the breathing, prodded at the thin arms and puffed legs. Shaking his head still, Dr. Lee went to report to the captain.

"Looks like we've got a case of beriberi aboard, sir. Pretty bad one, too, I'm afraid. Fella's close to death . . . "

"How can that be possible? I thought all these coolies were warranted healthy when we took 'em aboard? And this beriberi: isn't it slow to take hold, slow to kill?"

"Usually, yes. But who knows about this fella? If I'd seen him in Yokohama, I might have caught him then. If they'd told me sooner that he was sick below, I'd have given him medicine. But I saw him not, they told me not. How long has he been lying there, ignored by his mates? They're a callous lot, from what I've seen of 'em. All of 'em. In Siam. China. Japan. All alike. Indifferent to everything, sickness and death most of all. Fatalistic, I'd say. Inbred in 'em. Matter of religion. Or, rather, lack of it."

"Aye. Ain't no charity amongst the heathen, Dr. Lee. 'Each man for himself,' is their motto. 'Dog eat dog,' is their rule. And 'Devil take the hindmost' is their reward. See it all the time. He will die, you say, this fella? Best so, I guess. And what of the rest? Will they take the sickness?"

"God only knows. The way they're crowded in down there, they'll take it, every last one of 'em, if it is a contagion. Medical authorities differ upon this head, however, as it is a most mystifying disease."

"All I want you to tell me is whether or no 'tis a disease for which we'll be put in quarantine, in Honolulu."

"Not so far as I'm aware. Unless the Hawaiian government invokes other laws than civilized countries do."

"Glory be! All I need now is to be laid up with this voracious lot for forty more days and forty more nights."

"We can only wait and see, at this juncture. I have always maintained, sir, that a medical man can only ease the bodies of suffering men. God is the One Who giveth life, and Who taketh it away."

"Then let us hope, Dr. Lee, that on this ship He will take no more than one of those lives, down there below."

The next morning Wakichi-san died, gasping for breath in the Sad Woman's arms, as she tried to ease his agony. Saying nothing—for what can be said in the face of death—she and her brother laid him down in his cold bed. Life is a candle's light in the wind.

The doctor came, not to help Wakichi but to certify that he was dead. That being done he bade all the people who lived in bunks near Wakichi's to go above with him. By the clear light of day he examined them, in legs, arms, faces, chests, for signs of the beriberi. Toward the end of the inspection he became more cheerful, inasmuch as he found no sure sign of the disease among those passengers.

Sailors went down into the hold, bearing a length of old sailcloth, pieces of weathered rope, and a heavy stone. Using signs, they told Ishi to order his people to place the dead man upon the sailcloth. Ishi alone lifted small Wakichi from the bunk, gently laid him down upon his last bed. The sailors put the ballast stone at his feet, folded the canvas about him as a fishmonger wraps a flounder, tied the two ends with rope, and carried the burden away.

Soon after, Makino-san entered, bearing the bowl of holy water with which he cleansed Hold 3 and the dwellers in it of the defilement caused by death.

Captain Reagan wished to show proper respect to the dead, inasmuch as he feared Death more than he valued any living creature. Within the hour he summoned everyone in his ship to the funeral for Wakichi-san.

Once again the passengers stood in ordered rows. This time they faced the bow of the ship, toward the east, the direction where the days begin and all promises are fulfilled. Because Wakichi had been an infidel the captain did not read Christian prayers for the dead, but everything else was done as though a British sailor lay wrapped in that gray shroud. Wakichi's body, looking so small and so flat in that company of upright folk, lay upon a trestle against the port rail. On either side were ranged sailors and officers, all in clean uniforms, each with a hat upon his head. Above them the great grayed sails swelled like the breasts of doves in flight.

Makino-sama, daimyo, priest, and comforter to his people, spoke to them. He and the three other samurai wore the kamishimo, the "upper and lower" garments of their class, that is to say, the kataginu, or surcoat, wide and stiffened at the shoulders, and the hakama, heavy formal trousers, seeming almost like wide skirts. Without the two swords under their obi, however, they looked strange to the people, as though they were not quite properly dressed.

Knowing nothing about Wakichi the man, Makino spoke to them about the immortal spirit which dwells within each one of us during the allotted span of his life: "The wheel of his life has

turned and, in turning, has brought Wakichi's years to their destined end. Now his spirit has gone to stand before Emma-o and
his tribunal to be judged. So must the spirit of each one of us be
judged, when his wheel ceases to turn.''

The thought was not new: it was as old as are the fears and
hopes of mankind. The Nipponjin heard it impassively and unquestioningly, as they always do who are so accustomed to death.
Unlike Captain Reagan and his sailors, they did not fear death
because they knew that, for everyone except a saint, the end of
this life is only the beginning of the next: the Wheel of Karma,
set in motion by the Lord Buddha, who is kind, will allow them
another chance at a better life when this round is ended. Life and
death is man's lot. Birth and death are swift. Death is only a
floating cloud, through which we pass upon our journey toward
the sunshine of eternal life.

Many times had they heard the ''Sermon on Mortality,'' with
its reminder: ''Sooner or later, on this day or the morrow, to me
or to my neighbor, Death will come . . . So shall the rosy cheeks
of morning give way to the skull of eventide. One breath from the
wind of change, and the bright eyes shall be closed . . . ''

If they had been at home in Nippon for Wakichi-san's funeral
they might have enjoyed the occasion, and few would have listened to Makino-sama's words. But on this fragile ship, heeling
with the wind, they knew they were not at home. The setting filled
them with grim and fearful thoughts. The ship itself, stark and
gray, seemed lost upon an immense and trackless sea. Wakichi
lay bound up, as dead as a silkworm's steamed cocoon. No burning incense, no flowers, no memorial tablet honored him. They
themselves stood upon a slanting deck, with no solid earth beneath their feet, no hills or plains or forests beyond the rails to
serve as boundaries to a familiar home. Sorrow for themselves
clutched at their hearts, not grief for dead Wakichi, as they recognized how they had condemned themselves to the same lonely
end, without priests to pray for their spirits, without relatives to
care for their graves. Who, now, would chant for them, when they
died, ''The Threefold Refuge,'' or ''The Dedication,'' or ''The

Hymn to the Buddha"? Who would intone over them the "Amida Sutra," which promises the salvation of all living things, which tells of the numberless eons of time through which that salvation can be won?

Makino strove to comfort them, by reminding them of a thing they had forgotten: "Yet, we must remember, just as the wheel of Wakichi's life neared the time of its stopping, by the grace of the Lord Buddha a new wheel entered into the time of its turning— the wheel of Yotaro, son of Kintaro-san and O-Tomi-san. And soon the life of the child of Moshichi-san and O-Haru-san will begin. And after those will come other sons and other daughters, who will be born to you in the new land. With them to grow up about us, who can say that the new land will not soon be a second home to us?"

He is right, they told themselves, seeing things in the light of reason, forgetting for the moment the terrors of loneliness. He fastens our hope again, to the only truth, when he reminds us of the force of yo, the principle of immortality.

"Now let us say farewell to the body of Wakichi-san," said Makino. They wondered how they were supposed to do this, in such a strange place, neither temple nor shrine nor cemetery. Few had guessed what was to be done with the husk that Wakichi left behind.

Facing that meaningless remnant, Makino said, "Tonsho bodai. May he rest in peace."

"Tonsho bodai," the people murmured, as the wind of change ruffled their hair, pressed the flesh of their cheeks against the skulls beneath.

Makino lifted his hand toward Captain Reagan. The captain made a sign to the bos'n. He blew a short command with his whistle. As two sailors stepped forward, one at either side of the trestle, Makino bowed toward Wakichi's body, and to his spirit beyond. Following Makino's example, his countrymen bowed in the instant, all the men standing in exactly the same posture, the women bent forward even more humbly. The two sailors tipped the board upon which the gray bundle lay. More honored in death than ever he had been noticed in life, little Wakichi-san allowed his body to slip easily into the sea.

The Nipponjin could not forget their horror at seeing how casually these foreigners threw away the bodies of dead men. Without thought to give it life, they saw, the body is indeed but a log. After that moment of shock the wanderers yearned all the more strongly for the land. All the water in the sea could not wash away their feelings of helplessness.

"When shall we reach Honolulu?," they asked the Nankings and those sailors who spoke a few of the comforting words of Nippon.

"Ten days, perhaps," the answers came, "perhaps twelve, or fifteen."

The Wheel of Time, they learned, which hurries so quickly on the land, turns too slowly upon the sea.

Yet for Miya, the chaste prostitute, the Wheel of Time spun along as merrily as a pinwheel in a spring breeze. She had no chance to be bored or sad. For some strange reason, the farther away they traveled from Yokohama the more numerous her suitors became. Some of those importunate men tried to beguile her with toothful smiles and honeyed tongues. Some tried to charm her with little gifts, offered now, or with promised fortunes, to be delivered later. One brash Edokko, a potter from Imado in Asakusa, attempted to settle everything with his brute's strength. When he picked her up, intending to throw her into his bunk right then and there, she did not even have to scream. Her other suitors beat him with fists, geta, a pump handle fetched from the place of convenience, until he put her down. And then they beat him even harder, for trying to take advantage of O-Miya, not to mention all of her patient suitors.

"Kono yaro," she said coldly, pushing hairpins back into place, straightening her kimono. "I do not like a violent man. Either for a lover or for a husband."

O-Miya's scorn, the beating his former friends gave him, were punishment enough for the rogue, said Makino and his lieutenants when they were informed of this attack upon a woman of great virtue.

When she had thoroughly inspected the men in Hold 2 Miya went on visits to the other quarters. While there she helped the married women to wash and dress their hair in the marumage style, always a laborious procedure which leaves much time for pleasant conversation. Sometimes they assisted her with the more elaborate style of hair dressing she still wore. She found many an opportunity to engage the men in racy talk or in games of chance. She was a charming entertainer to everyone, and helped them, too, to while away the hours when they were not working at some small labor for the whole group or lounging about with their male companions.

As the days passed she actually became more beautiful, not only in the eyes of the men. The women, too, remarked the change in her appearance. The gradual whitening of her teeth, as the black dye wore away, accompanied the fading of the dark circles under her eyes. She used less rice powder, no longer feeling the need to hide wrinkles unbecoming in a whore but expected in a wife who has reached the age of thirty. Her unfailing wit, always clever but never malicious, the bright eyes, always searching for the one man she wanted above all other men, and, underneath all this, the graceful body of a woman who knew how to suggest without revealing, convinced many a fellow that he would pine for the rest of his life if O-Miya chose another to be her husband.

In addition to those strange men who are not interested in women, such as the pairs who were as good as wed, or the solitary ones who are content with themselves, Ishi was one of the few passengers who avoided her. Like Yonekichi he felt that her public search for a husband was not decent. Nonetheless, like most Nipponjin, he was not prudish about harlots in general, and certainly did not object to the honorable custom of a prostitute's buying her freedom in order to marry and have a family. But, he argued, this O-Miya was just too pushy, too unwomanly, for his taste. If she wanted a husband, he maintained, she should do what all decent woman do and ask for the help of a baishakunin, a matchmaker. With Makino-san, Daigoro-san, Tetsuo-san, and others available to serve in that honorable capacity, she could not say that she lacked a go-between. Naturally, the gossips soon carried talk of Ishi's strong opinions to her ears. Ishi had not known enough about his grandfather's example to realize that a man is safe from reprisals only when he keeps his mouth shut.

"Hmm," she said, with a far-away look in her eyes. "Who is this Ishi, that he should be so disapproving? I must have a word with him."

One day, as he rushed past her on deck, skittish as a colt fearing the halter, she stopped him with an uplifted sleeve. "Don't worry, dear," she tapped him gently with her fan. "You're too cold for my taste. And," she drew back a little, regarding him like an elder sister chastening an erring brother. "And, I think, too cruel."

"Too cruel?," he cried, who thought himself as being the kindest of men, the one most ready to help people in need.

"Oh, not with your hands, perhaps, or with words," she replied, giving him her patient, long-suffering look, the one she used upon men who must be taught that women, too, are feeling beings, not just holes to be plugged for men's enjoyment. "But in your heart. And therefore in your thoughts. But that's all right. 'The broad ocean does not mind the dust.' Please think of this, when you find the time. You're such a busy man, I notice . . . " With another admonitory tap from the fan she left him. Those proud lips of his were parted wide, that shocked man's mind was thinking very hard, indeed, as he watched her trip away.

So they sailed along, across the desert sea. The *Scioto* was not at all like the crowded vessel that carried the Seven Gods of Luck from China to Nippon. There were no gods aboard this foreign ship. And if, perchance, a certain number of fools were present, they were not as conspicuous as are the many who can be found on land. Dembei of Meguro, the bandy-legged man who shouted

"Fool!" when he strolled through the ship one night, did not repeat his unnerving performance. And no one ever saw a ghost or a fox-spirit lurking in the dark holds.

Yet beyond doubt the gods did hover above the ship—or some of the gods, at any rate—to watch over their people on the journey to Tenjiku. They allowed Wakichi to die, because his time had come to rest for a while. They allowed Yotaro to be born, because his time had come to suffer for a while. And Benten must have been there, at least briefly, to preside over the occasion when Koi, whose name means "love," put into Aiko, whose name means "child of love," the beginning of a child made with love.

The gods brought them safely across the wide waters, to the promised land. On the thirtieth day of their voyaging they saw many birds flying about, skimming the sea for food, and, towering above the horizon to the southeast, great masses of clouds. "Land is near," the sailors said, pointing toward the clouds, and the eager passengers gathered on deck to catch their first glimpse of it. Later in the afternoon they were rewarded: the clouds drew apart and floated away, and the people saw, green and golden in the slanting light, the rampart mountains of Kauai, lifted high above the sea. "There is Tenjiku," they said. "It is not a vision. It is a paradise ... "

"Tomorrow," the word went around, "if this wind does not fail, we shall arrive in Honolulu."

But the gods had one more affair to settle before they brought the pilgrims safe to harbor. In that memorable evening aboard the *Scioto*, all of them—beginning with the ancestral gods themselves—gathered around to help Benten, the Goddess of Love, as she helped O-Miya to choose her wanted husband.

Everyone was excited, naturally, except for Miya herself. She seemed to have no cares, no doubts. Not because she had decided upon the one man, but because, in her secret thoughts, she had narrowed the possibilities to three most pleasing candidates. Each was handsome, virile, and good in heart. Given such odds, in the gambles of fate, how can a woman be nervous? She delayed in making her choice merely because she wanted to apply one more little test. The man who won this test would win the love of her mind as well as the gift of her body.

O-Miya bathed and dressed for her wedding, singing a hopeful song:

I have no wish for
A frivolous or coquettish existence,
I want the deep life of love.

I have set up the double screen
Against a wind scented with plum blossoms.

Come to me and I will love you
In the tender light of the veiled moon,
I will love you, far from the plum trees.

O-Aiko and O-Haru, the day before, had helped to wash O-Miya's long hair and to dress it in the shimada style worn by many women of marriageable age. Checking in her memory the things she would need for this plighting, she felt the deep satisfaction of one who realizes that she has thought of every thing, and of every possibility. The one pleasure she decided to forego was the arranging of her hair in the style of a girlish bride. To do that, she felt, would be so presumptuous as to run the risk of offending the gods on high, not to mention the more critical people on ship.

During the evening meal both inquisitive neighbors and hopeful suitors hailed her with questions and expectant looks. "Later," she waved them off with a graceful hand, "later... Please be patient... "

With nothing to stake save their reputations as prophets, some men placed bets upon one suitor, some upon others. At the last count at least a dozen favored prospects were noted—some by their preening selves. When neighbors mentioned their names to O-Miya, in the hope that she might betray her heart's inclination with some inadvertent response, she looked at them in sweet dismay. "Oh, dear! I can never remember their names... "

By the time she and her train of suitors and their attendant supporters sat down to the usual game of Gomoku everybody was as overwrought as is the audience in a kabukiza, just before the three-colored curtain is swept aside. More people than had ever assembled in Hold 2 gathered there on this climactic evening, just to be among the first to know who would be the chosen man. Yonekichi, Daigoro, Ishi, many another scoffer, sat there, too, in the darkness at the sides of the long room, as did all the women, come to enjoy O-Miya's celebration. In honor of the occasion three lanterns lighted the space before the butt of the mainmast, where Miya and her court played their games of chance. Above the lanterns, in the shadows, hovered the helpful gods.

O-Miya knew exactly what she must do. Everything depended, as in any important engagement, upon the deploying of forces and the times at which they are used. Moving toward this end, she played—and won—a couple of fast sets of Gomoku with suitors who did not interest her. In the process of defeating them she contrived to maneuver herself and the Gomoku board into a place within conversational range of the three favorites. The field of battle having been so narrowed to support her strategy, she rested her white hands upon the board. The subtle test she had in mind did not require anyone to push little black and white pebbles around on a checkered board.

She began the test. "My, it's hot in here this evening," she said, fanning herself languidly.

"Too many people," growled one of the many, looking in disgust at all those intruders.

"Do you suppose that it's because the islands of Hawai are so hot?," she inquired, as though she earnestly desired to learn the multitude's opinion upon this most fascinating of subjects.

"Who can say?," replied two or three men, profoundly unaffected by this form of heat.

"You know," she said hesitantly, not wanting to impose her foolish woman's fancies upon a company of such stalwart men, "our coming to this new island reminds me of the time when our Heavenly Ancestors, Izanagi and Izanami, came down from the Celestial Realm to the Island of Onogoro."

No one could find a word to say. Half of them had never heard of Onogoro. The others could not understand what connection this austere conversation could possibly have with O-Miya's choosing a husband. A few, spectators as well as suitors, allowed themselves to entertain impatient thoughts about such chatter.

Undeterred by this great silence, she said, "On Onogoro—you remember?—they were alone. Only the two of them."

"Bakayaro," muttered the man who got that way sometimes. Dozens of fuzzy heads nodded, but whether in response to her or in agreement with him no one could be quite sure.

"Then, because they needed a home to live in, Izanagi stuck his Heavenly Jewelled Spear into the ground of Onogoro. And from it grew a Heavenly Pillar, and then a great palace, the Hall of Eight Fathoms, rose around them."

Utter silence, utmost puzzlement, rose around them in Hold 2. From the three favored suitors came not a sound, not a flicker of recognition for this most stirring of all Nippon's tales. They sat there, those three, those dozens, as though they were wayside stones listening to a wandering storyteller relating dull parables in a foreign tongue. They stared at her as if she were an idiot, not a woman hoping for a man to speak across the silence of others, to tell her that he, too, knew the myth of Izanagi and Izanami. Above all to tell her that, because she knew the wonderful story, he would love her for her mind as well as for her body.

"They looked at each other with open eyes," Miya continued bravely. "And with open hearts," she amended slightly the sacred lines. "And they talked of their desire to become man and wife."

Ahh! Now the listeners could understand where she was leading, this very clever woman. With sly nudges and merry winkings the audience came awake, taking a lively interest in this stimulating show. Miya looked expectantly at the hopeful candidates, at the favored three. But no one spoke to her, in words of any kind. They sat, as silent and unmoving as are the carven images of the Five Hundred Disciples of Shaka assembled in the Rakanji in Edo.

"Then Izanagi spoke to Izanami, saying—" In desperation, she broke off. This was the essential part of the test. They must respond, she cried in her heart, they must, else it will be of no use. Turning to the most favored one, thinking that he might be shy and in need of coaxing, she asked, "Do you remember what he said?" When he failed to answer, simply looking stupidly at her, she turned to the other two, no longer caring that, in doing so, she might reveal to the observant her heart's secret choices. But they, too, stared back at her, silent as the headstones in a graveyard, more ignorant than she'd ever imagined grown men could be.

"Oh, my," she sighed aloud, as cold despair moved into her heart, pushing out a foolish woman's futile hope. "Doesn't anyone know?," she made one last attempt, sending out her hope on its quest among the faceless crowd, beyond the three who had failed.

" 'How is thy body formed?' " asked a voice, deep and thrilling, from out of the darkness behind the mast.

Miya could not see him, but her heart leaped at his response. "And Izanami replied," she spoke quickly, for him alone, " 'My body is completely formed, except for one part, which is incomplete.' "

"Then Izanagi said," that deep voice took up the myth, " 'My body is completely formed, yet there is one part which is provided in abundance. Let us add to that part which is incomplete in thee the part which is abundant in me.' "

Ahh, the enraptured people thought, this is a fascinating story, so wondrously told. Ahh, thought Miya, here now is the man I have been seeking. Here now, at last, is the husband I have been wanting . . .

As in a dream Miya spoke the next lines of the myth: "Izanami replied, 'It is well,' " Holding fast to the dream, she talked with her heart: Who is this wonderful man? And why have I not met him? Never before have I heard such a voice! I am in love with his voice, before ever I see his body . . .

"Then Izanagi said, 'Let me and thee go around the Heavenly

August Pillar and, meeting on the other side, let us become united in marriage.' " His memory was as flawless as his voice. He knew what she was asking, this unknown man, he *knew*, and he responded to her need for him. She was his, she belonged to him, to his mind and to his body, no matter how he looked. He could be as ugly as a frog, as old and wrinkled as a dried persimmon, she did not care. She would love him because of that voice, sweet as the sound of choirs of apsara, strong as the tide of passion at its flood.

She put aside the Gomoku board, rose carefully to her feet, all but faint with joy. " 'It is agreed to,' " she said, into the darkness beyond the mainmast, toward the man who spoke now only to her.

" 'Do thou go around from the *right*,' " he ordered, emphasizing the direction she must take, thereby telling her that they two must avoid making the tragic mistake that Izanagi and Izanami had made when first they met. In their innocence—or was it, perhaps, in their eagerness?—Izanami went around the Sacred Pillar from the left, which is the privilege of males, thereby affronting the male gods of the Celestial Realm. "And I," he continued, "will go around from the left." As he spoke he moved slowly toward the mainmast, rising, like the Heavenly August Pillar, into the remote sky, where stars shine to light the Plains of High Heaven.

Scarcely knowing what she did, Miya glided toward the Heavenly August Pillar, to meet the man she had not yet seen, the man who was her destined husband. To the left he stepped, handsome as a warrior going to meet his lord. To the right she went, shy as a maid upon the path to a temple. Slowly, as if they walked alone on the Island of Onogoro, they moved, one toward the other, around the Pillar of Life, until they came together.

He spoke first, as is proper to the man. " 'How delightful! I have met a lovely woman.' "

And she, almost swooning, peering into the darkness to see the husband whom the gods had granted her, cried out in great joy: " 'How delightful! I have met a lovely man!' "

Falling upon his breast, she began to weep, like a true woman.

"Nani?," he chided her. "Are these tears for your chosen husband?"

"Tears of joy are these," she whispered. "And are those smiles for your accepted wife?"

He laughed. "Would I have submitted to taking your learned test if I did not want you for my wife?"

From the far side of the August Pillar the audience to this moving drama of virtue rewarded set up a great noise, demanding to see and hear the actors in it.

"Then, my husband, do you go before me, into the light, and I shall walk behind you."

"So shall it be," he said gravely. "We must follow the Way of the Gods, as Izanagi and Izanami have taught us."

When they came forward into the light all the smiling people fell silent, waiting for her to speak. Who would have thought that O-Miya the Huntress, who never lacked for speech, should so suddenly become O-Miya the Wordless?

At last, however, she held back those tears, found her voice. "Many of you have said that I should have asked a baishakunin to arrange my marriage. Therefore, I ask Ishi-san to come here now, to be my go-between, my father, and my family. The viewing-meeting, between my future husband and myself, as you see, has been most successful. Now I ask Ishi-san to present me in marriage to this fine husband, whom the gods have sent to me."

Amid loud applause and laughter for the happy couple, Ishi stumbled forward, blushing and apologizing at the same time. This Miya, he was thinking, this forward woman: she has taught every Nipponjin aboard this ship a number of valuable lessons. And I shall not be the slowest of her pupils.

"Here is the saké," Miya said to Ishi, "here are the cups. Just as in a wedding at home." Aiko came up, carrying a piece of board as a tray, upon which rested a small flagon and two tiny cups. Ishi took the tray and, kneeling, placed it on the deck at the couple's feet. Haru, wife to Moshichi, placed the tsunokakushi, the headdress of stiff white cloth, upon Miya's head, to cover forever the horns of jealousy. Yuki, the Sad Woman, almost smiling, slipped a kimono of white silk, lined with scarlet, over Miya's shoulders. In an instant they had transformed her into a bride. Everyone gazed in admiration upon this brave woman who, more than a month ago, had thought of everything she would need for her wedding, and now even provided the husband for it.

Miya held the kimono in such a way that only its white face showed. White is the color of death, and a bride wears it at her wedding because marriage means that she no longer belongs to her father's family. Yuki, in the place of her mother, led Miya to the right side of the hold, and sent her forth alone upon her journey. The women, prepared for this sad moment, began to sing the Farewell Part of the Wedding Song. Soon the men joined in, with their deep voices:

> From the shore
> A boat with lifted sail
> Rides toward the rising moon.
> On waves of the ebbing tide it sails,
> The shadow of the land falls behind,
> And the boat sails farther . . . farther . . .

With bowed head and faltering footsteps Miya made the journey from parent's home to husband's. At the far end of the hold, when the bride must turn and come toward the light, Koto, wife to Busuku, helped her to reverse the kimono. Now, clothed in scarlet, the color worn by a new-born child, to show that she was being reborn in the family of her husband, Miya came forward, toward the waiting groom. And all the people sang the Welcoming Part of the Wedding Song:

> On the sea
> A boat with lifted sail
> Rides toward the rising moon.
> On the waves of the flowing tide it comes,
> The shadow of her past lies far behind.
> And the boat sails nearer . . . nearer . . .
> To the shore called Happy Life.

And men and women alike wept with joy and sadness over this touching ceremony, so beautiful a reminder of home.

Ishi took Miya's cool hand and placed it in the warm hand of her chosen mate. He knelt before them, asking the pair to kneel beside the tray of saké. He poured the wine into the two little cups, offered them to the couple. Each sipped of the saké, exchanged cups, sipped again, once more exchanged cups, and once again drank of the wine. Three times did Ishi fill the cups, nine times did they drink of the sacred wine. And when the San-San-Kudo, the Three-Three-Nine Way, was finished they were wed, in the eyes of men. The gods, who arrange all marriages in Heaven, do not ask for such rituals.

Ishi stood up and faced the waiting crowd. The people stood up, most willingly.

"Banzai for the beautiful bride," cried Ishi, raising both hands high over his head.

"Ten thousand years for O-Miya-san!," the people shouted in glee.

"Banzai for the handsome groom!," Ishi cried.

"Ten thousand years for Daigoro-san!," they roared, making a noise that pleased the gods on high.

CHAPTER 12
THE WELCOMING

Thirty-three days out of Yokohama, the *Scioto* lay off Honolulu harbor, while the port physician examined her passengers and crew for evidences of unwanted diseases. Finding none, other than a few cases of the consumption and of the usual venereal afflictions, of which Honolulu already had aplenty (and having heard not a word about the mortal case of beriberi), he granted permission for the tugboat to tow the visitor in. "Thanks be to the Mercy of Christ Jesus and all His Saints," exulted Captain Reagan, out of habit as well as faith. Then, feeling the need to restore matters to their earthly perspective, he added, "And to the foine sailor who is this foine ship's captain." Salvation from perils physical and foes spiritual naturally requires votive offerings from a man so humble; and these he promised to make, in tumblersful of Ireland's smokiest whiskey, as soon as his fine ship was tied to one of Honolulu's stinkin' docks.

Turning a peeled eye toward the waterfront, he searched for that foreordained dock among the many. Half a dozen dirty coastal schooners cluttered the berths along the harbor's inner shore (the only one it might be said to possess, inasmuch as the outer shore was nothing more than a mud-covered reef), and about as many merchant vessels lay moored in the deeper waters at its head, stained with dirt from Nuuanu Stream. To right and left upon the land stretched the ugly town, a sprawl of shacks, sheds, lean-tos, warehouses, grogshops, more or less held in place by an occasional building made of substantial adobe, brick, or stone. Except for a few blighted coconut palms, all so curved in the trunk that, to Captain Reagan's poetical fancy, they seemed to be sinking in shame for their surroundings, this tawdry town might have been exuded from a river bank in New England. "What a cesspit!" Captain Reagan spat a wad of pollution into the defiled harbor. "What a sink-hole!" he enlarged upon the theme, wishing the damned tugboat would deliver him instantly from further seduction by such tropical beauty. Honolulu, by God's own inscrutable design, was even worse than Yokkahamm-a. Therefore, by God's own providence, reinforced by Reagan's own determination, he'd be out of here within the week, bound home for Hong Kong, the fairest harbor in all the world. Carrying profitable sugar in his holds, by Saint Peter's Crook, not a cargo of worthless grinning coolies . . .

From the *Scioto*'s deck the people of Nippon looked out upon the promised land. Mingled with relief at having arrived safely came disappointment. The tiny harbor, the shabby waterfront, looked like any little fishermen's village at home. The town itself, the three or four buildings of worth standing above the shacks and the dusty streets, did not appear to be a place where rich men dwelled or great wealth was stored. The bare brown hills at the rear of the city showed no hint of fields of sugarcane or streams of water. Indeed, those hills looked as if they had never known the touch of rain or the healing growth of grass. Only the jagged peaks and steep green cliffs of the high mountain ridge far inland, beyond the bare foothills, convinced the newcomers that the gods who send clouds and rain upon Nippon did not neglect to shed a bit of their kindness upon this island lying in the middle of the sea.

"This place is smaller than Shimoda," muttered Ishi. "And not nearly as beautiful. Shimoda's hills are green. The waters of its harbor are blue. The houses along its shores are cleaner."

"And where are all the green plains? And the empty places?" asked Koi, pointing to the ranks of houses, the many people walking about on the docks, or riding in carriages and wagons along the waterfront road.

"If this is the castle-town of Hawai," sneered Kuranosuke of Edo, "then please show me its castle."

They searched the battered town, the dry plain around it, the bare hillsides beyond, for the tall keep of a daimyo's castle and its strong walls of stone, but they could find none. They saw two tapering towers, raised upon stone foundations, and two others stuck up on wooden houses, but none of these looked strong enough to be a castle. Indeed, those slender tapering things did not look sturdy enough to be useful in any way, not even as watch-towers for firemen, and the Nipponjin could not imagine what purpose they could possibly serve.

"Perhaps the castle is up there, atop that bowl-shaped hill?" suggested Nagayuki. In his wanderings with his sad sister, he had seen more of Nippon's castle-towns than any man aboard the ship.

"Ah, so," said Kuranosuke the Edokko, and therefore the man to have the last word. "Yes. That would be a worthy place. It can be defended. Those other pointed things: they must be shelters for birds to nest in. I can think of no other reason for them."

They nodded solemnly, thinking how this desolate place was foreign indeed, despite its similarities to fishing villages in Nippon. Certainly the mountains were different here, and the trees, from what they could see of those. And the quiet. This place was as silent as a river bed at home in the heat of summer, when the frogs are asleep in the mud.

"Behold: our Isle of Onogoro," whispered Daigoro, the new-made husband, to his bride of two nights. She stood between him and the rail, her head resting lightly against his chest, her back and buttocks and fingers touching him in all sorts of subtle ways. He knew, rather vaguely, that an island lay out there, beyond Miya's scented body, but he could not have told you whether it was high or low, peopled or deserted, green with trees or white with winter's snows.

"Your Heavenly Jewelled Spear," she murmured, knowing what a great prize she had won in this gentle gift-man from the Goddess of Love. Blinded with bliss, she saw nothing, cared nothing about such trivial things as might be strewn about the world out there, beyond the embrace of Daigoro's strong arms.

"It does not look like Izu," declared Koi. "What do you suppose your friend was thinking of?"

"But those mountains are beautiful," said Aiko, looking at the distant ridge, sticking up like a backbone above the gaunt flank of the island. To her, a girl from Yokohama who never before had seen mountains so grand, they seemed to be covered with a green brocade shot through with threads of glittering silver and gold.

"Yes, but these are so far away," said Ishi, the running man. "You would have to walk for half a day, before you could sit in the shade of their trees."

Although their first impressions of Tenjiku were disappointing, they were eager to walk upon its firm earth. Their mouths watered at the prospect of tasting something other than fish, bland rice, and unvarying miso soup. They were bored with being idle. Hands reached out for work, just as feet yearned to push against the solid land. To tell the truth, thirty-three days of sitting around with no work to do are thirty days too many of uselessness. O-Miya-san was right: a man who likes to work is a better man for that. With nothing to occupy his hands and mind he can go mad with boredom, or fall into evil ways.

The best part about arriving in Tenjiku, they agreed, was the fact that it brought them nearer to the time when they would begin to work for those rich sugar planters. Thoughts of all the honorable money they were going to earn, visions of all the estimable gold they would save and all the respect they would receive when they returned home comforted them for the hardships they had endured during the voyage, strengthened them for the work that lay ahead. The discovery that this place was not really like the Lord Buddha's Tenjiku did not dismay them. Paradise must wait. In this world a man must do the best he can, to bear the life the gods have arranged for him.

The tugboat nudged the *Scioto* toward its berth at the China Pier, a roofless wharf sticking out into the harbor like a dirty tooth in an old man's mouth. From the pier a wide street led through the town to the foothills beyond. Buildings of white-washed wood or weathered stone lined this important thorough-fare. Although more numerous than the foreign buildings along the Bund in Yokohama, they were not nearly as handsome or as clean. Street mud fouled their lower levels, rain streaks and mold stained them from above. Strange markings, painted in colors upon the walls, looked like simple kana but kept their meanings secret from all Nipponjin except Makino.

"What do those writings tell us?," Ishi asked him. The samurai from Sendai had proved, in a thousand ways, to be the wisest man Ishi had ever known. The ryu master of Shimoda was an apprentice compared with Makino-san. Just as a man needs some one to love before all others, so does he need some one to respect above all others. To Makino, after this month aboard the *Scioto,* Ishi gave the respect and devotion he had never accorded any other man.

"E ... to ..." Makino shook his head like a baffled bull, sucked air through his teeth, giving all the signals that tell when a teacher cannot vouch for his opinions. "Shi Barua," he read aloud some of the nearest signs, "Tchi Heichu Debisu. Kasutam-su Hausu. Kahto Hausu. Ah-ren andu Ro-bin-sonnu ... Those are the names of the great persons who live in those big houses, I believe. Or perhaps of the rich merchants who own the shops in them, if they are not dwellings. I cannot be sure. After we go ashore, I can tell you better, perhaps."

Koi, his head turned sideways, made a sound of annoyance. "These foreigners! They are so smart in other ways. Why do they not write those kana properly?"

"Not that way," Makino laughed, "not from top to bottom, and from right to left, as we read. From left to right, in lines that go from side to side. You must remember that gaijin do almost everything different from us."

Koi put his head back up, where it belonged. "But still I can't see any kana that I know. Or kanji either."

"Those are not kanji or kana. Those are called letters. When letters are put together in proper order they spell words. And words tell them what idea is meant. It is a very slow way of writ- ing, I think, but gaijin seem to like it. You will see many ex- amples of how backward and upside-down they are. Their books, for instance: the front is where the end of ours is.''

"Why do they make things so hard for themselves?'' Koi asked. "Why don't they learn our sensible ways?''

"Well,'' said Makino, patient with foreigners as with everyone else. "You must be tolerant. Remember that they have had only a few years in which to learn from us, while we have known our ways for thousands of years, ever since Prince Ninigi brought them down to earth from the Plain of High Heaven. How long has it been since the Americans' black ships first came to Nippon, seeking our knowledge? Only fourteen years. I believe that, in time, foreigners will accept those of our ways that they like. Just as we of Nippon shall accept those of their ways that we like best.''

"And what of their women?,'' Koi wanted to know, the serious student in search of knowledge. "Are they, too, made different from ours of Nippon?—Upside-down, I mean, and backwards?''

With the air of a scholar contemplating the most difficult of problems, Makino replied, "I cannot answer that question with- out personal investigation. Still lacking.''

"A kind of experience you will never have, my husband,'' Aiko said firmly, thereby declaring herself no longer a bride but a wife.

At the *Scioto*'s rail and in her shrouds, where some of the younger men perched, including Ichigoro the Viper and his friend of the same age, Zembei, the passengers looked across the moat of water, diminishing as stevedores warped the ship toward the pier. A throng of Honolulu's citizens had gathered to watch the berthing, as they do for every exciting arrival and departure. Most of the spectators were native Hawaiians. Among them the few white men appeared to be uncomfortable and out of place. The Hawaiian women wore loose-fitting dresses of bright colors, big hats plaited from leaves of pandanus or stems of ferns, and, around neck or hat or both, garlands made of flowers, or polished seeds, or many-colored feathers. The Hawaiian men wore foreigners' clothing—shirts with neckcloths, trousers, hats, and shoes, but no jackets—although some preferred to shun both neckcloths and shoes. The few foreigners, to the last man, wore black jackets or frock coats over their tight-fitting white shirts and black trousers. Where the Hawaiians were cool, comfortable, and neat, the white men looked hot, wrinkled, and wilted. And lonely. Not a single white woman was present to keep them company.

"Maa," said many a Nipponjin. "How big these Hawaiians are! And how dark of skin."

But where are the children? the Sad Woman asked herself. In all that crowd upon the pier, no boys or girls played among the elders, no woman held a baby in her arms or carried one strapped to her back.

"And such strange garments these women wear," said many a Nipponjin. "They look like covers put over rice tubs, to keep the cooked rice warm."

"Look at those arms," said a man awed by such formidable women. "One of them is bigger around than four of mine."

"Ha!," cackled a ribald one, estimating the size of the covered parts on those splendid creatures, "think of bouncing atop one of those! Tossed about like a ship in a typhoon."

"More like a worm drawn into the mouth of a whale," said another, who enjoyed imagining such unlikely encounters.

The fine clothes worn by the people on the dock made the Nipponjin feel unhappy about their own. Their summer kimono seemed so poor by contrast, so wrinkled, sea-stained, and ragged from much use. And so dirty, because they could not be washed before the ship came to port. The passengers had succeeded in keeping their bodies clean, but the kimono smelled as musty as a lazy wife's unaired bedding. For this reason more than one poor man was resented by his neighbors, earning wrinkled noses and the unforgiving sneer that compared him and his rags to a "thousand-year futon."

Those people on the pier are laughing at us, for our small

bodies and our unsightly clothes, they thought, seeing the laughing mouths, the flashing teeth, the merry dark eyes of the Hawaiians. And they are scorning us for our poverty, they felt, seeing the frowns, the tight unsmiling mouths, the calculating eyes of the white men.

The laughing Hawaiians looked across the narrowing gap at the interesting new people who were coming to live for a while in their islands. New people were always coming and going. That's why Boat Day was always so much fun. To them, as to their ancestors, this land was a generous one, and they, as its hosts, offered aloha to all people, whether they came from far or near. The islands were big enough for everybody to live in comfortably and peacefully. There was plenty of land for all, and even more of the sea. No one ever suffered from hunger or from cold in this gentlest realm of a generous Iehovah. And always, because Iehovah was so provident, there was lots of time for enjoying the good things of life. Like going to the towns for entertainment. Like meeting your friends at the pier on Boat Day.

"Eia mai," said one massive woman to a monumental companion. "They are so small, these Japanese. And so young. Like boys and girls, before they are fully grown."

"And such strange clothes they have! Like the robes that haole women wear at home, before they dress to go out."

"Uiii, ka funny kine heads dey get," screeched another, lapsing into pidgin English, her special language for making jokes and provoking laughs. "All shave inna front, all long inna back. Jus' like wan—"

"Ah, ah, ah, ah," warned a neighbor who knew her too well. "Shut you' mout', you. Da mikanele going heah." She rolled her eyes in the direction of two black-garbed sons of missionaries who were standing nearby. They, knowing exactly what was being said, pretended not to hear.

Laughing at themselves, completely unaware of the effect their good humor was having upon the Japanese, the jesting women turned their attention to Captain Reagan, heroically bringing his ship to safety. Now there was something deserving shrieks of merriment. "Uuuuuiiiii, ka funny-looking buggah, dat! Jus' like wan cockaroach ... "

"At least they look clean," observed Mr. Albion Houghton, a rising young businessman, to Lúcius Grimes, his assistant, "in spite of those sullen faces." Pursing his thin lips, he wondered if he should give scandal to the younger man's ears, then decided that his eyes had already seen enough to taint even the most innocent of minds. Pointing a bony finger at the shocking obscenity drawing nearer and nearer, he hissed, "And those indecent clothes."

"They're healthy though, I guess," said the assistant, a thin missionary scion intent upon learning how to be a successful businessman. "Otherwise the Board of Health wouldn't have let them in." Having been born and raised in the islands, he'd seen so much naked Hawaiian flesh (despite the frantic efforts of his parents to shield him from such abominations) that he really couldn't understand what Mr. Houghton could be objecting to in these decorous Japanese.

"But will they work?," demanded the American, stressing the sacred word, honoring the paramount precept.

"They look strong ... "

"As they should, after a month's dawdling about in that pleasure barge. I certainly wish someone would give me a month's vacation like that. All expenses paid. Nothing to do but eat and sleep.—And read, of course," he added, a guarded Calvinist even in his censored dreams. Perhaps for that very reason he could not take his eyes away from those aliens, drawing near his citadel, threatening his immortal soul.

"Absolutely indecent!," he exploded, drawing a startled glance from young Lucius, still dallying with visions of sybaritic vacations enlivened by entertainments more alluring than mere eating or reading. "Those clothes, I mean. Or, rather, the lack of them. Bare legs. Bare feet. Bare chests on so many of those shameless men. Even their heads are half naked. People of very low morals, obviously." He would have expired, then and there, if a gust of wind had come along and blown aside the skirts of the kimono on the men clinging to the shrouds.

"The women do look modest enough, though," interposed Lucius, compelled by common charity to say something in defense of these strangers.

"Can't agree," snapped Mr. Houghton, spying out evil in all its manifestations. "Look at that wanton slut over there. The one in the blue and white bathrobe, or whatever it is. Leaning against the gross fellow behind her. Like a mare in heat. Look at that cow over there, nursing her babe in front of everybody." In two seconds he made Lucius Grimes more conscious of blatant sinfulness than ever he would have been had he come alone to watch the docking of this barque of perversity.

"We must get these coolies decently clothed, as soon as possible," ordered Mr. Houghton, not turning his back upon all those exposed limbs and parts, not permitting himself to see the elegant attire worn by Makino and his fellow samurai, or the fine bodies presented by ninety percent of those alien men. "Have you told Pfluger and Brenig to get their field clothes ready?"

"Yes, sir. Weeks ago, sir. Although they couldn't be quite sure about sizes and shapes. They used Mr. Center for a model, and made most of the clothes of a size to fit him. With some bigger and some smaller ones, just in case."

They studied Mr. Center, standing alone a few feet away. A genial and portly man who had lived in Honolulu for almost fifteen years, he appeared to be more Hawaiian than Japanese. And he was twice as big around the waist as were most of the countrymen he had come to meet.

"Oh, well," Mr. Houghton reached one of those decisions which made him so successful a businessman. "They can always tighten their belts. We've no money to waste on adjustments."

"Besides," said Lucius Grimes brightly, "the material is bound to shrink."

"That man," Makino pointed toward Sentaro, "looks like he might be one of us. Except for his foreign clothes."

"I wonder," said Ishi, not sure what to make of that man.

"How is it possible?," asked Kuranosuke, expressing the opinion of those who believed they were the first Nipponjin to come to Hawai. Ishi feared this waiting man might be even more sinister: the Bakufu, before it died, could have sent him ahead, to watch over them, a pair of eyes in attendance, no matter how far away they tried to go.

Noticing their interest in him, Sentaro approached the edge of the pier, opposite Makino. The samurai from Sendai, distinguished as much by his height as by the wide shoulders of his surcoat, drew from Sentaro manners and forms of speech he had not used since he left Japan. Bowing stiffly to Makino he called, "Dono-sama: irasshaimase."

Every passenger within hearing turned his head toward that sound of welcome. "Irasshaimase," Sentaro said again, bowing less formally to the common people at the right and left of Makino. They responded to the familiar greeting with smiles of pleasure and cries of thanks for his courtesy.

"Ah, they look happier when they talk," noticed the Hawaiians on the dock.

"Well! There's some life in 'em after all," judged Mr. Houghton.

Sentaro addressed Makino in Japanese. "I am Sentaro of Tateyama in Awa. I have lived in this country for about fifteen years." Enjoying the many exclamations of surprise that his statement drew forth, he added, "Later I shall tell you why."

"Center!" Mr. Houghton interrupted. "You know what to tell 'em?"

"Yes, sir, I know," replied Sentaro, tipping his lauhala hat to one of the honorable men in power.

As soon as sailors lashed the gangplank in place Mr. Houghton and his apprentice, impelled by the knowledge that time is money, dashed aboard in search of Captain Reagan and his "bill-of-lading," as the businessman could not refrain from calling the passenger list. Sentaro, not having to count the price of his minutes, crossed with more dignity. He ambled toward the *Scioto*'s quarterdeck, followed by two large Hawaiian men carrying a heavy cask slung from a shoulder-pole. On the wharf the satisfied townsfolk started upon their slow promenade back to Honolulu's streets and grogshops and offices.

Gravely bowing to each other, Makino and Sentaro introduced themselves in greater detail. The amenities being concluded, Sentaro requested permission to speak to the passengers, saying, "I bring instructions from the Board of Immigration."

"We are grateful for your help," said Makino. "To tell the truth, I have been worrying about how we would learn what they want us to do."

Summoned by Makino's lieutenants, the immigrants assembled amidships within a few minutes. "To our good fortune," Makino explained, "a countryman is here to help us. First he will tell us about himself, and how he came to be here. Then he will tell us what we must do for the officials of this government."

"Aloha," the transplanted Japanese began. "This is the word meaning 'welcome' in the language of Hawaiians. It also means 'farewell,' 'love,' and certain other things. You will hear it often in this country. It is a good word for you to learn—and to use." He paused, looking apologetically around at his audience. "Fifteen years have passed since I left Nippon. Please forgive me, then, if I have forgotten much of our language. During all those years I have had very few chances to talk with people from our homeland." He spoke slowly, in a dialect not very different from their own of Kanto, yet often searching for a word, often choosing a wrong ending for a verb, or using a countryman's expression that had long since gone out of fashion among the changeable folk of Edo and Yokohama. But the thing that Makino and Ishi liked best about Sentaro-san's speech was the fact that not once did he use the honorifics and expressions of deference that he would have been forced to employ had he been talking to these same people at home. He seemed to have completely forgotten that they were ever required.

"Sentaro is my name. I came from a village in Awa, near Tateyama. I was a fisherman there. One day, while four of us were working off the coast of Boso, a typhoon came up. When it ended, many days later, our boat was crippled, we were lost. We drifted, the four of us, upon the Great Ocean, for more than three months, keeping ourselves alive with raw fish from the sea and rainwater wrung from our sail. We were almost dead when an American whaling vessel found us. The sailors lifted us into their ship, fed and clothed us, brought us to this port. The people of Honolulu welcomed us, gave us work to do and houses to live in. I have stayed here ever since that time. Two others of our group went to California to look for gold. The fourth one died, unfortunately, soon after we came to Honolulu. If you ask why we did not go home, I must answer that we did not dare to do so, for fear that the Shogun's officials would kill us. That cruel law, I am told, has been changed recently. Here in Honolulu I have learned to be a carpenter, a maker of houses and furniture. A woman of this place is my wife. We have three children. You will see them later."

Listening to him, watching his manner, Ishi was interested to see how much this man from Nippon differed from his countrymen. For one of Ishi's aspirations, the reason for the difference was clear: Sentaro-san was a free man, who feared no one, neither samurai nor police, neither his father nor his lord. He smiled and gestured as though the people around him were friends rather than complete strangers. He was not awed by Makino-san's rank or gravity. Makino, despite his enlightened beliefs and generous intentions, was still stiff and formal, still the samurai in appearance if not in heart. Sentaro was good natured, relaxed, almost ill-mannered in his informality. Ishi, loyal in his respect for the sober Makino, yet liking the casual Sentaro, was instructed by the transformation that had been wrought in the fisherman. Will the rest of us be so changed? he wondered, after we have lived here for fifteen years? Is this how I shall be, he could not help asking, trying to see himself in that other man. That cormorant has learned to fend for himself, thought Ishi, glancing at Koi, who had told him about those dutiful dependent birds. That young man was listening carefully, as if to a prophesy about his own future.

"I am asked to tell you what will happen in the next few days. But first let me give you the welcome sent by the King of Hawaii. He is called Kamehameha the Fifth. He, too, says aloha to you, and he sends as a gift this cask of salted fish." Amid murmurs of gratitude from the nearer passengers the two Hawaiians deposited the cask at Sentaro's side and, not at all unnerved by their part in this historic event, shuffled off toward the gangplank. Fortunately for the spirit of aloha they could not understand the complaints being expressed by certain ingrates among the Nipponjin, asking why the King of Hawai could not have sent them pickled vegetables, or sweet potatoes, or tofu, or saké, or whatever other fresh food they craved the most, instead of a barrelful of thirst-provoking fish.

"These are the instructions from the Board of Immigration," said Sentaro-san, stopping those private mutterings with the news that all were eager to hear.

Obedient in act if not in thought, they remained aboard the *Scioto* for the rest of the day and night following. They enjoyed some consolation in their captivity, however. Endless supplies of water for washing their clothes were brought aboard through an amazingly long line of iron pipes. These pipes delivered not only water: into the washtubs flowed a few tadpoles, many small white shrimps, assorted insects, and flecks of pond weed. Even so, the water itself was sweet and untainted with mud, and it served to remove the dirt and the smells from kimono without replacing them with worse things.

And during the afternoon the Nanking, in thanks for the good help they had received from the passengers during the voyage (the ashes-throwing pranksters having been forgiven in the interval), sent ashore for cabbages, carrots, green beans, potatoes, onions, tomatoes, and whatever other fresh vegetables they could buy in the market stalls of Chinatown. Even though those viands were not pickled they were delectable. And with them to tickle the

tongue, the salted fish from the King of Hawai were quite accept-
able after all.

During the next two days they enjoyed the freedom of the city.
Obeying Sentaro's recommendation—"Be sure to see this fine city, and meet its fine people"—they ventured ashore, every one of
them. Wearing clean, if wrinkled, kimono, snow-white fundoshi,
and their slippers of plaited straw, they set out to discover the
beauties of Honolulu.

Once again they were disappointed. After the huge cities of
Edo and Yokohama, small Honolulu held nothing that could interest them. And beauty—when it could be discerned—came not
from the arts of men but only from the kindness of nature. The
King's Palace shocked them, it was so small and humble, not
nearly as big as the poorest daimyo's smallest yashiki in the most
run-down outskirts of Edo. The two stone churches, the largest
edifices in all Hawaii, reminded them of stables, or of storehouses against earthquakes. They were mean and dull and grace-
less, compared with the great temples at home, high and proud
and open, with their curving roofs, massive columns and strong
beams, and numerous ornaments of gilded bronze and glowing
gold. Even worse, these churches were dead. Whereas at home
temples and shrines are visited by crowds of people at all times,
here the churches attracted pilgrims and petitioners only one day
in every seven. "Saa," the Nipponjin decided, "the gods of this
place must be powerless indeed, if they are so neglected." The
immigrants were more charitable toward Sentaro-san, however,
saying that if he had known only his village near Tateyama of
Awa, then of course he would consider this Honolulu a fine city.

Although the town itself failed them the people did not. They
were most friendly. Everywhere the Nipponjin went they attracted crowds of curious folk, of all colors and stations. Men who
were called "reporters," writing for something called "newspapers," followed them about, scribbling furiously upon little pack-
ets of paper, making drawings of their faces, kimono, and especially of the heads of the few diehards who still wore topknots.

Storekeepers and housewives, calling "Aloha," offered them gifts of many kinds. "If the people give you things to eat," Sentaro had told them, "do not hesitate to accept them. That is their way of being hospitable."

The generous townsfolk thrust upon them things they'd never seen before—papaias, mangoes, bananas, pineapples, guavas, breadfruits, muskmelons, watermelons—and did not know how to eat until they were shown. Familiar foods were given also: apples, oranges, grapes, tomatoes, eggs, many kinds of fish, which they happily accepted, and quantities of animal flesh, which they politely declined. Never had they seen so much meat prepared for eating, and they shrank from those piles of limp carcasses, red with blood or black with flies. And they were repelled by the smell of butter: the town and most of its residents reeked of butter, that most offensive of all terrible things. The newcomers learned to hurry past foreigners' hotels and Chinese restaurants in order to avoid both the smells and the gifts that came from their kitchens.

Yet, search as they might, they could find none of those delicacies for which the mouth watered, the belly clamored: in all of Honolulu they discovered no pickled vegetables, no crisp daikon, no tofu, and—almost the greatest disaster of all—no saké.

Solace of another sort was lacking also. After thirty-three days of continence on that floating monastery every true man in the lot burned for the release that only a woman can give. When they trooped ashore on that first morning of their sojourn those men were not at all interested in seeing the Famous Views of Honolulu, whether they numbered three or three hundred. Their eyes darted about in quest of more pleasurable sights, seeking women as bees hunt for nectar. Their fundoshi, wrapped tight, were most necessary articles of clothing that day.

But how to find those special houses, in this town where they could neither read the signs nor speak the language? Where, in this clutter of houses and maze of streets, was the Yoshiwara of Honolulu? They expected to meet with some difficulty in their search for the Gay Quarter and they were most discreet in their questing about, because, more than anything else Sentaro had told them, they remembered his warnings about this most important subject:

"The haoles—that is the name by which white people are known here—are very queer. Be careful when they are near. You must obey their rules, or else you will get into trouble. Most of their rules are concerned with work, the protection of property, and sex. Let us now talk about their rules with regard to sex. For some reason I am unable to understand, they are remarkably ashamed of their bodies. They are most especially ashamed of the organs of sex and with the uses to which those are put. They cannot bear the sight of nakedness, even in children. That is why all haoles wear so many clothes, all the time. Even when they go to sleep. They cannot bear the thought of a man or woman making love with someone who is not a registered mate. They forbid the pleasures of love to their children, until they are married. They forbid prostitution—but many prostitutes are found here, in spite of the laws. They cannot endure the sight of a person relieving himself, even though the need to do so is intense. In times of greatest urgency they will run for long distances in order to reach the secrecy of a place of convenience, ignoring empty houselots, ditches, hedges, whole fields and forests that nature may be offering them in their need. And then they will lock themselves into that little closet, so that no one may see them.—Really. Do not laugh. You must believe me. I do not tell you untruths.—They are a most peculiar people. Therefore, take care in all those matters of the body. If you forget their rules, or disobey them, they will put you into that prison over there." He pointed across the harbor to a squat solid building with high stone walls about it, sitting like a brown toad at the end of a long causeway.

The Nipponjin shook their heads, aghast at such unnatural attitudes toward the most natural functions of men. Seeing their frowns, Sentaro gave them a thin reed of hope to lean upon for a staff: "Hawaiians, I should add, are not like haoles in these matters. They are more like us, sensible and relaxed about the body's needs. But Hawaiians too must obey the haoles' rules. Because of the new laws, I am sorry to say, some Hawaiians are becoming as fearful about the body as are the haoles. And those who disobey the laws are cast into prison."

Recalling Sentaro's lecture, the pent-up Nipponjin looked about the town with furtive glances from beneath lowered eyelids. But soon, amid all those friendly townsfolk, full of smiles and alohas, generous with offerings of food and drink, the excited men of Nippon became so confused that they could not have distinguished a whore from a temple nun.

As need intensified, and bladders swelled, and lust flared in their loins to the point where some were almost ready to assault sows sleeping in gutters, Takezo of Edo reminded his fellows of another insuperable problem: how were they going to pay for their easing, without money? These were the men who had squandered their fortunes in Yokohama, without heed for the future and such dire emergencies as this. The few provident ones who still kept some copper coins tucked away in their breechclouts would have increased their wealth by ten times if they had been willing to lend their zeni to borrowers at the usurous rates being offered. But those selfish fellows, as tight-fisted as they were small-hearted, would not part with a single cash, either for profit's sake or for a comrade's. Tempers rose, and many a fine friendship, affirmed during the voyage, ended forever in the dusty streets of Honolulu. Thus, once again, the old adage was proved that is taught by priests and forgotten by each generation of lay men: the desire for money and women will root out every hidden evil in everybody. Not for nothing did the Lord Buddha warn "In the presence of women, keep your thoughts tightly controlled."

Of course, during that day's foray quite a few of the better-looking and more clever fellows from the big cities proved also that the unspoken vocabulary of womanizers is the same in all ports of the world. Some women of Honolulu responded as readily as do those of Yokohama to a lustful stare, a ribald wink, a lewd touch, even to the shy but hopeful smile. Certain others among those hospitable women were moved by curiosity, they said, many having heard one thing or another about what a Japa-

nese man wears under his kimono. In any event, whatever the inducement, one by one the hunters dropped out of the pack. And
before long, without having to say a word other than "Aroha"—
and certainly without having to spend a single zeni—they were
happily engaged in playing the game that Izanagi and Izanami
invented, when they descended to another island in ages past.

Nonetheless, toward the end of a long dull day about sixty disheartened wanderers took their problem to Sentaro-san. They
surrounded him in the street outside the Bethel for sailors, near
the China Pier, toward which footsore Sentaro was leading them.
"We are not ready to go back to the ship," declared their
spokesman.

Sentaro listened to their woe with sympathy but no encouragement. "Whores in this town cost plenty of money. Can you pay?
A dollar, at least. The better ones will ask two dollars—or more."

They reckoned the sums involved, using nimble fingers and
quicker minds, even as bellies sank into the depths, to join with
their poverty. One dollar equalled three bu. Three bu equalled
2,880 zeni. The truth staggered them: if all sixty of those poor
men tossed all their zeni upon a spread-out fundoshi, they'd not
collect enough cash to hire a harlot for even one of them. Scowling with disappointment, they kicked at the dried mud in the ruts
of Bethel Street, wishing they were at home again, where a zeni
was something more than a worthless piece of copper with a hole
in it.

"The only hole you'll finger today," sniggered Kuranosuke
the pickler, thinking that perhaps now the time had come when
he should drown himself in the harbor, or throw himself under
the wheels of one of those heavy-laden wagons. Kuranosuke, his
companions were beginning to perceive, was a man easily discouraged and as easily angered by even the most trivial mishaps.
"Small wonder that he is a pickle-maker," his former friends
would say. "With a stir of his finger he could turn the sweetest
water into the sourest vinegar." But even they did not know how
frequently sour Kuranosuke's thoughts dwelt lovingly upon the
sweetness of death.

On either side of the dispirited men wagons burdened with

freight from the wharves came to a halt, carriages bearing important gentlemen home from their offices pulled to a stop. From the
nearest of those carriages a pleasant voice called. "Are you having some trouble, Mr. Center?"

Realizing only then that his charges were blocking traffic in
one of Honolulu's busiest streets, Sentaro acted with the skill of a
general. He raised his hat to the gentleman sitting in the carriage. "Yes, sir, Mr. Nihoa. Some small trouble. About this, may
I ask advice?" In the next breath, in sibilant Japanese, he
ordered his friends to move, and to move fast. They obeyed, instantly. Draymen cracked their whips, Mr. Nihoa's coachman
turned his team toward the curb, and traffic flowed once more on
busy Bethel Street.

From the sidewalk the Japanese examined the elegant ba-
rouche and the dapper gentleman who sat in its well. Although
undoubtedly a native, judging by the color of his skin and the
cast of his features, he was a small Hawaijin, about the size of the
usual Nipponjin. And, most obviously, he was a very wealthy
man: the carriage and its matched pair, the coachman in splendid
livery, proclaimed that fact. And the quality of his clothes, the
golden knob of the walking stick he held, the gold frames of the
spectacles he wore, announced that he was a rich man who enjoyed his wealth.

Withal, he was a kind man. Smiling in a friendly way, not with
the usual rich man's grimace, he said, "Sit here with me, Mr.
Center, and rest a while. You look tired. And tell me how I can
help."

"Ah, Mr. Nihoa," Sentaro's relief showed in every line of his
face. "You are sent from heaven, I think. Buddha heaven, for
sure. Jesus heaven, too, maybe."

Knowing that he need not shield Mr. Nihoa from pressing real-
ities, he explained the nature of his countrymen's plight. While
he talked Mr. Nihoa, nodding encouragement, surveyed the newcomers, lined up as though for his inspection. Different though
they seemed to be—with those interesting robes and those
astonishing variations in the methods of dressing their hair, not

to mention the differences in noses, lips, and eyes—he could see that they were men, not "shameless monkeys," as that niggling ass Albion Houghton had been describing them to his associates. And, Mr. Nihoa was not slow to understand, like all healthy men they needed comforts of the kind Mr. Houghton would insist upon denying them but that Hiram Nihoa made a business of providing.

"Of course, Mr. Center," he said. "I shall be delighted to help. Speak to the devil, when he appears, and all problems are solved." The lean brown face, the halo of pure white hair, the kind smile: for these and other reasons, people who knew him well called Hiram Nihoa "the Angel of Iwilei." Christian folk, knowing nothing about his good works, thinking only about the sources of his wealth, shrank from him in revulsion, calling him "that kanaka Beelzebub," "the Mephistopheles of Fid Street," "the Arch Fiend," and similar antique epithets from an outlived age.

"You will give to them—umm, how do you say it?—credit? They have no money for now."

"My goodness, no. Money will not be needed. Let us say that they will be my guests for this evening, as they are the city's guests for today."

"Ho!" Sentaro was appalled at what he'd done, aghast at the weight of gratitude he was putting upon himself and sixty of his countrymen. "Too much! Too many!" He waved both hands before his chest, as if to ward off that immense obligation.

"Not at all. I'm sorry, please believe me, that I did not think of this myself. They will be only a few, really, among the many. The many will call, and they can pay. But these few are chosen, and they can ride for free. Besides, it will be a new experience for my younger girls. I do not believe that they have entertained a Japanese as yet. In fact, I don't think we've had a Japanese guest in any of my establishments since you stole Abbie away from me, fourteen years ago." Inasmuch as Hiram Nihoa had paid for the wedding and given the bride away, Sentaro could grin easily at this perennial joke.

"Now, how shall we arrange this little ass-signation?," mused Mr. Nihoa, making a quick estimate of the number of guests awaiting his disposition. "It would hardly do for me to lead them to my hotels. 'A veritable parade of vice,' Henry Whitney would call it in his *Advertiser,* 'led by a piebald piper who should be arraigned for his depravity instead of esteemed for his lucre.'—Ah, forgive me, Mr. Center. I like to play with words. They are very entertaining. And so adaptable, in the telling of lies ... "

He searched among the inquisitive townsfolk, gathering around to stare at him and at the stolid immigrants. "But we are thinking about lyings of another sort, aren't we? Ah, there's a face I know. An old regular, as it were." Crooking a finger, he called, "Alika. Come here please."

Alika, delighted to be so well known, came at a run. A good-looking young man, with the air of saloons and gambling dens about him, he was even more familiar with Honolulu's waterfront activities than Hiram Nihoa himself.

"Alika, do me a favor, please," asked the man who could make or break Alika's fortunes with the drop of an eyelid. Part of Hiram Nihoa's power lay in the fact that he never flaunted it. Politely he waited for the expected "Shuah" before he stated his request, in a voice only Alika could hear. "Escort these fine young visitors, please, to my several places in Iwilei and Chinatown. I would say—let's see, now—about ten or twelve men at each place. That should be a fair division of labor. Tell the doorman at each house that they are to be my guests for the evening. Everything they want, without charge."

Alika's eyes popped, his mouth opened in appreciation of such princely generosity. "Dey no going believe me, I tell 'em dat."

"I think they will, Alika. They know that I do not send messages by men I cannot trust."

"O.K. I do w'at you say ... "

"Oh, one more thing," the old man tossed his head toward the dung-colored façade of the Sailors' Bethel. Although some residents of Honolulu hailed it as the guardian of waterfront morality and the preserver of mariners' purity, he knew very well how many scores of America's young men emerged each year from its Sabbath services to go and sin some more in Honolulu's brothels. "Take them by varied routes, please. Pretend that you are guiding them on a tour, to see the sights of Chinatown. After all, we must protect their reputations, if not our own."

"Shuah, Meestah Nihoa. I geeve 'um da tuah."

"Very good, Alika, thank you. For your help, you too must be my guest tonight. Tell Kimo, when you get there. You and Rosie have a good time tonight. On the house."

"Yes, suh, Meestah Nihoa. T'ank you. You wan guud man."

"There you are, Mr. Center. All arranged. Tell your friends to follow Alika."

Sentaro, tears brimming, stepped down from the carriage. "I am very grad," he turned to Mr. Nihoa, "knowing such a good man. I sank you for aroha to men of my home country."

"Not at all, Mr. Center. Some people in this town would not agree with that opinion of me, you know. But I have learned that what is good for the body usually is also good for the spirit, and so I try to help the one by cheering the other. Tell your friends to enjoy themselves, and that I hope they'll be happy in this beautiful land of ours." He shook Sentaro's hand. "Aloha, and give my love to Abbie and the children."

Sentaro went to tell his countrymen how Benten had sent the kindest man in Hawai to their aid. And Hiram Nihoa leaned back in his seat, while the coachman drove him away. Smiling contentedly, bowing to the many people who bowed to him, Mr. Nihoa enjoyed the warmth of aloha coursing through his own body and spirit. Hawaiians, haoles, hapa-haoles, Chinese: he felt aloha for all, as now he felt aloha for the Japanese, come to join him and all others in these islands he loved so much. He chuckled, more than once, rehearsing the details of this story, to have them all in order when, in a few minutes, he would tell it to his crony, Lot Kamehameha. They would sit in the fading light of the evening, on the lanai of Iolani Palace, talking about their past, worrying about their country's future. And how they would laugh over this delectable tale, which proved once again what all true men know: that all is well and good when ends can be made to meet.

The Sad Woman went looking that day for the fulfillment of her vision. Accompanied by her faithful brother, she parted from the others without saying where she was going. She herself did not know where her karma would direct her. She asked only to know if this was indeed the Tenjiku that the Lord Buddha had revealed to her.

In appearance this Yuki and this Nagayuki were not the same two people who had gone aboard the *Scioto* in Yokohama. During the long voyage they had changed in a mystifying way, so that even the most unobservant of their companions could not fail to see it. Some of the change, to be sure, could be laid to the loss of flesh which everyone suffered during the typhoon and those five days of starving. Everyone became thinner then, at least for the while, until the meals came down again from the galleys. When eating resumed almost everyone put back upon his lightened frame some of the flesh he had lost. But such was not the case with Yuki and Nagayuki. They remained thinner, although they ate as much as before, and they looked the better for being lighter. It seemed as if much water had been squeezed out of their bodies, to make the flesh less puffed up. Because of this, she walked more easily, although—as everyone noticed—her tongue moved no more freely than before and her silence remained as heavy. But the most remarkable change affected Yuki's eyes: they did not bulge so much, and she lost the appearance of a madwoman staring in terror at a ghost that only she could see.

The travelers talked about these improvements in O-Yuki's appearance—not to herself, of course—and hoped that, in its turn, her spirit would improve to the point where it would recapture its missing happiness. Until that time came, however, they supposed that they must put up with her silence and that grieving countenance.

On the day they went ashore in Honolulu, Yuki was excited within yet outwardly seemed no different than before. The sun, flooding sky and earth with light and warmth, flooded her memory, too, with the brightness she had seen in the vision. The strange trees, however, and the smiling Buddha holding a child in his arms, she could not see from the ship. And so she went in search of them in the city.

All the day long she wandered, until she and her brother were exhausted and confused. To her despair the trees they saw growing in yards around dwellings, in the park of the King's Palace, along the streets in the newer sections of the city, were not like those seen in her dream. The people they met were full of smiles and aloha, and now and then they encountered a man who looked somewhat like the benevolent Buddha. But not one held a laughing child in his arms. Even more dismaying, she found so few children, of any age and in any posture, whether sitting on the grass or running in a street. She grieved more over this absence of children than she did over any others of the Lord Buddha's rejections of her faith. How could she hope to bear a child in this land, when even the smiling people who lived in it were denied such precious gifts?

By day's end, grayer than the twilight with weariness and dejection, she trudged back to the dark ship. Racked with fear that, by some ill chance, she had come to the wrong place, that this was not the Tenjiku of her vision, she thought longingly of death. Only the memory of the morning's bright sun, and its promise, held her to life during the black night.

Ishi missed the chance to be one of Hiram Nihoa's chosen guests because he went with Makino-san, the three other samurai, Koi and Aiko, Daigoro and Miya, and the other married couples, to watch the preparations for a native feast at Sentaro's house. Inasmuch as Sentaro could not afford to entertain all his countrymen, he invited this smaller group to eat at his house and eased his conscience by accompanying the bachelors on their expedition through the town.

When he returned to his home, tired after so much walking but elated with Mr. Nihoa's kindness, Sentaro arrived just in time to join his guests around the eating-mat. The Nipponjin did not care much for the dishes that Abbie Center with her friends and relatives had spent the whole day preparing. They were repelled by the sweet thick poi that clung to fingers like joiner's glue; and they were disturbed by the mounds of hog flesh and of dog meat brought steaming from the earth-oven. But they nibbled at the sweet potatoes, bananas, taro, chickens, and tender fishes that emerged from the same smoky pit; and they devoured all the onions, tomatoes, and fresh fruits that Abbie had scattered about the eating-mat. The eating place was a beautiful thing to see— before the feast. Covered with green leaves, ferns, and fresh flowers, it looked more like a garden in spring. At the end it looked like a market place an hour after it has been hit by a typhoon.

Sated as they were with the foods the townsfolk had presented to them, Sentaro's guests were less interested in his feast than in his home. It fascinated them, being so different from anything they had seen in Nippon. To look at it no one would know that Sentaro was a Nipponjin. It held not a tatami mat nor a piece of silken cloth, not even a tokonoma in the main room or a god-shelf stuck up on a wall in the kitchen. Everything was made in the Western style: heavy chairs to sit upon, big tables and tall chests of drawers, and long mirrors to peer into hanging upon the solid wooden walls of the solid sprawling house. And great wide beds, standing up above the floor, always in place, with hard mattresses upon them, not soft futon put away each morning. Everything was too big, or too hard, or too high for the visitors, and their legs hurt when they sat in the chairs, trying them for the novelty. Because he had expected this, Sentaro advised his wife to serve the feast upon mats spread upon the grass under the trees in their yard. This was the Hawaiians' style, closer to the custom in Nippon, and everyone was the more comfortable for this escape from the upright haole manner of eating at a high table.

The spacious splendid house, the big yard, the lavish feast, the many relatives and friends who shared it with them, eating everything in sight so that nothing was wasted, convinced the Nipponjin that Sentaro must be a very wealthy man, and an important one in the castle-town of Honolulu. While they regretted that he had so forgotten his native land as to put no trace of it in his house, they admired the success with which he had amassed the treasures of the new land. They liked his big plump wife, with her friendly manner, even though they could not understand a word she said, and they were enchanted by his three handsome children.

At the end of the feast, in behalf of the guests, Makino complimented Sentaro-san upon his achievements and thanked him for his hospitality to the group. "You lead us to believe that, were we to do half as well, we should be very content with our stay in this land."

"Well," replied modest Sentaro, "this is the home of an ordinary man. I am not wealthy, as you are thinking, although I am not poor, either. But I work hard, I am well paid for my work and I spend my money wisely. In this I am guided by my wife." He looked fondly at the fine woman who, fourteen years before, had seen in him the one man she wanted to marry. Even though she was not a woman of Nippon, the newcomers agreed that she had been a good wife to Sentaro-san, and they bowed to her, trying to tell her that they thought she was most fortunate to have the chance to serve so respectable a man. "And," he nuzzled the head of the dark-skinned son he held in his lap, "we buy these things not for our sake only, but also for our children's."

Of all the treasures he saw in Sentaro's house Ishi envied him most that lovable son. Sentaro-san was showing him the next step along the way to which Nakamura-san had directed him, upon which Kannon-sama had helped him to set forth. Sentaro, sitting there like the Lord Buddha with a child in his arms, was both a promise and a proof that a man who owns nothing to begin with can attain happiness and wealth before his life must end. Just as the unsullied lotus can blossom out of mud in a pond, so can wealth be plucked out of the mud in a city's streets or in a sugar-cane field.

But what of happiness? Happiness does not come with wealth, as everyone knows, or with success in things of this world. Yet

Sentaro was a happy man. And he was happy not only because he owned property and was respected by Nipponjin and Hawaijin alike. Ishi, envying him those children and that loving wife, could not doubt the reasons for his happiness.

He looked at his friend Koi, his younger brother and yet so much wiser than he. Koi sat beside Aiko, holding her hands in his as they listened to Sentaro talking with Makino. In Edo, and on the voyage, Koi would tease Ishi, calling him "Three-stone Man," referring to the fact that he called upon the resources of the one that Kannon had given him while preserving those of the other two that every boy is born with. But, wise as he was, the teaser did not know about the fourth stone that Ishi bore within him, where his heart should be.

He looked across the mat at O-Miya sitting bright-eyed and happy beside her Daigoro. On the ship, turning upon Ishi like an elder sister, she had scolded him for being proud in heart. Surprising him, she had made him think, to consider if perhaps she was right. Now he knew that she had misjudged him. She mistook for pride the barriers that for so long he had put up as defenses against dread.

He looked at Sentaro, finding another reason for his happiness. Sentaro was a man free of fear. In all of Honolulu Ishi had not seen one thing to fear or one evidence of fearful men. Even the jail was only a place to be shunned, not feared. No Hawaiian samurai swaggered through the town's streets. No commoner fell upon hands and knees, pressing his nose into the mud when officials passed. All men were equal, in each other's eyes. And Sentaro's account of how Mr. Nihoa, one of the high nobles in the land, had helped sixty desperate Nipponjin, filled him with gratitude for the great man's kindness. Kindness was the law that ruled this land: it flowed from the people in everything they did, from the king down to his lowliest subject.

Suddenly, in an instant, there under the sheltering kukui trees in Sentaro's yard, Ishi felt his hard heart yielding to a new yet joyful pain. The thing he'd carried in his breast for so long, the poor thing that grief and fear and hate had made as hard and cold as a frozen stone, became warm again, soft and throbbing with need. The dread was gone, drained away as icy water will flow from under a bank of sun-warmed snow.

Ishi lifted his glass of this powerful new kind of saké, the liquid fire that Hawaiians call okolehao. He said, to no one, to everyone, "Aroha ... Happiness ... " He meant it for everyone there, for everyone in Hawai, for all the people in the whole world, and most especially for himself.

"Yes, a man can be happy here," Sentaro caught the sense of Ishi's pledge. "This is a good land."

"I think a woman, too, can be happy here," said Miya, forward to a degree she would not have presumed to reach in Nippon. She was not tipsy with okolehao although perhaps, as poets are wont to say, she was drunk with happiness. Few people noticed her un-womanly directness, so easily had they fallen into the Hawaiian habit of treating everyone as an equal, even a wife. "I like the way the men here treat the women," Miya explained. "I think this is a good way, for both men and women."

Tomi, wife to one male principle, mother to a budding other, could not agree with so shattering a declaration. Without realizing how forward she was being, she retorted, "But the husband must come first. Always." Then, embarrassed at having attracted so much attention to her ignorant self, she hid her blushes behind Kintaro's shoulder.

"Please excuse her," said that unchangeable male, bowing to left and to right. "She is not very bright, but she has a good heart."

Miya looked at them in amusement, seasoned with perhaps a trace of vexation. "Of course. The first rule of a good wife—as of a good prostitute—is to allow her man to think that he is the most important person in this world. But—," she lifted a shoulder, as if to say that the Rule of Manipulation is so well known as to require no further comment.

Makino thought this must be the moment to return the conversation to the man who would be most helpful to all. He bowed to Sentaro. "Please teach us. Many of us are bewildered in this new land. Tell us what we should know, what we must remember, as we begin our lives in it next week."

"This is a good land, as I have said. The land itself is kind. And it is a nation of good people. They are good, I think, because the land is kind to them. There are other reasons, to be sure, and you will learn of them in time.

"These good people have helped me to prosper, as you can see. And I am happy. At first, I admit, I longed for my home in Awa and my parents and brothers there. I was like Urashima Taro in that. But, unlike him, I do not think of them anymore, because now this is my home and my family is here. For you, if you wish, the same story can be told when you have lived among us for a while."

Ishi tried to imagine the time when he would be telling this same story about himself, in Sentaro's very words, to a new group of settlers from Nippon, come to live in this kind land. He would take Sentaro for his model, during the years ahead, not stupid Urashima Taro of the folk tale. That idiot, after having lived for a time in great luxury in his princess-wife's beautiful palace at the bottom of the sea, could not forget his starving old mother and his brothers and sisters and their miserable village at home in Nippon. Whereupon, like a fool, he chose to go home, giving up all that he had gained while dwelling in that hospitable land beneath the sea. And what did he find when he went home? That 300 years had passed, instead of 300 days. That his family was dead, he forgotten, and, where his home had stood, an ancient pine tree grew, sprung from the seedling he had planted when he was a boy. Moreover, as he stared up into the stiff branches of that tree of longevity, he aged by 300 years in an instant, and in that instant fell dead.—Bakayaro! Ishi dismissed him, the foolish man.

"If you like this place, you can do well here in time," Sentaro assured them. "The work is hard, but where is it not? The haoles are stern taskmasters, because they themselves work hard. But they are not cruel. Never have I seen a haole treat his workmen as I have seen masters at home abuse theirs. The haoles who live here have taught us something that is unknown at home—and, I am told, was not known in Hawai before the white men came. This is the thought that a man's life is of value, and that each man is entitled to his share of respect. Here, as you have seen, everyone is free, no one is a slave or an outcast. This freedom is a great gift, to men who know how to use it."

Momotaro the Peach Boy: he was Sentaro's model, Ishi realized, as he would be for Ishi as well. Momotaro emerged, a heroic boy, from a gigantic peach (just as Ishi, enjoying the notion, imagined himself emerging from the heart of Kannon's stone), to become the champion of the weak and the oppressed, first in his valley, then in his island. Later—and Ishi remarked the nice similarity to his own story—Momotaro adventured across the sea, subduing evils and conquering enemies, to earn the respect of other people and peace for everyone in his realm.

"The haoles have made many laws, and they respect their laws. They wish us, too, to respect those laws. They are fair with us, if we are fair with them. They do not like to be cheated, they do not like anyone to take advantage of them."

To Ishi, who had dreamed of people like these haoles—and about ideals for which he had no names, about which he talked with no one but Nakamura-san, back there in that other world of Asakusa—Sentaro seemed to be a learned teacher expounding the law, pointing him now toward a new path that branched off from the one upon which Kannon had set his feet.

"For this reason they write down the laws on paper, they write contracts, and rules, and regulations, so that everyone will know what is expected of him and what he can expect in return." Sentaro looked at his guests, all intent upon hearing every bit of advice he could give them, and he faltered. These poor innocents ... How could he tell them about the exceptions to his fine generalizations? How could he tell them, here tonight, when they were so full of hope, about all the troubles he foresaw for them, because he himself had met so many? Were they ready to hear that, while haoles in general are fair and merciful, they also are so very certain that their ways are the only ways by which men should live? Or that, in their opinion, all other nations of men are inhabited by inferior beings, who could never be invited to haole houses, could never be worthy of their friendship, could never be good enough to marry haole sons and daughters? The task was too great for him to accept. They must learn all this for themselves, in the course of time. Against that time he tried gently to prepare them.

"Because haoles do not understand other languages than their own, and will make no effort to learn ours, you must begin to learn their language as soon as possible. Only when you understand what they are saying to you, or what they are writing on those many pieces of paper, will you be able to protect yourselves from those few who do try to stretch the meaning of the rules to their advantage. Beware of those few. They are shrewd men, whose only god is gold. They are not necessarily cruel with their hands. But they can be ruthless in their thoughts."

The worried faces staring back at him told him that he had alarmed them enough. "Fortunately, such clever dangerous men are rare. And even they will pay you well for your hard work. Four dollars a month, together with free houses, food, water, lamp oil, firewood, and a doctor's care if you are sick, and free working clothes, to be given you when you sign your contract: where in all Nippon is the man who earns that much in money and in care? The houses are not those of daimyo, of course. I know, for I have helped to build some on this island. But they are much better than the house my family lived in near Tateyama. And much better, I suspect, than those many of you lived in at home.

"But you will see all this for yourselves, next week. At first, I am afraid, you will have some troubles, and some sadness. No doubt, too," he laughed, "some aches and pains, when you learn to use muscles that have been idle for so long a time. But do not be discouraged. Keep trying."

The boy in his arms stirred, said something in words the guests could not understand.

"My son says I talk too much. I think so, too. 'The clever priest preaches a short sermon.' Only one more thing must I tell you and then you need listen no longer. At home, as I recall, we have a saying: 'Remember the honorable men in power.' That proverb is as important here as it is at home. But the men in power here are not the Hawaiians, not the King of Hawai or his officials. Here the haoles are the men in power. Especially the English and the Americans. The ones who own the sugar plantations, their agents who manage the money for them, the bankers, the shop-keepers in the towns: those are the men in power. And they are the ones who rule our lives."

For the last time he looked around him, letting his glance rest on these grave young wanderers so far from home, for whom he felt an elder brother's affection, and an elder brother's worry.

"In this, I think," he finished quietly, "you will find that Hawai is not different from Nippon."

CHAPTER 13
THE DIVIDING

One more journey, one more landfall. And this last one is the best, thought Ishi, gazing across the sea to the beautiful island. Never had he seen a mountain so shattered, so cleft by deep valleys, so exalted to high peaks and narrow ridges raised above dark gorges one after the other, like the folds of a half-opened fan. Never had he imagined a place so bountifully watered: from every valley a stream rushed forth, upon every proud cliff hung a score of falls. This island was wild, untamed, undespoiled. It was rich in rocks, in water, and green growing things. It was empty of people. It called to him, across the sparkling sea, in beauty and mystery and loneliness. He fell in love with it at sight, and knew that he had found his home at last.

For two days the schooner *Mamokawai* had been under way, trying to sail the hundred miles between Honolulu and one port or another on the island on Maui. Freighted with obese Captain Agosto Antone, three huge Hawaiian sailors, seventy-four Japanese laborers, and a fouled bottom, she was crowded to the gunwales and very sluggish in the water. For more than a day she drifted in the lee of Molokai, scarcely moved by Captain Antone's loud Portuguese threats, her passengers' prayers, or lazing currents in the idle sea. Then, this morning, as though suddenly reminded of a duty they had neglected, fresh winds swooped down from the northeast, bringing full sails for the *Mamokawai* and rain squalls and white-capped waves for the entertainment of her passengers.

Because they possessed not a single mushroom to put in the

navel, as a charm to prevent seasickness, most of the passengers promptly got sick. Because the schooner had no hold into which they might crawl, all passengers, sick or well, lay upon the open deck, sharing it with rain and sun and sea spray, and with the surprised flying fish that sometimes fell among them. Those flopping malolo were the liveliest things upon the ship for several hours, while the people clung to each other, to the deck, to the low rail, in their efforts to avoid being thrown into the sea as replacements for the fish that had left it. None of the sick people gave much thought to food, fortunately; and, as usual, the few who were seaworthy men had to be content with memories and expectations, inasmuch as the owner of an inter-island schooner never bothered to provide meals for his captives. But no one thirsted on the *Mamokawai:* the rains were kind enough to fill the cask with more than enough sail-drippings tasting of salt, mildew, and ancient tar.

Those seventy-four passengers aboard the *Mamokawai* were the largest group to be split off from the company the *Scioto* had delivered to the Board of Immigration in Honolulu. The sugar plantations on Maui, being among the newest in the Hawaiian kingdom, had instructed their agents in Honolulu to send them as many of the new contract-laborers as their budgets could afford.

At eight o'clock in the morning of Monday, June 22, 1868, the Board of Immigration met at the Government Building in Honolulu, to calculate the cost of recruiting and transporting those laborers from Japan. The bills Captain Reagan submitted, in favor of Consul-General Eugene Van Reed of Yokohama and Jardine, Matheson & Company of Hong Kong, dismayed everyone in Honolulu, not least the parsimonious agents of the sugar planters. "Even in these days of high costs," Albion Houghton spoke for them, "seventy dollars a head is too much."

The Board of Immigration, perforce, remained firm. Mr. Jonathan Green, its chairman, rose to speak. Tall and bearded, resembling a Calvinist's vision of Jehovah, Mr. Green declared, with some acerbity, "His Majesty's Government has gone to a great deal of trouble and expense to help you sugar men. His Majesty's Government, as these accounts pending do show, is making no profit from this accommodation for you. Even more pertinent is the fact that His Majesty's Government's treasury has no funds for absorbing any portion of the expenses incurred. In view of these conditions, gentlemen, the cost per head for these coolies must be fixed at seventy dollars. Take 'em or leave 'em." Perforce, the sugar planters' agents accepted the terms.

Although, in general, plantation treasuries were in better financial condition than the kingdom's, they being considered more likely to return a profit in the long run, the agents still grumbled among themselves. "We'll just have to economize in other ways," Mr. Houghton advised his colleagues, with his usual perceptiveness. Sugar was on its way to being king in this dying kanaka kingdom, he foresaw, and he planned to be the new king's prime minister. "Pay the going rate," he counselled. "New hands taken on now will mean a loss this year, perhaps, but will certainly earn greater profits each year thereafter."

While these bargainings were being conducted in the Board of Immigration's office, the imported Japanese waited on the sidewalk before the paved courtyard of the Government Building, on the Merchant Street side. Reputable townsfolk, passing by on their way to work, to market, or the the Post Office housed in the *Pacific Commercial Advertiser*'s printing shop next door to the Government Building stared at these hordes of foreigners in their strange attire.

Promptly at nine o'clock, as announced, the plantation agents and others who were interested in employing the Japanese emerged from the Government Building. They stood for a moment at the head of the flight of stairs, wide as the building itself, leading down to the paved court. As was only proper, in this city of boundless courtesies, ladies and gentlemen in search of domestics were invited to make their selections first. Mr. Green waved a generous hand, made a gallant bow. Thanking him with dimpled smiles and tossings of their bonneted heads, lifting their hooped skirts ever so slightly, the ladies floated prettily down the stairs to the pavement, followed by their attentive gentlemen. Mr. Green and his secretary, trailing after, met with Sentaro and Makino at the foot of the stairs. The planters' agents, still at the top, snapped their fingers. Office-boys ran forward from the wings to receive instructions, lists hastily scrawled on scraps of paper, and other arcane information, all delivered with many waggings of sharp forefingers.

Doctor and Mrs. Owen Smithson, being the wealthiest couple present, took precedence, by common consent. After much uncertainty on the part of Mrs. Smithson (and saintly forebearance on the part of her husband), the while she flitted forth and back between the "cute" Aiko and the "very petite" Miya, she finally chose the older woman. Koi's fiercest scowls helped direct her to that decision; but more than likely she was captivated by the toothful smiles that both Miya and Daigoro turned upon her when Sentaro whispered the reason why this peculiar American female was studying them so intently. They had not dreamed that they could escape so easily from laboring in the fields. And when Sentaro told them the terms that Dr. and Mrs. Smithson offered, in return for the lightest of services as personal maid and houseboy, they accepted at once, without really knowing what those services entailed. But they did not give those a second thought: the promise of all that honorable money, and the chance to stay in Honolulu too, won their devotion instantly.

Enchanted by their modesty and politeness, the Smithsons swept off with these prizes then and there—or, rather, as soon as Mr. Green's brash secretary had made both masters and servants sign the contracts and instructed Dr. Smithson to put his signature upon an official statement whereby he promised to pay to the Board of Immigration, upon demand, the sum of $140 American. "We'll send you the bill," said this sassy Hawaiian youth, looking the irate doctor straight in the eye. Mr. Green, perceiving a little conflict of wills here, hurried off to attend the Reverend and Mrs. Harding while they made their selection.

Amid many cries and bows of farewell (and envious thoughts as thick as snowflakes in a blizzard), Miya-san and Daigoro-san departed from their companions of the ship. Not forgetting their friends, even in this time of greatest good fortune, Daigoro and Miya bowed very low, to left, to right, and to center, so that no one could feel that he was being left out. And they called, for all to hear, "Farewell. We wish you much contentment. Please keep us in your favor."

The haoles thought this a quaint little ceremony, but a bit time-consuming, and hoped they'd not have to put up with it when every one of these foreigners departed. The Nipponjin entertained mixed feelings about the deference that Daigoro-san and his wife had offered them. Most were gratified by the propriety, asking nothing more. But, as usual, there were some who sniffed and said, "Well, of course. After what has happened to them, they can well afford to show us such cheap kindness." As the wise saying reminds us, "With the same kind of smile the man below makes friends, the man above arouses jealousies."

Smiling not at all, because he was still furious with that insulting kanaka lackey, Dr. Smithson gave a street urchin a whole American five-cent piece to guide Daigoro and Miya to his fine home in Punchbowl Street, near the Queen's Hospital. But he forced the obligatory cheer to his lips when he handed his glowing wife into their carriage. "Where to, my dear?" he asked fondly, of this damned woman who spent his money faster than he could earn it and gave him damned little in return for it. And how, he wondered, did that damned black minion back there learn about all my debts?

"I think we'd best go straight home, dear," she replied, patting his hand affectionately, for all to see. "I want to be there when they arrive."

Reverend and Mrs. Abraham Harding, an elderly couple recently retired from the Congregationalist Mission, employed Kintaro and Tomi to be their servants. Sleeping Yotaro, strapped to his mother's back, did not hinder the arrangement. "Oh, dear me, no," Mrs. Harding told Sentaro, "we love children. There'll be lots of room for the little fellow. Our house is rather empty, now that ours have grown and gone away. The presence of children makes for a steady family, don't you think?''

The Hardings walked home, having no carriage of their own. Before they'd gone half way Mrs. Harding succeeded in getting Yotaro transferred from his mother's back to her own withering bosom. Behind her trailed Reverend Harding, long since subdued by Christian womanhood, and Kintaro and Tomi, converted by this woman's goodness long before they heard a word of Christianity's dogma.

Mr. Patrick Michael McInerny, a merchant who owned a fine haberdashery next to the Government Building, conceived the idea that he'd like a body servant for himself when he saw the Smithsons walking off with two of them. Not knowing one Japanese from another, yet fancying the tall lean ones because he himself was so short and round, he chose Nakasuke of Shinjuku, the tallest and thinnest one in the group. The doctor from the Board of Health was not present to tell Mr. McInerny that Nakasuke was thin because he was consumptive. Nor did Nakasuke know why he was so thin and tired, or why, lately, he had been coughing up flecks of blood. But his karma gave Mr. McInerny the dying body of Nakasuke to take home with him.

As word spread among them the immigrants waiting on Merchant Street became more excited, looking eagerly about for the persons who would rescue them from laboring in the fields. City men who had gravely assured Hamada Hikizo that they were devoted farmers, whose sole happiness came from working in mud up to their armpits, now remembered how delicately they were made, and how much of their happiness came from living in cities. Some, like Kuranosuke, would have given their service to a butcher of animals, working for him in blood, guts, and excrement up to their navels if he but promised to keep them in Honolulu. A few, such as hot-headed Koi, seethed with anger at the indignity of being examined like horses put up for sale; and Aiko still blushed after the scrutiny to which that pale prying woman had subjected her. Ishi, too, was not pleased by this kind of selling of human beings, but he said nothing for fear of arousing Koi to even greater complaints. That rash youth, full of fire above and of water below, drew titters from everyone who could hear him when he growled, "If they ask to see whether I am a man or a boy, I'll show 'em. I'll piss in their faces!" Only Ishi on one side and Aiko on the other prevented him from acting out the whole drama, right there in front of all those forbidding haoles.

Nonetheless, Ishi's tolerance was greatly strained when he saw Mr. Green leading a man to Makino-san. And Ishi was outraged when, after a few minutes' talk, Makino nodded happily, shook the hand the stranger offered, and went with him to sign a contract. Ishi was aghast. Makino-san a body-servant for that common foreigner, so short and fat and covered with hair! He almost wept for shame as he imagined Makino-san tied to a service so demeaning.

After Makino no others of the immigrants were chosen to be domestic servants, not even the boys Ichigoro and Zembei, trying for once to look both clean and dependable. As usual, high hopes gave way to groans of disappointment, and to low forms of humor. But joking stopped at once, although disappointment lingered, when the office-boys came down the steps, to take the rest of them into bondage.

They did this in true democratic fashion—alphabetically, according to the name of the plantation. The boy representing the first plantation on the list simply counted off the number of heads he'd been told to take, beckoned to them to follow him, and marched off to a table on the Government Building's broad verandah. There Mr. Green's vigilant secretary made each immigrant sign two copies of a contract printed in English. Sentaro and Makino stood by, to help with the signing if a man could not write his name and to explain for the few who thought to ask that this was a translation of the same contract they had signed for Hamada-san in Yokohama. When all the men destined for that plantation finished this procedure, the office-boy took one set of contracts and the signers to Brenig's clothing store, around the corner on Bethel Street. There each man received one set of work clothes made of Hindoo dungaree dyed blue with indigo, a pair of leather shoes with high tops, a pair of dark blue cotton socks, a light blue cotton shirt with long sleeves, and a lauhala hat. Herr Brenig, in a burst of artistry, thinking that so much blue needed a touch of color, added to each outfit a red kerchief of the sort that cowboys wear around their necks.

The first office-boy, despairing of being able to tell these aliens how to put on all those strange garments, pressed one of Mr. Brenig's Chinese tailors into use. For the rest of the morning that poor man silently put on and took off the same pieces of clothing, while equally solemn Japanese intently copied the process, and sweating Herr Brenig rushed about, acquainting them with the need to match buttons with buttonholes.

Once his men were dressed in the new fashion the office-boy led them upon the next stage of their journey. If they were assigned to a plantation of Oahu he took them to a livery stable and delivered them to a wagoner. If they were assigned to a plantation on another island he conducted them to the waterfront and delivered his charges to a schooner hired to transport them to their new homes.

All the haoles agreed that Mr. Houghton and his colleagues had set up a very efficient system for sending the laborers to work as soon as possible, with least expense of time and effort. The immigrants, too, marveled at its efficiency. They went through it as fast as water in a millrace—so fast, indeed, that most of them did not know where they were going.

After several batches of men had been spirited away, never to be seen again by their shipmates, Ishi, Koi, and Aiko were near the head of the line. The office-boy from Castle & Cooke came to count off his group.

"Where are we going?," Ishi demanded to know, very directly for a Nipponjin. He did not want to entrust himself entirely to the workings of Chance.

"To Maui," answered Sentaro, "to Haiku Plantation. A good place, I have heard."

"Is it a green island, this Maui? Does it have water?," Ishi persisted. "I do not wish to go to a dry island, such as this one of Honoruru."

Sentaro, never having been there himself, put the question to the office-boy. He laughed agreeably (which pleased the Nipponjin, this being the first kindness any haole had shown them that morning), and said, "More water than they know what to do with." Upon hearing Sentaro's translation of this answer they agreed to go to Haiku on Maui.

"Remember the name," said Sentaro. "Haiku."

"Hai," said Koi, in jesting mood again. "Haiku e iku. Ah, watashitachi wa Haiku e iku," he warbled in his geisha's voice, plucking at an imaginary samisen. Oh, we are going to Haiku, to Haiku of Maui across the sea . . .

At that moment C. Brewer's harried office-boy rushed up to confer with his cousin from Castle & Cooke. They reckoned that, between the two, the plantations they represented needed sixty-one men. "Why don't we hurry this job along," said the Brewer boy. A Harvard lad recently come to visit in Honolulu, he knew all the tricks for speeding events to his advantage. "Let's just take the next sixty-one in line. They all look the same to me. Then we put 'em aboard the boat before noon, and get 'em off our hands. I'm famished," he added by way of justification.

"But Wailuku comes near the end of the line, doesn't it?," said the Castle & Cooke lad, an honorable Punahou boy to the end.

"Only Kualoa lies between thee and me, friend. Wherever that is. And Mr. Wilder says, 'Sure, go ahead. I'm not much interested in hiring anybody yet.' "

"What about Kaalaea, Ulupalakua, and Waikapu? Not to mention Lanai, the Pasture of the Shepherd Saint?" A good Punahou boy's charity did not extend so far as to embrace Mormons.

"Oh, Heavens!," swore the malihini from Harvard. "How can you remember all these heathen names?"

"Don't fret. I'm supposed to sign up for a couple of those, too. Let's just grab off thirteen more, and then make a run. O.K.?"

"Such a job," sighed the Brewer man, dashing off to the secretary sitting in state on the verandah, "such a lot of pagans . . ."

In this way the Wheel of Chance affected Ishi's karma and that of his two friends. Through this improper collusion between a hungry office-boy and his agreeable and unthinking cousin, and the consequent confusion of papers at the secretary's table, Ishi, Koi, and Aiko, thinking they were going to Haiku Plantation, signed contracts that sent them to another place instead.

The great crisis of the morning came while those two haole boys were counting off the seventy-four heads they needed. Checking separately, each came to the same dividing place. "Here," they said, lowering their long arms right between Yuki and Nagayuki.

"Not good," growled Nagayuki, waving for Makino-san to come to their rescue.

"No, no," Makino said to the C. Brewer man, busy trying to push brother apart from sister, not looking at either in his haste. "Togedda. Togedda ahru."

"Oh?," said the haole. "Married?"

Makino, honest man, shook his head.

"Then," decreed the proper youth, "they must go to different places."

"Not good." Hissing at his inability to explain, Makino placed one forefinger against the other. "Togedda. One hausu. Orru same," he said carefully, "no not marry. Prease. You not part."

The youth stiffened. "Not married?" He blanched at such determined wickedness.

Makino recognized that wordless horror. Valiantly, he tried again. Unable in this emergency to remember the terms for brother and sister, he said, "Prease. You rook. Him. Har. You rook face. Fadda same. Madda same."

Slowly the message penetrated the Harvard intellect, at last the haole turned to look upon the victims of his zeal. Although to him all Orientals looked alike, even he could see that these two were most especially alike. "Ah, ah," he giggled, very much surprised to learn that not all coolies are as depraved as he'd been told. "O.K., O.K.," he conceded generously, "Together." Pushing Nagayuki into line beside Yuki, he yanked Number 73 out of it, and thrust him into the space Nagayuki had just vacated.

"S'ank you," said Makino, mopping his brow.

And that is how Yonekichi the scrivener went to a plantation on Kauai, instead of to one on the island of Maui.

Because in Christian countries women do not wear trousers, the Japanese women received skirts made of dungaree. They would have been less embarrassed had they worn trousers, but haoles did not know about mompei, those trousers-like garments that peasant women wear in Nippon. All others of the clothes they obtained in Herr Brenig's establishment, even the big shoes, were the same as those given to the men.

Some of the men looked very comical, enveloped in trousers too big for them in all dimensions. Quickly adjusting to the foreigners' strange ways, they filled the spaces by wearing two or three fundoshi at a time, or by wrapping a kimono around the waist before tying the trousers tight with pieces of twine or with the obi they had been wearing earlier in the day. The shoes were not so easily fitted: almost invariably the feet were too small to fill them. Mr. Brenig and his clerks showed the newcomers how to wrap sheets of newspaper around their feet, or to stuff paper into the toes of the shoes. Nonetheless, the shoes had a way of slipping off while the wearers were trying to walk.

In time, somehow or other, all got dressed in the stiff new clothes and plodded out of Brenig's store into Bethel Street. The coarse unwashed dungaree, smelling still of fulling and indigo dyestuff, chafed wherever it touched the skin. Those hard shoes pinched their tender feet. While they walked to the waterfront the wanderers felt hot and itchy and miserable. We clop along like a herd of tired horses on an icy road, thought Ishi.

This drab and ill-fitting uniform annoyed him. It had no style, no distinction. The livery of Lord Okubo's footmen was more elegant than the best clothes that haole men wore in Honolulu, and much more beautiful. He had never been ashamed of his uniform in Edo, much as he may have disliked the duties that went with it. But here, in Honolulu's streets, garbed in this blue stuff, he felt awkward and ashamed.

He need not have worried about the effect they made upon the townsfolk. With those uniforms, those big shoes and floppy lauhala hats, they were workers now, like so many others, not guests of the city. No one noticed them as they limped by.

At the piers where the schooners lay, Makino-san and Sentaro-san waited to say goodbye to the people in each contingent. Makino, the only Nipponjin in sight who still wore the clothes of home, looked especially handsome amid all those laborers in dungaree. They swarmed about, like dark grubs disturbed when a rotten log is overturned. Ishi, more ashamed than ever, tried to hide behind his companions, pulled that silly hat low upon his head. But Sentaro picked him out, being accustomed to the sight of people wearing such apparel.

"I cannot go," mumbled Ishi, when Sentaro told him that Makino-san wished to say goodbye.

"Because of those clothes? Don't be foolish. They are exactly the clothes you should wear in the field. We all wear them at our jobs. I, too, when I work as a carpenter. When you get used to them, and they to your body, you will not think anymore about them. Come, let's go over to Makino."

Noticing Ishi's discomfort, Makino turned it to his advantage. "Behold," with a sweep of his arm he indicated the line of uniformed people boarding the *Mamokawai,* "the samurai of sugarcane, going forth in suits of stiffest armor. But where are their weapons? And," he looked soberly at Ishi, "where is their leader?"

"That is my worry," Ishi said. "We shall miss you, Makino-san. Now we shall be as small sons without a father."

"Sons have a habit of replacing fathers," Makino said lightly. He wanted to free this serious man from his burden of loyalty. He wanted this borrowed son to stand alone. "I do not worry for this group. You will be with them."

"I?"

"Remember our talks aboard the ship? Remember how I asked for your help?"

"I remember. And how happy I was to be your lieutenant— once I learned that you were not jesting with me. I shall always remember . . . " He broke off, unable to trust his voice with words that could never say what he felt.

Makino realized that Ishi did not want to be freed from a tie that he cherished. To him this was more than the duty of a son to his father: it was the loyalty of a disciple to his teacher. And never, as long as both lived, could that tie be broken or dishonored. Swift as the falcon on the wing Makino changed his approach.

"You helped me well, Ishi-san, and I thank you for your loyalty. But you are not yet freed of your duty to me. This father of yours, if you wish to call him so, is a very selfish man. Unwilling to give up his power over his sons, he wishes to command them still. In other words, my friend, please continue to be my lieutenant on your island."

"You mean that you are still our daimyo? You are not going to be a servant to that foreigner?"

"Which foreigner?"

"The fat and hairy one whose contract you signed. Up there, at that other place."

"Ah, I see what you are thinking. No, not a servant. That man is Mr. Fenton Sengel, or Single, or Shingle, or something like that, I am not yet sure. He is a member of the British Legation in this country. At Mr. Van Reed's suggestion, and with Mr. Green's approval, I am to stay in Honolulu to help the Board of Immigration in its plans to bring more Nipponjin here in the future. Also to help settle any problems that may come up with this first group, as you go to work on the plantations. Mr. Green—a wise man, I think, and a good one—expects that we shall have many problems, just as the Chinese workers had, when they first began. Therefore, I am to remain here, to be in the middle of things. I shall live in the household of Mr. Sengel. Not as a servant but as a student. He will teach me English, I shall teach him our language, because he wishes to go someday to Nippon. And, best of all, I shall have the chance to study in a western school. Mr. Green says he will try to send me to school here, in a place called Punahou."

"A very good school, that," said Sentaro. "Very exclusive."

"So, you see, I am still responsible for the care of our people. And once again I ask your help. This time on Maui."

"Willingly, Makino-san," said Ishi, happy for his leader's good fortune, proud to be thought worthy of his trust.

"Ishi-san! Ishi-san!," many people called from the ship. "Please hurry! The boat is going ... "

"Good. Then I shall count on you as before," said Makino, offering his big hand. Ishi liked the warm, firm grasp. This was a better salute for men than bowing. And in this special case he knew it was more than just a touching of hands.

He turned and ran, before the tears spilled from his eyes. 'The eyelids of a samurai know not tears,' he had heard them say so often ...

Makino did not hide his sadness.

"A good man," said Sentaro, knowing how fathers like to think of their sons.

"A very good man. A man of light, too long sheathed in stone. He must be freed now from that sheathing."

"And you will be the carver?"

"No. The Lord Buddha, perhaps, will be the carver. Or perhaps Kannon-sama. Or some other god. I am but the man who sets the uncarved block of stone before him. And never have I found a better one than this."

Slowly the *Mamokawai* drew away from the pier, her passengers thick as blueflies clustered on a crab shell. They looked back at Makino-san and Sentaro-san, their last links with the past.

Feeling still the warmth of Makino's handclasp, the sting of his own grief, Ishi bowed to his teacher. Beside him, behind him, all the others bowed respectfully, in farewell to the two who were their protectors.

Makino stood on a crate, stiff as an image carved by an artist, looking more like a statue of kind Jizo than of a samurai. The travelers on the way felt their stomachs grow small. Why does he not say farewell? they wondered. What have we done to offend him? they whispered, as the distance widened between them.

Makino lifted his hand and waved, as haoles do, and Hawaiians, and all other people in this new homeland, as Sentaro was doing, beside their daimyo. Ah, now we understand, they laughed, learning from their teacher. Lifting their hands, they waved in farewell in this new manner, calling out, over and over again, "Aroha ... Aroha ... "

And now, at long last, more than fifty hours after that departure from Honolulu, the *Mamokawai* was sailing along Maui's northern coast, pushed by the trade winds toward Kahului Bay. Sitting beside the starboard rail, near the bow, Ishi wanted only to look at those spectacular ridges and gorges and watercourses displayed before him. This must be the place that Nakamura-san was telling me about, he thought. He must have engraved the picture of it upon his liver, to have remembered it so well. As I am doing now. How beautiful it is! How glad I am that I chose to come here, instead of staying on that desert Oahu. As is the way with trusting men when affairs are going well, Ishi too congratulated himself for having arranged his life so satisfactorily.

Yet, among helpless men, there are a few who can never forget the Turning Wheel. Such a one, sitting near Ishi, tapped him upon a damp blue sleeve. "Look at that," the man said.

"At what?" Ishi turned reluctantly from his contemplation of beauty.

"At that." Kuranosuke the Edokko pointed to the east, to the bulk of an immense mountain, blue and brooding in the distance.

"Ha!," Ishi grunted, as though he had been kicked in the belly. Instinctively, he drew back from that overwhelming thing, swelling like an ocean wave about to roll down upon them. Compared with that the shattered mountain seemed to be little more than an arrangement of mossy stones in a temple garden. "What is it?," he asked, wishing immediately that he had not asked. A place so implacable and aloof must have a name that men may not pronounce in vain. A place so cruel must be the abode of only the cruelest of gods.

"The Rim of the Wheel, rising in the east," said Kuranosuke, pretending that he jested. Then, seeing another resemblance, he said, not jesting, "A burial mound for dead gods . . . "

Ishi shuddered, and turned away. Kuranosuke continued to stare at it, as though waiting for the turning wheel to crush him.

CHAPTER 14
THE SETTLING

Maui, as haole map makers have revealed, is shaped like a humpbacked old woman sitting upon her knees. The sundered mountain forms her head, vast Haleakala the bulk of her body, clad in a muumuu for which the coastline from Makena to Hana serves as lace to the skirt. Breasts she has none, but she is gifted with a small point of a nose in Olowalu near Lahaina.

Upon this image Kahului Bay is nothing more than a crease in the nape of Maui's neck. A certain cynical rancher of Makawao, in one of his more acerb moments—when he felt justified in utterly disregarding the facts of anatomy—called Kahului "a supernumerary asshole." No doubt from his vantage at Makawao it looks like that—especially when, on rare occasions, after heaviest rains, nearby Kanaha swamp overflows, dyeing the sea with excremental mud.

In real life, because of its exposed position, Kahului is the perpetual victim of winds, waves, rains, and heat. They hurl themselves upon kneeling Maui's nape and the flat plain that is her neck and throat as if hating the poor cringing thing. And yet, try as they might, they do not destroy her. They build her up. Waves heap sand in great dunes above the beaches, winds shift the hills about at whim, scouring with grains of coral the dry dirt beyond. In this desert of sand and salt and dust the swift-falling rains are soon sucked up, the hardiest weeds cannot grow.

In this crease in the nape of the neck of Maui, Kahului's tiny wharf sits like an infinitesimal wen. Two small shacks, one a warehouse at the head of the pier, the other a Chinaman's store, each supporting the other, are the only upright things visible for miles around. Winds keep the sand away from their doors. Blasted and forlorn, they look as if soon they too will be torn from their roots and blown across the plain.

The only relief for the eyes in this bleakness is a thin verge of green along the shore, where coarse grass and pohuehue, the beach morning glory, cling to the wet sand, and the scum of seaweed covers the reef. The only hope for the soul is to get in and out of Kahului as fast as possible. Schooners stay no longer than they must; and even the Chinese storekeeper and his assistant do not go there except when ships come in.

"A fine town. With a fine view," said Kuranosuke, wondering for the millionth time why he had ever left Edo. He could not remember anymore why he had been such a fool. If he had hungered there, he was no stranger to hunger here. At this very moment his stomach was as empty as a pickler's crock in spring. If he lacked money there, or women, or respect and friends, he did not see any prospect of gaining these here, in this emptiness. Why? he asked, staring up at that cresting wave of blue rock, as if imploring it to answer him.

"Don't look at it," Ishi told him. "Look up there instead." He indicated the shattered mountain at their right, the mountain he was already claiming as his own. Surely that must be the place called Haiku. Although he had been surprised to find that it was connected by this sandy plain with that monstrous mound he did not like to see, he had not lost any of his love for his mountain. Its foothills were barren, its nearer slopes covered only with short grass, but the high peaks at the center were green and golden in the afternoon light. They were emblems of life compared with this dead flatland of Kahului, or the tremendous pile that so fascinated Kuranosuke.

Three great valleys had been gouged out of this eastern face of the sundered mountain. The two at either side were wide, open, welcoming. Sunlight slanting in from the west filled the whole valley on the left, touched only the farther cliffs in the valley on the right. But the one at the center was different. The sinking sun had no power to light up this deep gorge. Only in its hour of triumph could the sun penetrate that narrow, dark, mysterious place. It was like the birth canal of a woman during the last hundred days before she bears a child: then the seed-planting husband must not enter in. The valley was forbidden, secret, sacred.

Yet, loving it because it was a part of the mountain he loved, Ishi yearned to go to that sacred place. When he entered in, he promised, he must go only in the full light of day, with the high sun showing the way, when he himself would be a pilgrim cleansed of all defilement.

"And that," said Kuranosuke the inconsolable, pointing to the dark central valley, "that is the gateway to Emma-o's Hell."

"He's right!" exclaimed Koi. "Look! Smoke from the Hell of Raging Fire is coming out of it."

They saw two riders on horseback hastening toward the pier, one coming from the east, one from the west. On Maui, they recognized, there would always be this separation, this dividing into two parts.

Koi waved a casual hand toward the desolation beyond the schooner's bow. "That reminds me of an old man being married to a young woman."

"Why?" asked Ishi, the willing foil.

"Nothing in the middle," cried the tireless joker. Others laughed with him. They might as well laugh while they could, they knew.

"Where can they be going, those two?," someone asked, watching the galloping horsemen, the trailing plumes of yellow dust.

"They are coming to tell us to go back," said Kuranosuke. "That our being here is all a big mistake. Then they too will come aboard this fine pleasure boat with us. And we shall sail away ... "

Ishi wished that he could shake this miserable fellow by the throat until the brine poured out of him. But he dared not treat him so meanly. To do so would cause both the victim and his attacker to lose face, and Ishi knew that poor Kuranosuke should not be held to account for those worrisome remarks. What would Makino-san do? the loyal lieutenant wondered, to stop such hurtful talk. But no remedy came to his mind, except to speak the obvious and weighty truth: "Those horsemen are coming to lead us out of this place. Let us be ready for them."

The rider from the west arrived first, having had the shorter distance to cover. Whipping his steed until the last moment, he brought it to a halt in a cloud of dust and a scream of pain from the mare. As she reared and danced about, he looked down at the Japanese, bunched together in the shade cast by the Chinese store.

Sullen faces. Slippered feet. Holding bundles of rags. A couple of 'em with banjos slung over their shoulders. Skinny, scrawny, small.—And sickly. "Crissake!" he swore, "what a crew!" Something else about 'em, too. He couldn't quite put his finger on it. Something treacherous and sly. Something mean . . .

He slipped from the saddle, flung the bridle over the hitching rail in front of the store. Without wasting another glance upon the runty lot he loped past them, spurs jingling, boots kicking up as much dust as possible. Seeing the two Pakés looking through the store window, like ghosts from a haunted house, he aimed his usual friendly gob of spit at the pane, and made his usual direct hit. They recoiled, out of habit. "Shit!" he grieved for irremediable stupidity. "They never learn."

The Japanese did not know what to think about this tall thin man with the red hair and unbelievably long legs. They had been prepared to call "Aroha," if only he gave them the chance. But he was so unfriendly. He did not even look at them when he passed by.

"Perhaps he does not come for us after all," Ishi humbled himself. "No doubt he has other business with the master of the ship."

Some found the tall man's unfriendliness a bad omen. Others thought that it meant nothing, saying "What can he tell us, if he does not speak our language?'' A few who recognized the signs said bluntly, ''He is drunk.''

The horseman from the east arrived, quietly and without violence. He was only a boy, eleven or twelve years old, they guessed, with long black hair reaching to below his ears, skin the color of polished rosewood, and the most remarkable eyes. Gray they were, like the eyes in statues carved from stone.

He tied his horse to the hitching rail, gave the Japanese a boy's shy smile and friendly aloha. Feeling much better about this rider, they called out aloha and waved as he passed them on his way to the ship. His boots made no noise upon the planks of the pier, so light was his body, so easy his step.

After only a few minutes both horsemen came down from the schooner, each carrying a canvas mail bag in one hand, a packet of papers in the other. The man strode toward the Japanese. ''All right,'' he bawled, ''let's get moving. Who's for Wailuku?''

No one moved, no one answered.

''Christ! D'ja ever see anythin' so stoopid? How the hell they expect me to get any work outta such weakheads? O.K., O.K. Let's try again.'' Once more he roared, once again they failed to understand. Ishi, Koi, and a few others, who had been roared at by samurai and sergeants at home, rather guessed what the man might be yelling about, but because they could not be sure they kept their mouths shut.

The gray-eyed boy spoke. ''I suspect they don't know any English, Mr. Douglas. Let me try another way.''

''Well, they better learn damn fast. If they're gonna work for me. O.K., squirt. You shoot your piece.''

Inviting the attention of the Japanese, the lad pointed with his right hand toward the east, to the long shoulder of the great mountain sloping down to its meeting with the sea. ''Haiku,'' he said, very clearly. ''Haiku.''

Ho! Ishi exclaimed to himself, very disappointed. That is not where I wish to go.

With his left hand the boy pointed toward the west, saying "Wailuku."

Ah, thought Ishi, so that is the name of my mountain. Wairuku is the place where I wish to go.

With both forefingers the boy pointed to the whole group of attentive Japanese. With the right forefinger he drew an imaginary line in the air, directing it from them toward Haiku. His supple hands, his long fingers drew these airy signs with exquisite grace. The Japanese observed him with the eyes of experts, taking pleasure in the sight. Just so does a fine dancer use his body to tell a story, to express a message. The red-haired haole, seeing these same gestures, spat into the dust. "Goddam mahu! Shoulda been drowned at birth."

With his left forefinger the boy traced the line toward Wailuku. His students immediately sorted themselves into two groups.

"Well, I'll be damned!," allowed the admiring red-head. "Pretty good, there, squirt. Where'd ja learn that Injun sign language?"—By God! That's it! he thought. Put braids on 'em, feathers in their lousy hair . . . "Injuns, by God!," he snarled, "nothin' but runty Injuns!"

"Not at Punahou, you can be sure," said the boy, cutting off any sneers aimed toward that butt.

"Guess we'd better count 'em out. See if we got the right number of head." He stepped to one side, scratching the air with a dirty finger, ended with another "Damn! Off by three. Well, squirt, lessee you settle this one. I'm s'posed ta have twenny-three head, an' I ain't leavin' till I get 'em."

"The name is Hiram Bristol, Mr. Douglas."

"Your name'll be Shit, kid, if you don't get us outta here and home 'fore nightfall. I don't approve this idea of sendin' a boy ta do a man's job."

Like most half-Hawaiian children, Hiram Bristol was accustomed to hearing sneers and abuse from such superlative specimens of the preeminent white race as Jack Douglas. But, unlike most of his breed, he was lucky enough to have a father who taught him how to regard such abuses. "Think of them as unreasoned compliments, son, directed at you by people who insult you because they fear you. They don't know why they're afraid, but they are afraid, nonetheless. But you'll have nothing to fear from them, because they are bullies, cowards at heart."

Hiram Bristol inspected the contracts of the immigrants who had been recruited for Haiku Plantation, and did not find the least sign of a workman's name he could read. Brush marks at the top of each contract, looking like children's scrawls, gave him the clue he wanted. He thought for a moment. "Guess I'll need their help," he informed Douglas, as he turned toward the group intending to go to Haiku. He held up the sheaf of contracts, went to the first man in line, pointed to the brush marks, pointed to the man. Habit led him to say, "You?"

The man could not read any kanji other than those that spelled his own name. Not recognizing these, he shook his head. Hiram stepped to the next man in line, repeating the process. Ishi, realizing how slow this approach would be, stepped forward. He held out his hand for the contracts. The boy, recognizing a friend in this foreigner, released them at once. Ishi could read many of the kanji, but not all. He passed to their signers the contracts whose signatures he could decipher, called upon the others to identify their own. The closer he got to the end of the sheaf the more disturbed he became. At the end he was dismayed. Koi, Aiko, and he were left out. "Komatta naa," they worried together, "we are troubled. How can this be? Did we not choose to go to the plantation of Haiku?"

Douglas, furious with their stupidity, those blank looks, the bursts of excited chatter, started again to bellow.

"Don't yell at them, Mr. Douglas. They can't understand a word you're saying. Until they can understand, you've got to use signs. Let me have your contracts, please."

Once again the ingenious boy gave the papers to Ishi. With those supple brown fingers speaking for him, he asked Ishi to look for the contracts belonging to the disconsolate three. Ishi quickly found them—and the cause of their confusion.

After this short acquaintance with the ill-tempered man and the gentle boy, Ishi and his friends wanted very much to go to

Haiku. By use of signs he explained that the three had expected to go to Haiku, that they still most earnestly wished to go there. Dismay, pleading, and discreet hints of horror at having to submit to the commands of that cruel man over there failed to move the boy. To him, an American by association and his father's son by training, a contract was sacred, a covenant not to be altered except by agreement between parties of the first part with parties of the second part. Much as he liked the looks of these three Japanese, much as he regretted turning anyone over to the mercy of this brutal Douglas, he could only shake his head, saying, "No, I'm sorry. No. Wailuku," pointing to the west, but never losing his patience or his smile. At last they realized that they must obey so quiet an authority and sadly went to the end of the line bound for Wailuku. "Not good," they said, to each other and to all their neighbors. "Dame da!"

"Well, 'sabout time!" snarled Mr. Douglas, studying their unhappy faces, promising himself to remember these three troublemakers next time they got in his way.

Hiram Bristol, forgetting nothing, collected the contracts from Ishi, returned them to the gentleman from Wailuku. "They're all here, Mr. Douglas. Twenty-three, as per contracts."

"Buncha stoopid animals," growled Douglas, snatching the contracts, not deigning to thank the boy for his help. "C'mon you damn monkeys! Let's go!" Vaulting into the saddle, he kicked his horse. As she reared, her forefeet fell dangerously close to the gray-eyed boy. He did not move an inch before that coward's threat.

Douglas's Injun language was obvious enough to the Japanese. The ones who were to work for him picked up their bundles and trailed after him. "Farewell," they called over their shoulders, "keep in touch." They envied the fortunate people going to Haiku, to work with "the kind boy," as already they were calling Saul Bristol's first-born son.

The road from Kahului to Haiku is about ten miles long. Hiram Bristol led his charges along that long hot road until, about a mile east of the port, they met the four wagons the manager had sent down from the plantation to fetch them. The wagons carried baskets of food, earthenware jugs full of cool water, and mounds of dry grass for the weary travelers to sit upon. They arrived at their new home just before sunset. Hiram Bristol gave the fifty-one Japanese into the care of several foremen and delivered the contracts and the mail bag to the manager's house. Then he galloped home to Makawao, three miles away, to take supper with his mother and those of his brothers and sisters who were not yet put to bed.

"How do they seem, these newcomers?," asked his mother, when the chatter had quieted somewhat.

"Clean, and quiet, and so very polite. I liked them, Mother, even though we could not talk to each other. And I was sorry that I could not bring them all to this side of the island. Three of them wanted very much to go to Haiku. One especially. A tall man, who helped me to sort out those who were going to Wailuku from those going to Haiku. He and his friends looked very sad when I told them that their contracts said they had to go to Wailuku."

"Well, then, they will be helping your father, instead of Mr. Schapenhorst. Wherever they must go, I hope they will be happy here, on Maui.—Did you see your father?" How like his father this boy is, she was thinking, not for the first time nor the last. And yet how different, she acknowledged, seeing in him so much of herself.

"No, Mother. He sent Mr. Douglas to the harbor. I suppose he was busy. And Mr. Douglas did not give us a message from Father."

"Then we must wait, I suppose, until he comes home again on Saturday."

The road along the beach from Kahului to Wailuku village is little more than two miles long. While the newcomers walked it only once, Douglas traveled more than twice the distance, what with cantering, trotting, galloping, and prancing about on his nervous steed. Long before they reached Wailuku the mare's mouth was bloody, her flanks were rowelled into raw meat, and she was crazed with pain. Douglas was almost senseless with whiskey drunk from a bottle tucked in his saddle bag. Out of haste, not in mercy, he had chose to take his charges by the shorter and cooler way, first along the shore, across the patches of green grass and the tangled pohuehue vines, then inland on the dirt road following the bank of the Wailuku River. Had he not been in a hurry he would have made them walk up the long burning slope across the sand hills, where neither stick nor tree would give them shade.

Weak with hunger, hot and thirsting, the immigrants toiled along the path. Their feet, dyed blue by those cheap stockings, were sore and blistered by the heavy shoes that Douglas, very soon after they left the port, had insisted they must wear. Sweat ran down their faces, dripped into the blue cotton shirts and the heavy trousers, already encrusted with sea salt. They used the coats as towels, the lauhala hats as fans. Each man twisted his red neckerchief into a sweat-band, tied about the brow. The two women tied the bandana over their heads, trying to cover their cheeks against the sun and the wind.

They were deafened by the sound of the river, hurrying to empty itself in the sea. They were depressed, by the strangeness of this new world into which they were going; by the viciousness of this crazy foreigner racing around them on a crazed horse, shouting commands they could not understand; by the lengthening shadows of the dying day, closing in to trap them in deceitful darkness.

Beyond the tops of trees growing along the river road, the high peaks of West Maui's mountain flared briefly in the sunset, like torches lighted to guide them, then died out, to turn dark and sinister. Those who looked for portents in such things shivered in spirit. Until then Ishi had tried to take comfort from the fact that in Wailuku he would be closer to the mountain he had discovered so joyfully in the morning. But now he saw that it could wear other faces than the one he had loved at sight, and he grew afraid, as a man must who sees his beloved changing before his very eyes.

In the dusk they followed the rump of Douglas's horse across the river, stepping from stone to rounded stone, and up the mud-

dy path cut into its farther bank. Beneath overarching trees he
led them to a muddy clearing not far from the brink of the gulch.
Without saying a word he raised a heavy arm, pointed to a low
building. Then he rode away, vanishing beyond a clump of trees,
as though he were a ghost they would never meet again except in
their worst dreams.

They looked at the building. Never had they seen anything so
empty and desolate. They looked at themselves. Never had they
been so alone.

"Nasakenai!," someone swore, and a dozen others took up the
wail. "How terrible!" Aiko sobbed. Kuranosuke tried to snuffle
back his tears, and failed. Yuki sat upon a boulder, rubbing her
heavy legs. Koi groaned, "Another damned barrack." Ishi
pushed back the suspicion that Kannon had brought him here, to
this beautiful island, only to abandon him to the worst of men.

In the soft evening light the barrack looked neater and better
made than ever it would appear again. The dusk hid cracks between boards, empty knot holes, rough planks, and nailheads not
hammered down. Shadows merged with the trampled mud
around the building, with the dirt and dying grass and rocks beneath it.

One by one the wanderers went up the single step to the one
doorway, cut into the building's long side. They took off the muddy shoes, arranging them at either end of the step before they entered the house. It was nothing but a long empty box. No walls divided it into rooms. No windows let in light and air: these flowed
in under the eaves, through a space about a foot high, where the
walls did not meet the roof. No ceiling hid rafters and purlins, or
the backs of the shingles that made the roof. Down the middle of
the barrack marched its only furniture—a row of five posts holding the roof-ridge in place. From each post, at either side, trusses
reached out, like raised arms, to support the rafters, like the
branches of trees naked in winter.

"Behold Gohongi," tittered Eizo of Yotsuya in Edo, who knew
well the village of Roppongi. Six trees grew there, at the crossroads, to give that place its name.

"Heaven to hear about," mourned Kuranosuke, "hell to see."

"I wish I might see Hamada Hikizo dangling from one of these five trees of Gohongi," said Dembei, sinking to the floor.

"And Hambei the Pombiki," said Koi, through clenched jaws.

"And that crazy beast on the horse who brought us here," shouted Chikahei of Ochanomizu in Edo.

Soon each was vying with the other, calling out names of people whom he felt had harmed him in this life. Catching the rage, one from the other, they shouted and screamed and stamped their feet upon the floor, as small boys will do in fits of anger. And some wept and some laughed, because in no other way could they vent their disappointment and their fear.

At last they were quieted. And in the dark no one could see whose face was wet with tears, whose was dry.

After a long time someone said, "At least we have space enough to lie down in. For once I am not all tangled up in someone else's arms or legs."

"How can you say such a foolish thing?" squealed Koi, pretending to be a silly harlot. "I *like* getting all tangled in someone else's arms and legs ... " This Koi could cheer them without being seen. Beating his cupped hands upon the floor, he made a certain thumping sound that caused everyone to laugh, even Kuranosuke, huddled in Gohongi's farthest corner.

"Welcome home, everyone," shouted Koi in his own voice. "Sleep well."

Laughing (because what else could they do in this black hell?), sighing (because, despite the laughter, they were most unhappy), they settled down upon the floor, to sleep if they could, to suffer as they must.

Hunger kept them awake, crying in the belly as will an infant in its bed when it is sick with a fever. Anger smoldered in the liver, a dull but determined fire, like coals in a cookstove after the meal has been served. The more they tried to sleep the more they were consumed. Is this the kindness of haoles? they fretted, is this the aloha of Hawaiians? Is this the abode of wealthy men? they argued, as splinters poked into their flesh and cool air played about their blue feet. In desperation, while they stumbled outside in the dark to relieve themselves, they looked for some evidence of a house or a town where they might crawl to beg for food, but they saw nothing. Neither a light nor a glow of fire was there, not even a star overhead. Clouds above and trees below closed them in. They heard no sound of a living creature—unless one called the river a living thing. They could not keep from hearing that, running so close as to be almost at their feet, wild and gloomy as the river of Uji near Kyoto, an unceasing soughing and flowing as of wind rushing through a forest of pine trees.

For them this was like living in a world of the dead. Or like being dead, in the Hell of Black Clouds.

In the boat, when first they went into it in Yokohama, they had compared those bunks with coffins. Now, in Wailuku, they had not even those narrow boxes to lie in. Now they had nothing but a common grave. In the dark, at the end of the saddest day in their lives, they lay upon the hard floor, stiff and silent as corpses. Yet hunger and rage kept them awake, telling them that they could not die so easily.

Through the doorway streamed the light from a lantern. Boots stamped upon the stairs. "Aloha," called a cheerful voice, "e hele mai ai." They did not understand the words, but they heard the good will in the speaker. They saw a plump little Chinese man, dressed in a faded uniform of the kind they wore, with a white cloth tied about his middle. Guessing who he was, they leaped to their feet, greeting him with cheers and laughter. In an instant anger was put aside.

He waited beside the stairs, shining his bull's-eye lantern upon them while they pushed feet into shoes, not bothering to tie the laces. They followed his bobbing light along a path through the jungle at the back of the barrack. After about fifty yards or so the path entered another clearing, larger than their own, holding a pair of barracks much like theirs. These looked wonderfully festive, with light spilling from the doorways, glowing through the spaces under the eaves, twinkling through cracks in the walls. On stones, stools, chairs, stairs, half a hundred Chinese men sat contentedly, smoking little pipes, chatting, or playing cards. Flowers bloomed in small plots around the barracks, mingling their scents with tobacco smoke and the aroma of cooked food.

"I am alive again, after being dead," said Koi, almost dancing behind the Chinese leader.

"No wonder we could not see this place," said sober Ishi to anyone who would listen. "We looked in the wrong direction." And let this be a lesson to you, he scolded himself. Never give up so easily. Never believe the worst, until you have seen for yourself. Above all, never lose faith in the mercy of Kannon-sama.

"It is like Paradise," cried Kuranosuke, all mixed up, finding something nice to say for once in his life.

"Paké Camp," explained their guide, waving his free hand toward the glittering barracks. Veering to the left, toward an alcove cut out of the jungle, he took them to an airy pavilion furnished with tables and benches. It glowed like a shrine at festival time, smelling wonderfully of steamed rice and vegetables and other delicious things. The guide's generous hand waved them to the tables. As the famished travelers swooped down upon them the cook's helpers started to serve the food.

After the filling repast of soup, fried vegetables mixed with thin slices of pork, served with rice and tea, the cooks sat down with the newcomers to tell them certain facts about life at the Hawaiian Sugar Plantation in Wailuku. But words failed them. Chinese, Japanese, Hawaiian, English: of all the millions of words those languages call upon, guests and hosts shared only three in common, "Wailuku," "Maui," and "Aloha." With every good intention, they were baffled. Shaking heads, scratching scalps, sucking air through teeth helped not a whit. They looked at each other glumly. Smiles may be good enough for bedmates, but they are not the language used by men who want to make their fortunes.

Happily, one of the younger cooks bethought himself of an odd bit of information he picked up at temple school in Canton. While everyone watched him as if he had lost his mind, he ran off, fetching first a sheet of butcher paper from the kitchen, then a twig broken from a bush at the edge of the jungle. Calmly seat-ing himself at the table, he poured a puddle of shoyu into an empty dish, the while he chewed the tip of the twig into a fibrous brush. "Ahh," they said, in two languages, recognizing the cleverness of this methodical scholar.

With the brush, using shoyu for ink, he wrote two ideograms upon the paper. He was an excellent calligrapher. The few literate Japanese read the familiar kanji. "Tomorrow," they cried out. The calligrapher nodded at their response. The head cook beamed at this magical learning, invented in his ancient and esteemed country, which could break silences merely with the touch of a brush upon a paper.

The young cook wrote another character. "Eat," the Japanese read.

The cook touched his finger to the table. "Here," the newcomers understood.

Swiftly the teacher drew the signs for three numerals: 6, 12, and 7.

"Ah, so," the Japanese grinned, their stomachs settling back into place with this promise of being filled regularly.

Employing the ideograms that people of China and Japan use in common in their writing, but cannot speak in common because the sounds they have attached to those pictures are so different, the newcomers learned what they wanted most to know: where they could find toilet, bathhouse, and water to drink. All other things could come later. "Like," said Chikahei, nudging friends at either side, "where are the women such as we met that night in Honolulu?" Such as the laundry house, thought Aiko, who had so many dirty clothes to wash. Such as the temple, thought Yuki, where I can pray for guidance to the Lord Buddha.

They went home again, escorted by way of convenience places and water troughs, feeling much happier in body and spirit. The barrack was swarming with mosquitoes, but where in the world are those pests not found in summer time? Tomorrow night Ishi and his companions would make fires of green wood, as they did at home, hoping that the smoke would drive away the insects without suffocating the people. Tonight they covered heads and feet with clean fundoshi, or something that was not too heavy, tucked hands into the sleeves of their summer kimono, and, almost at once, fell asleep.

Before breakfast the next morning, while rain clouds hung low over the mountains, Jack Douglas enjoyed the pleasure of showing his boss the new laborers who had been dumped upon them the day before. "They strike me as being both stoopid and weak," said Mr. Douglas, in his most juridical manner. Douglas sober was not much different from Douglas drunk.

"Umm," yawned the new manager of the plantation. Remembering how this fellow regarded the Chinese workers under his care, the manager wished that this damned fool would stop being so damnably prejudiced. The manager himself, too full of similar biases when he was Douglas's age, tried to be charitable—as well as wary—with all malihinis from the States. Give 'em time, he said to himself as well as to others, they'll learn eventually. He himself had come around right smartly, having shed most of his prejudices since he'd learned to think for himself.

Of course, he'd had some pretty fine teachers to push him along, setting him good examples. He thought of them, remembering them with love and with pain. So many were dead now, in this doomed and dying nation. And those who still lived were so far away, almost in another part of the world. While he was here, almost an exile from that world, because he could not endure Oahu anymore. And he didn't want to go back, ever, to see the beautiful valley of Kaaawa. The Valley of Love and Delight . . . An Eden from which he had been turned out.

Talk about prejudices, he snorted. What an unmitigated fool I was then. He squirmed in his saddle, hating to think of those wasted years, all those screams of anguish, raised up against one god or another, in his frenzied pursuit of something he conceived of as grief. When all the time he refused to see that happiness, the antidote to sorrow, was right there for the taking. Shoot! Old Hiram knew the answer. All the time. And I was so damned slow to learn it.

"An' I expeck we'll have a helluva lotta trouble, gettin' any work outta 'em aroun' here," Douglas pushed on. "Talk ta 'em, they jus' stare back at ya. Not the slightest sign of understandin'. Or of brains."

"That so?" The manager brightened with a sudden thought. "Where do you come from, Jack? Where's your home, I mean?"

"Missoura. Bes' state in tha Union. White man's country, that."

Yup, the manager assured himself. Hawaii's full of men like this. Each coming from "the best place on earth," but none of 'em in much of a hurry to go rushing back to it. "Which would you prefer to do, Jack? Learn Japanese? Or teach our new hands English? Missoura English, of course."

Douglas saw no cause for humor in their predicament. "Damn it, Saul! We ain't got time to teach 'em anythin' but how ta work. And, believe you me, that's gotta be mighty soon. Them book-keepers over there in Honolulu are wantin' for us to make 'em some money soon. Not keep on spendin' it the way we bin doin'. Like it was water."

"They know as well as we do, Jack, that they've got to spend some money first, before they can make more money later. That's a basic rule of business. We're doing the best we can, with the materials we have on hand. And we're going to get the job done at the earliest possible time. Don't fret. They'll wait." They'll have to wait, he thought, knowing how much more remained to be done before this plantation could turn a dollar's profit. He had a mill house of sorts, a couple of years old, but no dependable mill hands because no cane had been harvested as yet. A couple of hundred acres of cane almost ripe for cutting. A thousand or so acres of land to clear and plant, to convert from barren hillside to green and flourishing fields. And to do that he needed water. There was water aplenty down there, in that raging river, but getting it up here, to the fields, was a problem he'd done nothing about as yet.

"An' there's a coupla wimmin in the lot, besides," Jack spat down into the clean mud. "Not that I dislike wimmin, mind you.

—Matter of fact, one's a rather cute little chit. Other's built like the square end of a barn.—But gettin' a good day's work outta them in the fields, after they bin up all night, screwin'—''

And, the new manager brooded, in order to make all this desert to blossom as the redolent rose, what talent am I given? Besides my superlative self, that is, and this egregious jackass who is somebody's brother-in-law? Fifty-four Chinese, of whom fifty-four would rather hang themselves than deliver an honest day's work in the fields. One rheumy rum-head, banished from Honolulu, to keep the books and count the pennies. Two Hawaiian youths, rescued from that missionary school at Lahainaluna, to be foremen. And now eleven untried Japanese, as new to the art of transmuting dirt into sugar as I was myself one short month ago. By the tits of Jezebel! 'Tis enough to make a grown man weep . . .

''An' I don't trust the looksa some a them Japs. Mean-lookin' bunch. Remin' me of Injuns.—An' you know what we say about Injuns back home.''

This concern with profits before losses are fairly sown. This dredging up of dregs, from Missouri as well as from Canton, to be transformed into farmers. Why don't they learn that Dame Nature cannot be hurried? Assisted, yes. Encouraged, yes. Maybe, even once in a while, beguiled. But never forced. Never raped. Dammit! If this wasn't exactly the sort of beguiling of earth and water and growing things that I like, if this wasn't the courting of Dame Nature's daughter Flora that I enjoy—and if I didn't need the money this job pays me—I'd tell that lot of money grubbers at C. Brewer to stow the whole deal, and I'd go back to the ranch up there in Makawao. Up there where I've already set Flora in a bower of her own . . .

As he did a hundred times a day Saul Bristol looked out across the sweep of central Maui toward the flank of Haleakala where, above Paia and Haiku, lay Makawao. Beyond the great dark mountain the rising sun was painting golden linings to the clouds. A good omen, he smiled, knowing it to be a delusion, but a pleasing one. And, as he did a thousand times a day, he wondered how Ululani fared, up there at Makawao, and those handsome sons and beautiful daughters she had given him, to his everlasting joy.

Picking their way through the mud, the horses brought them to Japanese Camp. Saul Bristol drew rein as soon as he saw it. "Damn it, Jack! The place isn't finished!"

"That's the best we could do with the time we had. Them Pakés ain't much as carpenters." Canny Douglas reckoned as how he'd best not say a word about the bookkeeper's refusal to spend one cent more upon one item more than he thought the Honolulu office would approve.

Careful not to disturb the shoes on the doorstep, Bristol entered the barrack. "Christ!," he said, stopping at sight of those dark figures, sitting on the floor, like effigies, in that one long room. When they stood up, faceless in the dark, small as children, pathetic as orphans, the rage he'd thought was forever stilled flared up with all its old strength.

He turned upon Douglas, ready to hit him. "Where are the windows? The beds? The cross-walls?"

"Pakés don't have 'em. Why should the Japs—"

"Why don't the Chinese have 'em?"

"They don't want 'em.—They said so."

"And these Japanese?—They've said so too?"

"Haven't any idea what they want.—Can't talk to 'em, like I said."

The manager considered his assistant, took stock of the situation, looked into himself. No, he decided, this is not the time for a display of the volcanic Bristol temper. Later, perhaps, when he could tear this fool apart, and try to put him back together again, a better man. But not now, in the presence of these specters, eery as witches met on a misty heath. Most especially not in front of the men this loose-lipped lout was going to boss.

Biding his time, he stalked out of the barrack.

At Chinese Camp, in the lanai where the workers ate, Bristol and Douglas sat down to take a cup of tea with Ah Siu, the chief cook. Ah Siu was one of the few members of the first group of Chinese contract-laborers who still worked on a sugar plantation. All the others had gone home to China as soon as their contracts ended, or died, or escaped to the towns of Hawaii, to run the tea shops, restaurants, bakeries, vegetable stores, public baths, laundries, and other such profitable and pleasant ventures. Ah Siu stayed with the plantations because he liked the country life and the profits to be squeezed out of it, in one way or another. During the sixteen years since he'd arrived in Honolulu, he had learned a fair amount of the Hawaiian tongue, and certain key phrases in the less useful English. He spoke Hawaiian at home, across the river in the village of Wailuku, where two Hawaiian wives ministered to his comfort and nine half-Hawaiian children ensured his immortality. He spoke whatever language was necessary in the whorehouse he operated on Market Street, just across the gulch from Paké Camp. He conversed in English in matters of commerce—unless, of course, the businessman was intelligent enough to speak Cantonese or Hawaiian.

Ah Siu and his boss chatted away in Hawaiian for ten pleasant minutes, laughing, rolling eyes, flinging arms about as though they were palm fronds in a gale. Jus' like a coupla damn' kanakas, thought Jack Douglas, disgusted with a white man who could fall so low.

At length the parley came to an end. Bristol rose from the table. With a farewell clap on Ah Siu's shoulder, a flood of jesting that sent the cook into shrieks of merriment, he strode out into the middle of the clearing.

"Come here, Douglas," he began. In no hurry to oblige, his assistant ambled over, to stand before this gutless nigger-lover he despised.

"First thing to remember, in our future association, is this: Chinese, Japanese, Hawaiians, Englishmen, Frenchmen, whatever other kinds of people you may happen to meet, even Americans from states other than Missoura, are human beings too, just like yourself. As such they must be treated as human beings, in as decent a fashion as we can manage.

"Second thing: don't you ever lie to me. Not ever. Your prejudices I can make allowance for. But your distortions of facts—that is to say, your lies—I cannot. I need to know the facts, if I am to be a good manager of this plantation. Note that word: good, I say, not profitmaking. You understand me?"

Pale with shock, Douglas asked, "What lies?"

"Here are some facts, as I have learned them. Our Chinese workers are being eaten alive by mosquitoes, every night. So, I suspect, will be our Japanese workers. Therefore, buy mosquito nets for all of them, from the stores in Wailuku. One net for each man."

Douglas gasped, as if the money to pay for all those nets was being drawn out of his bowels. "But the expense!," he cried, while Bristol observed with pleasure how a Scotsman's parsimony will subdue even his hate.

"Damn the expense! Aside from the fact that those nets will reduce the misery in which these people must live, at best, it ought to be clear to you and to those skinflints in Honolulu that if our men sleep better by night they will work better by day. Do you have a mosquito net, by the way?"

"Of course. But I—"

"Yes. But you . . . ? Go on."

"Never mind."

"As you say. Third thing: this morning Ah Siu and his helpers will learn from the Japanese what they want in order to make themselves comfortable over there in that empty barrack. We will fill all reasonable requests—provided, of course, that they are not too extravagant, and do not require materials that are unavailable in this center of enlightenment and culture. I mean to say, in that village across the crick. Our Chinese carpenters and the newcomers themselves will make whatever pieces of furniture they may need, such as bedsteads, chairs, tables, clothes-closets, and so on. And you will provide them with all tools, lumber, and whatever other instruments or materials they may wish to use. All clear?"

"Yeah."

"Good. Until they've made that barrack livable—and I expect they'll need a couple of days for that—you will not put the Japanese to work in the fields. Moreover, the women will not work in the fields at all. We'll find jobs for them in the camps, or in the mill house."

"Waste—"

"Finally, one more thing. And this ought to please your economical, penny-pinching heart. Only eleven Japanese will stay with us."

"But I brought up twenty-three! We need every one of 'em if—"

"Yes, I know. But you didn't read the contracts, did you? And you also brought up the mail. With it came instructions from our masters in Honolulu. With them we servants must comply. C. Brewer's secretary has informed me that four of these Japanese are supposed to go to old Walter Murray Gibson in his City of Joseph, over on Lanai. Four others are intended for Henry Cornwell's plantation up in Waikapu. And four are to be sent to Captain Makee in Ulupalakua. All should go today, this morning if possible. Send them by wagon or oxcart, whichever seems best. Tell the driver to leave four at Waikapu crossroads. To leave four at Kihei, with request to Anapuni to sail them across to Makee's landing. And to start the last four on the trail to Lahaina, with a letter to the Reverend Dwight Baldwin, asking his help to get them across the channel to Lanai. Don't worry. I shall write the letter. You arrange for the transportation. Ah Siu will fix food baskets for each of the three parties and for the driver. Whatever C. Brewer's minions may be thinking in Honolulu, I don't want C. Brewer's people to go hungry on Maui. As, Ah Siu tells me, they went hungry on that schooner. For two days, without a meal. Damn it! No wonder these poor people looked sullen and sick to you. Fortunately, Mr. Dunham had told Ah Siu to expect them yesterday evening. Most fortunately, Ah Siu saw you riding home. Otherwise, I suspect, they'd be hungry still."

"Who decides what Japs are to go?" He knew of two that he'd send, sure as shootin', over to that Mormon hell on Lanai.

"The Japanese will decide among themselves who will go, who will stay. With help from Ah Siu, if they want it. You're free of that burden."

Shit, said Douglas to himself. That ain't no way to keep these coolies in line. Give 'em an inch, they'll take a whole goddam mile ...

After the Japanese had broken their fast, Ah Siu and his helpers explained how once again the shrinking group must be divided. Ah Siu took them to the brink of the gulch through which the swift river flowed. At that place no trees blocked their view. He showed them the flat dusty plain stretching from Kahului on the north to Kihei on the south, and the long gradual ascent to the summit of Haleakala, the mountain that so oppressed Ishi and Kuranosuke. The cook with the brush had written its name: "House of the Sun," and "Taiyo no Ie" the Japanese called it, although they wondered when Amaterasu-Omikami ever found the time—or the wish—to leave her home in the Plain of High Heaven to dwell in that barren place.

Ah Siu showed them where Waikapu lay. It was the wide, light-filled valley they had seen yesterday from the schooner. He gestured vaguely toward the southwestern flank of Haleakala, at the end opposite Haiku, and said "Ulupalakua." Not at all sure about geography, he indicated an island lying beyond Kihei, a dull, gray thing, and named it Lanai. Not for several years would they learn that it was Kahoolawe rather than Lanai. Walter Murray Gibson's island was hidden by the high slanting ridges of Maui west of Waikapu. But on the day of separation the name of the place did not matter. The sea that flowed between Maui and Lanai was what mattered.

While Ah Siu was showing them the far places they looked too upon the near places that he neglected to name: the buildings of the plantations's sugar factory, seeming to be spilling down the far slope of the gulch; and, above and beyond it, the little village of Wailuku, with two of those tall towers that in Honolulu Sentaro told them were the marks of Christian churches. Smoke from the cooking-fires of Wailuku drifted inland toward the valley from which the river came.

There before them they saw the whole of their new world: a small island under an aloof sky, an island made of high mountains at either side and a plain of dry dust in between, shut off from all other lands by the blue encircling sea. Knowing what they were being told to do, they did not want to obey. Who would want to go to that smaller island across the channel? Who would ask to be sent to that far place at the very end of Taiyo no Ie?

The Sad Woman spoke. This was the first time any one had ever heard her say something of her own will. "I wish to go to that place." She pointed to Waikapu, but she could not have told her companions why she was moved to make that choice.

"And I, too," said her loyal brother, Nagayuki.

"And I," said small Ryozo of Kawasaki, who had found a good companion in cheerful Nagayuki.

But no one else opened his mouth. They stared at each other, each knowing that he was thinking first of himself, preferring to stay in Wailuku now that he could see what it held for him, rather than go off, once again, to perils unknown in places that might be much worse. Ishi, no different from the others, searched in his thoughts for a way to end this terrible waiting, for a means that would give each one a fair chance. But no thought would come. The river's roar deafened him, its water spilling over boulders, crashing over logs and uprooted trees, as if it were the river of time itself washing over him and his people, as if each of them was a small pebble being washed away from its home.

"Janken po suru!," Ishi shouted above the baying of the river. "That is the fairest way."

"Yes," they agreed, coming to peace again with themselves. Let the gods decide, they meant, with this game of chance. If I decide then I can blame only myself for my fate. But if they decide then my karma will be determined by them, and I shall be free of all blame.

Now Ishi worried about another problem. This is the fate of men who must lead, he thought ruefully: as soon as they settle one difficulty they are beset with two more. "Do we agree that Koi-san and Aiko-san must stay together?"

"Yes," they replied. It is easy to be generous when seventeen other fates lie between yours and the wrong choice.

"Then let them step out of the line," said Ishi. As they obeyed he wondered if they also stepped out of his life forever. He could see himself going off to Lanai, because that would be his karma, while they remained here, gazing after him as he trudged off to the island from which he would never return . . .

Eighteen men remained in a half circle, with a puzzled Ah Siu looking on.

"Play in pairs," Ishi called. "Ready?" He raised his right arm, hand clenched in a fist.

"Ready," they shouted, showing their fists. Ah Siu backed away, thinking they were going to fight.

"Jan!," Ishi shouted, punching air with his fist, as did the seventeen other men.

"Ah," smiled Ah Siu, seeing now what they were doing.

"Ken!," cried Ishi, repeating the gesture, while they did the same.

"Po!," roared Ishi, above the rush of the river, of the blood in his ears. Kannon's stone was his talisman, once and forever, and he was not surprised when his opponent showed two fingers—a weak "scissors" easily broken by the "stone" of Ishi's fist.

So it was with each pair: one man was the winner, one the loser, depending upon the wisdom of the gods.

"All winners step out," Ishi ordered. "Losers play on."

"Not fair!," the losers protested. "Two out of three matches! Two out of three . . . "

"No, no," laughed the winners, walking away, piously accepting the judgment the gods had made so swiftly for them that day.

Who were the winners that day? And who the losers?

Not for many years would they know how good or how ill their karmas would be. Some would not know until their lives came to an end. And some would not have time to make the reckoning, because for them death would come too suddenly.

But on that sunny day, when twelve of the group went away from Wailuku, standing up in a slow-moving oxcart, the eleven who remained thought they were the favored ones of the gods because now they need move no more. All were weary of moving, all yearned to take root. And the eleven who stayed believed that they could be happy if they took root in Wailuku of Maui.

Yet their hearts were sad, too, for the twelve who were sent away. Some were good friends, some were not, but all were countrymen, deserving of brotherly concern. Even sour Kuranosuke possessed some of the Eight Virtues in abundance, although he might be lacking in certain others. He weighed upon their consciences. Never, never would they forget him, clinging to the high pales of the oxcart, looking like a prisoner of the Bakufu being carried away to execution, yet calling himself a nobleman even as the squealing wheels bore him off. He tried to laugh, to be cheerful, shouting over and over again, "Just like a noble! Just like a prince!," because he remembered how, in Nippon, only princes and nobles ride in carriages drawn by oxen. But the tears ran down his cheeks, and his hands were white against the stakes, and the eleven who remained saw how he thought that both men and gods were forsaking him that day.

The four Nipponjin who were going to Waikapu jumped down from the oxcart at the crossroads. The low road went along the edge of the dry foothills, connecting Wailuku with Kihei. The high road led up the long slope of earth that spilled out of the wide valley. A high mountain wall, softened with ferns and grasses and low shrubs, closed in the valley's head; but at its sides the wall descended swiftly to meet the slope up which the four were walking. On either hand fields of green young sugarcane rustled in the strong breezes drawn up to the cool heights from the sun-baked plain.

The four travelers felt very small in that immense place. In all that spaciousness only they moved under the eye of the sun. Seeing neither village nor houses before them, they wondered if the oxcart driver had not made a mistake. But then, remembering the gestures he made at the crossroads and the signs Ah Siu had

made in Wailuku, they followed the road the gods had prepared
for them.

At length they came to the crest of the hill. In a shallow swale
lay a quiet little village. A dozen whitewashed wooden houses
stood around a central square, each in its own neat yard, green
with grass and low trees. Beyond it, surrounded by a grove of tall
trees, stood a larger painted house, with a wide verandah at front
and sides, similar to villas of wealthy men they had seen in Honolulu. Cows grazed upon the grass in the square, chickens stalked
about, dogs slept in the shade. And birds of many kinds flitted
from tree to tree, singing as they went.

Between hedges of sweet-scented flowers they walked toward
the village square. As they approached the clearing Yuki's heart
beat so rapidly that she forced herself to stop. Standing still,
breathing deep, hands held against her breast, she did not once
think of dying if that sad heart ceased to beat. No, she shook her
head at Nagayuki bending over her, do not worry. "This is the
place," she whispered, seeing the trees covered with big light
green leaves, hung with clusters of small creamy blossoms, just as
she had seen them in her vision.

"How can this be?" he asked softly, becoming faint in his
turn, with hope for his sister, and fear for himself if she should
die.

"Let us go on," she said, taking his hand as she had done
when they were children in Imaicho.

Almost like children they entered the quiet village. Before one
of the houses, on the smooth grass a brown man sat, half asleep in
the sun, enjoying the peace of noon. A child, just learning to
stand upright, climbed about on his father's belly, digging with
his toes against the man's thighs, clutching with his tiny fingers
at the man's shirt, chin, nose. Delighting in these soft little touch-
ings, the father smiled down at his son.

Yuki stopped. She waited for the Lord Buddha to fulfill his
promise to the last detail. For one so full of faith the Lord Buddha hearkened. With a touch of his little finger, perhaps, or the
softest of puffs of his breath, he caused the child to lose its hold

upon the shirt. As dozing fathers are wont to do, he caught the boy before he fell, turned him about, and, holding him in the cup of those big hands, seemed to proffer the laughing child to the air, to the sun, to Yuki, before drawing him in, to rest against his belly.

He did not see the four strangers standing wide-eyed in the road. He did not know how—with the Lord Buddha's help—he changed the Sad Woman that day into the Happy Woman.

The four men bound for Lanai arrived there safely, having been sent across the channel in a canoe by Dr. Baldwin of Lahaina. But of their lives there nothing can be said, because no one of their countrymen ever heard from them again.

Who can say whether his gods were kind or cruel to Kuranosuke of Edo? They sent him, according to the luck they put into his own fingers, to Captain Makee's plantation at Ulupalakua.

In that cool and lovely place, "the most beautiful spot in all Hawaii," as Captain Makee and many a guest said of his Rose Ranch—with its unsurpassed prospect toward the mountains of West Maui and over the near islands of Molokini, Kahoolawe, Lanai, and Molokai (and, on those occasions when the weather was clear, also of Oahu a hundred miles to the west); with its colorful flowers and lowing herds and fields of tasseling sugarcane; with its groves of fruit trees and troops of singing Hawaiian cowboys—Kuranosuke could think only of the joys of Edo, now forever lost to him. Overwhelmed by the solitude of Ulupalakua, terrified of that vast mountain of rock looming above him, he could not sleep, he would not work, he did not eat.

On July 4, the festival day of the United States of America, Captain Makee gave all his people a holiday, for resting, eating, feasting, and exploding Chinese firecrackers brought from Canton for the event. Morose Kuranosuke refused to join them. In the afternoon, when all the residents of Ulupalakua gathered in front of Captain Makee's long low white mansion for singing and dancing in the Hawaiian style, Kuranosuke sat alone in the bachelors' barrack. With a piece of charred wood he wrote upon the whitewashed wall beside the iron stove: "Too long have I lived in this sad world, gladly I go to the next . . . "

At dusk, purified by his bath, dressed in his best kimono, wearing the frayed rice-straw sandals, he went off alone, into the grove of fruit trees. It was the time of day when, at home in Edo, the "deep-toned curfew bell of Iriya sends forth its melancholy sound, filling the heart with sadness." Among trees from America, Europe, Asia, and Australia, thriving there as transplanted Kuranosuke never could, he bowed to the west, toward Nippon and Edo, the love of his heart, begging his ancestors to forgive him for having left them, asking them to receive with forebearance his penitent spirit. Then, fashioning a noose with his obi, he hanged himself.

CHAPTER 15
THE MEN OF GOHONGI

In Edo, Ishi of Asakusa thought he'd like to be a stone mason when he worked on a plantation in Hawaii. Beginning with the day he went to work, Kannon, in her kindness, gave him myriads of rocks to play with, all day and every day. So did she with the nine others of his countrymen who had expected to be tillers of soil, pullers of weeds, bringers of water to wilting canes. An infinitude of rocks she gave them in her limitless charity, from the time they went to the field in the cool of morning until they dragged themselves home each warm evening.

In his wisdom Saul Bristol put them to clearing the first of those thousand new acres he proposed to convert into sugarcane fields. It was work that such inexperienced hands could do; and it was a task that a luna could supervise, thereby sparing the newcomers the presence of Jack Douglas. Bristol kept him on a short tether, assigned to jobs in or around the mill house. Douglas was better at getting machines to work than at getting work out of men. Much as Bristol disliked him he did concede that Douglas had an instinct for setting up cumbersome mill-mounts, for laying out the routes by which harvested canes would be brought to the pits and from there fed into the crushing mills. If Mad Jack swore at the crushers, or kicked at iron stanchions, they did not suffer the megrims or fight back. Therefore, Bristol resolved, he would keep Jack Douglas indoors as much as possible. The field work he'd take care of himself, with the help of his foremen, Pilipo and Kawika. They did not know the first thing about machines but they had all the Hawaiian graces for getting along with people.

Pilipo was especially good with the Japanese. Each morning at half-past six he'd meet them at the mill house and lead them to the field. Carrying pick and shovel over the shoulder, a sharp cane knife and a lunch bag tied to the waist, they followed him in a ragged troop. If Pilipo had not been so waddling and unmilitant a man Ishi would have likened them to a group of foot soldiers following their leader in a raid upon a vegetable farm in Edo.

Often, now, he thought of Edo. Now that he was a free man he could remember with smiles the weeks when he carried a spear for Lord Okubo and the defense of the Bakufu. And when his thoughts moved on from those wasted weeks he would feel a stir of amazement at the great change his life had undergone in so short a time. In spite of his conviction that he never wanted to go back to Nippon, he would wonder what was happening in the homeland. The Meiji emperor, for example: was he still in power? Or had the mighty Tokugawa and their Inside Daimyo swept him back to Kyoto and restored the Bakufu to its supremacy? And what of his friend Nakamura-san? Had he chosen the right side when he went to help the Meiji emperor's party in its attack upon the Bakufu's navy off Yezo?

Somewhat to his surprise Ishi felt an interest still in the homeland, and a love that would never fade for certain things in it. The signs of summer would be starting now, he guessed: the unohana, those golden yellow daisies, and the irises might be past their peak, but the high grasses would be at their best, and the lotus blossoms, pure as Buddha's thoughts, would be rising from the muddy ponds, and the hototogisu would be singing their unending call through the long nights, "Ku-ku, Ku-ku," because they never slept . . .

—Because they never worked, that's why. Memories may be long, but the walk to the field was short, and labor in it promised to go on forever. The waste land to be cleared was immense, seeming to have no end. It lay across the river from Japanese Camp, beyond the crest of the bank above the mill. It began at the lower edge of Wailuku village and rolled eastward from there to the plain of Kahului. Its southern boundary lay out of sight, somewhere in the distance toward Kihei.

Each morning, for a minute or so, Pilipo would show them what to do, with gestures and, when absolutely necessary, with actual strenuous demonstrations. Then he would watch them, for perhaps as long as a minute, to make sure that they were capable of performing the difficult deeds he expected of them. They sprang to work, ten times more able than the lazy Pilipo ever wanted to be. He would nod, and say "Maikai," and go off somewhere to continue his sleep, while they attacked the desert for his sake and the Boss's.

For half the morning they hacked with sharp cane knives at shrubs growing in this dry dirt—guava seedlings for the most part, mixed with wild indigo, Spanish needles, spiny amaranth, the edible cactus, occasional clumps of wild tobacco, and a few entangling vines. They threw the cuttings into great heaps, which would be burned later after the plants were dried. During the rest of the day—except for the half hour allowed for lunch—they cleared the land of rocks.

First they picked up the loose ones, lying more or less upon the surface, and carried them to a pile at the river edge of the field. Then with picks and shovels they pried up the stones that could not be loosened by hand. If an apparent pebble turned out to be a buried boulder, too big to move by all the men toiling together, they left it in place. Later, Pilipo explained, a team of oxen would be brought up to drag the boulder away. Oxen, too, would pull the plow that dug up the roots of the bigger plants they cut down, so they were spared that laborious task.

On the first day of work Ishi was rather amused by Kannonsama's ready answer to his wish to work with stones. As he picked them up he observed the variety in sizes, shapes, textures, colors. Some were beautiful, most were plain, while a few were actually ugly. They were like people, he saw, in appearance as in heart. Some glittered with golden-green jewels, while others held no such little gems. Some were as full of holes as a sponge, and others as dense as the bone in a daimyo's head. But not one was as black, as smooth, as beautiful as the stone he carried next to his navel, the one Kannon gave him from her garden in Asakusa.

By late afternoon of that day, however, when the sharp edges to the prettiest of those rocks had cut his fingers in a thousand stinging places, and his back ached from picking up the countless things, and his feet hurt from trotting forth and back with those damned objects held like eggs against his belly, he was on the point of hating rocks, forever. And then, trying as always to be fair, he looked around him, at the dry stony slope on which he labored, at the great mountains rising near and far, yes, even at the ugly stone he was about to move, and he put aside his hate before it could take hold. "Do not hate your enemy," he reminded himself in words learned from the ryu master of Shimoda, "and you can conquer him." Rocks and stones, he saw, are not deserving of hate. They are the stuff of which mountains are made, from which earth and life are drawn. Stones are the jewels in dirt, as crystals are the jewels in stones. Stones are like people, in their numbers and in their variety, in their uselessness as well as in their usefulness. Why should I hate those stones, then, when all are brothers or sisters to the beautiful one I carry in my loincloth? When all are manifestations of the Kannon Ryo-i-nin who brought me here?

Ishi the Mover of Stones, not yet Ishi the Builder with Stones, remembered the lessons she had been teaching him all along the way: to have faith in her wisdom, never to doubt her mercy. If this is to be my karma, he thought, then I must accept it, as this stone accepts its fate.

In this Hell of Rains, Flames, and Stones, none of Ishi's companions shared his love for those earth gems. They hated those devices of torment with a fury that increased in proportion to their numbers. "Battle of Sekigahara," growled Eizo, shaking his head angrily as they stumbled across the field, carrying their enemies in their arms instead of charging upon them with spears and swords. Eizo's was a clever pun and, as puns are meant to do, it caused a laugh. Thereafter, among themselves they called this wide, dry, rock-strewn field "Sekigahara," that is to say, the Plain of Stones. This was a good name, because this field, in more ways than one, was to be a place of victory for them, just as in Nippon another Sekigahara (although that one was known as the Plain of the Barrier) was the battlefield where the first Tokugawa triumphed over all his enemies.

In the heat of the afternoon, as they sweated and toiled, the fury burned itself out, as happens with fevers. They hated no more. Stones became one with the universe of pains and afflictions. They were things to be endured, like sore muscles, mosquitoes, thorns, nagging wives, and grief for joys lost.

About this time, when they felt like slabs of fish being dried in the hot sun, Koi composed a song:

> Oh Jizo, help me!
> The spirit of a child am I,
> Toiling upon the Plain of Sai,
> Piling stones above the bank of the river,
> Making a high tower
> To reach Holy Paradise.

He stopped, hunching shoulders, glaring fiercely about, as if frightening away the old witch, Shozuka-no-baba herself, while his friends waited for more.

> Oh Jizo, help me!
> Do not let Shozuka-no-baba and her devils
> Steal my clothes.
> Do not let them pull down my high tower.
> Hide me in your wide sleeve, I pray,
> And carry me to Paradise.

"You have said it," cried Eizo, heaving his burden upon the pile. Yes, thought Ishi, he has said it well. And he murmured a prayer for his two dead sons, whom Jizo, he hoped, had long since carried to Paradise.

After Koi's song they considered that every stone they tossed upon the growing heap was like a pebble placed at the feet of an image of Jizo. Just as such an offering lightens the work and shortens the penance required of a child's spirit beside the River Sai, so did these stones piling up beside the River Wailuku promise to lighten their own labors in this world of trouble and travail.

Nevertheless, at each day's end they could see that they had done well the task assigned them. And each morning, when they returned to Sekigahara, they could tell that, during the night, no wicked old devils, from either this world or the next, had undone their efforts. They did not enjoy this work. What man could? But they persevered in it, out of pride and because of need. "This is what we are hired to do, and we must do it well," they told each other, "if we do not wish to bring shame upon ourselves." Whereupon some of them added, "And if we want to receive that honorable money."

During the first difficult week their hard work brought great relief of a sort to nine men, a serious deprivation to one. At the end of each day Koi wanted only to eat, wash, and go to sleep. "I must be getting old," he sighed to Aiko lying beside him, even more weary than he.

As the days passed, and muscles long unused became accustomed again to labor, and hands acquired calluses, feet hardened to shoes, and the pattern of their work put its marks upon bodies as well as clothes, the men of Nippon knew a kind of contentment. They were almost happy, at least for the while, with the security of the days and the comforts of the nights. Tired, dirty, reeking of sweat, they walked home at sunset, along a path grown familiar, and they recognized that they were thinking of this place as home.

Bankichi, the only farmer in the group, said so one evening as, shovel on one shoulder, pick on the other, the sugarcane samurai trudged back to Gohongi. "I'm thinking that this is like going home in Kanagawa, after a day's work in the daikon patch. Only here things are better."

"How?," asked Koi the fisherman, who loved daikon but hated the labor of growing it.

"Here we don't have to worry about many things, as they do in Nippon. There, as we say, 'one day's delay means one month's misfortune. And one month's negligence means a hundred days of disaster.' "

"And not only for farmers," said Eizo, the former printer of pictures for fickle Edokko to consider buying.

"There a cold night, a poor crop, or thieves, or typhoons, or tax-gatherers for the daimyo, a stray horse, leaf-eating worms, too much rain or not enough rain can mean hunger for a family. Sometimes maybe famine for a whole village."

"So also with fishermen who catch no fish," Koi remembered.

Determined to have his say, Bankichi continued. "But here the food is assured. We never go without it, because we do not grow it. That, I can tell you, is a great relief to this belly of mine. And to my head. I sleep better now because I do not worry about my next meal, my next day, the next thing I must not fail to do."

"Moreover," Ishi said, "we are free men here. No spies to frighten us into obedience, no samurai to hack us down, no daimyo to order us about."

"That is so," they agreed, with less interest than Ishi thought his reminder deserved. He did not know yet that to most men a full belly is more important than freedom can ever be.

"And, best of all, the thing I like about this place," said Heizaemon with a most happy laugh, "is the money we are paid. Four dollars a month. Imagine! I feel like a rich man already, instead of the poor thing I've always been. Imagine! Four dollars, just waiting to slip into my pocket, at the end of each month. With them to dream about I too sleep better at nights."

"Baka! Don't count your zeni until you hold them in your hand," warned Dembei. He was that same bow-legged little man with the deep voice who had wandered through the *Scioto*'s three holds shouting "Bakayaro!" the evening after they sailed from Yokohama. By now everybody knew Dembei of the unremitting gloom, who saw only the black rain clouds of life but never the shine of silver and gold beyond. No one except Ishi gave heed anymore to his forebodings: they were like scoldings uttered by a sour wife. But perhaps because they shared certain worries in common Ishi thought that Dembei was the wisest man in their group.

"Yes," the others responded to Heizaemon's sunny vision, "being rich is the best part of all," they crowed, thinking of the many necessary things they would buy with the first month's pay. After this, in the months ahead, they would have plenty of time to save the honorable money they would take home to Nippon. Thirty-five months would certainly be more than enough time in which to amass the fortune of a most respectable man.

Saul Bristol was quick to realize their worth and to encourage them with praise. They surprised him most happily when he made his rounds late in the second day of work. The Chinese, as he well knew, being old hands at conserving their strength, would still be chopping at the shrubbery, as if they had been asked to slice it fine for cooking. But these Japanese had cleared scrub and stones from more than an acre in less than two days.

"Good men," he said to Pilipo, diligently in charge of his crew ever since he'd spotted the Boss riding up from the gulch.

"Yeah. Good workers," replied the luna. "Not sick or lazy, as Mister Douglas says."

"Let's hope they keep this up," said Bristol, directing his black stallion toward the crew. No false pity sent him there, no sorrowing for sore hands or sweating bodies. To him, as to them, work was an inescapable burden of life, for only by the sweat of his brow can a man earn his bread and all the other things that he wants. These new men, like all others employed on his plantation, were well paid for the kind of work they did. Each of them cost the company about $12 a month, for wages and found. And, he believed, that's damned good pay. Good pay for a day's honest work was one thing, but approbation was a bonus he believed in adding wherever it was warranted. It cost no money to begin with, yet it earned excellent dividends.

He looked at these sunburned little men, their faces streaked with dust and sweat, bristly with black hair around the lips and on the chin. They stared up at him, expressionless as dolls. They recognized him by now, after he had come in the broad light of day to inspect the improvements to the barrack, and they knew that he was one of those honorable men in power about whom Sentaro-san had warned Ishi and Koi. As such, he must be accorded much respect. And, until they knew him better, this respect must be tempered with wariness.

Bristol welcomed respect. A man cannot be a good boss unless he commands respect. But he hated the look of fear that so often takes the place of respect. He had seen it too often in the demeanor of black slaves in America, in some of the Chinese coolies on this very plantation. Here, among the Japanese, he was glad to see in eight of the ten the evidences of respect for themselves as well as for himself, in the squared shoulders, the heads held high, the steady appraising gaze. And he recognized the signs of wariness: the eyes of men who have been hunted, the tenseness of bodies ready to run at the first threat of danger. But, thank the Lord, he saw none of the cringing that marks a fawning man. Even the two who did not look at him seemed to be embarrassed rather than afraid.

All to the good, he noted, while wondering again how men so small could be so tireless. And how men from so foreign a country could have acquired this Calvinists' zeal for work.

Lifting his hands, as though encompassing in them the extent of the clearing and of the workers' achievements in it, he said, "Maikai, maikai. Good, good," nodding and smiling as he repeated the words. They responded with quick nods and big smiles. He remarked especially a little guy standing off to one side. Clapping his hands in delight, he all but did a jig while he grinned—showing "a mouthful of missing teeth," as Hiram Nihoa might have said—and repeated the words Bristol had just said. Merely to see this kid and his antics made Saul laugh aloud, as if he were watching a comedian perform on a stage. Flicking them a quick salute, he sped away. How the hell am I ever going to talk with them? he wondered, not for the first time. Should I learn Japanese? Or teach 'em Hawaiian? Maybe I should start a night school, as old Schapenhorst has done over there in Haiku.

A relieved luna and crew watched him ride off.

"That's a good man, a very good man," said Koi.

"Why should he praise us for doing our work?," asked Eizo.

"Yes. A good man," said Ishi. "Just as Sentaro-san has said about these haoles."

"Well, about most haoles," Koi reminded them.

"Agreed," laughed Ishi, bending to pick up another heavy rock. The Boss's face, long, thin, and dark; his black hair streaked with white; and especially those gray eyes, seeing everything, missing nothing: all reminded him of the boy in Kahului. These two, the man and the boy, must be father and son. But if this is true, why do they live so far apart?

They had made Gohongi quite comfortable with the materials and tools the Boss had told Jack Douglas to provide. They built a wall across one end of the barrack, making a separate room for the married couple. Koi and Aiko did not ask for that. Mr. Bristol insisted upon it as soon as he learned that a man and wife were included among his workers. Having such privacy was a new experience for Koi and Aiko. They did not know what to do with it and were lonesome on their side of the wall, even though they could hear almost every sound their friends made in the larger room. Koi finally reconciled their loneliness with the Boss's determination by leaving the door open at all times. In this way neither the wedded pair nor their bachelor friends could feel slighted.

For themselves, the bachelor men preferred a single big room rather than many small ones. They built a raised platform along both longer walls of the barrack, exactly like the ones that monks have in temple dormitories and daimyo's footmen in yashiki barracks. Upon this platform each man was allotted a space for sitting, lying, sleeping, and for storing his possessions. There also he kept the smoothed log he used for a head rest. The floor space in the middle of the room was the common meeting place, for sitting as a group when they smoked or played the flower card game or just wanted to talk.

They drove nails into the walls and the five posts, from which to hang their clean clothes. Outside the barrack, under the eaves, they put more nails and strung pieces of rope for drying laundry and for airing their smelly uniforms at the end of each day.

Shutting out the mosquitoes presented a problem. All the stores on Maui could not have provided sixty-five mosquito nets at one time, even at Jack Douglas's demand. Douglas set his mind to the need, bought a bolt of the white netting, borrowed a pair of scissors from the Chinese tailor on Main Street, and told Ah Siu what to do. Under Ah Siu's direction Aiko cut pieces of the stuff of a size that could be nailed over the air spaces in the three barracks. Ishi and his gang nailed them in place. Left-over snippets were used to cover knotholes and cracks between boards. The entry ways, wide open for so long, were plugged with doors hung upon hinges cut from strap iron. All these devices kept out most of the mosquitoes. The few that did "pass the barriers without official permits," as the Nipponjin said, deserved the reward of blood for their cleverness.

A Chinese crew from the mill house laid lengths of iron pipe between their camp and the Japanese barrack, through which fresh water would flow at the turn of a spigot. And the Japanese, under the direction of the same Chinese crew, dug a cess-pit to receive their wastes. They disliked this haole kind of convenience place, not only for its inescapable stenches but also because it did not make proper use of excellent manure. But they suppressed their disapproval when the Chinese told them that haoles would permit no other means for disposing of human excrement. To put it upon growing plants was forbidden. Even to be seen relieving oneself was forbidden. The Japanese who had not heard this warning from Sentaro shook their heads over the absurd ways— and the wastefulness—of haoles.

All this labor took the better part of two days. When it was done the barrack made as comfortable a home as any of them had ever lived in. They acknowledged as much when, in the light of five coal-oil lamps, brighter than anything they'd enjoyed in Nippon, they sat down to talk.

"Oh, they are generous enough, I admit," Eizo said of the haoles whose wealth could give the lowest of their workers such an enviable place to live in. "But they have not given us everything we need."

They turned toward him in surprise. He was not known to be a grasping man. "What else can we possibly want?" asked Heizaemon.

"An o-furo," said Eizo. And, of course, the instant he mentioned it all realized how earnestly they needed that deep tub of hot water in which a man could soak his tired body for a few relaxing minutes at the end of a hard day. The Chinese method of washing oneself with a wetted towel, or the Hawaiian way of standing under the stream of cold water flowing from the iron pipeline, was good enough for getting clean—especially with the help of this slippery new stuff called soap that the plantation supplied—but it could never replace the admirable o-furo of Nippon.

"Hana yori dango," Ishi reminded them, "rice cakes before flowers," by which he meant that needs must come before luxuries. But they did not even hear him, they were so busy thinking of all the other things they considered to be needs.

"And we must have a place where we can wash clothes," said Heizaemon, the fastidious city man who could not bear the thought of being dirty after he came home. Each evening, the minute he reached Gohongi, he went—in the dark—to the river to wash his clothes and his body. "I don't want to spend so much time at the river's side, like the woodcutter's wife who found the peach with Momotaro in it."

"And I would like to have a place where we might make a cooking-fire," said Dembei. "So we can fix tea, in the evenings."

"But first we must get a teapot," Eizo reminded him.

"And teacups," said Chikahei.

"And tea," said Dembei mournfully.

"And money," sighed Heizaemon.

About a week after they arrived in Wailuku they began to get sick, not all at once but a few each day. At first Pilipo the luna was annoyed at the frequency with which the few sick ones trotted off into the bushes. He thought they were playing the usual trick of lazy men to steal a few minutes of rest. But when, as the morning wore on, they became paler and weaker, he grew alarmed. At midday he sent the sick ones home but kept at their work the five who were well. In the evening he himself went to the plantation office to tell the bookkeeper that perhaps a doctor should be called to care for the sick men.

Mr. Dunham, looking vaguely at him with bloodshot eyes, mumbled "Ah'll take care of it," waved him off, and went back to his books of figures and bottle of whiskey. "Evahbody gits sick," he observed to his ledgers. "Soonah oa latah. 'Specially 'roun' heah." Soon after he staggered home and fell into his nightly stupor. When he awoke in the morning, in his usual crapula, he'd forgotten all about the sick Japanese.

Pilipo was a kind-hearted man. When, as his duty required, he went to the barrack to check upon the absent men, he could see that they were not pretending to be sick. Even then he could have kicked them off their sleeping-shelf, as lunas were doing in other plantations, as Jack Douglas most certainly would have done at Wailuku. But Pilipo allowed them to stay close to bed and benjo that day; and, guessing how Mr. Bristol would feel, he did not mark them down in his time-book as being absent from the job.

So it happened with all the Japanese in turn. Each became sick with the bowel fever, each missed a day or two of work before he recovered. Ah Siu and his helpers cheered them considerably by explaining, with much laughter and very expressive gestures, that sooner or later all newcomers took sick in this way, but that few people have been known to die from it. "Kanaka ghosts from up there," he pointed to the narrow valley from which the river came—and the water flowing through their pipe lines—the while he ordered his scholar to write down the kanji for ghost. "Too muchee no good," said the scholar. Sick or well, the Japanese understood, and shuddered.

Ah Siu sent potfuls of jook, thick rice soup, to the barrack as a curative as well as nourishment. The working men came home with pocketsful of fresh young guava leaves, saying that Pilipo advised the sick ones to chew these tender buds as a medicine. Some patients took one remedy, some took the other, or both, or none, and all recovered eventually.

Aiko, unknown to everyone else, was the most seriously affected. About the time they came to Wailuku she suspected that she might be pregnant. And then, almost immediately, the bowel fever came and when it was over she was not pregnant. For this miscarriage, if indeed it was that, she was almost glad. To have a child now, before she would be able to care for him, was wrong. But she did not tell Koi about either of these events, not wanting him to feel responsible for causing the first or for correcting the second.

Sick though she was Aiko lost little time from her job. She washed dishes as usual, hauled water, helped to prepare three meals a day for sixty-five hungry people, cleaned Gohongi, and washed her clothes and Koi's.

Moreover, because she was the only woman in the two camps, she was in constant peril. Her countrymen did not attempt to push her down, but those of the lustful Chinese who did not have barracks-mates for lovers gave her much cause for fear. One of Ah Siu's kitchen helpers was the worst because he was always near by. She dared not complain to Ah Siu but quite by accident he saw what was happening. He picked up a meat cleaver in one hand, a firewood hatchet in the other, and, brandishing both, chased the screeching fellow all over Paké Camp, threatening to cut off the part of him that itched so aggravatingly. Aiko, thinking that Ah Siu was serious, ran after the two of them, adding her screams to theirs. Whereupon Ah Siu grandly, if noisily, relented, the forgiven man returned, frightened into decency, and Aiko burst into tears. When she recovered sufficiently to thank Ah Siu he allowed her to think that indeed he had acted to save her. But he was not safeguarding her virtue. Those dollar-making whores of his, in the village across the river, were the objects of his solicitude.

All the time the Nipponjin were learning to be "growers of stones and harvesters of rocks," they were also picking up new words in English, Hawaiian, and Cantonese. Some they comprehended immediately. These referred to things in the world about them, such as boss and horse, pohaku and lepo for stone and dirt, Paké and kaukau for a Chinese man and food. Other words were more troublesome, probably because the teachers used these terms so frequently that they forgot to define them. Thus, the newcomers had no trouble in understanding Pilipo when he said, at the end of a day, "Pau hana now. Paké Camp go, kaukau time." But when Ah Siu, or Pilipo, or anyone said, "Hello Japanee," they were baffled. "What is Japanee?," they asked each other for many a day. Finally, Ah Siu's scholarly helper instructed them: "Meeseetah Bilisitola, him haole. Me, Paké. Pilipo, kanaka. You Japanee. Ellyboddee pupule foa hana-hana dis damfool place." This last judgment the Nipponjin lost in their amazement at hearing that they were Japanee.

"Me Nipponjin desu," said Eizo, pointing to his nose, the indisputable identification of himself.

"Nah, nah," Ah Siu pronounced. "You Japanee." That settled that, for the present. But not for many months did they learn why they were known by this peculiar name. They accepted it, however, with their usual politeness. This must be another one of those strange foreign customs, they thought. After all, the Chinese and the Hawaiians also submitted to them. What possible connection can there be between Paké and Shinajin, for example? Or between Kanaka and Hawaiijin?

They were not the only innocents in this babel. The day after they arrived Mr. Dunham ventured across the river to Japanee Camp. Prissy as a lady piano teacher, he sat upon the barrack step, Record Book on his knee, bottle of black ink beside it, accountant's pen in his shaking hand. Trying to make Ah Siu or the newcomers understand that he wanted their family names first, their Christian names second, tested his patience so severely that he soon consented to write down the single epithet that each one professed was all the name he owned. A Southern gentleman still, Mr. Dunham began with "the little lady," and inscribed her as Aye-co. Coy followed, "husband of above." Mr. Dunham coped fairly well with Ee-shee and A-zo. But when Tametsugu and Heizaemon stepped up, poor unnerved Mr. Dunham, caring no longer about exactitude, settled for Tommy and Hay.

"Barbaric tongue," he mumbled, heading back to his dark office. "Even worse than kanaka."

In their evening conversations about this amazing country they lived in, the Japanese criticized many things, approved of even more. But the custom that most delighted them was the gift of every seventh day as a time of rest. They called it Ennichi, festival day.

"Such generosity," exclaimed Koi when, the first Sabbath having arrived, the Pakés convinced him that they were not teasing him with fables. "No work. Nothing to do but lie around."

"Doing nothing for the Boss, yet being fed. And fed especially well," gloated Tametsugu. "I cannot believe such luck."

"And the Pakés said, if I understood them correctly, that sometimes we shall have other holidays as well. I suppose these will be like our big festivals at home."

"Which reminds me," said Dembei, sounding like a voice from the world of the dead, "the time for O-Bon is coming soon."

"Already?," asked Chikahei. "Really?"

"How can one tell the time of year, in this land without seasons?," asked Heizaemon. "What month is this, what day?"

"You are right," Ishi spoke across to Dembei. "We must remember our dead. And our living."

"But how shall we know when the time for O-Bon comes?" Heizaemon persisted, the city man still. "Without priests, without temples to tell us?"

"Let us ask Ah Siu," suggested Ishi. "Perhaps he knows."

"I can tell you," said Bankichi.

How will you know? their faces asked him.

"My true heart will tell me," he said soberly, "with the help of the other five senses."

For once in the history of Wailuku, its Catholics, Congregationalists, and Mormons united in a common cause. Horror-struck at the information which had been whispered to one of them, the priest, the pastor, and the elder marched in a body to talk with Saul Bristol.

He listened gravely to their plaint, tactfully he suppressed a smile. Once upon a time he would have blasted them with scorn, driven them from his door with mocking laughter. But now he was older—and smarter. And more long-suffering, even with fools. Now he knew that Hiram Nihoa and he, with their fine ideas for raising up at Kaaawa a generation free of sinners, because they would not know anything about sins, were undoubtedly a few thousand years ahead of their time. They were outnumbered, in this generation and in those to come, by Mr. Grundys like this holy three.

"Eet ees your dutee, Messire Breestole, to stop zees—zees abominnashiyon," hissed the priest. Bristol noticed, with approval, that this young Frenchman, unlike others he had encountered in the morn of his life, was acquainted with the uses of soap. There's some hope for Holy Church, he conceded, if its professors are washing away the odors of sanctity.

"It is an exhibition devoutly to be suppressed," said the Mormon, who seemed to have a touch of humor—or else a very bad memory. Bristol hadn't quite made up his bias, yet, about these Mormons, so newly come among men and to Maui.

"*Acres* of naked flesh!," clarioned the reverend, given in this, as in all things, to repression and understatement. Bristol knew enough about Congregationalists to allow them no credit for charity, and damned little for truthfulness. But faith and hope they had in abundance—in the correctness of their own standards of belief and behavior. Thank God, he consoled himself, the meek are going to inherit the earth.

"Come, now, gentlemen," said the worldly manager of Hawaiian Sugar Mill. "All this fuss, just because they bathed in the river?"

"But stark nekkid, Mr. Bristol!"

"And on zee Sabbat, also."

"And there was a woman among them, in flowing tresses—but naught else."

"But who could have seen them?" Saul Bristol pretended to a naivety about Wailuku's people that he knew very well they did not warrant. "The only pool big enough for a party of—I mean a group of—that size lies quite a good piece—I mean a distance —upstream. In a place where there are no houses. And certainly in a place where no proper Christian would be likely to wander on a Sabbath morning." Innocent as a youth fresh out of Sunday School, he looked from one to the other, inviting their charity.

"They were *seen*," snapped the reverend.

"Does eet matter who saw zem?," smiled the priest, a Jesuit in Sacred Hearts' clothing.

"They hanged their wraps upon the willows," intoned the elder, "and did sport about without them." Out of the corner of his eye Saul studied this garbler of quotations. He was almost as good at the game as Hiram Nihoa. But, try as he might, Saul could not detect in this Deseret-dried prophet the slightest hint of Hiram's humor.

"Very well, gentlemen. I shall try to prevent its happening again. Explaining this to them, however, is going to be very difficult. A matter of language, of course. As well as of innocence, I suspect. From what I read, I gather that bathing is a common practice in Japan. There, it seems, they are not ashamed of their bodies."

"A common practice it may be. But practised in common it should be not."

"They ought to be horsewhipped," said the preacher of Christian love.

"Perhaps, rather, I should call upon you, gentle sirs? You, with your gift of tongues, might be able to speak with them better than I. After all, in Japan they have had little chance to hear—"

"But this, sir, is Hawaii. A Christian country. This is not Japan."

"So I gather, gentlemen." Saul Bristol opened wide the gate. "I shall do my best," he flashed his insincerest smile. When the gate was safely shut, he muttered, "for them." Confessing himself a coward in battles with men of certitude, he went out to find a man of charity.

Pilipo recognized at once the enormity of the offense, as his rolling eyes and happy laughter attested. Saul rode away from the field confident that in Pilipo the Japanese had another champion, one even more helpful than he could be.

The luna enjoyed this new responsibility: it added spice to a job otherwise very dull. With the supplementary gestures and dramatic expressions involving eyes, lips, nostrils, hands, the whole aghast body, he conveyed to the Japanese the information that hundreds of Wailuku's sensitive inhabitants had fled in horror from the sight of their lewd disportings in the river. Going on from that soothing beginning, he impressed upon the Japanese the lesson that they must never never do that again. They hung their heads, contrite as children, because without having intended to do so they had caused unimaginable trouble for Burisitoru-san and Piripo-san, and for all those many nice people in Wailuku whom they had not yet seen but who had seen them.

Pilipo's reproof bothered Ishi all the day long. He blamed himself for having allowed them to go bathing on that quiet Ennichi, in spite of Sentaro-san's warning. He had remembered the prohibition, and told them about it. For that reason they walked far up the river bed, until they came to a place where they thought no one lived. And then all they did was to wash their clothes and—while those dried in the sun—to wash themselves in a shallow pool among the rocks. They could not imagine why anyone should waste a second glance upon such a commonplace act. Ishi berated himself for not being a good leader. And yet, he could not help asking himself, what sort of people are these haoles, who follow a group of Nipponjin going for an innocent walk, who peep furtively at them from behind leafy branches, like boys peering for the first time at flower-women in the cages of the Yoshiwara . . .

That evening, as they walked home to Gohongi, Ishi said, "We must make an o-furo."

"How?" they wanted to know. "When?" No one, he noticed, asked "Why?"

"I don't mean a big one, for all of us to sit in together. We can make that later. For now I mean a small o-furo, for one man at a time. Such a bath as rich men sometimes have in their houses."

"Agreed," they said. "When do we begin?"

"Let me look around first, to see what we can use for making it."

His inspection showed that everything they needed was available—except for the most important part, a tub big enough to heat the water in. Stones for the foundation, bamboo for the walls and top, wood for the fire: they lay all around Gohongi, waiting to be taken. But nowhere could he find clay or metal with which to make the tub.

He reported his failure to the group. They sat in silence for a while, thinking. Then Tametsugu spoke. "Perhaps we could build another kind of bath. In the western provinces, I have heard, they make an o-furo that uses only one thin piece of metal. They call it the Goemon bath. Only a thin plate separates fire from water. The tub in which you sit is also the tub for heating the water."

"That's the way." Ishi saw the plan complete in his mind. "We can make that kind easily, once we find a piece of metal of the right size."

"Piripo and Ah Siu will help us," said Tametsugu.

"But how do you keep your feet from being burned in this— this Goemon thing?," Heizaemon cried.

"Bakayaro," Dembei growled. "You stand on your hands."

"You hop up and down, first on one foot, then on the other," said Koi. "Doing the Goemon dance."

"Hee, hee," Bankichi squealed, rolling his wide eyes even farther apart. "To save your feet, you cook your ass."

Ishi the Kind put Heizaemon out of his misery. "You will make the pair of geta, please, that each of us will use."

"Ah, ah, so that's how it's done," said Heizaemon, looking very enlightened. "And here, for all these years, I have been thinking that people from the provinces are not very smart."

"But first we must ask permission from Burisitoru-san," Ishi said.

Ishi's request went up through Ah Siu to Pilipo to Saul Bristol. The next day approval came back, along with the gift of a piece of cast-iron plate a quarter-inch thick and thirty-six inches square, and a bag of cement, rarer than gold. A Chinese neighbor who worked in the mill house brought up this bounty on a pack mule.

On the following Ennichi, carrying empty jute sacks borrowed from the mill, half the Nipponjin went to the seashore to fetch sand. The other half stayed at Gohongi, to begin work upon the honorable bath. Because, as the saying goes, too many captains will drive the ship up the mountain, Ishi sent his helpers upon all those errands in all directions, while he stayed alone to do his delicate job.

They finished it on the third Sunday of labor, with unexpected help from the Fourth of July holiday.

Saul Bristol strongly opposed such an American intrusion into the independent Kingdom of Hawaii, but here too he was fighting a losing battle. The sentiments of the honorable men in power over him ignored his disloyal own. From C. Brewer's head office in Honolulu came orders declaring a holiday. From the handful of American residents in Wailuku came a sermon at the Congregational church and oratory outside it afterward. Saul

Bristol excused himself from all such celebrations, declaring that he was a naturalized citizen of the Kingdom of Hawaii and a loyal subject of His Majesty the King. "This is Hawaii, not the United States," he took great pleasure in reminding the reverend. The dart failed to pierce its mark. The Yankee patriot could not imagine an American with soul so dead that he could not honor above all others that great and glorious land, and he promptly withdrew from the company of so black-hearted a renegade.

Ishi the experienced stone mason was prouder of this thing that he had made with his own hands than of anything he had ever done. Although it was not beautiful, as even he could see, it worked. It lacked beauty not because of the mason but because of the materials he was given to work with (an excuse which is, of course, the lament of every true artist). Moreover, the shape a Goemon o-furo must take actually prevents it from being a thing of beauty.

Ishi planned it all very carefully, sketching it on butcher paper with a charred stick—and with much help from nine noisy Nipponjin as ignorant as he of masonry or of the making of bathtubs. Nonetheless, by straining memories and putting common sense to work, they developed a plan that was as simple as possible and yet gave the promise of serving their need.

It was nothing more than a low box of a fireplace made of rocks, covered over with the metal plate upon which Ishi built another box made of stones. This upper box was broad enough for a man to squat in and held water enough to cover him up to his chin. To make this tub water-tight he plastered its inner surface with cement and sand. He did not forget to leave a small drain hole at one side. To help the fire burn well he made a chimney of stones, higher than himself, the tallest man who would use that tub, cementing these stones around a form Heizaemon made with strips of bamboo.

While Ishi worked lovingly upon this construction, other men brought stones from the river bed for him to use, laid the floor of the wash room with rounded pebbles taken from the same unlimited source, lashed lengths of green bamboo to make four walls and a roof, cut down trees in the jungle to stand as posts. The walls were a concession to haoles, not a comfort for themselves. They did not want any haole necks broken, or haole horror spent, while their owners climbed down and up the river's banks to look at naked Nipponjin. Aiko, with occasional assistance from Koi, gathered, cut, and stacked firewood for the time when it would be wanted. Everyone, of course, ever since the day they'd arrived, pounced upon every piece of precious paper he saw. Whatever they didn't use in the benjo would fill many another purpose, most especially starting the fire in the honorable furo.

At last everything was ready. Ishi decided that, after a week's drying, the tub's cement lining was ready to accept water. The faucet—that wondrous Western invention—was turned on, and Aiko was accorded the privilege of giving the tub its first scrubbing. This being done, Koi thrust the long wooden bung into the drain hole—with appropriate jests from bystanders—and the faucet was turned on again. And Ishi had the honor of lighting the first fire.

He had planned this ceremony ever since they began to build the o-furo. He could have sent Aiko to the cook-house for coals, or for some of those friction matches that Ah Siu flourished so wastefully. But Ishi wanted this occasion to be special, something that all his people would remember for the rest of their lives.

He washed his hands thoroughly, rinsed his mouth, cleansing himself of pollution. He scattered a small pinch of salt in each of the four directions to purify the bathhouse. He used his burning glass for the first time, to bring down to Maui's earth the life-giving warmth of Amaterasu, the Sun Goddess. No one could doubt that, as the glass gathered together the rays of the sun in one fiery spot and set the paper ablaze, Amaterasu's blessing was being bestowed upon her people. In silence filled with awe they watched the ritual gestures as Ishi lifted the blazing paper in his worn and calloused hands, stained forever now with dirt and cement and his shed blood, but beautiful still in the shape of their fingers and in the elegance of their every motion. Unhurried,

assured as a priest, he touched the burning paper to the dried
leaves and twigs that Tametsugu had laid in the fireplace. The
flames curled about uncertainly, the little coils of smoke waited,
as if for instructions from the goddess who had sent the fire.
Then, as the air began to warm and the draft took hold, the
smoke drifted inward, into the dark cave and up the long chimney, like incense on its way to Heaven. As the first wisps issued
from the chimney the spell was broken. Ishi's companions
cheered, congratulating him for being so expert a mason. Ishi felt
proud and humble at the same moment—because his friends
praised him, because the work of his hands was good, above all
because he was living in a place where, at last, he could see some
purpose in his life, some meaning in the things he did.

Aiko, beginning her duty, knelt beside the thriving fire. A kerchief covered her hair, the sleeves of her kimono were tied back
by straps across the shoulders. She was the priestess of the purify-
ing bath, as Ishi was the priest to this little community.

The men recognized that this was a day of great importance to
all of them. The smell of burning wood, of the bamboo form in
the chimney being scorched, was good. It filled the air, reminding them of evenings at home. With this o-furo, too, they had
made another link with home.

When Aiko came to tell them that the water was hot, they had
some good-natured argument about who should be the first to sit
in that fine tub. Nine men said that Ishi should have the honor.
He objected, saying that they should do Jankenpo for the choice.
"Let the gods decide in this," he said.

"No, no," Eizo settled the matter with a nice wit. "In the family the father always goes first. You are our father now, Ishi-san."
He meant this, although he laughed as he said it.

In their ready agreement with him the others too showed that
they had learned to like and to trust Ishi, and that from this day
on he would be their acknowledged leader.

Ishi, embarrassed yet pleased, could argue no more. He picked
up a clean fundoshi and hurried off to the bathhouse. In half a

minute he returned, looking very foolish. "Komatta naa ... We have forgotten the geta."

"What!," cried half a dozen desperate men. "What are we going to do?"

"Don't worry," said Heizaemon smugly. "Come, I will show you." He had made a pair of clogs from pieces of wood he found lying about in the mill yard. These he had hung on a nail behind the Goemon bath, where each man might find them if ever he should be first to enter the tub. Heizaemon also presented them with three little benches for bathers to sit upon while they soaped and rinsed themselves before entering the bath. The greatest surprise, however, was a higher bench, long enough for several latecomers to wait upon.

Aiko had laid them out, as well as the scrub brushes, the cake of soap, a small enamel pan for holding the wash water, the larger bucket for the rinse water. "These are gifts from Ah Siu," she explained, as they gazed in admiration upon these valuable articles. The soap itself would be worth a small fortune in Nippon, where it was unknown among common folk. There they used little cloth bags filled with rice bran for scrubbing the dirt from their bodies. Soap was a luxury imported from foreign countries, which only wealthy merchants and great nobles could afford to buy. But here, in this rich country, it was so cheap that the plantations gave it to people who worked for them.

"Ah, this is more like home," they said, approving the o-furo and all its splendid furnishings. "No one should bathe alone." While they inspected everything Aiko returned to her duties in the kitchen.

"And these," Heizaemon pointed to dozens of nails hammered into the posts and the crossbeams that held the hut together, "are for us to hang our clothes upon."

"Well, then, why do we wait?," said Dembei, beginning to unwind his fundoshi.

In this clubhouse they sat and gossiped and washed and soaked, one at a time, until the supper hour was near. When they swaggered on their manly way back to Gohongi Aiko got to clean up the bathhouse, to hang the geta in their proper place. She did not have a chance to bathe then because she had to hurry back to the kitchen.

Only when her work was done could she slip into the dark bathhouse and wash herself hurriedly before entering the honorable tub. By then the fire was long since dead and the water was only slightly warm. But she did not mind. In all her life at home in Nippon she was always the last to sit in the o-furo. That is a woman's lot, and she did not question it. A woman's lot is to follow her husband in everything, and to please him in everything. She smiled, even in the dark, for she was so happy with her husband.

Clean, smelling of soap, not yet so old and worn that she was too tired after a long day's work, she slipped into her kimono. Not bothering to tie the sash, she hurried across the dark clearing to Gohongi. In their little room Koi waited for her to please him. She hurried because he pleased her too. Very much, and in all ways. For this, she lifted her little face to the stars high above, she would be forever grateful to Benten-sama, who granted her such a good love.

They began to take root, these transplanted people, they began to think of the new place, too, as a home. When the o-furo was finished the men spent some of their free time on Ennichi in doing useful things. In the age-old hunger to draw sustenance from the earth some made vegetable gardens. They could not grow the variety of vegetables they had enjoyed in Nippon, being limited to those for which Ah Siu's helpers gave them starts. The Chinese were generous with roots of onions green and round, eyes of potatoes sweet or white, beans of several colors and shapes, and with seeds of tomatoes, cucumbers, squashes, and melons. Before long a tamer growth than the jungle grew in the cleared space around Gohongi. Bankichi, when he saw those onions and cucumbers growing so well, said, "We're going to have too many for us to use. Maybe we should send for that pickle maker to come and help us preserve them. What was his name, I wonder... I forget—"

Yet, even as they worked and built and planted, wanting to make a home out of this new place, they knew in their hearts that the barrack would never fill that need. For true contentment a man wants a house of his own, with a wife in it, and children. The men of Gohongi knew they must wait yet a while for these gifts. For the present they had only the promise that these might be gained in time—if the gods were kind.

Six of the men spoke frequently of the future when, their fortunes made, they would return to Nippon and to the life of men of property and esteem. Three of the Gohongijin kept quiet about the future, knowing only that they would not return to Nippon while they hoped that their fortunes would be found in this new country. One, not yet sure what he would do, said that he would wait to decide. But all agreed that, for now, matters were going well enough and that they were content. A man must wait, each understood, when he can do nothing to speed his fate.

Often the Nipponjin in Wailuku talked about others who had crossed the sea with them, and wondered how they were faring. What had become of O-Miya, for example, and Daigoro-san? Those two still excited the imagination—and pleasing gossip. Dembei, the cynic who thought that all people were fools, not least himself, was willing to bet the first ripe tomato from his garden that O-Miya as a wife would be worse than a witch. Heizaemon, on the other hand, offered a free haircut to the first one who brought him disproof of his contention that Daigoro would make married life a hell in this world for O-Miya. Only Koi and Aiko, the happy lovers—and therefore ill-prepared to offer judgments about anybody—argued strongly that O-Miya and Daigoro-san, being so much in love, would live happily until they were bent of back and wrinkled in skin and white of hair. At which point Dembei in disgust and Heizaemon in boredom changed the subject to one less inviting to sentimentalists.

They heard not a word from any one about their countrymen, just as no one ever heard about them. None of the Wailuku group, not even Eizo the printer of pictures, could write well enough to compose a letter. No Nipponjin from any place outside Wailuku ever came to see them. They did not even know what was happening to their fifty-one friends at Haiku Plantation, where the boy with the gray eyes lived. As far as Nippon was concerned, and the events happening there, to friends, families, the nation: ahh, that was another world, in another life.

They might just as well have been alone, on this island in the middle of the sea. This silence, this not knowing, they began to realize, was going to be the hardest of all troubles to bear.

"Now I can understand why Urashima Taro wanted so much to go home," said Tametsugu, one of the six who declared that they were returning to Nippon.

They would have been surprised, and exceedingly gratified, if they could have heard of the Sad Woman's fate.

When Yuki arrived at Henry Cornwell's plantation at Waikapu he was annoyed beyond measure to find that those nitwits in Honolulu had shucked a woman off on him, a laborer he could not put to work. And at a cost of seventy dollars, too, for her useless hide and head! Like Saul Bristol, Henry Cornwell could not be so ungentlemanly as to put a weak woman to work in the cane fields. Inasmuch as he was saddled with her he decided to employ the woman in his household, as a helper to his wife in the nursery and to the Chinese cook in the kitchen.

Yuki did her work well enough in the kitchen, once she learned the haole way of doing things (as amended by the Chinese tyrant who commanded both kitchen and Cornwells), but she was drawn to the nursery as water rises to the sun. Within three days, before any one quite knew what was happening, she had transferred all her devotion and most of her time to the two little girls. Mrs. Cornwell, a nervous mother, had not let them out of her sight during the five years since the elder was born. The attention of Yuki, dressed in a kimono, leading those dark-eyed little half-Hawaiian girls about with utmost decorum, reassured the mother and reimbursed the father for all his lamented expense.

Yuki thought that being a second mother was suitable employment for her until the time when she could bear her own child. Always smiling, so patient and so kind—yet, withal, so firm in persuading the girls to behave as young ladies—she charmed all the Cornwells without having learned a word of English or Hawaiian. She entertained the children with all the tricks a Japanese mother employs—the making of paper figures, the playing of games, singing and dancing, sewing dolls' clothes and coloring pictures, serving orangeade and cakes. Before long, to everyone's delight, these small girls could sing Japanese nursery songs and dance to the accompaniment of their own shrill voices and Yuki's clapping hands.

Within a fortnight she was invited to move to the Cornwell's mansion. They installed her in a bedroom of her own, furnished in the Western style. Happier than she had ever expected to be in this present life, Yuki went to sleep each night with a prayer of thanks to the Lord Buddha in her heart. He had been so good to her in the three short months since she left Nikko that she was not impatient. She could wait for the child of her body he had promised her.

Thus did they live, those Nipponjin in Wailuku of Maui. They worked hard, they hoped, they waited. The honorable men in power seemed to be pleased with them. Mr. Bristol waved and called aloha when he passed. Piripo-san, the kindest sub-boss they had ever known, won their loyalty, and they did not betray him. Mr. Douglas—thanks to the care of their protecting gods—worked in the mill house and did not come near them.

Although from early morning until evening their bodies labored for the plantation, their minds—and their eyes—still had time to wander. Some thought about the village of Wailuku, and the delights awaiting them there. Some thought of a farther future, others of the receding past.

Ishi would look up to the mountain from which the river flowed, wondering why it called to him.

And Koi would look to the sea.

CHAPTER 16
HONORABLE PAY DAY

For the Japanese in Wailuku the first of those troubles that Mr. Green and Makino-san foresaw came on the twenty-ninth day after they began to work in the fields. They counted the days according to the lunar calendar because they knew nothing about the Western one and its maddening variations in the length of the months. At breakfast on the twenty-ninth day, therefore, they asked Ah Siu where and at what hour on this day they would be receiving their honorable pay.

"Moa latah," replied Ah Siu, expressing the idea much more clearly with head and hands.

"Why?," they asked, very politely, sure that he must have misunderstood.

Ah Siu, finding this too difficult a question to answer in sign talk, summoned his kitchen scholar. He scratched his head, thought a long time before he reached for the writing brush and proper black ink, made with soot scraped from the cookstove. He recognized immediately the nature of the problem because Chinese, too, still observed the lunar calendar in their private ceremonies and rituals. The moon, regular in her cycles, is not so fickle a timekeeper as is the sun. In consequence, those crazy haoles, barbarians still who worshipped the sun, were always anywhere from three to six weeks awry in their greeting of the new year. Thereby they confused all civilized people on earth and affronted the gods on high. "Gott-tam sonakapitchee," he swore at haoles, for disarranging the harmonies of the universe, for making him think so hard in order to explain their ignorant ways.

"Look see nana," he began to draw the grid of lines depicting a calendar, whether it be lunar or solar. He wrote the characters for the days from top to bottom, along the right side of the grid, the numbers for the weeks at the top, from right to left. After crossing out the days already passed during this seventh haole month (which in truth was only the Fifth Month in China and Japan); and after having suffered through much excited commentary, from Chinese savants on one side of the table and Japanese calendrical experts on the other, he succeeded in informing the Gohongijin that this was only the twenty-fifth day in the haole month of Ju-lai. Pay, therefore, would not be given until six more days had come and almost gone.

Persuaded at last, less by the scholar's chart than by his earnestness and Ah Siu's vigorous table-thumping, the Japanese men went off to the field, grumbling all the way. They were fifteen minutes late, but Pilipo arrived even later. He found them hacking at the brush, as though each sapling was a most stubborn enemy.

On pay day, fifteen minutes before closing time, as was the custom, they went to the plantation office, next to the mill house. At his desk, with trembling hands and frequent reference to the Record Book, Mr. Dunham counted out the money that was due each laborer as he presented himself. The two Hawaiian lunas stood at either side of Mr. Dunham, to identify each laborer as he stepped up and spoke his name. Jack Douglas, pistol on hip, leaned against a wall, supposedly to guard all that money from bandits who never showed up. And Mr. Bristol sat at his desk, imparting authority and C. Brewer's blessing to the occasion. Nothing bored him more than this business, but he braced himself for it each time because it was a prescribed duty.

The Chinese, led by Ah Siu as honorable uncle, went first, as was only right. After them came the Japanese, with Ishi at the head of the line and Aiko at the end, as was only proper. Bowing stiffly, each received his wages in both hands, as though it were a precious gift from a daimyo, and hurried outside. Because these were the first foreign coins they had ever seen, none of them had any idea how much money he carried away.

The shock came at supper, when they asked their Chinese

friends to explain the meaning and values of all those different pieces of honorable money. When at last they had learned the lesson they sat in stunned silence. All kinds of terrible thoughts raced through their minds, many emotions gnawed at their livers. Each of the men had received exactly $1.96, instead of the $4.00 he expected. Aiko, being a mere weak woman, got 96 cents.

They looked down at the American silver dollars and dimes, the copper pennies, at the Mexican reals, the British shillings and pence, the French piastres, and all the other odd coins that passed for currency in the Kingdom of Hawaii. All those alien faces and foreign writings ... All those different sizes, thicknesses, colors, metals ... And all adding up to so little!

"Screwed again," said Koi in disgust, wanting to throw his paltry stack into the night, but keeping his temper in check, for Aiko's sake.

"Why?," they asked in anger, looking from Ah Siu to the scholar. Shrieking merrily, as though this were the funniest of jokes, they said that all plantations were run this way. The same thing happened to the Chinese each month: no man ever received all the money he expected or wanted. Indeed, some Chinese, who bought more things at the plantation store than they could pay for, received no coins at all. Laughing merrily, until the pigtails bounced upon their backs, their fellows on either side agreed with everything Ah Siu said. Laughter, they seemed to be saying, is the only medicine against poverty.

"The more words, the less sense," as the wise saying tells us. The Japanese could not understand these long explanations, and were in no mood to accept the consolations of laughter. They stumbled back to Gohongi, blacker in humor than the night. Anger churned in their bellies, hotter and more sour than a drunkard's vomit. Pride raised those stomachs to high indignation.

In the barrack, under the bright lamps, the hotheads burst out: "We've been cheated!" "We've been robbed!" "I feel like throwing all those stones back into the field!" "I'm going to leave this place. Tomorrow!"

They turned upon Ishi. "You said they were fair men, these haoles."

Ishi, as disheartened as any, recognized this as the worst moment in all their time together. The assaults of nature must be suffered, because men cannot sway wild winds nor calm furious seas. But the assaults of men—especially when they are planned—must be opposed, else the victim will never be spared. He wanted to protest this unfairness as fiercely as did his friends. He knew also that, once again, he too was on trial, being tested by those very friends for his right to be their leader. Yet, most of all, he knew that the haoles were being judged. And he could not believe that they would cheat anyone so meanly. Even Hamada-san and his henchmen were not that base.

"Wait," he held up his hand, just as Makino-san would have done. "Let us not bring disgrace and shame upon ourselves by making trouble without cause. What would the other people think about us if we ran around, shouting in anger and throwing stones, only to learn that we were in the wrong? Let us find out first what the truth is. Then we shall know what to do."

Most of his companions stared at him as if he were mad, or an abject coward. "How?," they objected.

"I agree with Ishi-san," said Dembei soberly. "Let us not make worse fools of ourselves than we are already."

"No doubt this can be explained," said Ishi, grateful for Dembei's support. "I cannot think they wish to cheat us. Let us be fair with them, therefore, until we have proof that they are not being fair."

"What better proof do you ask than this?," shouted Chikahei, throwing his money to the floor. The coins rolled in all directions but he did not spring up to retrieve them, as a man less angry would have done.

"Remember what we learned at home," said Tametsugu. " 'Peasants are like sesame seeds. The harder they're squeezed, the more they give.' "

"Have they shown in any other way that they want to cheat us?," asked Ishi. "Have we been given any reason to complain before now? Can you imagine Mr. Bristol—who has been so kind to us—wanting to rob us of our wages?"

"Fair face, black belly," growled Chikahei.

"Maybe we're paying now for all these things we thought he gave us, to fix up this barrack?," suggested Eizo.

That terrible possibility had not occurred to Ishi. While he thought about it Koi came to his aid. "What can we do, to learn the truth?"

"We must call upon Makino-san for help in this, I think. He said that he—"

"And how can we do that, when he is so far away?," asked Tametsugu. "Or do you have fox-spirits for messengers?"

"No, but we can try to write him a letter."

"But that will take so much time," shouted Chikahei. "Weeks!"

"And where will you be going in the next three years?," asked Dembei.

Ishi persisted with his one hope. "Who among us can write a letter, telling of our trouble?" The question was soon answered. No one in the group knew enough kanji to write a letter that would make sense. To compose a letter using kana alone was not worth the effort, because it would lead only to endless confusion in the mind of Makino-san.

Ishi turned to Koi. "Can Aiko write?"

"I don't know. I never asked her."

Dembei raised his hand. In his deep voice, so sensible and calm, he said, "I am trying to remember, fool that I am—What did Hamada-san tell us, before we signed those papers that we could not read?"

"Those useless contracts, you mean?," said Koi, who had double reason to remember them.

"But they took 'em away from us, I thought. Down at the harbor here. That gray-eyed boy gathered them up." Bankichi was a good man for moving rocks and growing tomatoes, but he had a way of confusing places and events that happened more than five days ago.

"No, not those," said Ishi. "The ones from Yokohama. Didn't Kimura-san give them to us? To keep? I seem to remember . . . "

"Yes, that's right!" said Koi. "He shoved them across the table at us, when he gave us all those zeni."

"Yes, that's how I recall it," said Dembei quietly, like a father coaxing his forgetful children to remember a matter of importance. "And where did we put them?" He winked at Ishi, telling him that he knew where he was leading this forgetful family.

"I threw mine away on the ship," said Tametsugu. "Why should I keep a piece of paper that I cannot read? Especially if it was given to me by a gang of crooks?"

"I wiped my ass with it," said Bankichi. "For the same reasons."

"So did I," said Dembei. "Bakayaro."

"I kept mine. I think," said Ishi. "Let me see if I can find it." While he rummaged through his sailor's bag others too searched for their contracts.

"What'll you do with it, if you find it?" demanded Chikahei. "Shove it—?" He was like a dog that bravely barks before its own gate.

"Perhaps all of us together can read enough of it to remember what Hamada-san said," Ishi replied, with more patience than the furious man deserved.

Koi found his copy stuffed into the cloth wrapping around the samisen he never had time to play. Ishi pulled his out of the box that held the burning-glass. It was so meaningless to him, this piece of cheap paper, that he had not even noticed it the other day, when he used the lens for the ceremony at the o-furo. Eizo lifted moldy remnants of his copy from a razor case.

"Let's see if we can read this thing," said Ishi, drawing the lamp closer to their task.

Only Eizo the picture-printer was schooled enough to make out most of the kanji in the contract that described the conditions of their service. Ishi could do very little except to encourage him to persevere whenever he wanted to quit this difficult task. In fact, Ishi and the others saw to their dismay, already they were forgetting many of the difficult kanji they had known at home, and even some of the simple kana were slipping away from memory's weak hold.

For more than half an hour Eizo puzzled over the document, making out a kanji here, another there, piecing out the meanings of the sentences with the help of the kana that kept the kanji in place, much as beads of clear crystal in an abbot's rosary will hold in place the richer gems.

"Well, at least it's not a false document, like the passport old Hambei gave us," Eizo announced, after he had studied it for quite a while.

Bored with this digression into the mysteries of the intellect, Chikahei developed second thoughts about the small fortune he had thrown away. Crawling about on hands and knees, he and his companions picked up the scattered coins, restoring them to him, every one. Then they lolled about, smoking little pipes, yawning, cleaning fingernails, ears, noses, while all repeated, in sixteen different ways, their disappointment at having been so definitely deprived, if not actually robbed, of their hard-earned wages.

At length, in deep despondency, Eizo spoke. "Not good. They are right. We are wrong."

"What! How is this possible?" Chikahei was ready to throw away his money again.

"The writing says: Half the pay for each month will be set aside, to be given to us in Yokohama when we return to Nippon. Remember?"

"That is the fortune of the future which will win us respect and women," rumbled Dembei. "Remember?"

Ah, yes, they nodded meekly. Now they remembered.

"Even worse," continued Eizo. "The writing also says that the money we were given in Yokohama—those thirty bu, remember?—"

"Of which Hamada's pirates took half, remember?," cried Chikahei.

"Yes, that's what I mean," said Eizo. "Those thirty bu were not a gift. That money was loaned to us. But without interest, let us be grateful for that kindness. With it we were supposed to buy the things we would need in this country. And we must pay it back to the government of this country. At the rate of fifty cents a month. That means—let me see—for twenty months."

"I do not remember hearing about this loan," said Tametsugu. "Did Hamada-san tell us?"

"No," growled Chikahei, echoed by Koi and several others, all getting angry again with Hamada and his school of sharks. In the midst of this uproar Ishi remembered the lizard man's features and voice, offering him a job "with my organization" when he returned from Hawaii. In Kannon's Name! Whatever made that cheating man think that I would want to work for the likes of him?

Dembei could neither read nor write, but he had a remarkable memory and a quick head with figures. "Four dollars less $2.50 leaves $1.50," he sang, like a priest reciting a sutra. "Then why do we receive $1.96—forty-six cents more than we are promised by the contract?"

They thought about this complication. They soon gave up, as much from shame as from inability to reckon in this new system of currency. To be paid more than they had earned, after having accused the plantation of cheating them: ahh, this was more subtle a punishment than such sensitive men could bear.

Severely now, a teacher scolding students who have failed him, Dembei said, "The forty-six cents are paid us for the three days we worked in the month before this one. This is not gift money, as you are thinking. It is money we have earned. But it also shows how fair these haoles are. As Ishi has said."

"Then we have not been robbed after all," concluded Heizaemon, almost disappointed.

"No. They have been fair, down to the last penny."

"More than fair," said Eizo. "They've paid us even for the days when we were sick."

Koi slapped his knee. "As always, the ones who robbed us were our own countrymen. Those pombiki in Yokohama."

"Beasts!" "May they choke on horse dung!" "May they die in

Edo's jail!" For a few seconds they turned their anger against those distant targets—until someone thought of a misery much closer to home.

"How are we going to live on this small amount? Only $1.96 a month?"

Dembei croaked, in Emma-o's own voice, "Not any more. From now on, $1.50 a month."

"Oh, we'll live all right," said Ishi, willing to forego many earthly pleasures now that his faith in haoles' fairness had been sustained. "What more do we need than we already have?"

"For a monk like you this may be enough," bawled the rude Chikahei. "But not for me. I can't even get two lays a month out of this'"

"Maybe Ah Siu will give us credit?," suggested Heizaemon, ever hopeful.

"Or a discount?," said innocent Akemi, the youngest man in the group.

Simpering like his favorite dansho, arching his body like a whore, Koi sang, "If you're hard up, I'll rent you my beautiful body. Only $1.00 a piece. 'Quality goods, at fixed prices.' "

Sly Eizo pushed $1.96 across the floor toward him. "Discount for two?"

His jest being called, Koi squealed like a pig threatened with slaughter, and threw himself behind Ishi. "Oh, Lover! Save me! Save me from that—that *terrible* thing!"

Once again Koi brought them back to earth from the clouds of wrath by the rope of laughter. And they felt better in heart, if no less poor in pocket.

"But tell me, please: how can we enjoy life at this rate?" worried Bankichi. "How can we buy all the things we need? When socks cost five cents a pair? And workmen's trousers cost all of fifty cents apiece?"

"And whores are a dollar a throw," mourned Chikahei.

"Is life to be enjoyed?," declaimed Dembei, enjoying this part very much, "or endured?"

"In this world," said Eizo, "there is no country where hard cash falls instead of rain."

"We must earn money in other ways," said earnest Ishi, thanking Dembei for his help with a wink of his own.

"How?," they asked, sitting up.

"Let us look around, and see what needs to be done."

"Feel sorry for the poor," said Dembei, looking ahead. "They have no leisure."

"But," said Ishi, as full of wise sayings as all commoners must be, " 'Poverty cannot overtake diligence.' "

Every one of the Japanese in Hawaii who worked on a sugar plantation had exactly the same shock on his first pay day. But many were not as restrained as Ishi in their reaction, or as polite in submitting to the reduction in cash payments. Saul Bristol was one of the very few managers who did not know that his new laborers were unhappy. On some plantations the Japanese protested very loudly; and lunas, pay masters, and managers were considerably annoyed to discover that the newcomers were not as tractable as they had appeared to be. On Oahu irate managers screamed to their agents in Honolulu, and they in turn complained to the Board of Immigration about the "intransigence of these coolies," who refused to work unless they received more pay. Mr. Green sent Mr. Makino to visit his countrymen, in an attempt to find the cause of these disturbances.

Mr. Green, at that moment, was contending not only with disgruntled agents and plantation managers. Mr. Patrick M. McInerny, much closer to home, was presenting him with a problem of another kind.

The day after he had hired Nakasuke of Shinjuku as his body servant, Mr. McInerny had been forced to take the ailing man to the Queen's Hospital. Within a week Nakasuke's sick lungs drowned him in his own blood. This sudden end to his plans forced Mr. McInerny to go to all the trouble of petitioning the Board of Immigration to grant him a refund of the $70 he had spent so fruitlessly. Mr. Green was sympathetic to Mr. McInerny's plea. This helped somewhat to mollify the haberdasher, very much irritated by Dr. Owen Smithson's refusal to refund the $7.50 he'd had to pay to the Queen's Hospital for medical expenses his unused servant had incurred just in the course of dying.

Mr. Makino had just written a letter to Mr. Van Reed in Yokohama in which he said, among other things, " . . . since leaving the ship here, we have been treated with exceptional kindness, including gifts of food. We are all finding out for ourselves that Honolulu is a much better place to live than we had been told in Japan."

Fortunately for his admiring opinion of Honolulu's hospitable people, Makino could not yet read English well enough to enjoy the weekly newspapers that supplied townsfolk with information, advertisements, learned articles, and comments about all the other odds and ends of life in civilized Christian countries. Had Makino-san been able to read, he might have been puzzled by an editorial that appeared in the *Pacific Commercial Advertiser* of July 11, 1868, for the entertainment of its public:

> GONE TO JAPAN.—One of the Japanese coolies . . . taken by Captain Makee, committed suicide on Wednesday last by hanging himself to a tree . . . All had one week's vacation at the plantation, to look around and become settled. But the Fourth of July was too much for at least one of them, who said he wanted to go back to his own country . . .

When he set out upon his trip to Oahu's plantations, Makino believed that all of the recent difficulties were caused by his countrymen's inability—or unwillingness—to read their contracts and to understand directions spoken in English or Hawaiian. He thought that by explaining the terms of the contract he could resolve most of their troubles. To his surprise, the terms of the contract turned out to be the least of their worries. The Nipponjin on other plantations had figured out, very much as Ishi and his comrades had done in Wailuku, that no one was trying to cheat them. The fact remained, however, that they believed they were not receiving enough money each month to sustain them in this expensive new country.

Far more serious were their accusations—on some plantations, but not on all—about cruel lunas who beat them with whips or clubs, who cheated them of work-time, or routed them out of bed when they were sick, or abused them in the fields. On some plantations, too, as Makino saw for himself, they lived in leaking shacks, more full of mosquitoes than of air at night. In some camps, so many men were put into a small hut that they could not sleep. In others, they disliked the food, the lack of bathhouses, they complained about the rain or the lack of rain, about the heat or about the cold. Most of all, they complained about having no one but themselves to talk to in this alien land. "What is happening at home in Nippon?" they asked, "what is happening to our friends in Honolulu and upon the other plantations?" Makino had to confess that he could tell them nothing about any of these subjects, because he was as uninformed as they.

Managers and lunas, too, brought their grievances to Makino, not remembering that their predecessors had had exactly the same troubles with Chinese laborers imported several years before. These Japanese, they declared, were lazy, surly, mean-tempered, too often sick, too often late for work. And, worst of all, they did not know the first damned thing about farming. Some of them couldn't tell the working end of a hoe. Others seemed never to have done a lick of farm work before. "These men claimed they were farmers," said a manager, pounding his big fist into a callused hand. "Somebody over there told us a pack of lies and sent us a bunch of bums."

Mr. Makino, thoroughly upset by these complaints from all sides, hurried back to Honolulu to discuss corrective measures with Mr. Green. Makino expressed his belief that ninety percent of the difficulties would end almost overnight if the laborers were paid their full salaries each month, rather than the half promised by the contract. "A man who feels the weight of money in his pocket can bear the burden of many inconveniences," he told Mr. Green.

Mr. Green knew that this was an adage of universal application. Within the month he summoned a meeting of the Board of Immigration, presented this and other problems to its members (including Mr. McInerny's petition for a refund), and persuaded them to adopt a resolution that urged the plantations to pay their Japanese laborers the full sum of their wages, "in recognition of the fact that prices in Hawaii are higher than in Japan and that $2 a month (or less) is not sufficient to enable Japanese laborers to buy clothes, tobacco, and other necessary items."

Most managers, or their agents, agreed with the recommendation and, as Makino foresaw, most of his countrymen stopped complaining about their wages. On a few plantations, however, no amount of money could make up for the misery of their lives or the cruelty of lunas. At Nuuanu Plantation on Oahu, for example, laborers lost one-fourth of a day's wages if they were ten or fifteen minutes late for work; lost two days' pay for each day of absence from work without permission; were fined twenty-five cents for each offense if they smoked, made noise, had visitors, or lighted the lamps in their dormitory after nine p.m.; and were charged twenty-five cents for each carelessly broken, lost, or stolen tool. And, of course, no increase in the amount of money they were given to spend could make farmers out of "city bums," or docile slaves out of men who, even in so short a time, had been given more than a glimpse of freedom.

Makino received letters from those few who could write, telling him of cruel treatment. These same men wrote also to relatives and friends in Nippon. Makino's patient efforts to improve the treatment of his countrymen on these offending plantations were unsuccessful. At length, on Christmas Day of 1868, more than six months after the *Scioto* brought the hopeful recruits to Honolulu, Makino Tomosaburo would wait no longer. He and Sentaro wrote a letter addressed to "the Kanagawa Government in Nippon," in which they requested "the Imperial Government in Edo to negotiate with the Government of the Kingdom of Hawaii ... to the effect that the labor contract governing the Japanese in Hawaii be carried out faithfully, and their treatment at the hands of field bosses be improved."

With that, as Jonathan Green's countrymen might have said, "the fat was in the fire."

CHAPTER 17
THE BATTLE AT SEKIGAHARA

Serious trouble, far worse than anything Mr. Makino would ever hear about, fell upon the Japanese in Wailuku on a blazing hot afternoon in August.

A few days before, a message came from Olowalu, a village near Lahaina, calling Pilipo home to attend his dying father. Mr. Bristol gave Pilipo permission to go and loaned him a good horse to carry him to Olowalu. Inasmuch as Bristol was much pleased with Pilipo's Japanese crew, he did not think that he needed to hire another luna to watch over them all the day long while Pilipo was gone. Instead, Bristol decided that he would start them off on their task each morning, and that Jack Douglas would check on their progress and send them home in the evening if he himself could not do so. Bristol was not happy with this arrangement, for several reasons, but in order to save bother and expense thought that he should do nothing else. Although Olowalu is only a short day's ride from Wailuku, he expected that Pilipo would be absent for a full week. While deaths among Hawaiians might come quickly, funeral ceremonies are always protracted. In the interval while Pilipo was away Bristol earnestly hoped that Jack Douglas would take to the field every bit of the relatively good humor he seemed to generate in his work at the mill house.

The system worked very well for four days. Saul took the Japanese in the morning to the new clearing, just below the edge of Wailuku village. He paced off the area he expected them to clear during the day, and marked its perimeter with bent branches or piles of small stones. Because Pilipo had told him that Ishi was their headman, Bristol addressed his instructions to him, while the others stood near, watching his sign language, seeming to listen to his words. Saul was favorably impressed by all of them at close range, and most especially by Ishi. He could see why the others had chosen him to be their leader. He liked the man's alertness, his quiet strength, the very manner in which he walked, as if he were a lord from that foreign land who wanted now to work for a while as a common man. But he could never get past the wall of respect and reserve that Ishi raised between them whenever he tried to show, in speech or gesture, that he was no stuffy tyrant. He sensed that, even if he spoke the purest Japanese, or Ishi the King's own English, this barrier of seriousness would always stand between them.

And yet when he looked at the toothless youth, all grins and merriment, eyes aglint with laughter, he saw how, with some people, words are not really needed. Just seeing the fellow made Saul lighter of heart. If jesters have that look, he thought, now I know why kings must have 'em. As he always did, he bestowed a wink upon Koi, as grandly as generous kings dispense rubies and ribbands and dominions among their favorites. Koi would grin, and everything was all right in the world, for both of them, for a while.

Despite Ishi's seriousness and the lack of words they shared, Saul soon learned that he could trust his Japanese crew to the full. Invariably, each morning when he returned to the field, Saul found that they had done exactly what he'd instructed them to do, and a little more besides. The rocks, for example, were not simply dumped in a loose sprawling heap. They'd been placed in neat stacks at the very edge of the field, where they would be out of the way of the ox teams that later would turn the earth for planting. The brush, cut down each morning, would be arranged in a fashion that speeded its drying. But never did they exceed the bounds he had established for them the morning before. They were telling him, he saw, that they knew how to follow orders to the letter. But they also wanted him to know that they could do more than follow orders: they could also think ahead, they under-

stood what he wanted to do with this hideous plain of raw earth
and limp scrub. By Heaven, he said to himself on the second
morning of his instruction, these are good men. I can trust them.
And I shall do so.

Invariably he expressed his pleasure in the good work they had
done the day before. But never did he increase the area he allotted them for the new day. If he could get from them such service
as they gave without his demanding it, he saw no need to push for
more.

Beginning with the fourth day Ishi's crew would be clearing
land adjoining the property of Mrs. Anna Hoomalu, in Saul's experience the most domineering female on Maui, if not in all
Hawaii. Bristol made doubly sure that Ishi and his gang understood what they must do beyond all possibility of error. "To here,
and no farther," he showed them, with hand signs, Hawaiian
words, lines scuffed in the earth with his boots, and, at the end,
with strips of his handkerchief, torn off on sudden thought, tied
to weeds a good two feet away from the stone wall that marked
the bounds of the Gorgon's back yard. Better strips of my handkerchief now, he assured himself, than strips of my flayed flesh
later.

Mrs. Hoomalu—the irony in that name never failed to bemuse
Saul: hoomalu means "to be peaceful, to make peace"—and he
had met before, in a number of encounters over plantation leases
that were anything but pacific. After those scarifying experiences
(which rubbed layers out of his very soul) he did not want to have
anything to do with the old beldame. He could imagine her now,
descending upon him in a fiery rage, like Pele borne upon a tor-
rent of molten lava, determined to burn him into cinders for having encroached upon her property if so much as one stone of that
wall were touched. In fancy (and he winced at the image), he
could see himself being dragged by the law's terrorized minions
into Wailuku's new court house, while she followed behind, accusing him, with jabbing finger and hoarse battle cries, of having
moved her damned wall solely in order to steal an inch or two of

her precious land for the greater profit of Hawaiian Sugar Mill and penniless C. Brewer.

Never had he met a more terrifying harpy, a more dreadful threat to the supremacy of a male of any size, color, or creed. Compared with her, the immense and imperious Princess Ruth Keelikolani, Hiram Nihoa's "bosoms friend," was a sylph, a zephyr, a saint. About six feet tall, 250 pounds of muscle and fat, with a voice that could bounce off the valley walls a mile away, Anna Hoomalu was every man's nightmare in sleep and his nemesis by day. Her husband had chosen the one possible way to elude her: he had died—"from exhaustion," the gossips said—almost as soon as he had sired the three silenced children who bore his name.

Even at half past six in the morning, when most of Wailuku still slumbered, Saul knew that this dragon would be on guard in her big brown house a mere fifty feet beyond the wall. If he could have done so, he would have made his horse tiptoe past that grim fortress.

But there are limits to what a man should be called upon to do in respect to the weaker sex. He was an expert in beating ignominious retreats. He made another one as soon as he was sure that Ishi understood his orders.

Standing behind the lace curtains in her bedroom window, Mrs. Hoomalu smiled. She had been watching this sharp Yankee Bristol's pointings, uplifted hands, tieings of strips of cloth to bushes, all raised up to protect her property as though he were a kahuna anaana laying his blackest spells. Fine, she said to herself. All this noise I've been making: it is doing some good after all. Here is one poor Hawaiian those sassy haoles are not going to run over and plow under. Not even when she's dead.

The hot August sun beat down upon them without a cloud to intercede, without a tree to give them respite, but still Ishi and his gang worked on. They were accustomed now to work, to heat, sweat, and thirst. They did not count the hours anymore. Only the days mattered now, and these they counted, because Sundays were the only occasions in their lives worth anticipating or remembering. All the other days melted into a blur of red dust, red stones, and red red sun. Even the skin of their bodies was dark red now, the color of Hawaiian fishermen and farmers.

At lunch time they bolted down the rice, tea, and bits of sliced meat, all equally warmed by the sun, that the Chinese cooks packed for them in the morning. After that they rested for twenty minutes, slumped in a kind of stupor against the walls of rocks they were making. Hats provided the only shade. Instinct told them when the half-hour recess came to an end. Respect for Mr. Bristol kept them from cheating.

At mid-afternoon they were working along the stone wall that Mr. Bristol had warned them not to touch. Ishi had been so affected by the Boss's worry that he would not let his crew cut down the wilted weeds growing within two feet of that protected rampart. The men were bent over their task, prying up rocks, when they heard a loud voice coming from beyond the wall. They looked up to see a huge native woman beckoning to them. She wore one of those loose garments that resemble sacks, her hair was piled up like a mountain on top of her head. And those arms! Saa, one was as big around as the boy Akemi at his waist.

They could not believe that she spoke to them. Ishi suspected that she was only watching their work, to be sure that they did not touch her property, and he turned once more to his stubborn rock. "E, Kepani," she called again, "e hele mai," and pointed to the wall before her. Upon it lay a tray bearing a large enamel pitcher and ten thick coffee mugs. "Come," she said, while she poured something from the pitcher into one of the mugs. "Drink!" she commanded, holding the mug toward them.

They stood up, looking from her to the mug and back again to the friendly face. She was offering them a kindness. She was like the people of Honolulu, so full of aloha. They put down their tools, moved slowly toward her, grateful but embarrassed. "Ishi-san," said Heizaemon. "You must thank her for us."

Ishi stepped forward. Clenching fists, squaring his shoulders, he bowed stiffly to the gigantic woman. "S'ank you," he said, making his first speech in the English tongue.

"Come," she invited him. "It is orange juice and sugar and good cold water."

They lined up, knowing no other way to behave in such a strange situation, Ishi first, Akemi last. Ishi smelled the fluid before he tasted it. Recognizing sweet orange juice mixed with water, he dared to sip it. "Ahh, oishii desu nee," he said to her, for his companions to hear. Then he drank deep, relishing it to the last drop. "Maikai, maikai, good, good," he said for her sake, as he backed away.

While his comrades took their turn at the kind lady's wall, Ishi stood to one side, fanning his head with the lauhala hat, drying his brow with the red bandana. During the three months since he had cut off the topknot his hair had grown half way to his shoulders, until it was as long and gleaming as a Hawaiian's. When she finished serving the other men, Mrs. Hoomalu turned toward Ishi, intending to offer him some more.

Eia mai! she exclaimed to herself, almost dropping the pitcher. This one! He is such a handsome man! He looks like one of us. Not like these others. They look like Pakés. Or worse. As all of Wailuku, and most of Maui, had known for a long time, Mrs. Hoomalu was not a charitable woman toward Pakés, haoles, negroes, whalers, sailors, Portuguese, Frenchmen, Hindoos, Lascars, sugar planters, peddlers, merchants, priests, loose women, spinsters, haole school teachers, Mormon missionaries, or stupid Hawaiians who did not conform with her expectations. And yet, as she had told herself throughout this long hot day, no good Christian can allow those poor mortals out there to toil away, in all this sweltering heat, without showing them some kindness. No matter who they are. For her, kindness was something to be offered to animals and perhaps to a rare stranger. Charity was more restricted: it began and ended at home, and she likened it to a mother's watchful love.

The more she studied Ishi, the more enchanted with him she became. She was like all those women in Lord Okubo's household, who fell in love with his face, his body, his walk, because he was so handsome, without ever having the slightest suspicion that his heart was as bitter and cold as an unripe persimmon fallen into a snowdrift.

Auwe, she sorrowed, if only I were young again. I'd drag this man into my bed before the day is ended. Dirt, sweat, salt, and all! Auwe, auwe . . . At times like this, in the past as well as in the present, Anna Hoomalu quite forgot that she was also a baptized Christian.

Conquered by him before ever she knew him, like all those other women in Ishi's past, she held out her hand for his cup. He sauntered forward, in that maddening way of his, offering her the cup. She did not take it, but put her hand upon his wrist, as though to steady the cup while she poured. Those eyes, she sighed. Black as night. Those teeth. White as the snows upon Haleakala. Those lips. Made for kissing. Those hands.—Naturally, the orange juice spilled out of the brimming cup, over those long fingers, elegant even though their broken nails were rimmed with dirt.

"Oh! I am so sorry," she cried, releasing his hand as she looked for something to dry it with. But he backed away, out of her reach, laughing, licking his fingers, making sounds and gestures telling her that he did not mind . . .

All too soon, for her as for them, the pitcher ran dry. Smacking lips, belching heartily to show their appreciation for so refreshing a drink, they put the cups on the tray. They bowed, said their thanks in many ways, and trooped back to work.

She bade them aloha, nodding and smiling vaguely. But her eyes were fixed upon Ishi, her mind was thinking about other things than orange juice and Christian kindness. This man! she exulted. He is exactly the one I've been looking for. There's one advantage to being older. By the time a woman is fifty, she knows damned well what she wants . . .

The next afternoon the orangeade party was repeated. The men went quickly to the welcome refreshment. Yet, alas, with few words in common, conversation was sadly limited. The Nipponjin were shy, talking among themselves in stilted phrases or saying nothing at all. Mrs. Hoomalu looked again upon Ishi, confirming her impressions of the day before (which, during an all but sleepless night, she had begun seriously to doubt). And he, the innocent man, did not have the slightest notion that he was being examined—and being found very suitable, indeed—for a place in the life of Mrs. Hoomalu.

Koi, Chikahei, and Heizaemon, men of the world as they were, saw those sidelong glances she turned upon Ishi. Koi nudged Chikahei, rolling his eyes in disbelief. In decency they waited until returning to work before they teased Ishi about his great conquest. "Dame da . . . Bakarashii," he laughed, not even blushing, because he thought them so ridiculous. "You imagine too much. This heat is cooking your brains."

While they worked, Mrs. Hoomalu's kitchen maid brought a second pitcher of orange juice to the wall for them to come back to, whenever they wished.

At about four o'clock Koi decided that he must slake his thirst with another cup of that fine drink. He invited Akemi and Bankichi to go along, because they were nearest to him. They were sipping the warm beverage when Jack Douglas rode up from the gulch. He was more than an hour early.

The instant he spotted the lazing three he kicked his horse into a gallop.

Akemi saw him first. "Ha! Watch out for trouble," he muttered.

"Don't run," said Koi, not yet afraid, thinking of his dignity. But Bankichi, who cared nothing for dignity, was already running back to his shovel. His fear saved him from Douglas's anger. Concern for their dignity did not save Koi and Akemi. The fact that they did not even pretend to fear him infuriated Jack Douglas. He charged down upon them, swearing all the way. Hearing the noise, Ishi and the others looked up in surprise.

"What the hell's goin' on here?," Douglas snarled, when he

reached the two criminals. "By Christ! If it ain't a goddam tea-party!"

As he usually did, Koi tried to ease a difficult moment with a jest. He imitated Mrs. Hoomalu in the act of pouring orange juice and a thirsty field-worker in the act of relishing it. Douglas chose to see no comedy in the show. "God dammit! Don't you sass me. Git back to work." He pointed to the field. "Git your ass out there. An' fast!"

Koi realized that he'd lost his bid for dignity. To work willing-ly for Mr. Bristol was one thing. To submit to the brutality of this hateful man was another matter entirely. Taking his time, he put the mug upon the tray. Akemi followed his lead, with elaborate tenderness, as if the cheap porcelain mug were a fine tea cup made by a master potter in Kiyomizu. Together they walked slow-ly back to their tools, while Douglas rode behind them. The other Japanese continued with their work, thinking that the two boys were fortunate to be spared a worse punishment. After all, they had broken the rule, and Mr. Douglas was only right to send them back to work.

"Git, goddam it, git!"

They moved no faster.

"Goddam." Douglas, scarcely able to conceive that he was the victim of such insubordination, cracked his horsewhip in the air above their heads.

They did not cringe, they did not hurry.

"God damn!" he roared, lashing them on back and rump, first Koi, then Akemi. The whip stung through the wet shirts, but those loose dungaree trousers protected their buttocks. Refusing to run, they marched as slowly as before, faces set as though carved in stone. When they reached the tools they had put down not five minutes before, they began to pry at rocks as if the red-haired demon were several hells away.

Such studied insolence was more than Douglas could bear. Mad with rage, he thought of a new torment. Flicking the whip at their legs, he made them hop. If they did not jump he whipped them across the back. They soon learned to obey that stinging black snake. "That's it, you bastards! Dance! Dance, you goddam stinkin' Injuns!"

With that masterful whip he made them trot, finding more sport in the hunt than in the dance. All thought of dignity gone, Koi and Akemi ran as he directed.

Ishi and his companions continued to work as if they were alone on the field, as though Koi and Akemi, dead to this world, suffered in a private and invisible hell of their own. This is the punishment that haoles deal out for breaking the rule, they thought, those men who had not yet met with punishment of any sort from their new masters. But no rule made by men of any land can keep their victims from hating them. With each crack of Douglas's whip he drew upon himself a load of hate that would freight a man's soul through a dozen reincarnations.

Koi and Akemi did not call to their friends for help. They knew that they alone must suffer for their fault. Out of loyalty to the group they did not draw the others into their trouble. But, in pain and in shame, they hoped that this punishment would soon end.

Drunken Douglas was not ready to let them go. Driven by demons from his own special hell, he whipped Koi and Akemi around the field, sometimes hitting them, more often not, until they gasped for breath and blood stained the sweat in their shirts.

When he saw the blood seeping through the wet cotton, the look of glee upon Douglas's face, Ishi realized at last that the whip beat down upon his friends not to correct but to kill. This mad haole was no better than a samurai driven by blood-lust.

Within him Ishi's stomach was fixed in resolution. "Enough," he said in a loud voice. Wanting Douglas to see him, he dropped the shovel, threw down his hat.

But Mrs. Hoomalu was ahead of him. Douglas's shouts and cracking whip had drawn her out of the big house. Behind her came an inquisitive youth just home from school. He carried a glass of orange juice in one hand, a thick slice of bread smeared with guava jam in the other.

"Stop it, you damn fool!," bellowed Mrs. Hoomalu the peacemaker, raising a big fist at Douglas. "You leave those men alone!"

Douglas pulled his horse up short. Koi and Akemi dropped to the ground. Ishi and his countrymen thanked their listening gods for sending the kind woman to their rescue.

Douglas rode slowly over to the wall. "What's it to you, you fat sow? You keep your big snout outta this." The boy beside her forgot to eat.

"You damn sassy son-of-a-bitch, you! You get away from here, before I call the police."

"Oh, yeah?" He flicked the whip, knocked the pitcher from the wall. She did not flinch. "If I was you," he went on, "I'd haul my black ass away from here, 'fore it gits whupped."

Without turning her head, Mrs. Hoomalu said, "Keoni. Go call Mr. Kalei. Hurry!"

Douglas unleashed the whip again, knocking over the tray with the mugs as the boy ran off. Furious at such havoc, Mrs. Hoomalu picked up a stone from the wall and threw it at Douglas, already jeering at her aim. She missed him, by a wide margin, and he laughed scornfully. "Better luck nex' time, ol' bitch," Then he went back to his more exciting game with those monkey-men. He'd played with them long enough. Now he was going to whip the shit outta them.

He kicked the horse into a trot. Akemi and Koi saw him coming. Each helping the other, they stood up to face their enemy.

Ishi moved in to stop him. In the effortless calm of muga, thinking nothing of himself, yet seeing every single thing from mountain peak to grain of dirt, hearing every sound from the flowing of Koi's blood to the jingle of buckles in Douglas's reins, Ishi strode across the field toward the man who was so full of hate. As from above he heard the voice of his teacher in Edo, saying: "Hate not your foe, for hate leads to rash actions, a waste of your spirit, a gap in your defense." Out of his past in Shimoda and in Edo—unbidden because it was always within him, waiting for this moment—came the knowledge that he was ready for this trial. Moving like the virtuous warrior he knew himself to be, Ishi walked across that rocky field toward Douglas on his prancing horse.

He stood between Douglas and his victims. "Dame desu," he said quietly.

"Don't you damn me," Douglas snarled. "God damn *you*, you proud son of a bitch!" He flicked that whip, once, twice, cutting Ishi on cheek and neck, drawing the blood he craved so much to see. "You proud bastard! I bin waitin' a long time for this day. Bleed, damn you, *bleed!*"

Ishi moved toward him. His eyes were hard, not with hate nor with pain, but with trust in his power. This mad thing before him, whip, boots, spurs, and all, was a weak and frightened beast: his own hate, seething within him, would bring him down. Ishi would be only the means of his humbling.

Crazed as he was Douglas sensed that he was being challenged by a force such as he had never met. Ishi's empty hands and expressionless face, above all that slow unstoppable advance, warned him that here was a man girded in an armor that all his hate could not pierce. Instinct urged him to run. Hate betrayed him.

He raised his arm to strike again. "So. You wanna fight, eh? Come on, then, you stinkin' Japanee. I'll show you who's boss around here."

Mrs. Hoomalu screamed as he struck.

Ishi leaped forward, pulled the reins from Douglas's hand, forced the mare's head back to make her stand. With nothing to cling to, Douglas slid to the ground. Like a cat, he landed on his feet, the whip still in his right hand. Ishi threw aside the reins and the mare fled.

"So that's your game! Sneakin' goddam Injuns!" Fearing attack from all sides, Douglas crouched low, whirled about, ready to lash out at the nearest enemy.

But Ishi alone stood before him. The others, seeing the vapor of his valor, recognizing his strength, stayed as still as the stones in the field.

Baffled by the lack of the least sign of attack from these creatures he could not abide, Douglas straightened up. Once again instinct warned him to turn and run. And once again a fool's pride pushed him to further violence.

From her position beyond the wall Mrs. Hoomalu watched in admiration and in fear. She did not move. She did not even think to pray.

Ishi took several deep breaths, dried against his trousers the sweat of muga gathering in the palms of his hands. Fifteen feet away Douglas waited, chewing his lips. In an absolute silence that enclosed the field and every one in it, Ishi lifted his empty hands before his chest, as if folding them in prayer.

"Crissake!," Douglas jeered. "A goddam prayin' preacher!"

Holding his open hands before him in the position of a man of discipline, Ishi regarded this weak and ugly thing who had never been a man.

"A goddam prayin' coward!," screeched Douglas, running as fast as he could toward his enemy, craving to whip him to death, to kick at his battered body until blood and guts and eyes and hair were—

Before he could lay whip or boot upon his victim he was hurtling head first through the air, screaming in terror. Everyone in the field and Mrs. Hoomalu beyond her wall heard the bones snap when he fell against the rock.

Anna Hoomalu cried out in savage triumph. Then, remembering a more imminent presence, she shouted, "Thank the Lord! Thank God!" After which, of course, she wept for joy. "Oh, that wonderful man!," she sobbed. "Oh, that brave man . . ."

Ishi and his countrymen walked over to look at the beast who had been tamed. He lay on his right side, in a merciful faint. His collar bone and right arm were broken. But his hard head and stiff neck were merely scratched.

"He will not use that arm again for hurting people," said Ishi quietly.

Akemi and Koi, pale as white men, stood before Ishi. "I have caused you this trouble," said Koi. "You must let me take the punishment."

"And I, too," said Akemi, "for I, too, am to blame."

"No," said Ishi gently. "The heat has cooked your mind for sure. Why should I be punished for this man's meanness? Do not worry. You will see. The haoles, remember, are men of justice."

When Constable Kalei and Constable Kaaiakamanu arrived a few minutes later, Ishi and Dembei had turned the insensible Douglas upon his back and propped his head upon the same boulder that had broken his bones. But only Ishi remained beside him. He had sent the others back to work.

Constable Kalei, aghast at the foulness of this attack upon a master by a servant, pointed at the fallen man, asked only one question. "Who did this?"

Ishi, understanding the gesture, pointed to his nose. "Me," he said, using one of the new words he had learned in the Land of Promise.

They brought Ishi in irons to Wailuku Court House and locked him in the jail. They called him the most dangerous criminal the town had encountered since its founding. People came to look at him through the bars in the heavy door, until darkness stopped any further viewing of so ungrateful a villain. He was forbidden a lamp, for fear that, in his determination to escape, so vicious a creature would set fire to the jail—and with it the Court House and all offices of government in Wailuku. And, naturally, no one thought that so thankless a brute should be given anything to eat, or even a cup of water to ease his thirst or to wash the blood from his wounds.

Ishi lay on the floor, in the dark, thinking. He knew that he was in great trouble. The honorable men in power, and the Hawaiian policemen who were their retainers, certainly had not treated him with the fairness he had been expecting. But he did not worry about them very much. Nor did he fear what they might do to him. Kannon-sama would take care to lead them to the truth about the events in Sekigahara this afternoon. The stone she had given him told him that. It lay warm in his hand, a gift and a promise. It was the one thing of his the policemen had allowed him to keep, other than his clothes, when they searched him, even down to his skin. The pocketknife, the few coins he carried in his money pouch, even his fundoshi they had taken away from him.

Upstairs, in the Court House, alarmed businessmen gathered, asking if it was true that those coolies down there on the plantation had risen in revolt. They took heart when brave Constable Kalei assured them that no, only one mad dog had turned to bite the kind master who fed him and that he, personally, had locked up the desperado in the cell downstairs.

On the Court House steps solid citizens remembered how, at Haiku Plantation only a few months ago, four Chinese coolies had murdered a Hawaiian man named Napua. "We don't want that kind of thing to happen here in Wailuku," avowed a haole businessman. Others urged the need for a quick trial of this Japanee devil—and for a quick hanging if the unfortunate victim of this unprovoked assault should die. Their mounting anger was interrupted only briefly when Saul Bristol and Mrs. Hoomalu hurried up the stairs and entered the District Magistrate's office.

At his request Mrs. Hoomalu told her story, twice. Each time the Magistrate questioned her most scrupulously about the point at issue.

The first time she answered, "No. The Japanese man did not lay a hand on that pig Douglas. I was watching all the time. That pupule Douglas was running up to whip the Japanese. And then, all of a sudden, he just flew through the air until he landed on his damn' collarbone. I think that he must have tripped on a stone just before he reached the Japanese man. I know that he did not hit the Japanese, and that the Japanese did not hit him. I am willing to lay my hand upon the Holy Bible, and swear that this is the truth I am telling you."

The second time she said, "Dammit, Solomon! I tole you the firs' time. He nevah touch da buggah. I was there. I saw. That damn' haole son-of-a-bitch tripped. Serve him right, too, for what he was doing to those poor Japanese. Too bad he didn't break his damned neck!"

"Now, now, Anna," said Solomon Kaunaoa wearily. "That's enough. The facts are all we're asking for here. The embroidery you can save for your friends."

"That jackass Douglas! Shia! He's no good, I tell you. He's rotten. He should be run out of town. He should be put in jail, to—"

Unable to stop her, as usual, the District Magistrate tried to ignore her. "Well, Saul, on the basis of the evidence supplied by this—this unimpeachable witness here, I guess you'll have a free man to take home with you."

"Thank you, Solomon," said Saul Bristol carefully. "May I say that, from what I know of the people involved, coupled with the evidence supplied by our unimpeachable eyewitness here, you are serving the cause of justice by giving my man his freedom. I myself think that he is a hero, and I am going to treat him as one. And I hope that you will assure the people of Wailuku that the police have jailed the wrong man this evening."

"I'll try to do so, Saul. But you know how they are, these— these people. Once they get an idea into their heads. And they're going to have a hard time believing that the vict—I mean Mr. Douglas—was so badly hurt just from a stumble. I have trouble believing that myself. However," he stood up, "let's tell Kalei to bring your man."

"I want to go with him, Solomon," said Mrs. Hoomalu, rising in all her impressive might.

Solomon the Wise looked up at his sister. "Blessed are the peace-makers. They get what they want."

As Bristol and Mrs. Hoomalu followed Constable Kalei through the Court House to the jail, Saul said, "I don't quite believe it myself, Anna."

"What?," she asked, smiling vaguely.

"How, in stumbling upon a stone, Jack Douglas broke his collar bone."

"Ah, a poet," she giggled, a massive schoolgirl. Then, suddenly, she stopped, very serious. "I will tell you, because you are a friend to the Japanese down below." The wide corridor was empty. Constable Kalei was already descending the dark stairs, but still she looked about for people who might overhear. "I did not speak the whole truth, in there."

He was not at all surprised, but he pretended to a Puritan's shock. "Anna!"

"But I told all the truth he needed to know. Solomon asked me if the Japanese ever laid hands on that jackass. I said no. That is the truth. No hands. But—" Once again she looked over her shoulder.

"But?"

"Solomon didn't ask me if any other part of him touched that damn' fool."

"And did it?"

"Well, to tell the truth, I don't know. I really can't be sure ... "

"Anna! You are the most maddening creature! What do you mean?"

"I am thinking of that man in the Bible. Oh, what was his name, now? I am so forgetful these days. The one who stayed up, all night long, wrestling with the Angel of the Lord."

"You mean Jacob?"

"Yes. Jacob. That was his name. The one who was chosen. And you remember how the angel won?"

Saul thought long and hard, dredging his memory for this pertinent fact. At last it came. "On the hip?"

She beamed. "Smart man." She frowned. "Only—"

"Stop teasing me, Anna!"

"Only in this case I don't suppose you could call it wrestling."

Constable Kalei opened the jail door with a flourish. Ishi stood up, blinking against the light from the bull's-eye lantern. Anna Hoomalu swept in, crying "Oh, you wonderful man!," drew the astonished Ishi into her arms, and kissed him.

Bristol edged into the cell. Poor Ishi was so embarrassed that he didn't know where to look. Saul reached past Anna's enormous hip and took his hand. As he shook it warmly, trying to draw Ishi away from the woman's clutches, he said, "I wish I could talk to this man, Anna, and tell him how grateful I am for what he's done. He's just rid me of the most obnoxious assistant I've ever known—or ever hope to meet. I can't thank this man enough—and yet I can't thank him at all. A sad situation. I'll have to ask Ah Siu to do it for me."

"I'll do it for you," she said, and kissed Ishi again. "What is his name, this beautiful man?"

"Ishi," said Saul, flashing a comradely wink at cornered Ishi, too flustered by Anna to be consoled by anything.

"Ishi: do you come with us." She held out her hand, a mother to her child. "We'll take you home now."

Ishi thought she meant to say goodbye. Gravely he shook her hand, once.

She laughed, that throaty sound that for many a gullible male transformed her from a dragon into a woman. "Oh, my dear. You have so much to learn!—And I know just the one to be your teacher."

"Now, Anna," said Saul, thinking of the terrified pupil. "A bit young for you, isn't he?"

"Oh, Saul!," she tossed her head. "How can you think such a thing?"

By the light of a quarter moon Saul Bristol and Mrs. Hoomalu took Ishi to the mill house, riding in her surrey. She drove, occupying the whole front seat, because that was the only way the rig would not turn on its side or collapse under her weight. Saul and Ishi rode in the back seat. Even if no cheering crowds lined muddy Main Street, muddier Market Street, and muddiest Mill Road to watch them pass, Saul thought of it as a triumphal procession of a sort. But, alas for honors to heroes. Mill Road stopped at the mill house, and there they were forced to deposit Ishi, in the indifferent if impressionable mud. Saul wished that they could find some better way to escort the returning hero to his home. But, in view of the Stygian darkness and ubiquitous mud in which the residents of Wailuku the Beautiful undoubtedly would dwell for the next millennium or so, he could think of nothing more to do. Cursing this lack of style, he descended from the buggy with Ishi, shook his hand once again (smiling toothily the while), said a loud "Thank you," and pointed in the direction of Japanese Camp across the gulch. He was relieved to see that the guest of honor took no offense because the festivities had ended so quietly. He smiled toothily in return, said a heartfelt "S'ank you," and left. Not one to stand upon the manner of his departure, thought Saul, struck dumb for once in his life.

Above him, an angelic presence, if somewhat earthbound, Anna said, for at least the thousandth time, "I like that man."

"So I gather."

"But not only for what you are thinking. For something else, too. He does what you haoles are always talking about, but don't often do."

"And that is?"

"He helps the dog underneath."

"Then we must help him. Such men are rare. And—need I remind you?—not only among haoles. Nor are they very popular among men of property."

"Get in, Mr. Pilate," she chuckled. "I'll take you home."

Gohongi was dark when Ishi came home, although usually at that hour it would still be full of noise and light. But on this night his friends sorrowed for him. Most of them counted him dead, executed by order of the men in power for his offense against one of their powerful officials.

In the little room apart from the others Koi lay on his belly, because of the whip cuts on his back. Wearing only his fundoshi, he waited for Aiko to return from her work in the kitchen. His heart was full of grief for Ishi, his mind full of bitter thoughts against beasts like Douglas, most of all against fools like himself. Everything that had happened this afternoon was his fault. And if anything happened now to Ishi he must be blamed for that too.

He dared not think beyond the time when he saw his friend being taken away, wrists bound by a short chain, ankles by a longer chain that dragged in the dust as he walked between the two policemen. He dared not believe that Ishi might be already dead. Torn between his love of the body for Aiko and his love of the spirit for Ishi, Koi did not know what to do. For him he would gladly die, but for her he must live. Koi put his head upon the floor and wept.

In the big room, among his comrades, Akemi brooded over his part in the afternoon's disaster. With less reason to feel guilty, he felt just as responsible as Koi did for Ishi's plight. "Ahh," he moaned, when, earlier, Dembei laid wet cloths over his wounded back. "Ahh, if only we had hurried to our work! If only we had not been so proud!" And Dembei had added to his hurt by saying not a word to comfort him.

Yasuo, who owned the keenest ears in Gohongi, perhaps because he was so tongue-tied, first heard the approaching footsteps. Who can this be? he wondered, thinking of Chinese cooks, angry lunas, vengeful haoles, and Ishi's ghost, in that order. But a ghost does not step so firmly, or kick pebbles about, he told himself, while his heart beat faster and the hair on his neck began to rise. And ghosts do not wear shoes . . .

In the next instant he guessed who it must be. Springing from his sleeping-space, he struck a match to light a lamp. In their places his companions looked up to see what alarmed him. "Iii . . . ," he stuttered, touching the match to the wick. As the lamp flared up, Ishi appeared in the doorway.

"Ishi!," they cried, jumping up to greet him.

Akemi started forward, uttering wordless sounds of relief.

From his room Koi came running. He too shouted Ishi's name. Instead of joining his friends at Ishi's side, he threw himself to the bare boards at Ishi's feet. Touching his head to the floor, he cried "Forgive me! Forgive me!" The others fell silent, backing away. "Katajikenai," Koi said, over and over again, that terrible word that means so many things. I have caused you trouble, it means. I have lost face. I am sorry. I accept the burden of gratitude. I thank you for your favor. All this it means, and more, as it makes the man who utters it forever bound in loyalty to the man who has favored him.

"Yamero," said Ishi in a low voice. "Stop this. Stand up, Koi, please stand up.—This is no way to greet a friend. This is the cormorants' way. Remember?"

Koi raised his head, the tears still flowing down his cheeks.

Ishi held out his hand. "This is the way with free men," he said. "Remember?"

CHAPTER 18

THE FESTIVAL FOR THE DEAD

The shortening of the days, the dying of the sun: these visible signs conjoined with the sense of the seasons in his blood told Bankichi the farmer that the time was come. And so, one evening, when all were gathered in Gohongi, under the lighted lamps, Bankichi kept his promise. "O-Bon," he said, bringing all of them within the compass of his wide-ranging eyes, and they knew at once what he meant. Perhaps this was because the nearness of the death they had imagined for Ishi a few nights before was still fresh in their minds.

"But what if no one in our families has died since we left home?," asked Tametsugu.

"Who can say?," Dembei replied. "What if some one has?"

"But will they come here?," Tametsugu persisted. "This far away from home?"

"Depends on you," said Dembei with one of his meaningful shrugs. "If they liked you in life they may like you well enough in death to take the trouble to visit you here."

Tametsugu frowned, not certain that he was being teased or taught. "We have nothing for them here. No memorial tablets. No priests or temples. Nothing." By this he meant not even a graveyard but he dared not say the word because if he did then, very soon, they would be needing a graveyard.

"We haven't even put up a god shelf," said Chikahei. "That shows how filial we are."

"Oh yes we have," Koi said. "Just beyond the wall. Aiko put it up, on one of the crossbeams, soon after we arrived. It will serve for all of us, I think. Unless you want something more in here."

He did not tell them that his brass image of Benten rested on the god shelf or how, in their devotion to the Goddess of Love, he and Aiko neglected to show much respect for all the other deities.

"I don't know what to believe," fretted Tametsugu. "About their coming this far from home, I mean."

"But what if they come, and we have done nothing?" asked Bankichi.

"Baka!" Koi borrowed Dembei's favorite epithet. "Don't forget us, too. O-Bon is for the living, too, not only for the dead."

"He is right," said Ishi the father. "This O-Bon will be more important for us, I think, than for the spirits of our relatives. Even if they do not come, the gods will be near—or their messengers. And we do not want to offend the gods, do we? Or lose all touch with home?"

Of course not, they hastened to say.

"So, then," Ishi concluded, "let us do the best we can, for the living as well as for the dead. It is proper to think of the past, but we must also think of the future. Are we agreed?"

All nodded, most solemnly.

Heizaemon spoke. "First, the god shelf. I shall put that up, since I seem to be the carpenter here. I think it should go right there, against the end wall."

"And I," said Bankichi, "I shall put the first fruits from my garden before it."

"And can you make memorial tablets for our known dead?" Tametsugu asked Heizaemon.

"They are not needed here," said Ishi. "Those are properly placed at home, where we left them, or in the temples and shrines of our families. Don't you think so, Dembei?" Ishi did not want to admit, to gods or men, the truth that he did not know whether his father still lived. Three years had gone by since he'd seen his father in Shimoda. And not once, during those three years, had he so much as thought of that grudging man who had given him life but little else.

"So do we pronounce," replied Dembei, "in our office as Abbot of the Monastery of Gohongi."

"And the prayers?"

"Each will say his own," decreed the self-anointed Abbot of Gohongi.

"And the dancing?" asked Koi, seeing how the orthodox Tametsugu was annoying Dembei if not Ishi.

"Ahh, now, that's better," said Eizo, cheering up. "They're what I'd come back for, if I were a departed spirit."

"Why bother?" argued Chikahei. "When you can't drink saké, or pinch the girls' bottoms, or take 'em into the bushes?"

"But you can watch, can't you?," Dembei told him. "Watch all those people making fools of themselves. And certainly you can whisper ideas into their ears. That's the only possible explanation for some of the crazy things that people do at Bon Odori." Unlike his companions, Dembei tried to find folly in everything because he saw the tragedy in the lives of all people, everywhere.

While he was still a youth, struggling to survive the claims of unrelieved hunger and perpetual fear, Dembei had perceived the truth in the Lord Buddha's message, "All life is sorrowful." Before that moment of enlightenment, gained in the alleys of Edo, not in some quiet temple, Dembei had learned through bitter experience the other face to this truth, that "Pain is the root of merit." Since that time, without help from the sermons of priests or the writings of sages, Dembei had passed through eight of the Ten Stages of Insight, whereby a man learns to endure in a world that is dreadful because it is nothing more than a place of emptiness and vanity.

Now, a wise old man in his twenty-fifth year of testing, he was attaining the Ninth Stage, wherein he would balance hope against despair, in spite of life's vicissitudes. He was learning another of the Buddha's lessons: to feel compassion for all men, at all times. But, because Dembei had been a youth so full of human feelings, he could not always shut out from his old man's mind the feelings of loathing, or disgust, or of hatred for the spectacle of this world that must be overcome before the seeker can attain to inner peace.

"That brings up another problem," said Koi. "Music."

"What! With all those instruments you have?," cried Tametsugu. "You're the musician."

"Who can't play a note—yet."

"I can pluck a few sounds from the samisen," said Dembei. "And I sing like a crow with a sore throat stuck on a snow-covered roof. But if some of you can do better ... "

"If I sang," Tametsugu assured them, "nobody would come. From this world, or the next."

Heizaemon loved woods, as Ishi loved rocks and Bankichi worshipped plants. With pieces of wood he had collected almost since the day he arrived in Wailuku, Heizaemon built not only a kamidana, a god shelf for the Shinto deities, but also a butsudan, a small altar for Buddhist divinities, and a tokonoma of sorts. Making a true alcove was beyond his ability as yet, because he lacked all the tools of a carpenter save his hands, feet, a few iron nails, and a stone for a hammer.

He brought in a tree trunk stripped of its bark. The wood, beautifully grained and elegantly twisted toward its top, was tawny in color, lighter than the valued hinoki of Nippon, and not nearly as smooth. Beautiful as it was, in Hawaii it served no other purpose than to make fence posts and hitching rails. He hung this trunk by a rope from the roof ridge in such a way that it looked like the post to a tokonoma. Two flat stones placed upon the floor to the left of the post supported a smooth board saved from the making of the sleeping-platforms. A few inches above that, and to one side, upon brackets of wood nailed to the wall (using a stone for a hammer), he placed the butsudan—a piece of driftwood from some unknown land. The sea had smoothed and bleached it. Heizaemon enhanced its beauty with a few drops of cooking oil from the kitchen. And high upon the wall, because believers in Shinto stand before their gods, he placed a similar shelf for those kami.

All this he did within an hour, during the evening after they agreed that they must celebrate the Festival for the Honorable Dead.

The others sat talking, smoking, watching him as he worked,

offering needless advice and foolish comments which he disdained. When he was finished Eizo said, "It is good. Already we live like rich men. Few poor men in Nippon have a tokonoma of any kind. And none can have one so fine as this, I think."

Although pleased by the compliment Heizaemon said, "It still lacks one or two things."

"Wait," said Bankichi. He ran outside and, after a few minutes, came back carrying a mossy stone out of which a small tree grew. Its roots had worked their way into the pores and crevices of the stone, drawing sustenance from it in return for beauty shared with the rock. "Maui bonsai," Bankichi said proudly, as he gave it to Heizaemon. "Found down by the river."

"Perfect," said Heizaemon, kneeling to place the symbol of life upon the floor of the tokonoma. Its small coin-shaped leaves, the oldest of which were dark green, the youngest almost red, were more enduring than any flower.

"Now," Heizaemon turned to the others. "The last thing. I don't suppose any of you brought your ancestral treasures with you? A hanging scroll or two? A painting of Saint Shinran, perhaps? Or of Kobo-daishi?"

"It just so happens that I presented my entire collection to the Lord Shogun, just before I departed from Edo," Eizo said, affecting an aristocrat's lisp for the moment. "He wanted them. And I preferred to travel without a lot of baggage, you know . . . "

"I have an idea," said Koi, dashing into his room. When he returned he carried his contribution hidden behind him. With all the drama of a kabuki actor flourishing a four-foot banner, he unrolled it before the group.

"Perfect!," everyone shouted.

It was one of the sleeves from his carp-covered kimono. Like a good wife, Aiko had taken it apart at the seams in order to wash it. But because she lacked needles and thread the pieces had not yet been sewn together. Now, in an unexpected way, the kimono's sleeve became a kakemono. Even Ishi, who had disliked the garment since the instant he saw it, had to admit that when Heizaemon nailed the top of the long slender panel to the wall it added beauty to that whole end of Gohongi. The carps still swam, they still strove to surmount all obstacles that nature placed in their way, but now they struggled quietly, and to some good purpose. Tapping Koi's shoulder, Ishi said, "That's the best of the things you brought from Nippon. The first of your family treasures."

"The god shelf," said Tametsugu the joyless. "It is still empty."

"The god shelf is *never* empty," declared the Abbot of Gohongi in his most oracular voice.

"Well, then, the butsudan," said Tametsugu the pious.

"Wait," said Ishi quietly. His sailor's bag lay not far away. From it he drew the green silk obi the old woman in the pawn-shop had given him on the day he escaped from Edo. She seemed to be in another world from this one in which he now dwelled, and a sadder one. "Will this help?" He gave the folded obi to Heizaemon.

The carpenter looked at it, cool and dark against his workworn hands. The fine silk threads clung to the roughened fingers. "A treasure indeed. And heavy. What's in it?"

"Images of the Lord Buddha, Kannon-sama, and Jizo-sama. To protect me on my travels."

"We'll just leave it folded, like this," said Heizaemon, placing the obi upon the butsudan. "Hidden or revealed, the gods will be here."

"Where did you get it?" asked Eizo. "It's worth a lot of money."

"An old woman gave it to me. Just before I left Nippon," replied Ishi, telling the truth—or as much of it as they needed to know.

"An *old* woman?," Chikahei asked, raising his eyebrows.

"Yes. My grandmother," said Ishi, proving again that, with some people, lies cause less trouble than truths.

The Christians' Sabbath came two days later, and all Wailuku rested. Although in Nippon the festival of O-Bon is accorded three full days and nights, because that is the length of time during which the spirits of relatives will return for a visit to their earthly abodes, at Gohongi, out of necessity, the celebrations were confined to one evening. "The spirits of our dead will understand our problem," Dembei convinced everyone.

Beginning at sunset, while Wailuku's good Christians sat at cold supper or listened to fathers read passages from the Scriptures, Gohongi throbbed to the beat of pagan music. Fortunately for all of Wailuku's inhabitants, the roar of the river, and especially the great distance between sanctified village and Japanese Camp, spared Christians the shock of hearing savage drums, bestial howlings, and the cries of lust that characterize all pagan bacchanals the world around. Pious Christians, when they laid themselves safely down to sleep, slumbered well because they never knew that, just across the river, a coven of infidels desecrated the holy Sabbath with lascivious dances, drunken revelry, and—most abominable wickedness of all!—commerce with the spirits of the dead. In Paké Camp, much closer to the scene and the spirit, Chinese men rather enjoyed the boom of the great drum, which was about all that they could hear of the O-Bon. Some even strolled over in the dusk to watch their Japanese friends offering proper respect to the spirits of departed ancestors. Patient as always, the Chinese knew that, early in the next year, the time would come for their own ceremonies of filial piety.

Just before sunset a lamp beneath the butsudan was lighted. The barrack door was opened wide, inviting O-Shorai-sama to come in. The "fire of purity"—made of thirteen dried stems of the sugarcane flower, the nearest thing to hemp that the Gohongijin could find—was set to burning at the foot of the stairs. Prayers were offered by each man in turn, as he knelt before the butsudan.

In the light of coal-oil lamps set upon the ground and of lanterns hung from the boughs of trees the ten young men of Gohongi gathered to welcome O-Shorai-sama. Dressed in their best kimono, wearing geta brought from Nippon, they came out from the barrack in Wailuku as though they stepped from homes in

Edo, or Yokohama, or Kawasaki, or Shimoda of Izu. Men from the cities carried folded fans in their hands, or tucked under the obi, on the hip. The country bumpkins, alas, never much instructed in matters of style, wore sweat-bands tied about the head and stuck their half-opened fans down into the kimono, at the nape of the neck.

They looked very festive, nonetheless, compared with the manner in which they usually dressed after dinner and the bath. Ordinarily, they sat around with only the fundoshi to cover the mara. The weather in Wailuku was so mild, even during the nights, that they did not feel the need for more clothing. But tonight, this being a most special occasion, they brought out their finery.

Yet their hearts were heavy. In their behavior, therefore, they were shy and stiff: gaiety was forced, voices were too loud. They missed the girls, and the women who, remembering how once upon a time they too had been young, watched over the girls. They missed the older men, and the children running around, the food-sellers' stalls, the smells, the strolling players, peddlers, musicians, above all the noise and the excitement, the feeling that they were part of a great community. Here they were by themselves, the same few who saw each other all day every day, and never talked with anyone else. They were like an unpopular family who tried to buy friends by holding a feast to which no guests would come.

Despite all their preparations this O-Bon seemed to be so futile. Yet, because respect for ancestors is the unbroken line which joins past with present and present with future, they dared not break the tie which bound them to their families. As each one took his turn in prayer before the butsudan—furnished now by Aiko's hand with food offerings of Kona oranges, balls of cooked rice, tomatoes from Bankichi's vines, and ripe guavas from the gulch—each one implored his ancestors to hold fast the line that joined him to them, and to bless him in the future. No one wanted to think that here, in this lonely land, his line would end with him. The death of a man in a family is one thing: although it may be sad it is bearable, because death must come to all men. But the death of a family is beyond accepting: it is like cutting down a great tree, so that it can never flower again and bear seed.

Knowing how uneasy they were, how they strained at banter, Dembei took up Koi's samisen and the narrow ivory plectrum, and began to tune the strings that had been loose for so long. He was more modest about his voice than it deserved: he sang very well, more like a deep-toned nightingale than a harsh crow; and he gave them words and tunes upon which to hang some genuine gaiety. Following his lead, Koi sounded the beat provided at home by the taiko, the great drum. Here in Wailuku he made that satisfying boom by thumping an overturned wooden tub with a guava branch. Bankichi added the hollow "thonk" of a shoulder drum by tapping the bottom of an empty gourd. Heizaemon clacked hardwood sticks one against the other or on a log, depending upon the sharpness of the effect he wanted. And Akemi suggested the tinkling of bells and the resonance of gongs by beating haole pots of different sizes with haole iron spoons. The only important instrument they lacked was the flute.

"Oi!" Chikahei shouted above the din. "You sound just like the band at home. Very expert."

"Start dancing!," yelled Koi between drum beats. "Dance!"

"Come on, you boburas! Move!," cried Bankichi.

Bobura, meaning "pumpkin head," was Bankichi's term of affectionate disdain, applied indiscriminately to uncooperative tools, stubborn rocks, balky mules, mulish friends who didn't think the way he did, and even, in moments of extreme exasperation, to himself. Big-city folk, like Ishi and Eizo, found it a strange new epithet—and for good reason. As Bankichi carefully explained, once, in his roundabout way, it is a word used among peasants in Nippon's southern provinces. While still a small boy he had learned it from the retainers of provincial daimyo when they stopped at his parents' stall on the Tokaido, near Yokohama, to buy mouth-watering daikon and belly-filling sweet potatoes. "But *no* pumpkins," they had bawled, thumping his big round head with their hard knuckles, scaring him half out of his wits. "We'll take this thing instead. This bobura!"

Chikahei bowed formally to Ishi. "Honorable Father: you must go first . . ."

Ishi pushed him good naturedly. "Children always lead the way at Bon dances. Right now, your tired old father wishes to listen to this heavenly music."

Seeing his reluctance, sly Dembei shifted to a lively sailors' song from Shimoda. Every fisherman in Izu knows it, naturally, and Koi picked up the rhythm in a most intricate battering upon his tub.

> I went out to the shore to look and
> A sailor off a boat just come in
>   has grabbed me and won't let go.
> "Let go my sleeve, let go my skirt.—
> I am my lady's servant, and have to work!"
> Ton-ton the falling pestle sounds: my poor mistress,
>   pounding barley in my place.
> Oh! if I could only get away from this
>   handsome fellow . . .
> Oh! if I could only get away . . .
> Oh! if I could only . . .

Ishi could not resist that call. Ishi danced, not as a priest, or elder brother, or father to the group, but as a man of Shimoda far from home. As a man who danced to please the spirits of his ancestors, about whom he knew so little, and of his dead sons, whom he had scarcely begun to know. But they must be pleased, all of them. Just as, someday, his new sons and their sons would dance to please his approving spirit . . .

And Dembei, who saw tragedy in everything, could not bear to look upon such grace and such beauty, wasted on so forlorn a dancing ground. Tears filled his eyes, sorrow took hold of his voice, bonds of feeling tying him to the sadnesses of this life. "Yosh," he broke off, pretending that he choked. "A mosquito in my throat.—I must wash it down." He poured himself a drink from the gallon jug of okolehao each man had contributed five cents to buy from Ah Siu's confederates. Smacking his lips, he sent the bottle on its rounds.

"All right! Let's go," said the recovered singer. "Everybody out." He started upon a cheerful Edo tune, full of "Yoi, Yoi's," that brought the rest of the men to join Ishi. Gracefully advancing, retreating, clapping their hands, swinging their arms, they danced in a circle around the great man-stone the ten of them had spent most of that day setting up in Gohongi's yard.

Bankichi had said that they must put up such a stone, if they wished to keep their virility during these weeks when they lived without women. Tametsugu maintained that the man-stone would help them to find women to marry and to get sons and daughters with in the years ahead. Dembei had snarled "Bakayaro" at the thought of all the useless labor that would be spent upon something that would do no one any good at all. Chikahei had courted the anger of heaven when he declared that, in his present state, he'd rather they put up a woman-stone, with a hole in it. Ishi, of course, worried about what the haoles might say when they saw such an unmistakable thing erected in Gohongi's precincts. Heizaemon pointed out, with irrefutable logic, that inasmuch as no haoles ever came anymore to Gohongi, and were not likely to come in the forseeable future, their disapproval need not be feared. All controversy came to an end when Yasuo, a couple of Sundays before, during his prowling about in the gulch, discovered just exactly what they needed—a slender stone about as long as a man is tall, shaped at one end to resemble the male principle. He found this image lying below a wide rock platform, overgrown with shrubs and vines. Ah Siu's scholar informed them that this was the site of an ancient Hawaiian temple, long since abandoned, and that the Hawaiians would not care what the Japanese did with their discarded god. Shaking their heads over such an affront to the most important of all earthly deities, the men of Gohongi resolved to rescue it from neglect. With Heizaemon's help they made a strong litter, and on this they carried the image to Gohongi. Once it stood upright, washed and glistening, in the clearing beside their home, not even Ishi and Dembei could regret that it had come to shed its benisons upon them.

When Chikahei and Yasuo took their places in the orchestra

for O-Bon, Koi and Akemi mimed the dance of a shy maiden pursued by her ardent lover. The musicians accompanied them with suggestive noises and rhythms, and Dembei sang descriptions of the lovers' charms that would have made the Shogun's police grow faint. So, with laughter they chased away the underlying sadness for a while, proving, as Koi had said, that Bon Odori are held for the pleasure of the living, too.

Later, when Aiko came home from the kitchen, her presence made everything seem more natural. Her woman's soft gestures contrasted with the strong grace of the men, with their stretched-out arms, their feet lifted high, the hard buttocks showing beneath the kimono, as proud as peacocks when they flaunt their feathers. But then, because she was the only woman, and because she was the wife to one, nine of the men fell to wondering, Where is my mate? And so the sadness crept into their hearts again.

Suddenly, they were more forlorn than at the start of the evening. Dembei watched the sickness taking hold, and knew the time had come to stop. "Yossh. Enough. My fingers are sore. The voice-box complains.—And tomorrow we must go to work."

Without a word of protest from anyone, the Bon Odori came to an end. They took the lighted lamps into the barrack, brought down the lanterns from the trees, put away their make-shift instruments.

They helped Aiko to place some of the lighter food offerings from the butsudan upon a small raft Heizaemon had made from pieces of bamboo. They carried it down the bank to the river, finding the path with the help of lanterns. Beside the rushing water Aiko asked Ishi to light the candle, Yasuo to place it in the square lantern he had made from oiled paper and pieces of fine bamboo, and Koi to put the frail craft in the river. They murmured "Farewell, O-Shorai-sama, farewell. Please come again to see us next year. We shall be here, waiting to welcome you."

The raft drifted away, slowly at first, then swiftly as the current caught it up. They watched it, a small glow in a great darkness, speeding on its way to the sea, guiding the spirits of the dead back to Paradise or to Hell.

The deep silence of Wailuku's night fell upon Gohongi, like a slide of snow burying a mountain village in Nippon.

In the barrack, as they prepared to go to sleep, Chikahei expressed the thoughts of almost everyone else. "The spirits, if they came, must have rushed away at once. If I were one of them, I wouldn't want to stay around this half-dead place for three minutes, let alone three days."

"At least we tried," said Heizaemon. "They'll have to give us some merit for that."

"If they came," sniffed Tametsugu.

"Didn't you hear any one out there?," asked Dembei. "I certainly did. Whispering in my ear. Sounded very much like my dear old grandmother."

"Really?" Bankichi lifted his pumpkin head from the log pillow. "What did she say?"

Dembei grinned. He was quite happy from all those soothing sips of okolehao. "Can't you guess?"

Without having to think everyone yelled "Bakayaro!"

In games of this kind Dembei could always win. "No, not that, for once.—Or not in that one word, at least. Although perhaps that was her intention . . . "

"What, then?" Bankichi insisted.

Imitating an aged woman's voice coming from on high, Dembei quavered, "What this place needs is more screwing . . . "

They yelled, they laughed, they swore. "It's not funny, Dembei," wailed Chikahei. If ever he went mad, Dembei thought, Chikahei would go in the noisiest possible way. If ever he were ordered to commit hara-kiri, he would do it with a pestle.

"Well," drawled Dembei, as somebody blew out the last lamp, "why don't we listen to what my dear old grandma said?"

CHAPTER 19
THE SEEKERS

Dembei's concerned grandmother started the fire, but their own juices fed the flames. All of a sudden they burned, as with a new fever. And of all the men in Gohongi only Koi was spared. Ishi suffered from it too: Ishi the celibate monk, who had suppressed this urge for so long that he thought it quite dead. But it was not dead, neither the desire in the flesh nor the yearning of the spirit for a wife, a home to put her in, and children who would rejoice him in his maturity, care for him in his age, and honor his spirit when he was dead. And he, poor fool, welcomed this softening of the brain that follows upon such a softening of the heart, just as though he had not learned how cruel the gods can be, who give such treasures to a man for three years or ten, and then, just as he is beginning to think they are his forever, wantonly take them away.

The men of Gohongi could talk about nothing else after the night of O-Bon.

"You're lucky," Chikahei accused Koi. "You have a wife." He looked like a man who has just received word that the police will be coming in the morning to strangle him.

"Well you could have done the same. Why was I the only smart one?"

"That's easy enough for you to say now. But who needed a wife then? Not I. As a matter of fact, I was trying to get away from two women, both wanting to be Chikahei's mate. Even now I wouldn't want either of 'em. I'm interested in something new. I like change . . . "

"Something new is what we all want, when we're tied down," observed Heizaemon. "But when we're bachelors something old and reliable looks attractive."

"And how did you become so wise?" asked Tametsugu.

"If the truth were told," said the carpenter, with a knowing look, "more than one of Hamada's happy band is running away from a woman he does not like. I am, you can be sure. Damned jealous hag. Thought she owned me, from topknot to toes. So when Kimura Hambei came along and told me about the beautiful women in these islands—"

"Beautiful women!" screamed Chikahei. "Where? Have you seen any? Any women at all? Other than that big fat one who gave us sour water to drink?"

"No. I must admit that I haven't seen any yet. But they must be out there somewhere, just waiting for us."

"And when are we going to find them?" asked Eizo. "Ever think of that?"

"Only during every waking moment," moaned Chikahei.

"What's the matter with Ah Siu's whores?" Koi inquired, most solicitously. "Aren't they keeping you happy?"

"Even with those cheap, broken-down old jugs, at fifty cents a throw how often can we see 'em?" snarled Chikahei. "I've been twice and now I'm broke. Empty in the pouch, but not in the bag."

"Besides," said Dembei soberly, "Chikahei's a frugal man. He hates to spend money on merchandise he thinks the owner should give him for nothing."

"Ah," laughed Koi, "my sentiments exactly."

"What we did not think about," said Chikahei, "is that we were coming to a land where we'd be set apart, like monks on a mountain top."

"Some Nipponjin are born to be stupid, I guess," said cheerful Dembei. "And others to be monks."

"We can send for some women, I suppose," suggested Eizo.

"Where from? Nippon? Or across the river?"

"Well, I was thinking from Nippon."

"Sure," said Dembei. "And who would recruit them? Who would pay for their passage? Hamada Hikizo?"

"Never!" Chikahei jumped up in rage. "That crook! He'd send us a load of maggoty harlots old enough to be your grandmother."

"With holes as big as shoyu tubs," sighed Tametsugu.

"Furthermore," Bankichi pointed out, "we'd have to wait a long time for them."

"Yeah, too long," moaned Chikahei, tightening his fundoshi as though his belly hungered. "I'm tired of lying with a lonely pillow."

"Well, then, who else is here? Where are the Chinese women?"

"In China," said Koi. "Why do you think we have Paké Camp over there. And Japanee Camp over here? No women, that's why. Only men. That's why."

"A cruel thing," said Tametsugu, "what these sugar plantations have done to us."

"Then what's left?," asked Chikahei, from deepest despondency.

"Hawaiians and haoles," answered Koi. "Take your choice."

"Given that choice," declared Dembei, "I think I'll be a monk. The ones I saw in Honolulu did not appeal to my fancy. Too fat. I like 'em skinny. Like me."

"Oh, I don't know," Chikahei gave full freedom to his fancies. "A big plump woman might be rather nice. Of any color. I'm not particular . . . But where can I find one?"

Ishi had seen more of Wailuku and its residents than any of his companions. "I'm sorry to disappoint you great lovers," he said. "There isn't much to choose from here, I'm afraid."

Dembei jabbed his pipe at Chikahei. "Isn't that the whole point of all this talk? We sit around here chattering all the time but doing nothing. We can look forward to lying with whores on Saturday nights, but not with the women who come out by day. We talk about looking for mates and we haven't even checked the goods in the market place."

"Why don't we look, then?," Eizo cried, expressing the singular thought.

"Shit! What's the good of only looking?," grumbled Chikahei. "Like going shopping, without being able to buy."

"Fine idea," said Eizo to Dembei, across the noise Chikahei was making. "Let's go next Ennichi."

"But let's not go together," said the tactful Chikahei. "Let's spread out. If I were a girl I'd be scared to death at the sight of most of you. If I were a girl," he hugged himself, "I'd pick a handsome man like me."

The next Sunday morning they gave over to discreet exploration. Despite Chikahei's repeated reminders that they should go separately, when the time came they were too faint-hearted to venture out alone. Freshly shaven, dressed in clean clothes, eight Gohongijin went together, across the gulch, through the mill yard, and up the hill to Market Street.

They took one look and groaned. Not a person in sight. Not even a pig sleeping in a mud hole. Empty as a rice pot during a famine. Tongue-tied Yasuo and Dembei were so discouraged that they wanted to go right back to Gohongi. But Chikahei, who never knew when to give up, insisted that they must go on. "Let's go and see what's around that corner," said he, a general urging on his troops.

Around the corner lay Main Street. Because it is longer than Market Street it looked even more empty.

"Ha," growled Dembei. "This is the deadest town I ever saw. Not a store open. Not a person in sight. Not even a shaven-pated monk out begging for food."

"These people must be suffering from a terrible pestilence," said Tametsugu.

"I'm going home," said Bankichi. "There's nothing here for me, that's for sure. You Japanees can stay, if you like. But not me."

"Wait, I'll go with you," Heizaemon said. "I'd rather fool around at home anyway."

Me, too, Yasuo told them by signs. Without another word the three started homeward.

"Yatchao," drawled Dembei, watching them go. "Let's get it over with. If a woman wants to marry me, she'll have to come and find me." And he, too, went back to the peace of Gohongi.

The valorous four who remained—and who wisely went their separate ways thereafter—were rewarded for their courage. Like carps in the streams and moats of Edo, they moved through Wailuku's six short streets and eight narrow lanes. They watched the village come suddenly to life as the bell in the Catholic church called its parishioners to seven o'clock mass. They saw people come out of their pretty houses and neat yards and disappear into the little church. Every dwelling-place in Wailuku, they judged, seemed to be the home of a wealthy family. The houses had so much grass-covered space around them, they were so full of costly furniture, they were painted in so many colors, and in their yards grew so many kinds of fruits and flowers and vegetables.

The explorers walked for hours, passed each other many times, with nothing of interest to report. They watched the few Mormons going to their chapel at ten o'clock, and the many Congregationalists streaming toward their church at eleven. But not a single person from the village spoke to any one of them, or offered food or drink. The people of Wailuku, they concluded, are not as hospitable as are those of Honolulu.

Of the four only Akemi came home with an adventure to relate. Soon after eleven o'clock this youngest Nipponjin went into the big white temple at the highest point in the village, to see how the people here worshipped their gods. He clumped noisily up the stairs, just as everybody does in temples and shrines at home, and kicked off his shoes at the porch, even though he saw no others arranged there. At this very moment a scowling haole with a bushy brown beard and a finger raised to his lips tiptoed out to the porch, saying "Shhh!," grabbed Akemi's arm, and took him—on tiptoe—to a seat in the nearest bench. From the rear of this bare white hall he saw many other captured worshippers sitting upon great long benches, listening to another haole with a bushy brown beard talking at the front of the room. Every now and then everybody would stand up and sing, very loudly. A strange, weird, unpleasing kind of music it was, for the most part. When they had strained their voices and his ears to the limit, they stopped shrieking and sat down again for a while, to listen as the man at the front talked some more. It was all so confusing! And so long . . .

Poor Akemi. Trapped between those two bearded, fierce-eyed guardians of the temple, just as frightening in their way as are the Ni-o, the two ferocious kings who stand watch over temple gates in Nippon, he squirmed with boredom for almost an hour. Understanding nothing at all about the complicated ritual, he yawned repeatedly, wishing that it would end. Whenever he dozed off the singing would start up again. This was a scheme, he realized after a while, intended to keep everyone awake who otherwise would try to sleep. As if anyone could really sleep in those uncomfortable benches in that bright white room, with sunlight streaming in through the tall open windows. This was the ugliest temple imaginable, too, having not a single image to look at, no candles, no decorations, and only a small bunch of flowers stuck in a jar on a table at the front of the hall.

Akemi did have three experiences in that bare room, however, which he did not relate to his fascinated countrymen. They were too private for a boy to reveal to men who might laugh at him, as they had aboard the *Scioto* when he suggested that they should send their thanks to the Meiji emperor for saving them from the typhoon.

One of these was the thrill that went through him when certain sounds came out of a huge musical machine that was piled up against the back wall of the church. The thing reminded him of a gigantic sho, with an uncountable number of golden pipes of different lengths, arranged like the reeds in a sho, or like lengths of bamboo stacked against the fence in a lumber yard. My! but those deep sounds the man drew forth from it were even more satisfying than the ones given off by the great drum when a priest beats it during a shrine ceremony, in order to call the god's attention to the prayers being sent up to him.

The second experience was the gift of money. The bearded guardian at the door to the hall passed among the people a big wooden bowl holding coins of all sizes. Akemi saw that the people in front of him dipped their hands into the bowl, taking what they needed. How nice, he thought. Usually, the people in a town must give to their temple. But here, I suppose, the temple is so rich that it gives money to the people. When the bowl came to him, at the back of the room, it was still full of coins. Not wanting to be greedy—because, after all, the plantation gave him almost everything he needed—Akemi took only a quarter of a dollar before handing the bowl, with a polite nod of thanks, to the fierce custodian. For some reason or other he was looking outside, through the open door, and he did not see Akemi's expression of gratitude.

The third experience was by far the best—and yet the most upsetting. Toward the end of the service, while Akemi was yawning and stirring restlessly, a Hawaiian girl sitting at the far end in the bench ahead glanced back at him and smiled. After that kindness he did not mind so much the slow-moving minutes. He studied the curve of her cheek, the long braid of black hair hanging down her back, the black lashes protecting those dark eyes. He hoped for another glance, another smile, but she did not look at him again.

The end of the service took him by surprise. When everybody got up to leave he had wit enough to stand and wait for her to pass. She could have gone out another way, he noticed, but she chose to walk past his bench. And as she came slowly toward him she looked him full in the face and smiled again. She shattered forever his peace of mind with that glance from those soft eyes, that parting of those full red lips.

The day was not entirely wasted for the four who went home to Gohongi. "By losing, gain," as Dembei consoled himself. While Bankichi fondled tomatoes swelling on the vine, pulled weeds, dug a new bed (and quietly applied to his younger plants the dung from the privy that he had been aging for a month), Dembei sat under a tree playing tunes on Koi's samisen, sipping okolehao to make tongue and throat smooth, fingers nimble. " 'Alone I play, alone I sing,' " he sang, " 'and this brings joy to my heart.' "

Heizaemon and Yasuo went exploring in the other direction from Wailuku village, and soon reached the sandy wastes lying between Japanese Camp and the seashore. Once more they turned back to Gohongi. "This is not our lucky day," Heizaemon was saying, when they stumbled upon parts of a cow that had died a long time before. Only bones and hide, hoofs and horns remained. The hide below was rotted, but that above was still firm and usable, although the hair had been weathered away.

"Ho!," exclaimed Heizaemon. "Not bad luck after all. Just what I need."

"Why?," asked Yasuo.

"For making zori."

With sharp knives of splintered leg bones, made on the spot, they cut away the useful parts of the hide, salvaging almost half of it.

"I feel like an eta," said Yasuo, who could speak well enough when he was not excited.

"We have no eta here," Heizaemon said with a laugh. "Haven't you noticed? Only daimyo and peasants." For the first time in his life Heizaemon could say the hated word without fearing that someone would discover that it applied to him. But even with this close friend he dared not reveal his secret. Until the day he died no one else must know the shame that he had escaped.

They loaded the pieces of hide upon a shoulder-pole ripped from a tree and started toward home. Along the slopes above the gulch they found patches of wild tobacco plants growing among the rocks.

"Please wait a moment," said Yasuo. "I might as well pick some of these leaves. Why should I pay Koi a good price for that stuff he brought from Yokohama, when I can make my own?"

Ah Siu generously allowed Aiko to take a rest on Sabbath afternoons and evenings. He did not want either her or Koi to complain that she received no holiday at all. Mr. Dunham assumed that, like all other employees, she received a full day's rest each week. Koi and Aiko did not dream that she deserved more free time than Ah Siu gave her. So, in the usual way of accepting folk, every one was happy, Aiko most of all. After the midday meal had been served, and all the dishes were washed, she could be with Koi. He would be fresh and full of energy, having slept the morning away.

On this last Sunday in August they went to the beach, to look for seaweeds, shrimps, crabs, squids, limpets, anything that would taste of the salt water for which they hungered. Aiko was almost sure that she was pregnant once again, but she decided not to tell Koi until she could no longer be in doubt. They walked along the familiar river road to Kahului bay, talking happily about many things, and laughing often because being together was so good.

A number of Hawaiian people from Wailuku were at the shore when they arrived. From a small outrigger canoe at the edge of the reef, where the waves broke, two men and two boys laid a long net, hung with many dried leaves, hoping to catch in it some of the smaller fish. The net's upper line was kept afloat with small stoppered gourds filled with air, its lower was weighted with small stones. In the shallower waters nearer the beach a few women searched for things to eat. Along the shore naked children scampered about, playing on the sand or splashing in the warm water.

Aiko tucked the long ungainly skirt under her belt and was ready to go in. Koi removed his dungaree trousers and cotton shirt. His fundoshi was much like the loincloth that Hawaiian men wore when they went into the sea or worked in their fields. He loved the heat of the warm sun upon his skin, and he would have gone naked if the haoles were not so strict. Since the day the policemen took Ishi off to jail, Koi had developed a strong respect for haole laws.

Koi and Aiko waded about on the slippery reef, in the shallow tidal pools, and saw many sea creatures. But these were so different from those of Nippon that they did not know which to gather and which to shun. "Let us ask her," said Koi, indicating a woman nearby, made doubly big by the air trapped under her wet muumuu.

With his talent as a mimic Koi had no trouble putting the question to the native woman. She showed them which plants to pick, how to clean the fronds, bade them chew some crisp red ones, approved of their responses. They tasted so good, after all these months of having none. Then the woman took them closer to the shore, among the rocks that were not covered by the sea for part of each day, and showed them how to gather pipipi and opihi, the limpets small and big, and how to pull the fleshy morsels out of their shells with long spines broken from sea urchins, and how to crack open those armored things to get at the spongy meat within. In half an hour she taught them all they needed to know about gathering such tasty fare.

When Koi acted as if he were a shrimp the woman looked puzzled and Koi realized that such creatures were not found here. He asked about crabs and she told how the edible kind appeared in great numbers upon the beach, but only at night. During the day they slept deep in the sand.

Thanking the friendly woman for her help, Koi and Aiko went off to fill their flour sack with seaweeds, sea urchins, and limpets. They picked enough to take back to Gohongi, for all their companions to share at supper, and for the Chinese too, if they wished to partake of such fresh delicacies.

On the way home Koi said, "A strange thing, back there. Did you notice? Along that whole shore, during all the time we stayed, I did not see a single man with a fishing pole. They were setting out nets, so fish must be there. But no one used a pole and line. I wonder why?"

"Why don't you try, then?" asked Aiko, in the way that wives have of pushing husbands into doing things they want to do.

On this day of adventuring Ishi went at last to his mountain. No doubt he could have gone sooner if he had thought more of himself than of his companions. Yet, in a way, he was afraid to go. He did not fear people, or ghosts, or hardships he might encounter on the path. He feared to be disappointed in his expectations of the place. He wanted to find beauty there, and mystery. And, this world being what it is, he feared that when he arrived at the goal within he would find ugliness, a desert, a wasteland, the end of a dream. When other duties at Gohongi held him back he felt relieved.

But now, on this special day, he could find no excuse to stay at home. Moreover, in the willingness of his companions to venture out, alone and full of hope, in search of new lives for themselves, he foresaw the end of the brotherly group at Gohongi. From now on, he suspected, they would be more contentious, less friendly. Already the whining Tametsugu, the argumentative Chikahei, were causes of annoyance to the other men in the barrack. Chikahei especially—that mouth-wrestler! At times he could strain the compassion of the Buddha himself. And when companions begin to wear upon each other they must get away, as much as possible. Yet where could they go, in so small a place as Wailuku?

For Ishi the answer was clear: he would find his refuge in the mountains. The early morning sun was bright and warm. Now, at last, the time had come to make his pilgrimage.

After the eight brave explorers went off to Wailuku he stood for a moment in the peace of Gohongi. As they had done when they departed, he bowed before the tall man-stone, asking the blessing of the Great Force that rules the life of men. It was stirring in him as much as it did in Chikahei and in all his other countrymen.

Dressed in old work clothes, soft and comfortable after so many washings, he walked along the trail beside the river. In the gulch the many trees and ferns, spray from the dashing water, made the air feel fresh and cool.

But when he'd gone little more than half a mile, as he approached the mouth of the valley, a canopy of clouds shut out the sunlight. The valley lay shadowed and somber, a cleft in the mountain that rose unseen on either side.

Along the river the very trees seemed to change their shapes and colors. Bright crimson fruits grew upon some of the tallest trees. These strange things had almost no stems and looked like apples stuck to branches, twigs, even the trunks of the trees. A few half-eaten fruits lying on the ground told him that he could safely try one. It tasted like rose petals, although its juicy flesh was purest white.

At the pool where all the Nipponjin had bathed he wondered again how anyone could have seen them, or why anyone should have wanted to look at a happening so ordinary. Today, when he purified himself, no one would see him. Even if he had to bathe out of the cup of a flower, under the shelter of a leaf, he would be most careful, because he did not want to cause any more trouble for himself or for Mr. Bristol.

To Mr. Bristol he owed his life. And to that huge Hawaiian woman also, he supposed, because she must have hurried to tell Mr. Bristol what had happened during that afternoon of torment and worry. He was sorry because so much hurt had come to the second boss because of him, but he did not know how else he could have stopped that evil man from dealing greater hurt to Koi and Akemi.

And he was awed still by the power of budo. It had not failed him when he needed it, so unexpectedly. "Evil falls before the power of good," the ryu master had said to his disciples. Until the day of Ichiro's murder the boy Genzo had believed his master, in all his teachings, even though they were not addressed to him, the lowly farmer's son. But after that day he no longer believed, because he had seen Ichiro slain by evil.

Yet here, in another land and at another time, without his thinking about it, certainly without his daring to ask for something that he had no right to claim, the power of good had come to help him, the man Ishi who had grown out of the boy Genzo. Humbled by this proof of the power of good, Ishi the man felt strong and complete, as Genzo the man had never been so strengthened. And Ishi understood why this was so: during all those years, he had been a man unfinished and weak because, in his hardness of heart and smallness of spirit, he had wilfully rejected the teachings of budo.

Ishi hissed at himself, shook his head. He had been so hard-hearted! And hard-headed, too. The power of good must have come to his rescue only because that man Douglas was so much more evil than he himself was small-minded. And for this help, and this awakening, Ishi would be forever grateful to the budo master of Shimoda and to the judo master of Edo.

—Just as he would be forever grateful to Mr. Bristol for his kindness. In spite of their fears Mr. Bristol was not angry with the Gohongijin over their small battle at Sekigahara. In fact, as Ah Siu and his scholar explained to the Japanese, the Boss was very happy that Mr. Douglas was going to leave Wailuku as soon as the doctor said he was well enough to travel. "Him one no-goot son-a-ka-piki," Ah Siu said gleefully, adding nothing to the comprehension of the Japanese. "Me too muchee solly he no maké yestadee. Moa betta maké now. Bimeby too late."

Mr. Bristol's assurances, delivered through Ah Siu, made Ishi feel much better, but the best sign of the Boss's forgiveness was his handshake, given more than once since the night he took Ishi away from the prison cell. Compared with that the other evidences of Mr. Bristol's kindness were unimportant. The raise in pay, for example. Ishi did not approve of receiving $5 a month more than his friends did, just because he was their headman and temporary luna. "Shut up and take it," they shouted, when he started to tell Ah Siu that he did not want all that extra money. "What will I do with it?," he asked. And they hooted and howled and pounded his back, giving him a hundred suggestions within the minute for spending the money on them if he could not find ways to enjoy it for himself. So he yielded to their good will, hoping that his being set apart in that way would not make them envious and bitter later on. "It is not good for a man to be set above his companions," he said, because he believed this to be a truth. Too often had he seen what happened to such a man in Nippon. "The nail head that sticks up," as they said at home, "must be hammered down." And they did pound it down, quite cruelly in most cases. The man who was different from his fellows, in thoughts or in deeds, was very rare. And when he did survive, he was either mad or so evil as to be worse than mad.

Another message from Mr. Bristol pleased Ishi more. This was the promise to make him a luna, like Pilipo, as soon as he learned enough of the English language, or of the Hawaiian, to be able to understand the manager's instructions. This offer he liked very much, because it gave him a chance to gain respect for his countrymen as well as for himself, and advantages for all of them that would be related to their ability to work. He thought that he could be a good luna, a better assistant to Mr. Bristol than ever Pilipo attempted to be. Pilipo was a kind man, as he had shown so often, but he was not a hardworking luna. He lacked loyalty, as Ishi defined that virtue. And in Saul Bristol, the man who was his new lord, Ishi had found a daimyo to whom he could give his unquestioning loyalty. He would not give loyalty that was demanded and unearned. But loyalty he could offer out of respect and liking he would give gladly.

Well, thought Ishi, we shall see what happens. 'The world is just as a person's heart makes it.' He knew better than to plan too far ahead. More than a day, less than a season seemed to be the limits to any reasonable man's plans for the future. Man hopes, the gods decide: always this is the lesson to be learned from life. But, he argued, a man can help himself to gain those hopes, can he not? This is the message that priests will teach. And, in truth, this was the knowledge that Kannon Nyo-i-rin had sent to him, on that fateful day at Sensoji in Asakusa. Since that day he may have worried, but he was never without hope—or without plans to help himself to move along the path she had opened up for him.

And now, in the land to which she had brought him, he hoped for a good life. He liked this place, the kindness of the climate, the gentleness of the earth and all the creatures on it. This is a good land, as Sentaro had said, and it is full of promise. And I want to take my place in it, he told himself, forgetting so soon the capricious gods, dreaming ahead, by many seasons, to the time when he would be a man content.

Above him the walls of the valley closed in. The river rushed through its narrow gorge, cutting ever deeper into the hard rock.

From the right side a small stream crept into the river, the child
of a waterfall born in the mist far above. Ishi could see, beyond
the sparse trees, the wet black cliff down which the water flowed.
No houses could possibly stand beside it, no people could possibly be present to watch him as he bathed. He crossed the river,
followed the little stream to its head. And there, standing in a
small pool as near as he could get to the foot of the cliff, like an
ascetic mountain priest, he purified himself for his entry into the
valley beyond. Only the gods of the place saw him in his nakedness, and they are never offended by piety or by beauty.

Not far beyond that stream the valley walls opened out, the
river flowed more gently. Groves of twisted trees with big yellow-
green leaves grew amid clearings where stood the works of men:
taro patches, vegetable gardens, stone walls, ditches through
which water moved slowly, and thatched houses, such as Hawaiians dwell in. Farmers' tools lay about in the yards, strips of
leather from cinches and girths, the wooden forms of ancient sad-
dles littered the stone walls, wet clothes hung upon bushes. The
scents of foods being cooked filled the air, although Ishi saw
neither a fire nor smoke. Nor did he see any people. The settlement was as deserted as a seaside village about to be raided by
pirates.

Where have the people gone? he wondered. Do they run from
me?, he entertained himself with an unusual touch of humor,
from the fearsome bone-breaker of Wailuku? And then, his
thoughts coming back to sober fact again, he concluded that
surely the many people who lived in this village would not be
afraid of a lone stranger wandering past, without sword or staff to
threaten them. They must be working in the fields, or gathering
food in the valley, or gone off to pray at the temple. Even so, he
hurried past the empty houses in his concern to give their owners
no reason to suspect him of any wrong-doing, if they happened to
be watching him. He remembered all too well the saying from
home: 'Don't tie your sandals in a melon field. Don't straighten
your hat under a plum tree.'

The trail, well used and easy to follow, led him farther into the valley. The clouds hung low and heavy upon the mountain. He could not see its peaks or judge the height of the cliffs. He moved as a snail might, at the bottom of a moat, where the water lies above rather than below.

Soon after midday the water above began to come below. The clouds spilled heavy rain for many minutes. Although he took shelter under a tall tree it did not protect him very well. Soon he was as wet as if he were standing out in the open. For a while he feared that his tree might be struck by lightning, and he with it, until he realized that no flashes lit up the gloom, and that the noise he took for thunder was nothing more than the roaring of the swollen river.

When the rain ended the clouds did not lift. Waterfalls, plunging down the lower walls of the cliffs, told him that here the mountains must be very high. The promise of greater beauty is here, he saw. But I must come back some other time to see it. Today is not a lucky day for me. And this must be an evil direction for me to take, on this unlucky day. I should have turned back when the sun hid behind the clouds. Now, too late, he remembered his vow to come here only in the full light of the sun.

When both weather and time are inauspicious, the wise man does not leave home. The smart man who is gone from home when he recognizes these bad omens turns back at once. Ishi started homeward.

Always, the return goes faster than the approach. Within a few minutes he was near the silent village. At a place not far above it he saw a cluster of trees laden with those bright red fruits that tasted of roses. Because he was hungry he waded through the wet grass, stepped across a few puddles and slippery stones, to reach the closest tree. He stretched out his arm to pick one of those shining scented apples. But his fingers did not close about the tempting fruit. Six feet beyond them he saw a woman, standing among the trees on the bank above him, as motionless as they. Her eyes were opened wide in fear, her lips were parted, as if to scream.

He leaped back in surprise. His shoe slipped upon a rock, he lost his balance and fell backward into the wet grass. By the time he gained his feet, and looked up to tell her not to be afraid, she was gone. He could not find her although he searched everywhere. She had disappeared, as a fox-spirit might, or a ghost. Or the goddess of the mountain . . .

All the way home he thought of her, trying to remember everything that his eyes had seen. But almost everything about her had slipped away, as she had—as though she were made of mist that had drifted, only for the moment, among those trees. All he could remember were those great dark eyes staring in fear, the opened mouth. And a brown hand lifted to her breast, where a hint of white lace hung, falling like foam from the high collar of her dress, gray as mist upon the mountain.

When he passed the houses beside the path he heard people talking and laughing within, and saw preparations for a feast being laid under the trees in the yard. Mats had been placed upon the wet grass, with stones at the corners to hold them down. But no people sat upon the mats, no one was there to call aloha and invite him in. For all he knew the voices he heard might have been uttered by fox-spirits, those mats and stones might have been illusions put there by demons. Just as the woman among the trees might have been a fox-spirit sent to lure him to his death.

"The head is concealed, but the back is exposed," as the proverb says of the man who is afraid of ghosts. Ishi did not allow himself to run from that eery hamlet. But he could not shake off the feeling that he was being watched as he walked away from it. The muscles in his back tightened, the hair upon his neck stood up, as he thought of what those evil spirits might be wanting to do to him.

He left his fears at the place of purification. For this cleansing he did not remove his clothes: he simply stood beneath the falling water and let it wash away defilement and weakness. When he emerged from this yamabushi's ritual he was whole again, and safe.

But his mind was not washed free of thoughts about the mist-woman. He could not really believe that she was a fox-spirit. The lace against her breast, the flesh of that brown hand, those eyes and lips: they were too substantial to be worn by a spirit. And why should a fox-spirit be afraid of him? He seized upon this fact with relief: it proved that she was a woman of flesh and blood.

Then, if she is a woman, he vowed, he would go back, again and again, until he found her there, in the valley. She called to him now, more than the mountain did. In his rejoicing over this proof of her being real, Ishi did not recognize that the mist-woman had bewitched him just as certainly as if she were a true fox-spirit sent from the world beyond to entrap him.

CHAPTER 20
YO AND YIN

For all the people of Gohongi the week moved too slowly. When at last the day of rest arrived each of the men knew what he must do.

Akemi went to the white church on the hill. As before, he understood nothing of the service, thrilled to the music, deftly drew a quarter from the wooden bowl, melted at the sight of his Hawaiian girl. At the end of the hour, when everybody got up to leave, he said "Aroha" to her as she passed. She smiled at him, whispered a shy "Aloha," while her mother looked in surprise from one to the other. Akemi was very pleased with the girl's response: it promised more to come. He was young, he had lots of time to wait for the rest. But he was inexperienced in the customs of this new land. What, he pondered, could he say to her next time, to prolong the moment of felicity? And where, he wondered, could he find a go-between to arrange the marriage with this girl whom he had chosen to be his wife?

Chikahei, Tametsugu, and Eizo wandered aimlessly through the village, sat under trees, felt as lonely as they looked. Together or alone, they met no one who spoke to them. On Ennichi, they concluded in great dejection, this town of Wailuku is closed up tighter than the door to a money-lender's shop when a poor man knocks. "How can we meet anyone," they complained, "when no one ever goes out?"

"The Four Happy Hermits of Gohongi," as they called themselves, were thoroughly content not to go anywhere. They made a rule to stay out of each other's way for the whole day. Bankichi worked in his garden. Heizaemon made slippers from the pieces of hide he and Yasuo had brought home from the sand hills. Yasuo, the tongue-tied one, made bamboo cages to put singing birds in, although he did not have the heart to trap the birds. And Dembei sat under a tree, playing Koi's samisen, singing softly to himself, sipping okolehao, until in mid-afternoon, he toppled over, like a round-bottomed daruma, and slept.

Koi and Aiko went again to the beach. He carried a long bamboo pole. She carried everything else: a bucket, his box of fish hooks, a length of twine cut from Ah Siu's stock, and, wrapped separately in pieces of newspaper, scraps of meat, vegetable peels, and a few earthworms to test as bait.

They waded out to the edge of the shallow reef, where the small waves were breaking. Following his instinct, Koi put an earthworm on a hook of moderate size and cast the line into the green water.

Hawaiian men and women on the beach watched this strange fellow with his long pole, wondering what he was trying to do. Within two minutes they saw very clearly what he and that new device could do, when Koi pulled in a fine papio. Five minutes later, when he hooked a weke, the native fishermen gathered around Koi and Aiko, eager to learn the secret of their success.

"And that," as Koi would say in later years, never tiring of the tale, "is the true story of how pole-fishing and surf-casting came to Hawaii. Before that day Hawaiians used long nets to catch their fish with, or lines with a hook tied at one end and a canoe at the other. But never a bamboo pole. Funny, no? How they never thought of tying their lines to poles. Or of using earthworms for bait. Just as they never used small throw-nets. That method, too, they learned from a Japanee. But I had nothing to do with that..."

Ishi thought that surely this fair and sunny morning betokened a good luck day. With faith in Kannon's infinite mercy, but not much hope of meeting so soon the woman of the mist, he repeated his journey into the valley. He purified himself in the same secret stream, he entered the narrow gorge. This time no mist hung low upon the mountains, no wreaths of cloud floated across the faces of cliffs. Today earth showed yet another of her many humors. The tremendous precipices, the soaring peaks, stood up in all their strength and beauty. Ishi, walking below them, felt like an ant striving toward a hidden goal he could not know how to reach.

He passed the thatched houses, empty as before, but with that aroma of cooking food just as heavy in the air. At the unforgettable place where the mist-woman had appeared to him he looked among the trees to see if she, too, might have returned, summoned by messengers from Kannon-sama if not by his own imploring thoughts.

All through the week, by day and by night, he had thought of her. She would not let him go: her image was fixed in his memory, as the ink from a painter's brush is fixed to the fibers in a sheet of paper. At first he had tried to wipe it away, using annoyance for a cleaner, and mockery, directed at himself for being a fool. But then, as the image persisted, he welcomed it, enjoying it as does any man with a hidden vice or a secret dream. At last he supposed that he was in love, with this image in gray, this woman made of mist. Bakayaro! he sneered at his folly, even as he smiled over his yearning.

This was a new experience for him. He had seen its effects upon susceptible lads like Koi. He had heard about it from the gossip of Lord Okubo's servants and footmen, from visits to the Yoshiwara, the kabuki, the bathhouses, and from the stories related by wandering tellers of tales. But never had he thought that he would be a victim of this strange disease. At home in Shimoda he had neither received nor given love, not with his surly parents or with his drudge of a wife, found for him by his father. What farmer has time to waste upon love? Even so, his heart had not been entirely dead: he was beginning to feel love of a father's kind for his sons, before they were taken away. But when they died he thought that love had perished with them, that only grief and dread had taken its place.

Yet now, here in Wailuku of Maui, to his amazement, he was

showing all the signs of this sickness. Ridiculous! he snorted, at first. Why now? he sighed, toward the end of that week of delectable misery. But he did not go so far as to ask, Why me? Instead, he took to yearning for the body of a woman whose name he did not know, whose house he could not find. And, as he yearned, he wondered if she were, indeed, a fox-spirit who had succeeded in bewitching him. Or if, perhaps, his body's need for a woman had fixed his mind upon the first one he'd seen in this new land who pleased his eyes. He did not think to ask if, like a man bewitched, he yearned for her because she was beyond his reach.

He watched for her among the trees, but she was not there. Neither were the red fruits he had lifted his hand to pluck: they, too, were gone, and only their sour, rotting remnants, teeming with fruit flies, lay upon the mossy stones. How short is the time of life, they told him. How vain are your dreams . . .

Disappointed by this omen, but not yet unhappy, he continued to walk along the path, following the left side of the river. The high precipices accompanied him at either hand, scored in places by tall narrow ravines, little more than grooves cut by waterfalls. Quiet streams flowed from them, to nourish the central river. After several days and nights without rain the river too was quieted.

Beyond the point at which the storm had stopped him on the Sunday before the valley widened again. Above the trees he saw the great curve of the cliffs forming the valley's head, closing it in and completing it. He stood in the very womb of the mountain. And now he understood why, from the very beginning, he had looked upon this mountain as being the abode of a great goddess.

Ishi went on, slowly now, marveling at the perfection of this immense womb of living rock, and of the long narrow birth canal through which men must enter in and leave. A few minutes later the path brought him to the crest of a low hill above a bend in the river. And there his marveling turned into utmost awe.

"Ho!," he cried out, stopped short. Thrusting up from the valley's floor rose the most magnificent man-stone he had ever seen. Taller than the height of a hundred men, it stood up, proud and firm, the fertilizing god to this fertile goddess. Ishi sank to his knees before these tremendous symbols of Yo and Yin, the male and female principles, so wondrously conjoined in this silent sacred place.

These great deities of life filled him with reverence. But the silence in which they dwelled distressed him. He could not believe that so holy a place could be so deserted. At home in Nippon such a male-stone would be wound about with thick shimenawa, those sanctifying ropes plaited from rice straw, which mark a thing as being the manifestation of a divinity. Shrines would have been built at its base, if not upon its summit as well. Shinto priests would attend it, offering prayers to it and to its fecund mate, invoking their blessings upon the land and the people. And thousands of those people would be coming here each day, the men to ask for their little share of his unfailing potency, the women to beseech the fruitfulness promised by her immense encompassing womb. Yet here they stand, these two divinities in their mystic concourse, neglected and unhonored. In truth, this land is as empty of people as is this shrine. With these great deities of fertility to protect them, how can the people of Hawaii fail to offer them the respect they deserve? No wonder the Hawaiians are a dying race . . .

The sun at its zenith flooded the valley with light and warmth. Every leaf responded, every bird and insect throbbed with the gift of life. And into worshipping Ishi, too, the deities of the valley poured their power.

Now, indeed, was Ishi most unhappy. Driven by the primal need, and not knowing where to appease it, he rushed back toward Wailuku, to the cloister of Gohongi. As he fled he prayed to Kannon-sama, who had helped him before, and to the great gods whose abode he had just discovered. He thought longingly of the mist-woman, especially when he passed the grove where she had appeared to him so briefly. He needed her. He wanted her, body and beauty and spirit. Suffering in his loneliness, he hurried into the clearing where the thatched houses sat among the taro patches and the gnarled trees with the pale green leaves. "With a stride like a lion's, as beautiful as a deer," did he come out from the sacred grove.

To his surprise he saw a family sitting around an eating-mat laid out upon the grass, just beyond the low stone wall. White-haired elders, vigorous younger folk, and two small children sat in the shade of the trees, talking and laughing. They were equally astonished to see him, bursting out of the jungle as though he were a boar trotting to the river for water. As their merriment for themselves faded, courtesy for him appeared. "Aloha," they called, "aloha ia oe."

Ishi stopped, out of habit, bowed stiffly. "Konnichi wa," he said. Then, remembering greetings learned more recently, he waved, saying "Aroha," and gave them his very brightest smile. Sorrows within, he had been taught since childhood, must not be revealed to strangers.

"E komo mai. E hele mai ai," the white-haired woman called, beckoning him to join them with one plump hand, while she pushed her husband with the other. He rose and went toward Ishi with a friendly smile and an extended hand. "Come in, come in," he said in English. "Come in and have a little something to eat." The words slipped past Ishi's ears, but he could not mistake the invitation. For the briefest moment he thought to flee from these people too. But the need for friendship, not hunger for food, overcame his shyness. "S'ank you," he said, "Maharo," and stepped through the gate.

The old man perceived that Ishi did not understand his cheer-ful conversation. He turned to his family. "I believe that he is one of those new Japanese men from the plantation, who came to Wailuku not long ago. They do not speak either Hawaiian or En-glish. Auwe, Tutu: what are we going to do with him?"

"Oh, Papa. What does it matter? Let him eat. He must be hun-gry, if he's been up in the valley all morning. And we can talk with hands and eyes, if not with tongues." She pushed herself up from the mat, gasping and grunting, with aches and pains of age, with too much heavy fat upon her small bones. With waving hands and bright commanding glances she welcomed Ishi and led

him to her place at the mat. He tried to pull away when he saw
that they had finished with their meal, but she would not release
him. She pushed him down to the mat, and he obeyed. Women at
either side removed leaves and wooden bowls from which Tutu
had eaten, men quietly explained to the children who this
stranger might be. Ishi smiled and bowed at everyone, especially
at the big-eyed children. He tapped fingers on knees, swallowed
hard, wished he were at home in Gohongi when, in a flash of terror, he realized that all these people were going to talk to him.

"Kinau! Kamamalu!" Above his head Tutu shouted: "Bring
some more food. A guest is here."

"A guest? So late?" The young voice expressed annoyance,
complete with pouts, not pleasure.

"And who can it be?," asked another kinder voice, as the
owners of both came out from the cook house. Ishi looked up as
they appeared.

And there she was: the woman of the mist.

In a great silence, from which all sounds were shut out, Ishi
saw her eyes open wide, the hand rise to her breast, the lips part
in a gasp of surprise.

"Never mind who it is," Tutu pretended to be cross. "Just
bring the food. You can talk to him later."

Surprise yielded to something else. Perhaps amusement. Perhaps modesty. Ishi could not be sure. The mist-woman smiled,
more to herself, he thought, than to him, and slipped back into
the cook house as quietly as she had come. Ishi's heart began to
beat again.

The other woman, younger and very brazen, appraised him
cooly, from head to crotch to foot. She reminded him of O-Miya
at her harlot's worst.

"Kinau!," screeched Tutu. "Don't be so rude!" With a lift of
the shoulder, one last and undisguised glance at Ishi, Kinau too
drifted away.

Ishi began to hear sounds again: birds calling, water flowing,
seeds sprouting, plants growing . . . And the noise of Tutu complaining, far above his head. "Oh, these girls! This is what I get

for letting her go to that terrible Honolulu! She goes away nice and sweet. She comes back spoiled and sassy."

"Man-crazy," one of her married daughters said, giggling at the persistence of the family's perennial problem.

"Not like her elder sisters," one of the tamed husbands confided to all who could hear.

Ishi sat among them, struck dumb but not blind. His voice-box could not have made noise enough to cover the chirp of a cricket. He fixed his gaze upon the place from which she had vanished, as though she were still there, bewitching him. For a whole week she had been haunting him, and he had suffered from that sorcery. But now that he knew she was real, a woman of warm brown flesh, not a thing of cold gray mist, he gave himself up gladly to her magic.

She was more beautiful than he remembered. The dim light among the trees, her fear of him, had stolen for the moment the beauty she possessed at all other times. His own fright had played other tricks, too, upon his memory: she was taller than he expected, and older. She was not a mere girl, like that other leering one. She was a woman in whom sorrows seemed to have burned out all falseness and all foolishness, so that only peace remained within. And grace. The way she moved, the very manner in which she held her head, pleased him. She pleased him, in every respect. And he yielded now, completely, to her spell.

"Eia mai," said Tutu's oldest daughter, nodding toward enchanted Ishi. "This one hungers for more than fish and poi, I think."

"Kia! Watch your tongue," scolded Tutu, not wanting to give ideas to the children.

"Kia," said Papa to his sons-in-law. "And so would I, were I his age again."

Kinau and Kamamalu came from the cook house carrying bowls and plates of food. They knelt beside Ishi, one at either side, to set the dishes before him. The younger one went away quickly, sullen because he did not look at her. The elder stayed with him, spending more time than was necessary at the simple task. He could feel the warmth of her body. His cheek tingled at her nearness. She breathed deep the scent of his flesh, studied the strength of his thighs, the hang of his long hands. Ishi thought of how Daigoro had won O-Miya, and wished that he could tell this woman the words that Izanagi said to Izanami when they met beside the Central Pillar of Heaven. And Kama-malu thought of her hollow life and empty bed since the police-men had taken her husband away, of how much she wanted a man to fill his place. A man like this one . . .

Ishi tried to think about the food. But how could he eat, in his confusion? He looked about, to see whether he should use spoon or fingers at this feast, when he wanted not to eat but simply to gaze upon her.

With all these people staring at him, watching everything he does, thought Kamamalu, he is shy. Well, then, he must be helped. "Please eat," she said in English. "Before the meat gets cold."

He looked at her dumbly, dazed and soft-eyed as a fawn seeking its dam. With all these strangers around, he fretted, feeling her so close, seeing the sweep of her lashes, the smoothness of her skin, how can a man declare his thoughts?

She looked at him, seeing again what her eyes had told her a few minutes ago, a whole week ago: here is a man most hand-some. When first she saw him, reaching out toward her, she feared that he had come to rape her, up there in that quiet ohia grove. In her fright she could not run, she could not even scream. Only when he fell back, in his alarm at discovering her, did she realize that he had not known she was there, picking mountain apples among the trees. And yet she had run away, fleeing from the man who meant no harm. From the man for whose touch she had yearned ever since that moment . . .

Papa spoke from the side of this fascinating show. "Malu, he does not speak English. Or Hawaiian. You must try some other way."

"Auwe!," she cried, turning her gaze upon Uncle for the brief-est of instants. This was a most unwelcome barrier. "Then what language does he speak?," she asked, just to have something to say.

I shall try every possible way, she vowed. During the week her thoughts had turned again and again to him, to the memory of his long fingers reaching out toward her, of the handsome head lifted toward her, of those full lips parted as though about to speak. He had haunted her so much that, this morning, in foolish dreaming, she had hurried up to the grove as soon as the family returned from church, hoping that he would be there. But he was not there, and she had sorrowed ever since, afraid that she would never find him again.

"We do not know," said Papa. "I think perhaps he is Japanese."

"Oh, is that what he is? I have been wondering."

"He seems to be very nice," Tutu said, to everybody. "Such a nice smile . . . "

"But needing help," added Lukila, encouraging Malu with giggles and little pushings at her back. "Help him."

Kamamalu turned to their guest. "This is how we eat," she began slowly, in soft Hawaiian. With her supple fingers she showed him how to pick up the pieces of pork, how to take a dab of poi in the spoon of two fingers, how to carry that to the mouth without spilling any on the way. Both teacher and pupil gave fullest attention to every detail of this extremely difficult lesson. Papa, Tutu, cousins, children, all disappeared into nothingness, as Kamamalu bound this prize to her with dainty fingers, caressing voice, glances meant for him alone, all held together with the glue of poi and the unbreakable bonds of love.

This time she would not run away from him, nor let him run away. This time his hand must be made to pluck the fruit so close to his grasp. She knew, in her reason as well as in her heart, that he had come today in search of her. A few minutes ago, when he looked up and saw her by the cook house, his face had told her everything that she needed to know.

Ishi watched her every motion, rejoicing in the grace of the hands, hearing the welcome in her voice, seeing the softness of love in those eyes. When so many signs were being given to him his shyness melted away, taking with it a lifetime's fears. The ruins of the old defenses against pain and sorrow crumbled and fell away. No longer afraid, because Kannon-sama was giving him now his time for happiness, Ishi reached out and took the mist-woman's hand in his. Love needs no words, his fingers said. She did not draw her hand away.

"This man's a fast worker," said Lukila's husband, in deepest admiration.

"And all without saying one single word!," said his wife.

"When have these two met before?" asked Papa, always the most charitable member of his family, and always the least informed.

Tutu lifted a kerchief to eyes filling with tears. "At last," she sobbed.

Kamamalu took Ishi's hand in both of hers, claiming him for her own.

Ishi bowed to his love, thanking this woman of flesh and blood for her goodness to him. "Maharo," he whispered to her, to her alone.

CHAPTER 21

THE BLESSINGS OF BENTEN

Ishi, Kannon's favorite, received Benten's blessing as well, and
no doubt those of the great beneficent deities of Iao Valley to
whom he had offered reverence earlier in that Sabbath day. The
gods of learning and of wisdom gathered around also, at Kannon's command. As the day progressed Ishi made a fine beginning upon the study of the Hawaiian language. Before the day
ended he had learned a heartening amount about Hawaiian people in general, and about one lovely Hawaiian in particular.

He was a man much enlightened when, soon after dawn on
Monday, he joined his comrades at the morning meal.

"Where have you been?" they cried, turning heads, opening
mouths, as excited as hungry fledglings in a nest when the father
bird comes home. If they had only looked at him they might have
guessed where he'd been. But the early hour and the dim light
made them dull.

"We were worried," said Koi, more quietly perhaps, but just
as slow-thinking as his comrades. "Where were you?"

A man of wisdom and learning knows when to talk, when to
keep his secrets. "Up in the valley," said Ishi, stifling a yawn,
touching his sore lips. They were very tender, after all that rubbing, biting, licking, nibbling, tasting, and simple pressing of
mouth upon mouth that Kamamalu had taught him in quieter
moments scattered among many other kinds of lessons. "Kissing," she called it, this new game, another way for lovers' bodies
to meet that he'd not known before, because it is an art pro-
scribed in Nippon. And very exciting it was, very pleasing. But,
alas, it caused such a chafing and swelling. Ishi hoped his lips

would be healed in time for his next kissing lesson, planned for
very early the following Sunday morning.

That far-away look, that absence of mind: Koi finally recognized the signs. "Ah, so," he laughed, happy for his quiet friend.
"And how far did you go? In that valley, I mean?"

"To the end," said Ishi, smiling.

"And where did you sleep?," asked suspicious Tametsugu.

"In Paradise," said Koi quickly.

"Yes. That's what it's like, up there," said Ishi. "Tonight I
shall tell you about the great gods who dwell in that place."

"Where have you been?," cried Mrs. Hoomalu as she stumped
into Kamamalu's parlor. The little house trembled with each
heavy footstep. Kamamalu, still half asleep, trembled at the
sound of that voice. "You're never at home! I've been looking for
you for a week. Driving around. Sending messages." She settled
into a huge rocking chair. The chair creaked, the house ceased to
quake. "Kia! Such a gad-about!"

"Oh, Mama. Why do you exaggerate so much? Three days I've
been away, not a week. And I've been up at Aunty's house, in the
valley. Where else would I go?"

"I thought as much." Mama's sniff was as necessary as breathing. "And how are all those back-country folk?"

"They're well. They all send you their love." Kamamalu, full
of love this morning, resolved to be Mrs. Hoomalu's peace-
making child for as long as she possibly could.

If Mama had been in truth the suspicious woman she claimed
to be, she would have seen at once, in that dreamy smile, those
roughened lips, this absence of mind, how her daughter fared.
But, as usual, Mama had other matters in view than a daughter's
contentment. "I can imagine," she snorted at such a ridiculous
message. Love, indeed! Not much of that commodity had been
passed from her to the family of her late husband.

Kamamalu, Peace Child, so named by her hopeful father, did
not take up the ancient challenge. Today of all days she did not
feel like fighting with Mama. All her life, it seemed, she had been

fighting with Mama. Screams and shouts had replaced cuffs and blows as she grew up, but still the two of them fought, about almost everything. Whatever one said or did, the other was almost certain to be annoyed. They were like two cats who can not endure each other and yet must live in the same house. Papa used to say that they bickered so much because they enjoyed all the noise. Mama claimed that she talked so much only because she wanted Kamamalu to grow up to be a good and sensible woman. And Kamamalu felt that Mama was a tyrant, who *knew* that she was right about everything, who maintained that anyone disagreeing with her was absolutely wrong. "Just like the haoles," as Kamamalu said to others, as well as to Mama, who waxed even more furious at the charge.

Mrs. Hoomalu dismissed those country relatives with a wave of the hand. She didn't want to fight today either. But with this girl, God knows, quarrels developed like thunder clouds in a clear sky. This child is so feckless! She never looks ahead, never plans for tomorrow, never worries about next month or next year. She is enough to drive a worrying mother to distraction! Not only feckless, but stubborn, too. Not that she is stupid. She just refuses to learn to do things right. Like picking up her clothes. Mrs. Hoomalu, who after years of trying had finally taught Kamamalu to put things away just about the time she left home to marry Keolu, inspected her daughter's parlor with distaste. Look at this house! A mess! Clothes flung all over the place. A petticoat here. The muumuu there. The chemise . . . Shia! Almost as if she'd started pulling them off at the front door . . .

"And where's the boy?," the doting grandmother asked, her face softening into something intended to be a smile.

"With Aunty. He was too sleepy to bring with me last night, when I came home. I'm going to get him later this morning, after she comes back to town with Kinau." She did not hide her yawn. "That's why I was sleeping late this morning." Here it is, only eight o'clock, and I wanted to sleep until ten, at least. Oh, Ishi, Ishi . . . He didn't want to sleep . . . Thank goodness I closed the bedroom door. Mama would have a frothing fit if she saw that.

"And have you heard from Keolu?" asked Mama.

"Yes. Last Thursday. A sad letter. Written only three weeks ago. Poor Keolu. That Kalawao must be a terrible place. Even worse than people say it is. He says he's lucky to have a roof over his head, a bed of leaves to lie upon. He thinks that he will die soon. The sickness is spreading fast in him now. Poor Keolu." Tears of pity gathered. She searched through nightgown and robe for a handkerchief and could not find one.

"Again I say," said Mama for at least the hundredth time. "You shouldn't have kept him hidden up here for so long. If you'd sent him to the doctors in Honolulu he might have been saved." Here was just one more proof of witlessness. Both of them! Hiding him here in this house, for so many months, until even Keolu realized that he could find no hope for a cure in that stupid kahuna's useless medicines. "But that's in the past now. What of the future? Again I ask: has he written that will yet?"

"Oh, Mama. How can you make me ask him for such a thing?"

"Easily. Look about you, Malu. Look at this house, at this fine expensive furniture, at this big piece of land. What will happen to them? If he doesn't take care of you before he dies he cannot do so after he's dead. If he doesn't write a will leaving all this to you—and all that land out at Waihee too—then, under these damned new haole laws, everything must be sold, so that his useless brother and sister will get their share of the property. Don't be so stupid! You must take care of yourself and your son. His son. Those other two have enough as it is."

She did not tell Kamamalu—because the girl had no head for business—how that nice young Henry Baldwin had told her that the Waihee land was going to increase in value as Christopher Lewers' sugar plantation enlarged its acreage. And Henry ought to know what he was talking about, in his position as head luna for Chris Lewers. Mrs. Hoomalu, who cherished an innate dislike for missionaries, made a blanket exception for all members of the Baldwin family. And of these she put young Henry at the very top of her exceedingly short list of "decent" haoles.

"I know, Mama, I know. But I cannot ask Keolu to write a will.

To me that is the same thing as asking him to die. And he will think so too. I cannot do it.''

''You are so superstitious. And so stubborn. And he is so stupid. He should have made his will long ago, before he went to Kalawao. If I'd been here at the time, I would have made him write it before I let him step out of the house. Ohh, you two! Children who never grew up. Well, what's past is past. I'll stop again at the Court House and poke Uncle Solomon about it. Maybe he can tell Keolu to do something before it's too late. Before you become a widow, with a small son and no money. And only me to come home to,'' she finished grimly, well aware that both of them would find no joy in that proximity.

Kamamalu wiped away the last of those tears upon the sleeve of her robe. ''Do what you think best, Mama.'' Always, in practical matters, this was how her rebellions ended.

''There's something else I want to talk to you about.''

Kamamalu sat up in alarm. Good Heavens! Has she heard about my Ishi already? ''Yes?,'' she asked, very carefully.

''I need your help, next Sunday afternoon. All day, really, I suppose. I'm giving a supper for some of the new workers at the plantation. The poor things are wandering around through the town like ghosts without places to haunt. No friends. No entertainment. No Iwilei district or Hotel Street, like in Honolulu. Only Ah Siu's whore house—if they can afford his high prices. Our charitable Christians of Wailuku have closed all their doors, since that damn' fool jackass Douglas hurt himself.''

''But how can peop' talk to these newcomers? They speak only Japanese.''

''And how do you know that?''

''Ah, well, ah—Uncle Abraham told us so. Yesterday. He was telling us about them.''

''Well, it's true that they cannot speak Hawaiian or English. How can they, when they've had no chance to learn either? That's all the more reason why they should have the chance to learn from us. The best way to learn, I think, is for each man to meet a family who will take care of him. And teach him our ways. I feel sorry for them.''

Kamamalu raised her head. This was the kind of talk from Mama that she could never let pass. "Sorry?" You never felt sorry for anybody in your life, she meant. Not for Papa. Not for Keolu. Not even for me, is what she meant most of all.

Mama knew very well what she meant. "And how do you know what I feel, inside of me? E? But never mind. In this case, I admit, maybe you're half right. I have a special reason for giving this feast. I've been watching those Japanese, in the fields back of my house. They are good workers. They would make good husbands for some of our Hawaiian girls. Better than those shiftless kanakas they've been marrying since time began. Or than those damn' drunken haole beachcombers from Lahaina."

There she goes again, thought Kamamalu, running the lives of everyone. But Kamamalu was weary of arguing with Mama on this point. Arguing never changed Mama's opinions by one hair's breadth. And besides, Kamamalu decided, I have something better to do next Sunday. "I'm afraid I can't come," she said, as firmly as she had ever spoken to her mother.

"Of course you can. Your favorite aunty and uncle will be coming too. So will all their children. I need them for cooking the food. Those country relatives are good for something once in a while."

Kamamalu almost wailed. How could she meet Ishi next Sunday morning if Aunty and Uncle were not going to be at their house in the valley? Who would take care of her son if his cousins were kept busy in town?

Mama did not notice Kamamalu's distress. "I want you there, too. And I want you to bring some girls. Nine or ten should do. *Not* girls from the Female Seminary, though. Young girls, pretty if possible. *Not* old maids. These Japanese are not old men. They're young and—well, most of them are good-looking. At their worst they are still better to look at than most of the married men in this town. Hawaiian, haole, or Paké."

"But how can I ask nine girls to—"

"Of course you can. Girls haven't changed that much since I was young, I'm sure. They're always interested in looking over the market. Just as men are. Trouble with you is that damned Female Seminary: it's made a hypocrite out of you. You forget what you're put here on earth for.''

Oh no I haven't, thought Kamamalu. "But at the Seminary we learn that there are other important things in life, too," she said primly, knowing full well how such mealy-mouthed talk angered her mother.

"Besides," said Mrs. Hoomalu, overlooking sickening piety in favor of a more important issue, "your sister is going to marry one of them. You will meet him on Sunday."

"Kealia? When did she get back?''

"Oh, she's not here yet. I've sent for her. Told her to come home, where she belongs. She's supposed to arrive sometime during this week. She'll meet him at the party.''

"Mama! You can't do that to her!''

"Why not?''

"What if she's met some one in Honolulu? What if she loves another man?—Or does not love this one you've picked for her?''

"Love. Shia! See what happened to you, when you married for love. First, a husband who was not so lovable after all. Or so loving. Second, a man who was already marked with the leprosy, and you too blind with love to notice it. Kealia is not going to make the same kind of mistake. Neither is Keoni, when his time comes to marry. I'm picking Kealia's husband. And, I must say, I've got a good one for her in this Japanese. If I were ten years younger, I'd keep him for myself.''

"Mama! How can you say such awful things?''

"Why not? Do you young ladies from the Seminary think that mothers and fathers are not made of flesh and blood? Shia! How do you think you were made? I tell you, no matter what people are saying about us, your father and I were happy in our marriage, before that damned haole disease made him so sick. And why were we so happy? Because my mother and father chose him to be my husband. I had nothing to do with it. I did not even know how he looked until we were betrothed. Theirs was the wisdom, mine the reward. Think about that for a while.'' She picked up a lauhala bag, heavy with gifts for her grandson and bundles of food for Kamamalu's kitchen. "Here," she thrust the bag at Malu as she stood up to go.

"So, come early on Sunday. About eight o'clock in the morning. I'll need plenty of help. Fixing the food for the imu. Setting the mats. You can go to church, though. If you must."

Resenting those bribes in the lauhala bag, resenting most determinedly her mother's unrelenting control over her life, even now, four years after she had married Keolu, Kamamalu said coldly, "Mama. I do not want to go. I have something else I'd rather do on Sunday."

"Like what?" The old woman looked directly at this sullen daughter of hers. All her life she'd been pushing away her mother's love. And even now she fought off these evidences of a mother's concern. After so many years of trying, Anna Hoomalu sighed, she didn't know anymore how to act or what to say in this girl's presence, or how to prove to her that she loved this first-born child so much more than she did the other two. Because she was so weak, so helpless ...

All the excuses Malu dared to make were hopelessly weak when raised against this irresistible parent. But she could not submit. "Prayer meeting," she blurted, throwing discretion to the winds.

"You can go," said Mama, sweetly reasonable. "After the party. With the pastor. He will be there, too, to give the blessing. So also will the Mormon elder and the Catholic priest, to say more prayers and ask more blessings. Nothing like a little competition in the market place, for souls as well as for bodies. This is going to be the most goddam Christian party ever given in Wailuku. Those Japanese are going to find friends if I have to kick down every closed door in the town. And just to make sure that it's successful, I'm going to hide a couple of kahunas out in the back, to bless the pig and the poi. *And* the party."

She planted a kiss on the top of Kamamalu's bowed head. "See you on Sunday, if not sooner," she said, as she waddled out of the room, slamming the front door behind her.

Too crushed to weep, Kamamalu sat in her dim parlor, listening to the quiet stealing back into it.

At midday, when Malu went to claim her son, she told her troubles to Aunty Deborah. "How can I get out of going?," she wailed. "I want to be with Ishi."

Aunt Deborah, sister to Kamamalu's dead father, had been putting up with his wife and widow for almost thirty years. "Don't worry. Go to the luau. Ishi will have to be there too, if she's inviting all the Japanese. How many of them are going?"

"I don't know. I didn't even ask. Dozens, for all I know. But why should Ishi go? I'm sure he'd rather be with me."

Aunt Deborah studied this unhappy niece of hers. "You're sure you want him? As a husband, I mean, not just as a bed-mate?"

"Yes! He is wonderful, out of bed as well as in it. And you saw how he was with the children. I *want* to marry him. As soon as—"

"And will that be soon?"

"Auwe for Keolu. He thinks it will be soon."

"Auwe for poor Keolu. But he gave you a beautiful son to re-member him by. What of Kekapu?"

"I will keep him, of course. He is my darling."

"And yet you want to marry Ishi? Does he know about Keolu? Does he know that Kekapu is your son?"

"He knows about Kekapu. That was easy to explain. I'm not sure if he understands about Keolu, although I tried to explain. But—well, after last night—I think that Ishi does not mind that I have had a husband before him."

"You want to be the wife of a common laborer in the fields? You who are the daughter of chiefs?"

"What is wrong with being a laborer in the fields? Do not you and uncle work in your taro patch? And besides, Ishi will not always be a common laborer. He is meant for something better."

"And how do you know that? You cannot even talk with him yet. He is a foreigner, who does not know our ways. And you do not know the ways of his people. How many troubles that alone will cause."

"But he wants to learn our ways. 'Please say to me,' he says all the time, asking me to explain about everything. And he remembers most of what I tell him.''

"You really are smitten with this man.''

"I love him. Since the minute I saw him. A whole week ago. Not as with Keolu. Keolu was fun to be with, and pleasing to look at—until the sores came. And I thought I loved him. Now I see I married him only to get away from Mama. But I was faithful to him, even when he was not faithful to me. Yet he was really only a spoiled boy. He did not pull the love right out of my heart—and out of my body—as Ishi does.''

"You and he made us wonder very much, yesterday. We could not understand how love could take hold of two people who had only just met. Uncle, especially. He's still shaking his head.''

"You were so good, all of you. To help us the way you did.''

"My dear: looking at you, seeing you so happy, we knew that we might better try to tie down the wind from Ukumehame than to stop you from going off with him.''

"Nothing could have stopped me. Not even Mama.''

"We saw that. As Uncle whispered to me, 'Better in the bed at home, no hoi, than here in the grass of Iao.' But just don't let the Christians in this town find out how heathenish we all were yesterday. 'God is love,' they preach. But they do not mean that kind of love.''

"I think even Mama will approve of him, when I tell her about Ishi. In her hard way, she is more full of love than are most of those haoles from America. This feast for the Japanese is an example of how she tries to help the people who are left out. 'The dogs on the bottom,' as she calls them. Whoever they are she tries to take care of them.''

"That's why the rest of us don't get too mad at her. As your father used to say, 'She's all right, as long as she thinks she's having her way.' The trick in handling her, your father and I learned a long time ago, is to let her think so. But then to do whatever we want. Your father was an expert at doing this.''

"And so is Kealia, I think. I know that Keoni is. But I: I never learn. I always try to argue with her. It's a bad habit. And I always lose. So, then, I suppose I must go to help her, like a dutiful daughter."

"That's the only way. And you and Ishi can go to your house afterwards. For prayer meeting," she laughed. "We'll bring Kekapu home with us."

"How can I tell Ishi not to go to your place up in the valley next Sunday? I don't even know where he lives. From what Mama says, I think he's working in the fields near her house. But I don't dare go near there, looking for him. If I do, she'll be sure to see me."

"I'll ask Pilipo. He ought to know something, even if he is so lazy."

"You're very kind to do this for them, Anna," said Saul Bristol, to the finest woman in Wailuku, enthroned in her sagging buggy.

She looked down upon him, standing in the mud of Mill Road. Here is another handsome man, she was thinking, going to waste in this damn' mud patch. Men are such fools, chasing after money, or adventure, or dreams of one sort or another. Instead of staying at home, where they belong, bringing up their families, as they should. "Don't tell the reverends," she said, "but this wild party is being arranged just to get those lonesome Japanese men into the beds of lonesome Hawaiian girls. Have you noticed that this damned town holds twice as many women as men? The damn' fool men have gone off to Honolulu, or to sea, or to the gold fields in California, or some place else. Any place else. Instead of staying at home, making more kanaka babies like themselves, they're running around, wasting their money and their seed in far-away places. No wonder we don't have enough Hawaiians at home any more. Sometimes I think that we are a dying race because we don't do anything to save it. So, if kanakas will not stay at home, to make more kanakas, then I'm all in favor of filling up this place with children half-kanaka and half-Japanese. If they're as good looking as these half-Paké kids who are showing up here now, then I won't worry any more about the future of Maui."

"You remind me of a friend of mine from Honolulu. Hiram Nihoa. You and he—"

"The little runt who owns all those whore houses?"

"Well, that's one of his claims to fame, I guess." Saul never ceased to marvel at the guise in which fame chooses to alight upon the shoulders of the great. Hiram would be remembered for his whore houses, not for his service to five Kamehameha kings, his labors for the nation, or for his epic *History of the Reign of Kamehameha IV,* if ever he finished it. And, perhaps, in about another eighty-nine years or so, for his *Account of a Journey around Oahu for the King,* locked up now, at Saul's own insistence, in a strong box bound with chains and seals.

"Can't say that I approve of his business," Anna Hoomalu said, to Saul's amazement. "Not that I've got anything against whores, mind you. Sometimes I wish I'd been one myself. But because I think that all those men should be turned loose upon the women in a town, not herded into those damned 'hotels' stuck away in one corner of it. All that screwing makes men like Hiram Nihoa rich, but it doesn't do anything to populate the country."

"You've got a point there. I hadn't thought of it in that way."

"Of course I've got a point. I've always got a point, whatever I do. And, I don't mind telling you, the chief point to this party next Sunday is to get that man Ishi into my daughter's—well, let's say bed. When I think of the good-looking kids those two can make, I am ready to burst with impatience to hold them in my arms.—The kids, I mean.—At least a dozen of them. How's that for being a virtuous mother?"

"The world needs more mothers like you. And less virtue of the sort that missionaries preach. But I thought your daughter was married?"

"The one up there on the hill? That's the first daughter. Ishi's for the second one. Speaking of virtue, how is that drunken pig? I ask out of wicked curiosity, not charity."

Sometimes her changes of subject were confusing to the uninitiate. This one Saul took in stride. "He's mending well enough, the doctor tells me. Killing the pain with whiskey. But he'll not be able to travel for another month or so."

"Too bad he didn't break his damn' neck. You be careful of him, Saul. He's no good. Who's taking care of him?"

"His Chinese cook. A man accustomed to abuse."

"What about that Irish girl who's staying with him, taking his abuse?"

"She left. The day after he got hurt. Glad to get away, I guess."

"Why don't you and Ululani come too?" Mrs. Hoomalu headed off on a subject more to her liking.

"You tempt me to break my rule, Anna. But we cannot. She's nearing her time, and won't be able to ride so far from home. And I want to be with her and the children for as long as possible, when I go up to Makawao on Saturday."

"O.K., O.K. It's funny, though."

"What is?"

"You being so virtuous. You have the look of a shark, as we Hawaiians say. And the chastity of a Catholic priest. Kia! Such a waste! Growing sugarcane is all well and good. But you should plant kids, too. All over the place. Not only in Makawao, but right here in Wailuku, too. On week nights."

Before Saul could think of an answer to that she yelled at her horse and started off. Over her shoulder she shouted, "Don't forget to tell the Japanese."

The Eight Melancholy Monks of Gohongi rejoiced to learn of Mrs. Hoomalu's kindness. They were especially pleased when Ah Siu said that he himself would take them to the feast, inasmuch as he too was going to be a guest. With him to show them how to behave they felt less worried about attending this great event in the foreign style. They did not really know what to expect. Some hoped for the same conclusion that Mrs. Hoomalu had in mind, although one more immediate: they envisioned her party as being something like a Dosojin Festival at home, or a Bon Odori, during which young men and women made offerings to the gods of fertility in the sincerest possible manner.

Chikahei especially could hardly contain himself at the thought of the prodigious sacrifices he was willing to make, most sincerely, upon the altars of fertile friendship. Ishi said little, knowing that he would not be present for the occasion. Bankichi, his wall-eyes bigger than ever, declared he would not go, because he preferred not to leave his vegetables. But soon he was persuaded to change his mind by Ah Siu's hints that the mere sight of Mrs. Hoomalu's extensive kitchen gardens would more than repay him for the effort of attending. All agreed that, for the sake of amity and good will, they would even try to eat poi, about which they'd heard from Koi and Ishi. But they drew the line at eating dog, despite Dembei's jeers that, in all likelihood, they would never know what they were being served by the waitresses at Mrs. Hoomalu's inn.

At times like this Ishi would feel a warm affection for his companions. By now they were much more than mere strangers who, brought together by chance, had crossed an ocean and shared the same hardships. Now they were almost like brothers: after living and working together for these four months, each knew the others' strengths and weaknesses, almost their every thought and dream. And, as must always happen if people are to live in harmony, they took care not to grate too much upon each other's sensibilities. Good manners, taught since childhood, loyalty and good humor, learned since boyhood, stopped quarrels before they could well begin and guided opposing opinions along cheerful courses. Despite Chikahei's noisy grievances (which each one recognized as voicings of his own complaints), despite Dembei's deep-voiced gloom (which some realized were expressions of the universal worries of mankind), the Gohongijin were happy with the life they led in Wailuku of Maui—at least for the present.

"We are fortunate men for having come to this place," Heizaemon had said one evening, in response to some remark that Tametsugu made. Ishi, already lying in his bed space, listened for Tametsugu's answer.

Eizo, the printer from Edo, was the one who replied. "At first I did not think so. But now, when my body no longer objects to working so hard, I am inclined to agree with you."

"And what of you others?," Heizaemon asked. Six said that now they wished to stay in Hawaii for the rest of their days. Four men still thought that they would go home to Nippon when their term of service ended.

"And you six," said Tametsugu, one of those who would go home. "Why do you want to stay?"

Dembei was the first to answer. "Because now as never before I have some hope."

Ishi was surprised to hear this one of all possible words come from Dembei's mind. He himself had been about to say that he wanted to stay in this land because he found freedom here. Yet upon reflection he saw that these two were but different faces upon the same precious jewel that some men call happiness, others contentment.

"Hope," said Tametsugu with a shrug. "What good is that? You can not eat it. You can not spend it."

"Hope?" asked Akemi. "Hope for what?"

"You are right," Dembei replied to Tametsugu. "Hope cannot be spent at the store or at the whore house. Nor can it be eaten. It is a funny thing. Yet, without it, a man can be eaten away from within. Therefore, I say that it is an important thing. It can only be stored within. To comfort a sorrowing heart. To repair a cracked mind."

"What are you talking about?" cried Chikahei, a man never without hope, and therefore a man with a very sound mind. "I don't understand—"

Dembei laughed. Tonight he chose not to be the Abbot of Gohongi. "I mean, really, that here in this country I am given a second chance to become the kind of man I want to be. At home in Meguro I missed my first chance. Without quite knowing how it happened, I was a failure, sinking to the bottom of the pit. And in Nippon, as you know, when a man starts to sink he does not usually have a chance to rise."

They thought for a moment about Dembei's charge. Ishi sat up in his bed, the better to see their faces.

"Here," said Dembei, "there is no pit." He moved both hands parallel to the floor. "Only the level land. And lots of space in it."

"And," Koi slapped his knee, winking at Ishi, "no cormorants!" The others stared at him, wondering what cormorants had to do with hope.

Ishi broke in, before the cormorants swallowed them whole. "Makino-san said very much the same thing as Dembei. He believed that many of us would—" He stopped, mouth open in surprise, as he recalled a conversation upon an evening before ever he saw Makino Tomosaburo. "Ho! Not only Makino-san. Hamada Hikizo-san, too, thought that some of us would be glad for this second chance."

"What?" cried Koi. "He actually spouted such priestly talk?"

"Yes. Into my own big ears."

"Well!" Dembei set his jaw in a grimace like Hamada's, curved his fingers in the manner of the Lizard Man. "If, as people say, the tortures of Hell are graded according to the size of a man's fortune, his kind thought for us should be counted to his credit, don't you think?"

"What?" Chikahei shook a fist a Dembei. "You want to get him out of Hell sooner than he deserves?"

"If you hate anyone," gentle Heizaemon reminded them of another wise saying, "let him live.—In Nippon."

"If some good can be found even in a crook like Hamada," said Eizo, very seriously, "then there's hope for a wily seducer like you, Chikahei-san."

While Chikahei exulted in the compliment Eizo thought his way into a profound observation. "Did you ever stop to think how the Lord Buddha chooses some very unlikely folk to be the agents of his will? Imagine! Hamada-san being the one to turn my wheel in this direction ... "

"Please instruct me," Chikahei began reverently, bowing to the Abbot of Gohongi. "Why would the Lord Buddha arrange for an eleven-wheeled carriage to be built in Wailuku of Maui, using parts made in Nippon?"

"Let us commit an act of piety," suggested Ishi, "and slit this doubter's tongue."

"Nah, nah," warned Koi. "Then he'd talk twice as much."

Dembei blew out the lamp, the signal for sending them to their beds. But for a long time some of them lay awake, tittering over their fancies about that impossible vehicle of Chikahei's imagining.

"And ten male parts at that," mourned Tametsugu, darker than the dark.

"Brace up! Take hope, take hope!," said Chikahei brightly. "I am seeing a vision. Female wheels are rolling in our direction ... Soon, very soon, we shall meet ... "

Through Ah Siu, by way of Pilipo, Ishi received Aunt Deborah's message that she and her family would meet him at the feast on Sunday, not at their house in the valley. Fortunately for Ishi's peace Ah Siu delivered this communication to him alone, not to all the Japanese at once. In private matters, as befits a whoremaster, Ah Siu displayed a gentleman's delicacy.

Ishi understood at once that the message meant that his beloved, too, had been invited to the party, undoubtedly to be his companion. Kia! He shook his head admiringly. This Mrs. Hoomalu is remarkable. She must know everything that happens in this village of Wailuku.

After that he was just as eager as his fellows to go to her party.

Yet, as always, in the midst of happiness trouble did not fail to push its way in. The question of Kamamalu's husband bothered Ishi, like a grain of dust caught beneath an eyelid—or a crack in a lip made for kissing. He could accept her son without difficulty: the boy was a merry child, almost two years old, full of smiles and play. He and Ishi became good friends immediately. But the boy's father was a problem not so easily resolved, about whom

Ishi remained very much in doubt. Kamamalu had tried to tell him about the absent man, but her explanation so confused him that it might better have been left unsaid.

The man was not dead, but neither did he live on Maui. Apparently he had gone away, but she did not know when he would return. Remembering Mr. Bristol and his gray-eyed son, Ishi wondered if the custom of this country required husbands of great rank to live apart from their families, just as in Nippon the shoguns had forced daimyo and other important warriors to live apart from their families for long periods of time. In that case, the distressed lover worried (because he wanted to be an honorable man as well as Kamamalu's registered mate), am I to be denied my woman just when I have found her at last?

—Kannon-sama, he prayed, once again I turn to you for help. Benten-sama, he addressed the one who took good care of lovers whether or not they were honorable, I beg you to come to my aid . . .

Ah Siu took his duties seriously. After consulting with Mr. Bristol he announced that proper dress for the occasion would include—no, not kimono, tabi, and geta as Eizo and Chikahei had predicted—but clean work shirts, work trousers, stockings, and shoes. The shirt was to be worn "haole style, not Paké style"—that is to say, with shirt tails tucked inside the trousers. And shoe laces, he said firmly, must be tied. Neck cloths posed some problem to the consultants, until Ah Siu suggested they wear clean bandanas, just as cowboys do when they ride into town.

No one needed to tell the Gohongijin that their faces must be shaven and their bodies freshly bathed. Most of that memorable Sunday was given over to such washing and grooming as those young men could not have received since their mothers last attended to them. Once clean, some of them scarcely moved about Gohongi, for fear that they would sweat too much before the party began. Stiff as a shogun's generals in conference before a battle, knees wide apart, hands resting upon thighs, they perched upon the edge of the sleeping platform, waiting for Ah Siu to summon them.

"Too bad we cannot be carried in palanquins," said Eizo.

"But why do you worry about honest sweat?" asked Chikahei. "The smell of sweat can be very exciting ... "

"Sometimes. Not always," advised Bankichi, who knew about farm girls' unbathed bodies and planting rites.

"I wish to be clean," said gleaming Akemi, thinking of that maiden in the church. She could not possibly be so gross as to sweat.

"Yossh! That's enough," growled Dembei. "You're like a bunch of whores in a Yoshiwara cage. Chattering away about nonsense. We're going there to eat, not to screw. I will bet you that we'll return here tonight as unbedded as we leave. You watch."

"Nasakenai," whined Chikahei. "How terrible! If we do, I shall not live through the night."

"There are ways to relieve that pressure upon the dike," cried Bankichi.

"There are?," asked Chikahei innocently.

"Yeah," Dembei seized this chance. "Hang by your tail from a tree. Then you will see how lust makes monkeys of us all."

"But—" Chikahei, still seated with knees apart, flung out his arms, stiffened his fingers, curled his lips most fiercely, and, glaring like a triumphing hero, made a mie that would have won him acclaim in Edo's foremost kabukiza. While his enchanted companions watched this superlative performance, he moved his head proudly from side to side, as, in a hero's loud voice, he informed the world, "*my* lust has no bottom!"

CHAPTER 22
THE JOINING

According to the plan, at four o'clock on that special Sunday afternoon Ah Siu would come from his house in Wailuku to the corner of Market Street and Mill Road. Standing at that vantage, he would wave his white handkerchief in the direction of Gohongi across the gulch. When, as he said, "You Japanee look-see-nana me, you come wikiwiki chop-chop fas'."

As the appointed hour approached Ishi volunteered to be the lookout for his companions, so carefully refraining from sweating. He was less concerned about perspiring a bit than wishing to gain a rare moment of privacy. Unlike most Nipponjin, Ishi did not mind being alone at times; and of late, he noticed, the chance to be alone with his thoughts was especially welcome. He attributed this form of contemplation not to boredom with his fellows, because in truth they were never boring, but to an increase in his need for peace and quiet, when he could think more clearly about the events that were shaping his life.

Dressed in clean clothes, faded from so many bleachings in Maui's bright sunlight, he came out from the barrack into the yard. He bowed to the male-stone Gohongi's men had erected on the day of O-Bon, invoking Yo's blessing. Anyone else seeing Ishi that day would have thought that the request was not necessary: it was obvious, just to look at him, that Yo had been favoring Ishi since before he was conceived. Even so, he never learned the complacency of such good-looking men as Daigoro, or the prideful preening of others such as Chikahei. Because of this modesty, no doubt, Ishi gained higher regard from both gods and people, for—as is well known—the gods are ever pleased by humility, and a humble man's friends are instructed by his virtue.

Ishi sauntered over to a boulder at the brink of the gulch. His smooth skin, darkened by Maui's sunshine, the long glossy black hair worn like a helmet shaped to his head, made him seem more Hawaiian than Japanese. Had he walked past his companions among Lord Okubo's footmen in Edo, they would not have recognized him. Only his eyes—narrower, longer, more hooded than the big round orbs with which Hawaiians are endowed—would have told the perceptive observer that he was not a man of Hawaii. The full lips, happily healed by this time, were neither exclusively Hawaiian nor distinctively Japanese. They were merely, as everyone knows, the mark of a passionate man.

He sat upon the warm boulder, cleaning and trimming his fingernails with the English pocket knife brought from Yokohama. Occasionally he glanced toward the corner where Ah Siu was expected, or toward the long slope of West Maui falling away to the central plain and the sea. When he finished with the knife he put it into his trousers pocket, to rest in its usual place against his right thigh. On the left side, in the position of honor, lay his greatest treasure, the stone of Kannon. These two things: they were like the two men in himself, the new and the old, the changing and the changeless, the Hawaiian and the Japanese.

Sitting upon the great boulder, like a king upon his throne, he gazed out over the grand sweep of Maui, from the sundered mountain at his right to the mighty House of the Sun far to the left. He was no longer afraid of Taiyo no Ie: now, after many weeks of seeing it daily, in all its moods, he looked upon it with reverence and awe, but not in fear. Why this should be so he had not yet determined. Almost it seemed as if the great mountain had been placated, by some sacrifice offered up to it of which he remained in ignorance. But he would learn in time, if the gods intended for him to know. For the present he was content to wait, content to know that the long valley of the sundered mountain had given him his happiness.

The plain joining the two parts of Maui shimmered in the heat. Wind-devils of red or yellow dust whirled like frenzied guardians around Kahului. In the distance, toward Makena and Kihei, mirages dotted the desert with lakes of quicksilver. They were as transient as anything Ishi's eyes had ever seen, as false as anything his mind could imagine. Yet they fascinated him because they were illusions that appeared to be real. They were like dreams about to come true, hopes soon to be fulfilled. They were intimations that no boundary lies between this world and another, hints that perhaps sometime, somewhere, a chosen man could enter one of them and, in doing so, would step from this world into that other. Ishi, poet enough to think of the possibility, was realist enough to shrink from the thought of being that chosen man. "This world," he said to himself and to the listening gods, "is good enough for me."

This good world of Maui lying spread out before him, he saw, was not a place of beauty. And yet neither was it a place of ugliness. It was stark and raw. It was brutal and untamed. And, just as Nakamura-san had told him, it was empty. For that reason, he understood, it was unfinished. In all that expanse he saw not a single human being, not a single bird or beast. Such emptiness, beyond his comprehension in crowded Nippon, astonished him even now, when he lived upon its very shore.

And yet he knew that it was not as empty as it appeared to be. Even in that seeming desert certain small plants grew, some tiny animals crept. And wherever on Maui's hard body water lingered life could be found in abundance. Along the banks of the river flowing past his feet, in the high-walled valley from which it came, many kinds of trees, ferns, and grasses thrived. Around the edges of the swamp near Kahului, and on the northern shoulder of Haleakala, where clouds gathered and dropped their rain, the green of life sprang up, to show that the earth beneath is good.

Water, the gift of the gods, is the giver of life to earth. Wherever it weds the earth, there does the land bloom and yield up its bounty. And when this dry empty plain is given the boon of water, it will be empty no longer.

The labor of many men will be needed to bring water to this thirsting plain. This river at his feet could be the conduit for that bounty from those great gods who dwelled up there, at the heart of the sacred valley.

The labor of many men, for many months ... Ishi knew that he and his fellows were going to be among the laborers who would dig the ditches that would transform this land. Pilipo had told them about Mr. Bristol's plans for the great ditch that would bring the water of life from Iao Valley.

Ishi, looking toward his future, found that it too was good. His life, until recently little more than a desert of despairing, was already being transformed, by the kindness of the generous gods.

He did not ask for much. He who had had nothing would be content with very little. Yet, to his surprise, he saw that what little he had asked for was being given. And with that little he was content. For what man, if he is wise, will demand more than the gods wish to give him at any one time? Theirs is the mercy, his the reward.

He drew from the pocket at his left side the stone of Kannon. It lay in his hand like the dark sky of night, its little crystals glowing like stars.

"Kannon-sama," he addressed the presence in the stone, the goddess in the heavens beyond, "I thank you for your kindness to me. Please keep me in your favor."

Responding to Ah Siu's summons, the residents of Gohongi walked in single file along the same path they took twice each day, on the way to and from work. On those ordinary occasions they found much to talk about; but on this day they went in silence, feeling nervous because they did not know what awaited them at the inn of Mrs. Hoomalu.

Aiko went last in the line. Of the eleven Nipponjin only she wore Japanese clothing: her best kimono, of plain cotton in narrow stripes of brown, blue, and black, with a big obi of dark brown brocade embroidered in yellow and red. Koi had helped to dress her hair in something that resembled the marumage style worn by married women at home. Without the thick oil to stiffen it, the many combs and ties to hold it up, they were not very successful, but, as she was the first to say, "Who is to know the difference?" And Koi advised her not to put on the white tabi and straw slippers until they were close to Mrs. Hoomalu's ryokan, lest they be spattered with Wailuku's mud.

Ah Siu was a wonder to behold: resplendent in a haole businessman's garb, from tall silk hat and frock coat to shining high-
topped shoes, he was even better proof than Sentaro of Honolulu
had been that a plantation laborer could gain wealth and respect.
In Ah Siu they saw themselves, a few years in the future: prosperous, sober, and stolid, secure and respected in this world because
they worked hard and spent their money wisely, on worthwhile
things. None of them realized as yet that Ah Siu's wealth, if not
his station in the community, came from other enterprises, not
from wages paid by Wailuku's sugar plantation.

"Maikai, maikai," Ah Siu sang in approval, beaming like a living Buddha as they gathered around him. They walked beside
him along empty Market Street, feeling confident in his company. Pilipo met them at the corner of Main Street, in accordance
with Mr. Bristol's suggestion and with Ah Siu's cheerful concur-
rence. While Aiko washed the mud from her feet with water
dipped from a horse trough, her nervous companions straightened bandanas, ran bamboo combs (made by Heizaemon)
through their long locks, tightened fundoshi in preparation for
the ordeal ahead.

At last, when Aiko's feet were clad in those snow-white tabi, the
sugarcane samurai marched to their fate, like true warriors.

As ahaaina go, Mrs. Hoomalu's was a modest affair. Only thirty guests were invited. This meant that, with friends, relatives,
and friends of relatives who came to help, only sixty people would
be present at the feast. Five hundred of Wailuku's other residents looked on from outside the stone wall marking the front of
Mrs. Hoomalu's broad yard. They came to see not the feast itself,
for that was nothing new to them, but to inspect the guests who
were bid to the festivities.

Earlier in the week horses, cows, and goats had been allowed to
crop the weeds under the spreading koa trees in the front part of
the great enclosure. In the shade of these fine trees, standing
upon lauhala mats laid over the short grass, Mrs. Hoomalu and
her children greeted the guests as they arrived.

The hostess looked almost womanly, with her graying hair arranged in a soft pompadour rather than in the severe bun she usually affected. She wore a muumuu made of black calico, with a high neck and full sleeves. The dress rather successfully covered the rolls of fat she had added to a body that once upon a time was as slender as Kamamalu's. A lei of red and yellow feathers rested upon her full bosom. Her feet were bare. Her daughters knew better than to try to correct Mama upon that point of behavior.

They stood behind her, being only accessories to Mama, so to speak, on this occasion as on all others. Kamamalu wore a holoku of pale green calico, the color of young leaves, the color of new life, and a lei made of black and yellow feathers close about her throat. Her long black hair, parted in the middle, fell in soft masses over the ears and was gathered in a coil at the nape of the neck. Tall and slender, she was the most beautiful woman at the party, as everyone acknowledged. Yet every female pitied her, and every man avoided her, because she was so misfortuned. The sickness of Keolu was too fresh in their minds. No man wished to draw it upon himself, by offering to take Keolu's place. And the women thought that now, for Kamamalu, all happiness must be ended. For, with a husband like Keolu in her past, what man would be so foolish as to want to take his place? Leprosy, the people of Hawaii were being told, most falsely, by some foolish physicians in their chambers and by frothing preachers from their pulpits, "is the punishment for sin. It is the fourth and last stage of loathsome syphilis, the Great Destroyer." And, in this country of aloha, no one needed to be told by what sinful behavior the first stage of syphilis might be acquired. Not that anyone accused Kamamalu of such wantonness. No, that blame they heaped upon the charming and profligate Keolu. Yet when they looked at Kamamalu they could not help but wonder how soon the evidence of his punishment would begin to show upon her lovely body.

While they pitied Kamamalu, and shunned her, the men in their thoughts circled about the flame of Kealia. Where Kamamalu was beautiful and gentle, Kealia was handsome and bold. She had her mother's strong features and much of her hardness of manner. Where Kamamalu gave, Kealia took. They were like Hiiaka and Pele, in the legend of old. At the age of twenty Kealia had all the vitality of a young woman untouched by sorrow, because she had not yet loved anyone other than herself. As though flaunting her youth and freedom, she wore a close-fitting holoku of red silk and, for jewelry, a white cameo hung upon a chain of gold. Her hair was done in the style recently brought home to Hawaii by the Dowager Queen Emma after her visit with Eugénie, the Empress of the French. Kealia, fresh from the elegant soirées and ballrooms of Honolulu, bedazzled everyone in Wailuku who was fortunate enough to see her.

Well aware of her power over men, she did nothing to tame it or to gratify them. She was like that fickle goddess Pele whose color she wore: unpredictable, cruel, and often violent, she disdained men, using them only to conquer them. Barefoot also, in a clever acceptance of Mama's style, and at the same time as a sign of contempt for the country people of Wailuku, Kealia looked about at all these bores and bumpkins, and her spirit yawned. She resolved to escape from Mama's clutches and Maui's wastes as soon as she possibly could.

Behind the females of his family stood Keoni, not yet counting for anything because everybody thought a boy of fifteen was much too young to matter. Bored, petulant, handsome, and spoiled, he slouched about, wishing he could get away from this mob of aged imbeciles. He could find much better entertainment in the house next door, where—anytime he cared to tap upon her wall—the young widow Halawa was delighted to admit him to her kitchen and her bed.

Ah Siu and Pilipo led the eleven guests of honor along Waiale Road, lined by crowds of people kept in order by vigilant Constable Kalei. The policeman greeted Ishi like an old friend, not holding against him his failure to be the worst criminal ever imprisoned in Wailuku jail. The villagers gaped at Aiko's kimono, obi, and tabi, the first they'd ever seen. Opinions ranged from "funny kind!" to "how beautiful!" but everyone agreed that this was one fancy foreign fashion the sensible women of Maui were not likely to adopt.

The guests of honor looked with interest upon the residents of Wailuku. "Well," grumbled Dembei, "and where were they, when we went in search of them?"

"Aroha! Aroha!," Chikahei, Tametsugu, and Eizo called happily to every pretty woman they saw, "Aroha gozaimasu."

"Monkeys!," cried Dembei, embarrassed by such antics, yet amused as well.

"Keep smiling!" Chikahei implored his companions. "Look your best! Our many nights depend upon this single day."

"Funny," observed gardener Bankichi, his eyes swerving so furiously that one seemed to be looking at Iao, the other at Haleakala. "Some women are shaped like sweet potatoes, others like daikons. I guess I like best the ones that look like—"

"Pumpkins!," cried Heizaemon, setting everyone to laughing.

"You would think that they have never seen new people before this time," said Aiko primly, trying not to step upon her husband's heels.

The valorous troop entered Mrs. Hoomalu's yard. For a few moments they were enveloped by silence and shade, while they walked along the carriage drive.

"Hey!," said Chikahei, explaining the obvious. "This is not an inn! This is the other side of her house . . . "

This is a woman of power, thought every one, as Ah Siu and Pilipo led them to the place where the kind lady awaited them. This is indeed a woman of power, each one said to himself when he saw her, standing there, like a daimyo's wife surrounded by her court.

Ah Siu presented them. He had lived in this strange land long enough to know that here, at least on public occasions, women took precedence over men. He began with Aiko and her husband, whom he introduced as "Meesus and Meeseetah Koi."

While Ah Siu performed his duties, Ishi and Kamamalu gazed lovingly across the narrow space that separated them. Ishi grew soft within at the sight of his beautiful woman. And she, of course, thought him the most handsome male she'd ever seen, by far the most splendid man in all of Maui.

Mrs. Hoomalu's certitude was jarred for a moment. No one had ever told her that these Japanese had brought their women with them. My goodness! she muttered, what if Ishi already has a wife? A quick glance along the line, an imperious question shot at Ah Siu, restored her composure. "Oney one Japanee wahine," Ah Siu assured her, as he took Koi and Aiko by the wrist, intending to tug them away.

"Isn't she pretty," Anna Hoomalu said flatly, much as she might have said "the sky is blue." Her daughters were much more interested in Aiko than she cared to be. Mama thought her unwomanly, a thing apparently without breasts, body, or legs beneath that lounging robe. Kamamalu examined her as a specimen of all the women in Japan who must have slept with Ishi, to teach him all those tricks that he knew so well. And yet she could not believe that this modest little thing, bowing so formally before Mama, could be a woman of fire and passion such as she was herself. Kealia studied the kimono, the obi, the hair dress, scarcely seeing Aiko's delicate face or the stupid husband standing open-mouthed beside her. "My, what beautiful brocade!," Kealia exclaimed, wondering how she could lay her hands upon such a piece of fine stuff.

As he stared at this gorgeous creature in red Koi forgot Aiko, Mrs. Hoomalu, Maui, everything else. Not once, since that day long ago in the Yoshiwara, had he thought of the oiran who had so impressed him with her beauty. But now, in the blaze of Kealia's presence, his old yearning burst into flame. Maa, he cried to himself, as lust raced through his veins. This oiran: why should I not have her, before my life is ended?

After the thrill of seeing her man had quieted a little, Kamamalu found the wit to notice that he stood last in the line of Japanese. Only nine men, she counted, not including that first married one. Then who is the one Mama has chosen for Kealia? She looked at each Japanese in the line, from one impassive face to the next, from one slight body to the other. And then she saw that, among the nine, only one could possibly be worthy of Mama's choice. Reeling with the shock, she moaned, raised a hand to her breast. Ishi, only a few feet away, saw the gesture but did not hear the cry of pain. He thought that she lifted her hand for him.

The line moved faster after Ah Siu pushed Mrs. and Mr. Koi into Pilipo's care. Pilipo left them with his wife and returned to catch the next man as he fell from Ah Siu's grasp. Mrs. Hoomalu, saying "Aloha," shook each man's hand cordially as he, bowing stiffly, gave his name. She did not bother to introduce them to her daughters. These little men did not matter: they were only excuses for drawing that one man here, bringing him within her reach.

Having received strict instructions from his Aunty Anna, Pilipo knew exactly what to do with eight of these bachelors. During his planning the week before, he had indulged himself in some splendidly entertaining pairings: of short and bow-legged Dembei with tall and scrawny Kaulana, for example; or wall-eyed Bankichi with cross-eyed Makalei from Waihee. But here, in Aunty's very presence, he restrained himself, out of wisest cowardice, and matched the men as best he could with girls who might be interested in them. Pilipo had all the finest instincts of a good match-maker. And, as time would tell, he was remarkably successful in the pairings he arranged on that important day.

Only once did he make what might have been a serious mistake. This happened when he thrust young Akemi at little Puana Kuahiwi. Akemi did not even see poor smirking Puana. He walked right past her, seeing only the girl from the church whom he had chosen at first sight to be his mate. Kaala saw Akemi and glided forward to meet him. Pilipo, aware that some matchings are made in heaven, shrugged and left them, happy—if speechless—with each other.

The puzzle that Pilipo could not solve concerned Ishi, the best man in the lot, and the one for whom he could easily have found a dozen eager women. Aunty had said, "Leave him for me. I'll take care of him." And Pilipo, even in his fantasies, dared not dwell too long upon the possible meanings to that staking of a claim.

Ishi stood at last before his hostess. He bowed. She took his hand in both of hers, smiling broadly at this most favored man. "Ah, Mr. Ishi. Aloha. I am happy to see you." Pilipo hurried to her side, to be present at the judgment of Ishi. Many people watched, to see why Anna Hoomalu should be so cordial to this special one.

Ishi responded with a big smile of his own. He did not fear this woman of power, who had rescued him from prison and from death. Why should he not be easy in her presence, and thankful for her hospitality?

Mrs. Hoomalu rejoiced at the rightness of her choice. "Come," she purred, drawing him toward Kealia, "I want you to meet my daughter."

Kamamalu thought that she must die now, of grief, right here, in front of everyone. Aunty Deborah pushed her. "Go get him! Now!"

Kealia, not having been informed about Mama's plans for her, hardly noticed Ishi. To her he was just the last in the line of Japanese laborers in whom, for some whim of her own, Mama chose to take such great interest. Kealia waited to be released from this dutiful attendance at Mama's rear. She wanted to go and gossip with old acquaintances, standing over there by the eating-mats.

Ishi said, in almost perfect Hawaiian, "Aroha to you, Mrs. Hoomaru. How are you this afternoon?"

"You are learning our language!," she exclaimed, the smile becoming an expression of surprise and joy. "Very good! And who is your teacher?"

Ishi's stock of social exchanges in Hawaiian having been exhausted, he looked helplessly from her to Kamamalu just beyond.

Kamamalu swept in. She took hold of Ishi's other hand and drew him toward her. "I am, Mama. He is mine. I saw him first. Two weeks ago." Behind Mama's back Aunty Deborah folded hands upon her belly, looking wonderfully satisfied.

Mrs. Hoomalu glared down at this daughter, as if to demolish her with a blast of rage. Kamamalu, head up, glared right back, ready to fight for her man if she must. The screaming, the biting, the pulling of hair: she and Kealia had fought often enough over lesser things. Now she would do it again, to win the biggest prize they would ever contend for.

Ishi looked from one to the other, not understanding the meaning of this tugging.

Kealia began to laugh at the sight of this helpless man about to be torn limb from limb by those two predatory females.

With the speed of lightning Anna Hoomalu's mind considered all the possible interpretations to Kamamalu's declaration, and rejected all except the right one.

"Well! I'll be damned!," she cried. "I didn't think you had it in you." She too began to laugh. "Most sensible thing you've ever done." She gave Ishi's hand into Malu's keeping. "Take him, my dear. With my blessing."

She gripped Ishi by the shoulder. "Welcome to the family, my boy," she said. Then, as the tears of happiness began to gather, she pushed the lovers away.

As Kamamalu led her man aside, Ishi whispered, "Say to me, prease: Mrs. Hoomaru you know?"

Kamalu wanted to throw her arms about him, to kiss him, to shout with triumph now that she had won this prize. But she dared not do so in front of all those watching people, who remembered that she was still the wife of Keolu. So she pressed his hand, the while she smiled like a princess upon her mother's subjects, and said, in Japanese words learned from him, "Anata . . . Ato de . . . "

Ishi, the beloved husband so addressed, understood that he must wait until later for an answer to his question. But Aiko, who overheard this verbal caressing, looked in surprise at the beautiful woman who had done it so well. Where had she learned to speak Nippongo, Aiko wondered. And who had been her teacher? She tugged at Koi's sleeve, to put her question to him. Reluctantly giving his attention to matters so ordinary, instead of to that fiery attraction across the yard, he listened to Aiko's rapid questioning, turned to watch Ishi being dragged off to her lair by that possessive woman. So that's the one, he exclaimed to himself, deciding in the instant that he did not like her. "Ato de," he muttered to poor Aiko, no wiser than before.

Among all the guests only lazy, sleepy-eyed Pilipo saw the whole puzzle falling neatly into place. Eia mai, he smiled benignly, a dusky Cupid happy to know that in this pairing, too, he had a helping hand. But for once in his life he kept his big mouth shut, his gossipy tongue in its cave. Affection for Cousin Malu, not fear of Aunty Anna, made him not only kind but wise.

Anna Hoomalu, dabbing at those unwonted tears with a crumpled handkerchief, allowed herself a moment of motherly satisfaction over so unexpectedly happy an ending to a tale that she had feared was going to be unrelievedly sad. This Kamamalu, she clucked. Imagine! . . .

Now other matters, lesser worries, demanded her attention. Planning for Kamamalu and Ishi would have to wait until later. At least until this party had come to its blessed end.

"Everything is ready to serve?," she asked Deborah, still gazing fondly at her favorite niece and that captured lover.

"All ready, says Abraham. Whenever you say. But where are the haoles? They haven't come yet."

"They're not coming," said Anna, effacing them from this world with a swipe of her hand.

"What? None at all?"

"None."

"Auwe nohoi e!—How can they be so rude?"

"Easily. That is a haole habit. I invited eleven of them, five husbands, five wives, and one priest. When I spoke to them all told me they would be delighted to come. But since that day everyone of them has sent me a polite little note, or a message mumbled by a child. All regretting that they cannot be here today. Shia! The damned liars! The only one who tells me the truth

is that little priest. He has to go to a funeral in Waihee. I've
checked on that. Old Mrs. Kaaiakamanu died last night."

"Auwe for Tutu Kaaiakamanu. But why should the haoles
change their minds?"

"Can you not guess?"

"Yes, I can guess."

"My friends tell me," Anna burst out, unwilling to settle for
mere guesses, "that some of those haole women, twittering like
birds in the trees, have said, 'Why should we go? We have nothing in common with those ignorant laborers.' "

"Nothing in common? What do they mean?"

"That's what I ask. They don't mind their husbands or their
friends putting Hawaiians, Chinese, Japanese to work for them in
their damned sugarcane fields. Their husbands don't mind selling us things in their money-making stores."

"Or fooling around with some of our girls. But never marrying
them, of course."

"But when I invite them to meet with us as friends, they suddenly discover that they have 'nothing in common' with the workers. Shit! I should have known better. I shouldn't have been so
stupid."

"You are not the stupid one, Anna. They are the ones who do
not think. And they are blind as well. One of these days they will
learn that the first shall be last, on earth as in heaven, and the
last shall be sitting on the top. They tell us this in their churches,
but they don't remember it in their homes."

"They also are the ones who say that charity begins at home,"
said Anna, denying them access to her charity and her home, for
ever and a day. "Come, my dear. Let us take care of our friends."

"Who will say the blessing?" asked Deborah, as the two enormous sisters-in-law moved toward the guests as gracefully as
clouds drifting with a breeze. "You want Abraham to come?"

"I'll do it. I'll think of something."

In response to urgings from Kamamalu and Kealia the guests
were gathering around the eating-mats. These, covered with
green leaves, ferns, flowers, foods, and fruits of many kinds,

resembled a bountiful land as seen from a high hill. The late afternoon light, subdued by clouds hovering in the west, by the crowns of the koa trees overhead, softened the hard lines of the earth and all things on it, hid the blemishes in people, the wrinkles in their clothes. The guests, standing in pairs or in small groups, listened, laughed, conversed with more than mere words. No one was left out, no one was sad.

Aunt Deborah giggled, being as expert in this art as her daughters. "I am thinking that, as is usual with them, those haoles are right. They are right to stay away. They really do not have anything in common with us. They don't know how to enjoy life. If they were here now, they would be as stiff and cold as tombstones. And this would be more like a funeral than a feast."

"I agree with you," Anna clapped an approving hand upon Deborah's sloping shoulder. Like most members of the Hoomalu clan, she could be counted upon to pluck laughter even out of the pit of disaster.

"I'll go tell Abraham to begin," said Deborah cheerfully, floating off to inform her family working around the earth oven in the back yard that now was the time to serve the kalua pig, the steamed fishes and chickens, the baked taros, sweet potatoes, and ti roots they had prepared for this sumptuous feast.

Mrs. Hoomalu took her place at the head of the largest eating-mat. Hawaiian and Chinese members in the company fell silent, knowing that an ahaaina always begins with a prayer. The Japanese guests, recognizing the sudden hush, stopped for a while their lessons in this new language, the learning of names, the exciting flirtations that conveyed so much meaning with so few words.

Once again Kamamalu took Ishi's hands in hers. Seeing this, Koi felt the stab of guilt that torments an unfaithful man. Turning his back upon the Hawaiian oiran who fired him so hotly, he tried to make amends to Aiko by taking her hand. The other men of Gohongi, monks no longer, at least in their thoughts, immediately adopted this congenial Hawaiian custom.

Mrs. Hoomalu, never at a loss for words with which to address either gods or men, looking out upon the company like a mother upon her children, saw that no prayer from her was necessary to ask the blessing of heaven for this gathering. Heaven had already given its blessing. The great gods were already here among them.

Speaking slowly, in her native tongue, for every one to hear, Hawaiians, half-Hawaiians, Chinese, Japanese alike, because all alike were people of this new Hawaii, she said the words that the common people of Hawaii had already learned to say to each other: "Aloha ia oukou. Malu, malu nui loa ia oukou." "Love to you all. Peace, much peace, to all of you."